What Reviewers Say About E

KIM BALDW

"*Force of Nature* is filled with nonstop, fast paced action. Tornadoes, raging fire blazes, heroic and daring rescues…Baldwin does a fine job of describing the fast-paced scenes and inspiring the reader to keep on turning the pages." – L-word.comLiterature

ROSE BEECHAM

"…her characters seem fully capable of walking away from the particulars of whodunit and engaging the reader in other aspects of their lives." – *Lambda Book Report*

GEORGIA BEERS

"Beers weaves a tale of yearning, love, lust, and conflict resolution. She has constructed a believable plot, with strong characters in a charming setting." – *JustAboutWrite*

RONICA BLACK

"*Wild Abandon* tells how these two women come to realize that 'life was too precious to be ruled by…fears, by…demons.' While these two women struggle with their issues, there is some very, very hot sex. If you enjoy complex characters and passionate sex scenes, you'll love *Wild Abandon*." – *MegaScene*

GUN BROOKE

"*Course of Action* is a romance…populated with a host of captivating and amiable characters. The glimpses into the lifestyles of the rich and beautiful people are rather like guilty pleasures…a most satisfying and entertaining reading experience." – *Midwest Book Review*

CATE CULPEPPER

"…an exceptional storyteller who has taken on a very difficult subject …and turned it into a spellbinding novel. As an author, she understands well that fiction can teach us our own history." – *JustAboutWrite*

JANE FLETCHER

"*The Exile and the Sorcerer* is a mesmerizing read, a tour-de-force packed with adventure, ordeals, complex twists and turns, and the internal introspection of appealing characters." – *Midwest Book Review*

Erotic Interludes 5
Road Games

edited by

RADCLY*f*FE and
STACIA SEAMAN

2007

ROAD GAMES

ISBN: 10-DIGIT 1-933110-77-5
13-DIGIT 978-1-933110-77-6

THIS TRADE PAPERBACK ORIGINAL IS PUBLISHED BY
BOLD STROKES BOOKS, INC.,
NEW YORK, USA

FIRST EDITION: MAY 2007.

CREDITS
EDITORS: RADCLYFFE AND STACIA SEAMAN
PRODUCTION DESIGN: STACIA SEAMAN
COVER DESIGN BY SHERI (GRAPHICARTIST2020@HOTMAIL.COM)

Contents

INTRODUCTION

Sometimes the games we play are in our minds, sometimes they're on the field—and the very best are in the bedroom…or the elevator…or the back of a low-rider. This collection of thirty-one stories from some of the best erotica writers working today takes us down twisting, turning roads that are sometimes metaphorical and other times very real in search of games of seduction, conquest, and danger. From tee-time with two golf pros to end-of-shift for a hot and horny cop, these are out-on-the-edge lesbians willing to play the game for the ultimate thrill. Join us for a guaranteed scorching ride.

Stacia Seaman and Radclyffe 2007

WINNER TAKES ALL
MEGHAN O'BRIEN

My cell phone buzzed at one o'clock in the morning, just as I was about to get into bed alone. I glanced at the display before I answered, even though I knew who it was. She was somewhere in the hotel, no doubt gambling and losing, and I had just about given up hope that I would hear from her before I fell asleep. I flipped the phone open.

"Nice of you to check in."

"Lindsey." I heard raucous laughter in the background, female voices. "You need to get down here."

Turning back the covers on the bed, I slipped between the sheets. Smiling, I went along. "No, I don't need to do anything. I'm going to bed."

"I found a game, Linds, and I lost. I, uh, need you to come bail me out."

A game. My heartbeat picked up.

"Come on, Linds," she said when I kept silent. "Please, honey. I need you."

"How much?"

Juliet cleared her throat, and I knew she was on the hook for more than just a few dollars.

"How much do you need, Jules?" I mustered up my most frustrated voice, as though this was a routine we always played out, and at this late hour, I simply had no patience for it. "Tell me."

"Just come to room one-oh-six. I'll explain everything."

"Fine." I threw back the covers and rolled out of bed. "Give me a few minutes, okay?"

"No problem. I appreciate this."

I granted her a long-suffering sigh. "I bail you out, you come back to the room with me. Understand?"

"I understand," Juliet said. "Thank you, sweetheart."

I snapped the cell phone shut without another word.

❖

I didn't bother putting on my clothes. I walked to the elevator in my favorite satin pajamas, uncaring that I might run into any night-owl guests. Would Juliet be surprised when I showed up looking like this? I wanted the other players to see that she was dragging me away from the comfort of the lush hotel sheets because she was lousy at cards.

The door to room 106 was slightly ajar, and I gave a light knock before poking my head inside. "Hello?"

At the sound of my voice, Juliet turned to greet me with a too-wide smile. "Hey, sweetie."

It was the smile of a woman who knew she was going to be in trouble.

Three other women sat around the table in the middle of the room. Three pairs of eyes looked me up and down as I stepped inside, no doubt taking in the sight of my informal attire. I sized up each woman in turn. "So who's the winner?"

The biggest of the three, whose brown hair was cut short against her head, broke into a toothy grin. "That'd be me."

I walked to the table, ready to cut to the chase. "How much does she owe you?"

"Now, sweetheart—"

I held up a hand to cut off whatever explanation Juliet was going to give me, never breaking the gaze I shared with the poker champion. The woman was buff. Her biceps strained the sleeves of her gray T-shirt, and her muscular thighs looked ready to burst the seams of her jeans. Great. If I couldn't pay up, she could easily beat Juliet's ass.

"Just tell me what she owes you so we can take care of this and I can go back to bed."

The winner raised an eyebrow, flashed me a grin. "Actually, darling, it's you who owes me."

My stomach flipped over. "Excuse me?"

"One hour. To be spent at my discretion."

My jaw tensed when the meaning of her words hit me. With effort,

I kept my expression neutral as I turned to face Juliet. Her face was flushed deep pink, and she gave me a sheepish smile.

"Linds—"

"You *bet* me in a poker game?"

"It wasn't like…I mean…I didn't—"

"You told a complete stranger that she could *fuck* me?"

Juliet's mouth hung open, but no more words came out.

I turned back to the winner, who watched us with a vaguely amused smile. "What's your name?" I asked her.

"Grant," she said. "You're Lindsey?"

Without answering, I regarded Juliet once more. She cowered in her chair, clearly trying not to meet my eyes but also seemingly unable to stop herself from darting her gaze in my direction every few moments. The other two women at the table watched the three of us play out this scene with an obvious air of enthrallment.

"I'm not yours to wager, you know." I stepped close to Juliet and bent to talk quietly into her ear. "I should just walk out of here and let you clean up your own mess."

"Honey—"

I put my hand on her shoulder to stop her from speaking. "But I'm not going to."

"You're not?" said the woman who sat next to Juliet. She had short blond hair, impeccable style, and gorgeous green eyes that sparkled with interest.

Juliet sat up a bit straighter, as though alarmed, and swallowed. I turned to Grant with the sweetest smile I could muster.

"I'll settle her debt," I said. "But we do this right here."

Grant leaned back in her chair and placed her big hands on her thighs. "Sounds good to me," she said, then grinned at her tablemates. "If you all could excuse us for about an hour—"

"No," I interrupted. "We do this right here, right now. Juliet can watch."

I swore I could see the blood drain from Juliet's face. She went absolutely pale and wide-eyed.

"After all, this was her bet." With that, I got to my knees in front of Grant and covered her hands with mine. "She can pay it off with me."

Grant tipped her head back and laughed, a deep, throaty chuckle. "Right on. I can handle that."

"Can *you* handle that?" I asked Juliet.

She cleared her throat and averted her gaze. "I guess I'll have to."

"I guess so." I reached for the button of Grant's blue jeans. With the other hand, I cupped between her legs. I found what I hoped I might. "You're prepared, I see."

"Never leave home without it," Grant murmured and shifted her hips so I could unzip her jeans and pull them down to expose gray boxer briefs. The bulge between her legs sprang to life impressively. "After all, you never know when you're going to get to fuck another woman's girl."

I glanced at Juliet, who stared at us with what looked like sick fascination. She blinked rapidly as I reached into the opening of the boxer briefs and pulled out a thick, flesh-colored dildo. I shifted so that she would have a better view of what I was about to do for the big winner.

"No, you never know," I murmured. Then I bent and took the head of the dildo into my mouth.

I heard Grant moan, and the other two women at the table whooped in delight.

"That a girl!" one of them shouted. "Suck that cock."

I wrapped my hand around the base of the dildo and started pumping it as I sucked at the head. I made my movements slow and deliberate, wanting Juliet to see every detail. I licked up and down the shaft, occasionally glancing up to meet Grant's eyes with the most subservient expression I could muster. I wanted this woman to take me, and I wanted Juliet to bear witness to my surrender.

Grant's hand landed on the back of my head, and in no time her fingers tangled lightly in my hair. She began guiding my motion, clearly turned on by my performance. "Your girlfriend is a good little cocksucker," she murmured.

Juliet said nothing.

"I bet her pussy tastes good too, doesn't it?" Grant taunted. "I think I'll find out for myself." She pulled me off her cock with a fistful of my hair. "Take off your pajamas," she demanded, and held out her arm to help me to my feet.

I felt a shiver of self-consciousness as I began to unbutton my top. All four women in the room stared at me openly. I looked right back into Juliet's eyes. I let my top fall to the floor. Goose bumps raised when the satin slid over my bare arms. My nipples immediately hardened into painful points, and I grimaced.

"Now the bottoms."

I obeyed Grant's order. I stood naked in front of everyone and resisted the urge to cross my hands over my pussy. I refused to let any of them know how difficult it was for me to be on display like this.

"Sit on the table." Grant swept a pile of poker chips to the side and pushed back from her spot at the table. "Right here, in front of me."

I took a seat with my thighs pressed together. Juliet was to my right and a brunette woman of about forty to my left. Grant sat directly in front of me, her face roughly level with my belly.

"Lie back, darling," Grant said, and pushed against my shoulder until I complied.

In this position, I could turn my face to the right and look Juliet straight in the eyes. She was close enough to touch. I kept my gaze locked on her as Grant pushed my thighs apart with her hands.

"Hold your pussy open for me, Lindsey."

I reached down with both hands and spread myself open. I could feel Grant's gaze burning into me and my eyes slipped shut just as she said, "I'm going to lick you until you come in my mouth."

Then I felt the barest touch of her tongue on my labia and nearly came unglued. My eyes shot open and I saw Juliet's face, jaw tense with some indefinable emotion. Nostrils flaring, she stared in the direction of Grant's head moving slowly between my thighs.

Grant ran the tip of her tongue along my labia, up one, down the other, then moved down to circle my opening. She pulled back and breathed, "Fuck, this pussy tastes good."

I squirmed on the tabletop, caught between humiliation and arousal at being talked about like a mere object. Grant lowered her face and covered my labia with her hot mouth again, running her tongue along every dip and crevice of my pussy. She explored me thoroughly, in no rush, and in no time, I was shocked to realize, I was dripping wet.

"She likes it," Grant mumbled, and flicked my clit with her tongue. I picked my head up and watched her lick me, even as her gaze was locked on Juliet. "Does she get this wet for you, Juliet?"

Juliet kept up her silence. Maybe she figured there was no right answer to that question.

Grant sucked on my clit, a noisy, slurping kiss. Almost unconsciously, I spread my legs wider and pulled my pussy open even more. I knew my clit was swollen, and in this position, it was most likely jutting out like a proud little cock. I wanted to give Grant better access, because it all felt so goddamn good.

"Suck me off," I groaned, then arched my back. This was as much for my own benefit as it was for Juliet's. Grant knew how to use her mouth, and now that I was in this position, I needed relief. "Please make me come."

"After I do, I'm going to fuck you," Grant said as though she were warning me. "You want this hard cock inside your pussy?"

I nodded, still squirming around on the table. "Yes. Please. Whatever you want."

Grant bent and wrapped her lips around my swollen clit, then moved up and down on it while her tongue played fast circles all around. My thighs began to tremble, an imminent sign of climax, and I struggled to keep my hands on my pussy. I thrust my hips into her face, aggressively seeking out the pleasure she was delivering. When I came, I whipped my head to the side and squinted my eyes and clenched my teeth. I couldn't keep in the throaty growl that burst from my lips as she lapped up my juices, the soft rasp of her tongue prolonging my orgasm to a dizzying extreme.

When she finally pulled away, my chest was heaving with exertion. Sweat beaded on my forehead and between my breasts, and my thighs were sticky with it. I lay spread out on the table for everyone to see, still quivering with aftershocks caused by every little thing: the breeze blowing across my overheated sex, the lustful gazes of the two woman whose names I didn't even know, and the sound of Grant's chair being pushed back so she could stand between my spread thighs.

I gazed up at her from beneath half-closed eyelids. She put her hands on my knees and smirked around the table.

"The hard part is figuring out what to do first," she said to the amused laughter of her companions. Juliet licked her lips and said nothing.

I groaned as Grant slid a hand between my thighs. She ran her fingertips through my wetness, then pressed a finger inside.

"You like having your girlfriend watch me finger-fuck you?" she asked.

"Yes," I said, and it was the truth. I looked at Juliet, whose chest was moving in time with her labored breathing. Between Grant's touch and Juliet's gaze sliding all over me, I was nothing but nerve endings drawn bowstring taut with pleasure.

"Feels good, right?"

I groaned and arched my back to draw her deeper inside. She twisted her finger around and rubbed all my most sensitive places, then pulled out and pressed in again with two. She was showy with her touching, and a little rough, and it got me so wet that Grant raised an eyebrow in surprise as I ejaculated just a little on her arm.

"Damn," Grant said, and grinned. "This girl is ready to go."

I sat up as far as I could, reaching for Grant's cock. My fingertips grazed the head, but I wasn't able to get a grip before she put her free hand on my shoulder and pressed me back onto the table. She withdrew her fingers from my pussy and gripped the dildo at its base.

"Is this what you want?" She stroked up and down the shaft, as though preparing herself to give it to me. "All you have to do is ask."

"Yes," I said.

Grant raised her eyebrow again, and the corner of her mouth twitched. I looked into playful green eyes and found that she was having fun with this. I returned her smile and propped myself up on my elbows.

"I want your cock," I asked sweetly. "In my pussy. Now."

Without a word, she guided the head of it to my opening. She pushed in slowly, and my head fell back and my mouth dropped open as my pussy strained to accommodate it.

"This is pretty big, huh?"

"Yeah," I said, and collapsed onto my back again. She made no move to slide deeper. With just the tip of it inside me, she reached down and rubbed her finger along the sensitive flesh that gripped at its girth.

"Just relax and take it," she murmured. Grant kept her eyes locked to mine as she eased a finger inside me, pressed close to the dildo, stretching me impossibly more open. "I promise it'll feel good."

It did feel good. I bit my lip and whimpered as she rubbed her finger along the length of the dildo, stroking inside me. There was something so decadent about having both her cock and her finger inside me. It made my nipples ache with pleasure-pain.

Grant withdrew her finger, then her cock. I groaned in disappointment, a noise that turned into a guttural moan when she pressed the cock back inside.

"Look at her," Grant said to Juliet. "She loves being stretched open around my cock."

Juliet met my gaze. Her eyes were dark, and her cheeks were flushed. She shifted in her seat.

Grant pulled out again, then thrust back in. I jerked at the suddenness of the penetration, the small jolt it sent through my arms and legs. Grant hiked my leg up over her shoulder and leaned in close, burying her cock as deep as it would go.

"You like getting fucked?"

"I love it," I whimpered. I threw an arm over my face, biting my lip as she delivered another sharp thrust. "Please don't stop."

"Oh, I plan on getting my full hour's worth out of you. That's what your girlfriend promised, and that's what I'm going to take." Grant took hold of my other leg and placed my ankle on her shoulder, grabbing onto my calves as she set up a driving rhythm deep into my pussy.

I glanced at the woman to my left. She stared at my pussy, the point of entry for Grant's cock, and licked her lips. Her eyes were open wide, like she couldn't believe what she was seeing. Then her gaze darted to me and she caught me staring, and stared back. I let my eyes slip almost all the way closed and moaned, smiling at her as Grant fucked me hard. The woman looked like she was about to pass out.

Suddenly Grant pulled out and didn't push back in. Startled, I lifted my head and gave her an incredulous look.

"Oh, I'm not done, Lindsey. I just wanted to try something new." Grant grabbed my hip and forced me to turn on my side. "Get on your stomach." She smacked my ass, harder than I would have expected, and said, "I want you bent over this table so Juliet can watch me fuck you from behind."

I obeyed and rolled over, wincing when she delivered another stinging slap to my already sensitive flesh. She kneaded my buttocks in her hands, spreading me apart as though for inspection, then released me and delivered two more sharp blows.

"You're a little slut, aren't you?" Grant said. She pulled my labia open with one hand and rubbed the head of her cock over my pussy with the other. "Gonna be a good girl and lie here so I can fuck you like the slut you are?"

She breathed on my pussy as she talked, so cold on my red-hot flesh. I could feel my wetness on my inner thighs. I thrust my ass into the air, subservient, and silently prayed for her to start fucking me again.

"That's right," she growled and spanked one cheek, then the other. "Get that ass up there. Let everyone see that wet pussy."

Then her fingers were inside me again—three of them, it felt like—thrusting and twisting and stroking my g-spot. She drew out some more ejaculate and laughed heartily when the woman sitting at my head cheered her on. Grant pulled her fingers out and, reaching under me to play with my nipples with her free hand, guided her cock back into me from behind.

Once again, she played it slow at first. Opening me up, sliding in so gently, so deliberately, before finally giving in to all-out fucking. She grabbed my hips and pulled me on and off her cock, every so often withdrawing completely just so she could give me that thrilling shock of penetration again.

My clit was painfully engorged, my whole pussy felt heavy and sore with the need to come. Grant kept up a deliberate pace, keeping me balanced on the razor-sharp edge of orgasm. Every so often she would pull my buttocks apart, exposing my slick anus to the cool air and causing my internal muscles to clamp down even harder on her cock.

But instead of releasing me from the exquisite torment, Grant pulled out of me again. I felt her step away, then felt her hands on my arms, helping me to stand. I stumbled as I got to my feet and moaned at the delicious sensation the movement caused in my pussy. Everything felt good, but nothing was quite good enough. I needed more, and I was desperate to make Grant give it to me.

"Please," I murmured, and wrapped my arms around Grant's shoulders. I dropped one hand between her legs and pressed the base of the dildo into her body. "Please, I need to come."

"I've still got a few minutes left," Grant said and disentangled herself from me. She pulled her chair out from the table and sat down facing Juliet. "And I want you to ride me when you come."

She didn't have to ask me twice. I climbed onto her lap, aware that Juliet had an excellent view of what was about to happen. My back was to her, so I wouldn't be able to watch her face. I could imagine her reaction, though, and just thinking about it made me hot.

I reached down and grasped Grant's cock and guided it into my pussy. I sank down onto the length of it, down onto her lap, until her face was even with my breasts. I threw my head back and moaned when she leaned forward and sucked a nipple into her mouth.

Immediately Grant's hands were on my hips, guiding me up and down on her cock. I rode her unashamedly, fucking my pussy hard, desperate for release. She pulled up on my buttocks, no doubt showing Juliet how she was filling me up, how tight I was around her. I closed my eyes and watched the scene from outside myself: Juliet sitting passively watching this butch fuck her partner. I pictured the sight of the flesh-colored dildo disappearing into my pussy over and over again, of Grant's almost masculine hands grabbing at my ass and spreading me open to display me to my own partner.

That last thought nearly made me come right then and there, and I would have if Grant hadn't pulled me up off her cock and held me suspended above it, even as I struggled to impale myself on it once again.

"No," I whimpered. "Fucking...*please*, Grant, please just let me—"

"I know you're close," she whispered to me, and gave me a sympathetic smile. "Turn around and I'll make you come. I promise."

I didn't so much turn around as she moved me herself, using her hands on my hips to guide me so that I was looking at Juliet. We locked gazes and kept staring at one another even as Grant pulled me down so that I was poised above her cock again, my back to her chest. This time Grant guided the dildo into me and pulled me sitting with both hands on my thighs. The fingers of her right hand found my clit and started rubbing light circles over the swollen ridge of flesh.

Juliet broke our gaze briefly to look down at Grant stroking my clit, and at her cock buried deep in my pussy. Then she looked up at me and flashed me a subtle smile. I smiled back, then threw my head back and cried out as Grant finally let me come. I squirmed around on the cock as best I could as I rode out the orgasm, and Grant kept stroking me with the pads of her fingers, milking every last bit of pleasure from my body.

When I started to come down from my climax, Grant reached up with her free hand and gave my nipple a hard tug. At the same time, she seized my clit and made a motion as though she were jerking a tiny cock off. I was so swollen that it almost felt like that was exactly what she was doing, and I found myself thrusting my hips into her hand, like I was trying to fuck it.

My second orgasm hit me then, and took my breath away. Juliet just watched wide-eyed as Grant devastated me completely. By the time my pleasure ebbed, I was limp in her lap.

Grant kept her hand on me for long moments, just playing with my pussy. I sat and let her caress me, enjoying the intimacy of the gesture. Juliet exhaled slowly and uncrossed her legs. She watched Grant touch my labia and toy with the skin of my opening, which was still stretched tight around her always-hard cock.

"That was nice," Grant said. She gripped my hips and helped me off her cock, then stood with me. She turned me around and pulled me into a gentle hug, then gave me a chaste kiss on the lips. "That really was nice," she whispered under her breath. "I'm sorry your girlfriend did that to you, but it was cool of you to play along."

I smiled, and patted Grant on the back. "It was nice. Thank you." Then I bent to gather my pajamas and put them on. "Juliet, come on. We're going upstairs now. I'm exhausted."

Juliet stood without a word and followed me to the door. I could feel three pairs of eyes on us as we left the room. No doubt they assumed that I would tear her apart as soon as I got her in private. We walked in silence to the elevator and waited for the next available car without speaking.

When the door opened, I stepped inside first and pressed the button for the sixth floor. As the door slid shut behind us, Juliet finally turned to face me. And she smiled.

"So did that live up to your fantasy?"

"It was perfect," I said, and grinned. "And she was hot!"

"I know." Juliet gave me a self-satisfied smile. "As soon as I saw her, I knew you'd be happy."

"Oh, I'm happy."

"You deserve an Academy Award, by the way. For a minute I was really freaked out that you were pissed at me."

"I am," I teased, and put my arms around her. I leaned in for a rough kiss, nipping at her full lower lip with my teeth. "You ready for your punishment?"

CARPE DIEM: LUST, WRATH, AND OTHER DEADLY SINS
STORY ONE: JUST UNDER THE SURFACE
RONICA BLACK

The impact of steel on steel reverberated up the club, stinging my hands enough to make me curse. A small group of birds flocked noisily from a nearby tree, their peaceful morning ruined. I swung again as hard as I could and nearly slipped on the dew on the lush lawn. The next impact stung again but I embraced the pain. Breathing heavily, I lowered the club and looked around at the gray light of dawn and the progress I'd made thus far. I shook my head in disappointment.

"I can do better than that." I returned to the standing golf bag, speared the damaged club into the appropriate slot, and fetched the only club left. I angled it up for inspection and grinned at the thick, oversized head of the driver. "Time to tee up, boys and girls." I brought the club back over my head and powered it down onto the windshield. The glass splintered and caved but didn't shatter. This time, however, the car's alarm started to sing.

"'Bout fucking time." I swung again, knocking the driver's side mirror so hard it hung swaying from the door. "It's only a hundred thousand dollar machine." Laughing, I rounded the vehicle, swinging my mayhem down upon its hood and side windows. I cursed as I brought the club up to find the head broken off. As I studied it, I heard movement from the trailer.

"What the fuck…" a voice called out. The door to the double-wide banged open as the owner of the clubs and car came rushing out. "What the fuck are you doing!" he shrieked over the car alarm, running down the steps to the grass where he slid to a stop. He stood there in his boxer briefs, the blood draining from his face. I regarded him with calm indifference and stabbed the shaft of the club into the windshield, my attention once again on the trailer.

A woman appeared in the open doorway, completely nude save for a sheer, short robe that flapped open as she moved. Her breasts had the full, perfectly round look of implants, both nipples pierced. She started shouting as well, but I couldn't make out the words. Tired of the noisy alarm, I climbed on the hood and jumped up and down, caving it under my motorcycle boots. The alarm slowed and quieted to a weird slur of sorts, as if it were dying.

Boxer-brief boy continued to scream at me, grabbing fistfuls of his hair in frustration and then falling to his knees in defeat.

I had known all along that he wouldn't try and stop me. He knew who I was and he knew I'd been hunting him for over a week. No, he wasn't going to do a thing. He was going to stand there and watch me do this.

Whistling, I crossed the lawn to my truck and returned with a red gas can. The luxury car looked like a silver pincushion, clubs sticking up out of it at various angles.

"What are you doing?" He was getting worked up again as I approached the car and set down the can. "No, no! What are you doing!" Suddenly, he had courage. He squeezed my shoulder in pure desperation and I backhanded him sharply. The woman screamed as he stumbled backward, his fingers touching the blood that trickled down his chin.

"I'm calling the cops you, you crazy bitch!" she yelled, breasts heaving.

"No, you won't," I said with little concern and set to work pouring the gasoline onto the car.

When I finished dousing the vehicle, I tilted the can and let what gas was left trail onto the grass, then tossed the empty can into the jagged mouth of the back window. Much to my amusement, boxer-brief boy was at the car, hurriedly trying to salvage what was left of his custom-made golf clubs. The bitch was still yelling, though this time at him, while dragging him away from the car.

I walked a good distance away, lit a cigarette, inhaled, and narrowed my eyes, staring at the couple through the smoke. When the woman finally managed to pull him back toward the trailer, I flipped open my Zippo, struck a flame, and let it fall to the grass. A small whoosh sounded from near my feet and the trail of fire took off through the lawn. I smiled at the couple clinging to one another, thinking of how happy he must be with his stripper mistress, who was well known for her cowgirl persona.

A true movie buff, I couldn't help but be reminded of Bruce Willis in *Die Hard*. Giving the terrified couple one last wave, I turned my back and said, "Yippee-ki-yay, motherfucker."

An earsplitting explosion shook the ground behind me, the heat from its hungry flames nipping at my back as I walked away.

My name is Diem Rushton. I am a vigilante. This is a day in my life.

I blew smoke out the side of my mouth toward the open window as I drove away. In the rearview mirror a plume of black smoke swirled into the morning sky. I nearly laughed aloud as I thought about the jerk's lame attempts at trying to hide from me. The double-wide was owned by a friend of the cowgirl, a fellow gentleman's club entertainer who was nice enough to lend it out to a friend in need. And boxer-brief boy, he just couldn't stay away. It was only a matter of time before he rolled that brand-spankin'-new car up the green lawn.

That's all it ever takes, really. Time.

Self-centered and self-serving people can never go without for any length of time. Their selfishness and impatience always gives them away.

And that's where you'll find me. Right there waiting when it does.

I sighed, thinking of how a good job always excited and exhausted me.

Tired and needing to relax, I took a quick shower when I got home, washing away the scent of gasoline and smoke. Then I took a nice, long nap. When I woke, I wandered around the house for a while, checked my messages, which alerted me to two more potential clients, and then realized I was nearly out of cigarettes.

With a new purpose, I climbed on my black Suzuki GSX-R750 sport bike and reveled in its appearance. I'd had it painted the year before, something more "me." Silver ghost flames licked all the way back to the seat. She was sleek, sexy, and felt fucking phenomenal between my legs.

The ride soothed me considerably as I streaked down the road, wind in my hair and demons forever on my tail. The convenience store on the corner was typically busy for a late Friday afternoon, but I lucked out and pulled in up front next to another large bike, killed the engine, and hopped off.

The door dinged and the store smelled just like they all do—like old, overheated hot dogs, coffee, and Twinkies. For some reason it always comforted me. I was staring at rows of nicotine sticks behind the counter when I heard it.

"Diem? Is that you?"

I turned.

Her eyes lit up and my initial attitude eased a little as I remembered that I liked her okay.

"Hi," she said.

I smiled and nodded.

Her name was Vivian and I had worked with her, back when I was teaching school, back when I was a good girl. (That's a whole other story.)

She was a thin blonde with an infectious smile and bright blue eyes. Very attractive by straight-girl standards, meaning she definitely spent a lot of time on taking care of herself: mannie-peddies, highlights, makeup, designer clothes, the works.

"It's been a while. I wasn't sure if it was you," she said as those bright eyes scanned me carefully once, then twice. Her face gave away her thoughts. Back when I taught, I had always prettied up for work myself—makeup, nice clothes, you know. But now my hair was short, spiky, and blond and my T-shirt was black and sleeveless, a tattoo of a cross on my upper arm.

Her eyes went up and down one last time and then rested on my tattoo. When they eventually came back to my face I knew that she knew.

"This is my riding motif." I felt I owed her an explanation for my rather butch attire, or maybe it was engrained fear from years of teaching, years of hiding who I really was.

Her cheeks colored a little. "Riding?"

I watched her closely, wondering about the blush. "As in motorcycle."

"Oh!" She shook her head. "Sorry, it's been a long day."

"School?"

"You know it." She smoothed down her gray skirt as if worried about her appearance, as if somehow hers didn't measure up to mine.

That perhaps she was dressed *too* nicely. "I really miss you," she confessed, her eyes sincere. And then she seemed to realize that maybe her words were a little too sincere as well. "I mean, *we* really miss you."

"Yeah, well, you know..." Jesus, what was I supposed to say? *I left a very noble career in teaching for the dark side, righting people's wrongs?* I put the focus back on her. "How are your kids?" I knew she was married with two little ones. Their photos had been all over her desk.

"They're good, real good." I glanced in her handheld basket and noted the chewy fruit treats and small boxes of Cheerios.

"Good, that's good. And the husband?"

Her diamond sparkled on her left hand.

"He's fine."

I nodded and smiled, pleased for her. "Well, I should probably get going..."

She touched my forearm as her eyes flashed with excitement. "We should go out sometime. Tonight, let's go out tonight!"

Stunned, I merely stood there, echoing, "Tonight?"

"Yes!" She touched me again.

"I don't know, I just got back into town..."

But she didn't give me a chance to explain. She pulled me up to the counter and hastily laid out her items. I raised two fingers to the clerk, who knew what I smoked from my frequent visits. He pushed two soft boxes across the counter and Vivian pushed him a twenty, holding up a hand as I started to protest. Bobby gave her change that she shoved into her purse as I grabbed the plastic grocery sacks and held the door for her.

"I'm over here." We crossed the pavement and she opened the tail of her SUV. I noted the car seats in the back and wondered why in the hell this straight, married woman wanted a night out with me. I loaded up her groceries, pocketed my cigs, and she shut the door down tight.

"Where are you?"

I slid on my shades and pointed to my bike.

She shaded her eyes from the brightness of the setting sun. "That's nice. Real nice."

"Thanks."

"I can picture you on that." She grinned slowly and I noticed a spark in her eyes. She opened the driver's door to the SUV and hid her purse under the seat. After retrieving her D&G sunglasses from the visor, she slipped them on and locked up the vehicle.

Wickedly sexy, she placed a soft, warm hand on my bare bicep and whispered, "I want a ride."

Hot from her touch and the low purring of her voice, I shook my head in disbelief. "I don't know," I said slowly.

"No arguing." She squeezed my arm. "Come on, I've got a little over an hour." She started toward my bike, strutting confidently across the pavement.

"Don't you want to go change first?"

She turned to face me once she had her hand resting on the black and silver flamed tank. A smirk lifted the corner of her mouth as I approached. "I can manage in this."

I was still reeling at the idea and trying to mentally catch up. I wasn't one who handled loss of control well.

"You need a helmet, a jacket…"

"You don't wear them." She glanced around quickly and then hitched her skirt up to her upper thighs. With practiced grace, she swung a gloriously long leg over the bike and settled herself on the higher back end of the seat.

"Come on." She patted my seat and the smirk grew.

My throat tightened at the sight of her. Skirt cinched up so high I could see where her stockings met her garter. I flushed, wondering what color her panties were. If I bent my head just a little, I knew I would be able to see them.

Motherfucker, this is insane.

She patted the seat again and raised an eyebrow.

Hurriedly, before I melted from the creaminess of her exposed thighs, I swung my leg over and started the bike. Her arms wrapped around me tightly and her legs were warm and firm against my sides, her grip strong and sure. I walked us to the slanted cement exit and realized that somehow, within the space of twenty minutes, I had lost all control of my evening.

"Where to?" I asked.

Her lips brushed my ear. "The air force base."

My heart thudded like a caged wild animal within my chest.

As I pushed off onto the main road, I could tell that she'd ridden before by the way she pushed against me, leaning forward into the wind. She moved her hands up and over my shoulders, gripping me tighter, her breasts firm against my back.

When we glided onto the freeway, she shrieked into the sunset-streaked sky. It was at that moment that I realized that I didn't have an average, soft-spoken, married history teacher clinging to my back. No, this was a woman. Flesh and blood, vibrant and wild.

We pressed on into the night and she clung to me tightly, howling into the wind, loving every second of it.

My cheeks stung at my own smile. I felt so alive, more alive than I felt during or soon after a job. This new alive was incomparable.

A purple heaven had settled in by the time we flew along the road beside the air force base. I slowed the bike, unsure, and then followed my headlight as she told me where to pull over.

The tires kicked up dirt as we turned off the two-lane, little-traveled road. I turned the bike to face the base, killed the engine, and kicked down the stand, leaving us all alone in the dark beneath a fresh, silver-shining moon. The desert smelled fresh and alive, as if it had just been raked by the hands of God.

I pushed my shades up on my head and sat and stared through the high fence in the distance at the small red dots of the air traffic tower. My body was humming like electricity through a live wire.

Vivian's hands were on my thighs and her voice once again stirred my insides.

"That was some ride."

The wind blew a few strands of her hair against my cheek, startling me. They smelled like her perfume, like the raw sexiness of a woman, contained in a bottle. I closed my eyes as her hands traveled up my thighs, over my middle to my breasts. I shuddered, truly startled.

"I want you, Diem." Her hot tongue flicked my ear as she squeezed my nipples. A soft cry of surprise escaped me and my center flooded with arousal.

"I have always wanted you."

I'd had no idea. None. She had always been friendly and professional. And now she was against my back, straddling my bike, touching me with her burning hands and flaming words. My heart thudded in my ears. I remembered the close scrutiny of her eyes in the convenience store, when I realized that she knew. And then it all made sense.

"Mmm," she groaned, grinding herself against me. A fighter jet took off, screaming and rushing right over our heads, a phantom in the darkness, and I jerked under her hands. The wind of the jet actually blew against us, heightening all that she was doing.

"Yes," she growled, rolling my hardening nipples with her fingers.

I cried out again and her teeth found my naked neck as her warm hands inched up my shirt to massage my exposed breasts. "You feel so good," she crooned, nipping at me, driving me wild. "It's been so long. So long since I've felt another woman." Her tongue pushed into my ear and her hand rubbed at the denim seam in my crotch.

"Oh God, Diem. I can feel how hot you are."

I leaned into her, my head tossed back, overcome with pleasure. She sucked on my shoulder, hard and determined. Then she pulled away as another jet soared loudly overhead. I felt her absence against my back, cold and empty. I opened my eyes, not realizing they were closed, and watched as she moved from behind me, bunching her skirt up over her hips. Sheer stockings covered her long legs up to her thighs, where a dark garter belt held them in place. I swallowed hard, realizing there were no panties, just the dark blond, neatly trimmed hair of her pussy.

Instinctively, I scooted back and she swung her leg over the bike to straddle it just in front me. She licked her lips, hungry eyes fastened to mine as she unbuttoned her blouse. Grinning, she eased out of it, plucked the sunglasses off her head, and then turned to hang them both over the handlebars. Next she unlatched her dark bra, which matched her garter, and flung it over the other handlebar.

Her gaze held mine for a long moment, and I knew she was enjoying my attention. My face was burning white-hot with desire and my chest was rising and falling fast with my hastened breathing.

She took my hands and placed them on her warm breasts, whispering, "Touch me."

My body burned so fierce I thought I'd glow in the dark as I squeezed and massaged her small breasts. She threw her head back in pleasure, gripping my shoulders tightly.

"Suck me, baby. Put your mouth on me." She lifted herself up to me. I extended my tongue to lick and flick at her firm nipple. Her hands knotted in my hair. "Oh God, hurry. Please suck me."

Eagerly, I lifted the small weight of her breast and took it into my mouth, sucking hard. She clawed at my scalp and howled like a coyote crying into the night. My shades fell from my head, but I didn't care, nothing else mattered. I sucked and swirled my tongue around her, feasting on her breasts while she thrust herself into me. I worked her nipples with my teeth over and over again.

Face heated and lips swollen, I tore my mouth away from her, needing to breathe. She sat heaving in front of me, her wet breasts catching the red lights of another departing jet. Her hair flew in the wind and she looked like a wild creature of the night, hungry and willing to do anything to feed.

She raised her hands to her slick breasts and caressed them as she began to undulate, rubbing her bare sex against the seat, her bunched skirt like a halo around her waist.

"Mmm," she moaned, biting her lower lip. "This feels so good." She arched her back and quickened her hips, her knees bending to bring her feet up off the ground. Her skin was bathed in the silver of the moon, rocking, straining, pulsing. Between her legs, the folds of her flesh were slick with arousal, wetting the seat as she writhed. "I'm so close," she whispered. "I almost came three different times on the way here. I love the way the bike feels, the way you feel."

The easy accessible skirt was the reason she hadn't wanted to change. And as I watched her fuck my bike in her stockings and garter and heels, nothing in the world could've turned me on more.

She leaned forward and fastened her mouth on mine as the sound of jets echoed through the desert. Her tongue was long and fierce, pushing against mine for dominance. Her mouth was blazing and demanding, letting me know just how close she was to breaking. Running my hands over her bare flesh, I eased her back against the tank of the bike. She wrenched her mouth away and stared up at me, eyes flashing in the moonlight. Carefully, I scooted back to the very edge of the seat and ran my hands down over her breasts and stomach.

Feeling the tickle of silken hairs, I glanced down at her wet, shimmering flesh. Her cunt was swollen, glistening, waiting.

I closed my eyes as I dipped and explored her wetness, just wanting to concentrate on *feeling* it.

So hot, so slick. *Jesus.*

A strong hand gripped my wrist as she urged, "Hurry."

She arched as my fingers slid up and inside. I groaned at the wet, tight feel of her and nearly came against the seam of my jeans.

"Do you feel me?" She sat up and gripped my shoulders. Her hips began their magical dance again, fucking my fingers.

"Yes, I feel you," I whispered.

"God, I feel you," she said between clenched teeth, tossing her head back.

She thrust harder and harder, riding me fast and frenzied until her cries were short and sweet. And then, just before she came, she stopped. Breathing slowed, she held on to my shoulders and moved so her cunt slid up and down, on and nearly off my fingers, long and slow. Her nails dug into my back as she drew out the pleasure, milking it for every last drop.

"You like it like this?" I asked, mesmerized.

"Mmm, yes," she whispered, sweat lining her upper lip.

I clamped her shoulder so she couldn't move, ensuring I was deep inside her. "How about this?" I curled my fingers against her g-spot and rubbed firmly.

"Oh God," she rasped. "Mmm…" She sped up again, grinding and writhing, bucking her hips back and forth. "Yes," she said. "Oh God." Her eyes clenched shut and her muscles tensed in the moonlight.

Hand soaked in her excitement, I pressed my thumb against her firm, thick clit. Her nails dug deeper and she made only noises, words long gone.

Another jet flew overhead and her eyes flew open. She pulled me to her, kissing me with a hard, wet tongue, swirling and taking. Her hips thrust three quick times and then she tore her mouth away, threw her head back, and came into the night sky, jerking and pulsing. Her cry was loud and throaty against the noise of the jet, her body absorbing the pleasure in powerful, uncontrollable undulations.

"Oh God," she finally managed to croak, clinging to me, still fucking me for dear life. Her manicured nails pierced my back and her mouth latched to my neck, biting and sucking, groaning against my skin. She held me to her for a long while until her body finally slowed to ride me in long, full, heavy thrusts.

I closed my eyes, too overcome to stop myself. Her nails, her mouth, her teeth, her cunt, all of it clinging to me, driving me over. I rubbed myself against the seat, once, twice, and then shattered into a million pieces, offering them up into the night. She laughed all throaty in my ear, realizing I had lost it, and then kissed me so hard and long I thought I'd pass out.

Eventually, she pulled her mouth away, parting with short, wet sucks of my lips. Then she rested her cheek on my shoulder and we both just listened to one another breathe. We stayed like that, holding fast to one another in the dark quiet. After another jet broke the peaceful sky and flew away, she stirred, lightly kissing her way up to my face.

"Diem?"

"Yes?"

"Can we ride home like this?"

I chuckled. "Not if you want to actually make it home in one piece."

Her eyes found mine and her hands held my face. "Why did you leave?"

I glanced away. "That's another story for another night."

She seemed to understand that I didn't or couldn't talk about it at that moment.

"Can I see you again?"

I looked back to her. My breath nearly caught at the sight of her flushed, vibrant face, full lips, and daring eyes.

"Maybe."

"It's a little late to play hard to get."

She still seemed able to pin me with her words. Who would've guessed what lay just under the surface of this seemingly conservative, married teacher? Or boxer-brief boy, who was married, successful, and attended church regularly? No one really truly knows someone else. It's all an illusion.

"Come on." I moved from the bike to hand her her clothes. Then I bent and picked up my shades. "Let's get you home. I bet your kids miss you." I didn't want to get attached or make promises I knew I didn't want to keep. She was a strong, confident woman, the first one who'd ever assumed control over me. It was as unsettling as it was exciting.

She smoothed her skirt back down a little and fastened her bra, then slipped into her blouse.

"My kids are fine." He eyes flashed. "Mommy needs a little fun every now and then too." She finished buttoning her blouse and swung her leg over the bike.

I slung my leg over and started the bike. Her teeth held my lobe and her fingers pinched my nipples, ensuring that I couldn't and wouldn't move.

"There's no sense in running, Diem." Her voice played in my ear, igniting me once again. "I'm not finished with you yet. Not by a long shot."

She released me and licked my neck, long and slow back up to my ear. "Now, take me back hard and fast. I want to come one more time before I go home."

Circuit
Evecho

Leti thumbed the worn suede of her favourite wallet; crepe thin and supple, it slipped easily into the rear pocket of her jeans on a nudge and hugged the melon curve of her arse, leaving no lines to mark the nakedness underneath. She was dressed minimally for maximum effect: white on black, open topped in a singlet with one-inch straps trailing over the packs of her shoulders and in and out of the sloping crevasses of her collar. Square chest muscles built beyond the edge of the white bands flexed in support of iron arms. She was ripped like a brick mountain and she had brought the payoff here—a honey trap in the form of a Friday night gay bar.

As she leaned in to signal the bartender for a second draught, a cheerful drawl with hints of countries farther south than the Gulf intruded from the side.

"That good, eh?" It was a curvy, clipped accent that could turn her hot and cold in a switch. Leti ignored the comment but straightened her neck, her booted foot landing on the chrome pipe below.

Dirk had been admiring Leti's impressive physique from the moment she trod up the stairs to stake a berth by the benchtop. Leti stood on chunky legs with one hand pressed into her waist. Her index finger just dipped into the seam of her back pocket and the rest fanned along the upper indent of her buttocks, nicely pushing her succulent buns out. Her ribbed top was stretched by precision slabs of muscle shifting like oiled plates below the surface of her pale skin, except where the material fell into her lean waist. The image worked.

"I'll carry her tab," Dirk instructed the keep.

"No, thanks." Leti kept her tone neutral and her gaze on the bottles. "I can buy my own."

"Dressed like that, I'd buy you anything you want."

Leti clenched her jaw to stop a retort, but her nostrils flared and her neck muscles tensed. Her grip on the glass tightened all the way up her arm.

"Hey, sorry if I offended you, kid." Dirk was not at all apologetic.

"I am not a kid," Leti growled. "I haven't been for a long time. You know that."

"I remember when you looked a lot different."

Leti set her glass down with a determined thud and cut her gaze toward the voice. Dirk had soft styled hair that flopped long over her face but stayed short in the neck. In a long-fingered gesture, she pushed one side back over her ear, only for the other side to draw down in recompense. Brown strands slid over each other, dark and rich as rum. Inviting. It was enough for Leti to notice the wide mouth and sharp jawline underneath.

Bluntly, she said, "I'm not selling."

Unsurprised by the answer, Dirk replied calmly, "My unlucky day, then." Her shot glass alighted empty onto the bar. The bartender exchanged it for a fresh drink at her nod. "Thanks, mate. Her drinks are on me." She swiveled her bar stool away from the liquor display and touched her feet to the sticky wooden floor. Off the seat, she was a little taller than Leti.

"Don't worry," she said, still with that inscrutable half-smile. "I'm only interested in what you're not selling." Then she slipped away into the depths of the club.

Leti barely heard the words, mesmerized as she always was by the attractive disparity of Dirk's wide mouth set in an angular jaw, and agile lips that could shape anything. The other parts of her appreciated the symmetry of shoulders, square to hips, unbroken by breasts in the GQ fit of a long-sleeved tee. Lined neatly into the waistband, a slim belt buckle shone against the darkness of Dirk's black trousers—a loose lock to flat hips—one she would like to feel digging into her back.

An unmistakable tightening had gripped her below the waist upon hearing that voice. Unusually beautiful gender-fooling women, like Dirk, were her weakness, and Dirk had been inspecting her with an appetite.

Shit, she had just blown an opportunity.

Leti sat for several minutes, slowly draining her beer and a tingling awareness. The apologetic rejection still prickled under her skin. She could have a bevy of offers tonight, but all she wanted was to hit her knees for a smooth urban butch. It had been too long and Leti was hungry for it. They would find each other again later. That was how they always played it.

Unsolicited feathery brushes swept Leti's back coyly, drawing her out of her mood. In response, she dropped her left hand and traced the swell of hips under a frock. The woman behind was salsa-ing a vigorous cocktail into her back. At her accepting touch, thong-cuffed buttocks swiveled firmly into the seat of her palm, and the dance changed from tentative to boldly provocative.

Wet hair whipped her neck as the woman impressed a body mural through gyrations into her rock-steady back. Thighs thick as anchors in black jeans, Leti planted her legs to ground her position. She hooked her arm backward around the petite woman and rolled her shoulder blades into nipples raised by resistance. Her powerful hand spread against the woman's spine, bringing her in, while her other hand lifted the closest leg up to parallel her own. Supported by Leti's grasp, the dancing woman reached between them and opened herself up to thrust her cunt repeatedly against the edge of Leti's bar stool. Long veins mapped up along Leti's arms and ran tributaries through delts already round and hard as marble. Leti closed her eyes and wished for heavy limbs around her waist, a rough tongue in her ear, and bites hard enough to bring sweet pain.

The music became wilder, the woman breathed harder as the cushion's external seam plied rigid against her clit. She gasped and shrieked softly with each bounce, head shaking tempestuously as she danced to the urgency in her loins. Leti remained still and imagined the body humping behind was moving steely thighs knowledgably into the back of hers.

Sweat sheened on her scalp and her body strained from holding on till the woman came victoriously, gliding up her back on a long glissando and griping her shoulders hotly. Her thanks—a kiss and a squeeze of her biceps. Leti did not turn around to face the anonymous woman. The vertical wave of her body was the only memory they would share. That, and the heat between their legs.

Dirk kept her eyes on Leti's stony expression throughout the performance. It was this contrary manner, after her tender-shaped behind in the fit of low-slung jeans, that made her watch. Leti was prime meat in a place like this and Dirk knew she would come to her when she had made her point.

Tense with a restless pressure, Leti could feel the interest racing through the crowd after the little show. She needed to start something soon. She slugged back a shot of absinthe, soaking her tongue in the distilled magic of wild aniseed and herbal alchemy. Then, from her pocket, she extracted a white capsule, brought it under her nose, and snapped it. The popper's acrid hit sped up her brain to banish the numbness and latch onto her heartbeat drumming to the pervasive weight of the music. It was time.

She was on the dance floor in three strides. Head bouncing to the call, arms stretched upward for the riffs and punching to the synthetic pulse, her muscular body rocked to a stimulating mix of arousal and adrenaline. The ridged material of her ribbed top flitted over her puckered nipples, bringing them out. Ghostly bodies moved in through the rolling fog of dry ice to rub against her; in front, behind, touching her wantonly. Leti lifted her face toward the lights and spun, searched for a familiar face above and level.

Dirk was pleased, and starting to twitch, from following Leti's dance moves. The abandonment with which she threw her body into the music, the flexible way she begged and teased with her trim hips, her arms supplicating for a top—to Dirk, Leti was wanting tonight.

Leti found Dirk watching the floor, watching her. She locked onto her location and headed toward where she was leaning against one of the pillars hedging the floor. Yanking up the front of her singlet, she slid her hand under it and thrummed her abs slowly, continuously, as she walked over to her. Legs apart, fingers wedged into the top of her jeans until they threatened her fly, Leti cocked her groin toward her target. The returned lusty look tested her whole demeanor. When it dragged up from her crotch, she simply said, "Wanna get out of here?"

Steady eyes assessed her for a minute but Leti held her ground—barely. The pop of speed had impelled her arousal until she was almost crying out from it. She was hot and full and ready. Too many hands had touched but not enough with intent. She needed to fuck now, and she wanted it from this person.

Dirk smiled knowingly. Leti's impatient fingertips and the hunger in her eyes gave her away. Curtly, she said, "My way, my rules."

To which Leti moved in, close enough to share heady midnight breath. "I want to suck your dick. I'll do anything you want."

Dirk snaked an arm around Leti's waist and dug her fingers into the arse that had tempted her all night, promising, "If you're good, I just might let you."

❖

"Where are we going?" Leti yelled above the roar of the wind rushing over the cabriolet's front shield. The topless coupe was flying over the limit but all the controls were in the hands of the driver.

The edge of a tattoo peeked above Dirk's forearms where her sleeves were pushed up. Arms locked on the sports wheel and soft hair rising in the drag, she said, "I thought we could take a drive. Go somewhere nice."

"Fuck nice. I wanna blow you, man. C'mon." Leti reached over and squeezed the material covering Dirk's crotch. Her thumb pressed into the top of the fleshy slit underneath. "Don't you want it?" She wiggled her thumb deeper between Dirk's thighs and dragged it up roughly between the lips of her pussy, scraping the tip of her clit on the way.

Dirk's hips nearly flew off the bucket seat. Her legs opened instinctively but she quickly grabbed Leti's hand and clamped it to rest on her thigh. "I'm not letting you do it till you come down from that high."

"I'll come down when I go down on you." Turning her whole body on the seat, Leti used both hands to undo Dirk's pants, reckless of the control Dirk was trying to maintain.

"All right, okay. Oh, Jesus!" Leti's fingers had found their way into her briefs and she was rolling her knuckles around Dirk's pussy, bumping and massaging the underside of her clit and her sensitive peehole. Leti's hand was a compact vibrator with flexible phalanges and knobs playing all over her cunt, slipping below impudently and drilling through the soft slopes of her vulva.

Thighs spreading, Dirk hurriedly signaled and turned off the road into an industrial estate. The area was poorly lit by lonesome streetlamps and security floodlights that only faced the hulking buildings. She found the first empty car park and screeched to a halt under the shadows of a tree. Deserted and occupied only by the night, they were invisible once the engine was turned off.

Dirk hastily unclipped the safety belt and pushed her seat backward, her pants lowering in the same move. Her eyes were already closed to everything but the grinding between her legs. "Yesss." She placed one hand on Leti's surging upper back where bunched muscles flushed with heat. Her nails scratched across the ribbed top in uneven catches as her hips counter-rolled into Leti's half-open fist.

Leti's fingers changed shape and direction, flicking and strumming in upward strokes from the base of Dirk's clit to launch off the tip. Dirk groaned louder, her hips now hiking forward in the direction of her clit. Leti heeded the escalating grunts and moved her hand faster. She held Dirk open while her thumb whapped unerringly on the rising clit head. Dirk's legs instinctively rowed wide. Nerves singing to overload, tremors jumping to her toes and tits, she came with a hollow shout and snapping hips. Leti washed her fingertips in warm come squeezed out by the deep drawing shocks still gripping the depths of Dirk's pussy, before withdrawing her hand.

Dirk grabbed Leti by the neck as she rose, pulled her face close, and drove her tongue into her mouth. Leti met her hungrily. They battled with rough kisses, locked open mouth to open mouth, used teeth that bit and tongues to wrestle. Dirk slowly squeezed Leti's neck in the vulnerable spots, the pain a warning that she could easily snap it. Leti tried to move back.

"Next time, not when I'm driving," she hissed. She kept Leti arched in position until she felt her nod, then she released her hold and pushed her in the shoulder. Leti fell back into her seat. It was too dark to see her face but Dirk wasn't interested in what she might be thinking at the moment. She opened a storage compartment and took out a firm friend.

"Here, put this on." She tossed a small bulk into Leti's lap.

Leti encased the familiar shape in her palm. It was thick and short. "Where's the strap?" she asked.

"You won't need it this time," Dirk said, pulling on her pants. "I want you to stick it in your jeans and place it where it feels good. Leave the other buttonholes undone."

Leti ripped her fly open and tried to jam it between two button spaces but had to use three—it was a fat cock. She moved it around until the inner ridge lay above her sweet spot. When she jacked down, it would pound or press on her clit depending on how she played it.

She was doing just that, fisting and pumping the cock, feeling it move in her jeans, when Dirk's mouth took over. She relinquished her hold on the dick and leaned back. She laced her hand through Dirk's fine hair and imagined how the cock would look swinging, then hammering, into Dirk's wide mouth.

The primal smell of sweat and open sex leached out from their bodies. Sounds of pleasure guided seeing hands, and the air was replete, heavy, with the taste of secretions. Leti held on to the headrest and let her pelvis ride the blowjob. Her granite quads and strong back fucked along, not allowing Dirk any rest, not when she had been ready all night.

Dirk wasn't about to lose control of the scene. She had Leti's dick in her mouth but she was still the one directing. Boring two fingers past the bottom of Leti's open fly, she ran them up the side of Leti's clitoral shaft, curled them into hooks, and pinched her clit between them, soft then hard, up and down, alternating the squeezes with jacking her clit.

The hand in her hair started roving. Dirk used the curve of her hooked fingers to draw out the length of Leti's clit, then slammed the cock down on its unprotected head. Leti's thighs trembled and grew rigid. Dirk repeated the concentrated movements faster, turning the boi helpless under her mouth.

"Yeah yeah yeah," Leti urged, hips churning and punching like a jackhammer. They rose and lowered to the stiff member rubbing itself urgently between Dirk's clamped fingers.

If the dildo was longer, Dirk might have choked from the ferocity and speed of Leti's bucking hips, but instead, her fingers worked on pulling the crest of Leti's clit through the waves of a mighty orgasm, if Leti's hoarse refrain was any indication. Come-soaked jeans and a damp leather seat was proof enough for her.

Dirk yanked the cock out of Leti's jeans, turned it around, and sucked on the under-ridge. The whole phallus had taken on Leti's welcoming scent. She couldn't wait. She unzipped her pants hurriedly and thrust a hand under her briefs, seeking the slippery aching point in her pussy. Dirk looked at Leti—her legs would still be splayed, fly open, and her body wasted for the moment. She rubbed spaded fingers hard and furious over her clit, thrashing it like she would a bratty boi, and shuddered quickly to an orgasm.

"I could have helped you with that," Leti offered, slow and contented, from the other side.

"You will." Dirk started the car, still catching her breath. "At my place. Now, be a good boi and keep your hands busy with that cock. I'm going to want a taste of your sweet ass when we get home."

BOTTOMS UP
GEORGIA BEERS

I'm nervous. Why am I nervous? This is ridiculous. It's *Kara*, for God's sake. Kara, who loves me. Kara, who has pledged to spend the rest of her life with me. I have nothing to be nervous about. Nothing. Right?

That's what I've been telling myself the entire three days she's been on the road, off on one of her business trips again. But the other thing I've been doing while she's been gone is thinking about our conversation a week or two ago…the one that finally gave me the solution to the problem of why we adore each other more than life itself—*still,* after ten years—but don't have very much sex.

We were in bed, me on my laptop and Kara next to me reading a book. I was racking my brains, thinking, *So what the hell is it? Why do we go weeks, sometimes months, without having sex? We've got built-in babes here! We're in a committed relationship, we're both attractive women who are attracted to each other, and we're both right there for the taking. It's the benefit of marriage, isn't it? Yes, we have full-time jobs and we do come home tired on occasion, but we have no children, so that's really not a great excuse. What the hell is it? Why aren't we ripping each other's clothes off a couple times a week? I don't understand.*

I was reading some erotica online and I tried to focus on that when I suddenly came across something so simple, so logical, something that made so much sense that I almost couldn't believe it. I read again, rolling it around in my head and wondering how I'd missed it before. I looked over at Kara, who was engrossed in her lesbian romance novel, and just blinked at her. She finally felt my stare and looked at me through her reading glasses (which make her look damn sexy).

"What?" she asked.

"We're both bottoms." That's it. That's all I said.

She held my gaze with her arresting green eyes and we stared at one another, absorbing this new information for several long minutes.

"My God," she said at last. "You're right. We totally are."

"We totally are."

We laughed about it. We both felt relieved that we'd finally found the answer to the question that had been plaguing us for the better part of a year or two. We hugged. We cuddled.

Then we went to sleep.

We're so damned predictable.

I take a deep breath now and blow it out as I pace in our kitchen, mentally picturing her rejecting me. Or worse, laughing at me and my feeble attempts to take control. I've got all my introductory moves planned out in my head, but I have no idea if I can pull them off. I'm new to this game. My hands are shaking and I'm starting to sweat, which sends me into a mini-panic. I don't want to sweat! I need to smell *good*, not like I just went for a run.

"Christ," I mutter, pressing my fingertips into my eyes. "Okay. Come on. Pull it together." I wander into the living room and inspect my reflection in the decorative mirror for the tenth time in as many minutes. Not too shabby. My hair is neat, loose and wavy the way Kara likes it. I've touched up my mascara and dabbed on a little bit of the perfume she bought me for my birthday. I'm dressed simply in jeans (Kara's favorite pair) and the clingy white T-shirt that she says I don't wear often enough because I'm self-conscious about how it glorifies my breasts. Glancing in the mirror now, I have to admit that I like the look.

My head snaps to the side as I hear a car pull into our attached garage, and I head for the kitchen. I actually whimper aloud with the worry that suddenly floods my system hotly. My heart is pounding and I can't believe how difficult this is already. Is this how all tops feel? I think I'm probably being silly, but I can't seem to help it.

She walks in through the side door and I am momentarily stunned by her beauty, as I always am when I see her after days apart. Her dark, sleek hair is straight and shining, reaching just to her shoulders and tucked behind each ear. She's wearing the black pantsuit I helped her pick out a couple months ago. It makes her look powerful and sexy at the same time. The pants are tailored nicely to fit her compact body, the fabric snuggling firmly against her ass. The jacket hangs unbuttoned and open, as it usually ends up when the day is finished, and the red silk blouse underneath it is suddenly begging for my fingertips. It's revealing a dangerous amount of cleavage, something I've mock-scolded her about in the past, and a single diamond glitters at her throat, dangling from a silver chain around her neck. It was an anniversary present from me and she wears it every day.

I swallow hard because she is so fucking gorgeous, I'm not sure what to do with myself.

"Ugh." She tosses her keys on the counter with a clatter as she sets her leather briefcase on the floor. "What a day." She kicks off the black leather heels and settles down to her real height, about two and a half inches shorter than she just was, and much shorter than I am. My Kara is a petite little thing, that's for sure. She looks up at my face.

"Hi," I croak. The startling green of her eyes always makes me feel like she's suddenly shined a spotlight on me.

Her gaze scans over me and I can almost feel it. "You look great." She kisses me quickly on the mouth, then turns her back to me and opens the refrigerator to peer inside. "What do you feel like for dinner?"

Now or never, now or never, now or never.

It's my mental mantra and I know if I don't obey it, I'll chicken out completely. I will my feet to move and am shocked when they actually obey me, getting me across the linoleum floor in four steps. I press up against Kara's back and wrap my arms around her middle.

"You," I answer close to her ear, my voice husky.

Her shoulders shake as she chuckles. "No, really."

I balk slightly and realize this is my out. It would be incredibly easy to give up right now, laugh along with her, and make dinner. But I'm annoyed that I balked at all and so I steel myself to try again. I press my lips against the pulse point at the side of her neck and suck on it, lightly at first. She shrugs her shoulder up with a girlish giggle, but when I increase the pressure and use my tongue, I hear her swallow.

"What are you doing?" she asks softly.

"Taking what I want." *God, what a great line! I'm so butch!*

Kara laughs again and turns in my arms, the refrigerator door closing with a slap behind her. "Honey. Seriously. What's going on?"

I poke at the inside of my cheek with my tongue. Jesus, is it always this difficult? No wonder I'm not a top; it's too much damn work. Again I think how it would be the easiest thing in the world to drop my arms to my sides, chuckle about what a funny joke that was, and go on with our very loving yet sexually not-so-satisfying life.

"I want you," I say matter-of-factly, knowing I don't sound quite as confident as I did a second ago. Before Kara can knock me down another notch, I cover her mouth with mine. She's surprised; I can tell by the muffled gasp that escapes her as I press her against the refrigerator. I don't let up. I don't want her to speak right now. My self-assurance is hanging on by a thread. One more hesitation and I'm done; I can feel it. I run the tip of my tongue around her lips, requesting access, which she grants me, much to my surprise.

I sink into her, reveling in the softness and warmth of her mouth as I kiss her. My hands slip under her jacket and her blouse is like velvet beneath my fingers. The heat from her body radiates through the fabric, and it almost makes me swoon. I catch myself, though. I'm supposed to be in charge here, but I realize with slight horror that I didn't think I'd even get this far, that my plan doesn't go beyond this point because I had such little faith in myself. Surprisingly, I hadn't hesitated. Well, okay, I had a little, but I got myself back on track. I was stronger than I'd expected. Which is a good thing, but still…what the hell do I do now?

I continue to kiss Kara while I have this internal conversation. I'm surrounding her, trapping her between myself and the refrigerator, and I'm a bit taken aback to realize that I like it. I like the feeling. I like being the one in control. I understood when I was planning this little ambush that the only way I'd be able to do the right things at the right times would be to imagine the shoe on the other foot. My brain quickly tosses me an image of the situation reversed, with Kara in control, and I think, *What would I like her to do next?*

I slide my hands up and grasp the lapels of her jacket, pushing it back over her shoulders and down her arms as I wrench our mouths apart. The red blouse is sleeveless and the freckles on Kara's pale shoulders wink at me, causing my mouth to water.

"God, you're beautiful," I whisper with reverence as my eyes rake over her. Her chest is heaving and she blinks rapidly, her eyes cloudy with confusion and desire. I latch my mouth onto one bare shoulder, pressing my teeth in more firmly than she's used to. She inhales sharply and fists her fingers in my hair. The feeling is not unpleasant.

"Honey," she says and her voice is strained. "What—"

"Shh." I silence her with my lips. I'm getting into this, much to my own astonishment. It helps that Kara is so much smaller than I am. If we were the same height, I don't know that I'd be pulling this off, but as it is, I'm able to subtly steer her around the kitchen until she's backed up against the part of the counter that sticks out like a peninsula.

What would I want next?

While my tongue is buried deeply in Kara's mouth, I feel my way along her blouse and unfasten each button with impressive dexterity. Soon she's standing in the kitchen in her bra and slacks and when I pull away to take in the view, her eyes are clouded and her lips are swollen a deep pink. She looks like she's been blindsided. In a good way.

This power trip I'm suddenly taking is pretty damn cool. Being the top has its advantages, I have to admit. The way she's looking at me, the way her breasts are rising and falling rapidly and her chest is flushed red...*I* did that. Holding her gaze, I reach for the front of her slacks. The button pops and she flinches. I quirk one eyebrow and slowly lower her zipper, then give the fabric the gentlest of nudges. It falls to the floor silently, pooling around her ankles in a silky black puddle. She's wearing a red bra and matching red panties, and my machismo falters slightly as the sight of her in all her underweared glory makes me go weak in the knees. I swallow hard, determined not to screw up when I've come this far.

What would I want next?

I kiss her again. Hard this time. Demanding. Feeling like I'm in charge. Showing her who's the boss at this moment. *Here's a hint, doll: it ain't you.* I capture both her breasts in my hands and knead them through the silk and lace of her bra. She moans into my mouth, which sends a rush of wetness into my panties. I cup her ass and lift, catching both of us off-guard as I deposit her on the counter. Now we're face-to-face and I have much better access. Kara wraps her legs around my hips and pulls me into her tightly. All the air seems to leave the room, but I keep kissing her. I can't remember her ever being quite this hot.

Our mouths still fused together, I find the clasp of her bra and open it. I give her no time to notice before I slide my palms around to the front and grab a handful of warm, pliable flesh in each one. Her nipples poke at me, making themselves known and demanding more attention. I pull reluctantly from her lips, loving the whimper of protest that escapes her, and take as much of one creamy breast into my mouth as I can fit. Then I suck hard and with enormous greed. Kara tosses her head back and groans an erotic sound I've never heard before. It sends a fresh, hot rush of wetness to my panties. Good God.

Long minutes go by as I love her breasts, licking and sucking and rolling and pumping. Kara's nearly hyperventilating, hands braced on the counter, her head still thrown back, and she's the sexiest damn sight I've ever seen. I'm absurdly proud of myself at this point. I've taken her from chuckling over a supposed joke to being half naked and panting on the kitchen counter. In our everyday sex life, I might have been annoyed by now…annoyed that I still have all my clothes on and that she's made no attempt to get me out of them. But I'm okay with that because I think I'm beginning to understand how this works. It's all about the one on the bottom. She's got all the control; she just doesn't always know it. I see that now. At this moment, Kara could ask me to squat on the floor, flap my arms, and cluck like a chicken and I'd do it for her, as long as it meant I'd get more of her once I was done.

Trailing a path down her quivering belly, I absorb the softness of the skin there, the faint smell of her arousal suddenly tinting the air. I stand up straight and catch her eyes. Their usual green is now almost completely overtaken by the black of her pupils. I smile at her, trying my best to put a wicked glint in my expression and hoping I succeed, not having much experience with such things. Stepping closer, I wrap an arm around her waist and lift her slightly. Our lips are millimeters apart, but I don't kiss her. Yet. With the fingers of my other hand, I catch the waistband of her panties and pull them down and off. My eyes never leave hers as I lift the panties up and dangle them from my finger before letting them fall to the floor. Kara's nostrils flare and her tongue darts out to wet her lips.

I've never been so turned on in my life.

Not making eye contact any longer, I stare at her body instead. Her skin is creamy white; she hasn't had much opportunity to be in the sun yet this year. She's petite and compact, but oh so womanly, with curves in all the right places. Her taut brown nipples look painfully hard and the coarse, dark triangle of hair between her thighs is glistening. Putting a hand on each knee, I push her thighs apart slowly, listening to her breath hitch in her chest. I stare at her, at the evidence of her extreme arousal, and she lets out a tiny whimper.

"Please," she whispers.

I stifle a triumphant hoot because I just made my girlfriend beg for my touch simply by looking at her. This is a power trip in the extreme and I am almost unable to keep myself from diving at her and devouring her completely.

Instead, I take a small step forward and kiss her, pushing my tongue into her mouth at the same time I slide my fingers into the warm wet that's waiting for me. We groan in tandem at the contact. She's totally drenched and I'm suddenly honored that she saves this part of herself for only me. My fingers seem to move of their own accord around and through her heat and I suddenly feel relief, like I'm home. I know this feeling; I know this body. I slide into her and she wrenches free of my mouth, a gasp forcing its way from her throat. With her arm, she pulls my head to her shoulder, my name and God's interchangeable in her heated whispers of pleasure. I push in and out of her slowly, slickly, and when her head falls back, I run the flat of my tongue up the long column of her throat, tasting the salt on her skin, almost tempted to take a bite.

Her hips jerk and I know she's close. I'm thoroughly in control here and I realize once again how much I like it. I'm suddenly, inexplicably grateful that I tried this little experiment; it seems to be working for both of us. Kara moans and I know it's time to release her and bring her home. I pick up the pace and pull my head up so I can watch. There's nothing more beautiful than actually being able to pinpoint the moment she tips over the edge. Her breath catches and she raises her chin. Holding tightly to me, she hisses my name before catching her bottom lip between her teeth and squeezing her eyes shut. A long, guttural hum issues from deep in her throat and I feel her entire body go taut like the string on an archery bow. Her legs clamp around my middle and I push into her one last time, holding her to me to keep her from sliding off the counter.

God, she's beautiful.

"I love you," I whisper as she comes down, her body relaxing little by precious little. She drops her forehead onto my shoulder, trying to catch her breath. My fingers are still buried in her warmth and I feel her inner walls twitch.

"I love you too." Her voice is soft, muffled against my T-shirt. We stay in this position for several long minutes before I feel her shoulders shaking and realize that she's quietly laughing.

"What?" I pull back with a smile and try to catch her eyes.

She looks up at me, and her green eyes are sparkling with a gorgeous blend of satisfaction, love, and amusement.

I want in on the joke, so I ask again. "What?"

"Did you just top me?" she asks.

I feign surprise. "Me?" I try unsuccessfully to suppress my knowing grin.

She slaps at me playfully and pulls me in for a hug. I notice with great joy that she hasn't ordered me to remove my fingers yet, so I wiggle them ever so slightly and am rewarded with a little intake of breath.

Yup, I could get used to this game. Being the top is pretty fucking cool.

ROAD GAMES
RADCLYFFE

O kay," I said, "let's play I Spy."
        "Another stupid game I don't know how to play," Christie
grumped.

I felt her pouting all the way in the front seat, but I didn't dare
take my eyes off the snow-covered road to check her pretty pink lips.
'Course, I didn't have to see them to know exactly how they'd look—
full and wet and puckered just a little bit, like she was ready to blow me
a kiss or flounce away.

Except she wouldn't be flouncing anywhere for quite some time,
and neither would the rest of us. Not at the rate the snow was falling
outside and given the fact that we still had 150 miles to go before we
reached the condo we'd rented with some other friends for Valentine's
Day weekend. Crap. It hadn't snowed all winter, and now out of
nowhere, a blizzard.

"Come on," I cajoled. "It'll pass the time and it beats singing 'A
Hundred Bottles of Beer on the Wall.'"

"*Again*," Christie muttered. "It figures I'd get locked in a car with
two jocks for a week."

"It hasn't been a week," I pointed out reasonably. "Only twelve
hours."

"Feels like twelve years."

I heard Christie huff and risked taking my eyes off the narrow,
twisting road for a second to glance into the rearview mirror. She was
sitting sideways with her legs up on the wide rear seat of my 4Runner,
looking miserable, her chin on her knees, her long blond hair falling
around her face. I felt sorry for her. I felt sorry for all of us.

Kit turned in the seat beside me to peer back at her girlfriend. "Aw,
baby, it'll be fun. Just give it a chance, okay?"

"Okay, whatever."

"This is the way I Spy works," I said hastily. "The first person picks something outside but doesn't tell the rest of us what it is. Then they say, 'I spy something with my little eye, something starting with the letter *P*.' Then the first person to gue—"

"Little eye?" Christie snorted. "You mean, like the one in your *little* dick?"

"My dick doesn't have an eye," I said, grinning despite myself. Kit and Christie, my two best friends. I loved them, I really did. But being stuck in a car with them for half a day was starting to wear on my nerves. "But it *does* have a great *big* fabulous head."

Next to me, Kit chuckled. The SUV bounced and shimmied a little and I clutched the wheel.

"Are you watching the signs?" I demanded of Kit, peering through the increasingly heavy snowfall and cursing my decision to try a shortcut to beat the traffic on I-95.

"What signs?" Kit gestured to the window. "Like I can see anything through that."

"You've got a point," I conceded. "Maybe I Spy isn't such a good idea." I racked my brain. We'd already been through Twenty Questions, Change a Letter, the Name Game, Alphabet, and Countries. "I guess we can just listen to a CD again."

Christie and Kit groaned simultaneously.

"Okay, then the radi—" I broke off as the shimmy became a shudder. I fought the wheel, which was jumping around in my hands, and just that fast, we went into a slide. The back fishtailed off the edge of the pavement and hit the snow-covered shoulder and the next thing I knew, we were spinning. "Hold on!"

Christie shrieked, Kit swore, and I tried to remember everything I'd learned in driver's ed about not flipping over in the middle of a skid. *No brakes. No brakes. No brakes,* I chanted silently while aching to stomp my foot on the brake and put an end to the dizzying motion. With a huge *whoomp* the SUV plowed into something, a mountain of snow geysered up around the windows and cascaded over the windshield, and we jolted to a standstill.

"Jesus," Kit gasped.

"Everybody okay?" I shouted, twisting under my seat belt to check my passengers. "Christie? You okay back there?"

"Was it the crack I made about your little thing?" Christie said, her voice shaking.

I laughed, loving her even more for being tough in a clinch. "That'll teach you to bad-mouth my equipment, won't it?"

Kit popped her seat belt and leaned between the seats into the back. "You're not hurt, are you, baby?"

Christie shook her head. "Nuh-uh." She leaned forward and kissed Kit. "How about you, honey?" Then she wrapped her arms around Kit's neck and dove in for more before Kit had a chance to answer.

"Don't mind me," I groused while they were kissing and cooing. "I'm just fine. Thanks."

Kit came up for air and grinned, shaking her head to flip her short dark hair back out of her eyes. "Feels like we're in a ditch. I guess we should take a look. What was it, do you think?"

"I'm not sure. Axle maybe." Whatever it was, it'd felt bad. That plus the weather did not equal a good night ahead. "I've got flares in the back. We better set some out if we can't get out of here."

I climbed out after checking the rearview and side mirrors to make sure I wasn't going to get picked off by a passing motorist. Not much chance of that. We hadn't seen taillights or headlights for miles. Kit joined me, and we tromped around the SUV in knee-deep snow, the visibility so poor we could barely see the road.

"Going to need a tow," Kit observed.

I had to agree. The ass end of my truck was practically invisible, half in a ditch and buried in a snowdrift. We set out the flares and hustled back inside. Then I dug out my cell and called the number on my emergency road service card. Fortunately, Kit had been following our route on the map and we had a very good idea of where we were.

"It's a holiday weekend, and with this storm," a very nice woman advised me, "it's going to be at least three or four hours before we can get to you. Do you have adequate warm clothing?"

No, I wanted to say, *we came out in shorts and sandals.* But I could tell she was reading from some sort of emergency checklist card, and it wasn't her fault I had detoured into the backcountry, so I just said, "Yes."

"How much gas do you have?"

"Better than half a tank," I said, mentally whispering a quick thank-you to whatever gods had prompted me to fill up just before we'd gotten off the interstate.

"Don't run the engine unless you clear the snow from around your tailpipe, and turn it on sparingly if you start to get cold."

"Okay. What about—"

"The temperature is well above zero, and you should be in no danger if you stay inside your vehicle until our emergency truck arrives."

"Thanks." What else could I say? Forget about all the other stranded motorists and come and get me first? That's what I wanted to say. But we really weren't in any trouble. We had enough munchies, soda, and water for a solid day if we had to wait that long. Which we wouldn't need to.

"I'll call you in an hour and a half with an update," the nice lady said. "You keep your phone nearby and don't use it to call anyone else."

She suddenly sounded a lot like my mother, and I felt myself sitting up straighter. "Okay. I've got it."

I disconnected and explained the situation to Kit and Christie.

"We're going to be stuck out here all night!" Christie practically screamed. "We could freeze out here!"

"We're not going to freeze," I said testily. "We'll be out of here before morning. Try to sleep or something."

"You're not supposed to go to sleep," Christie retorted. "Besides, you two are sitting up there where it's warmer!"

She was right about that. I hadn't been wearing a jacket while I was driving, and it was still warm enough in the front seat that I was comfortable in only my sweatshirt. Kit squeezed between the two front seats and clambered into the back. Putting her arm around her girlfriend, she murmured loud enough for me to hear, "I won't let you get cold, baby. Don't you worry about that."

"Well," Christie said, "I guess you could think of *some* way to keep me heated up."

I glanced in the rearview mirror, saw them go into another clinch, and figured they'd survive the wait. Easing my seat back enough to stretch my legs out underneath the steering wheel, I closed my eyes. Sleeping would pass the time until help arrived.

It was very quiet in the truck. Very very quiet. Except for the sound of kisses. Funny, when you're not actually doing the kissing, they sound different. They don't sound slippery and soft and tingly, they sound like someone drinking after a trek in the midday sun or eating after a long fast. Wet and thirsty. Hot and hungry. Small murmurs of pleasure and satisfaction interspersed with urgent pleas for more.

They probably thought they were being quiet as they sighed and shifted and murmured softly. It hadn't been that long ago when Kit and I had shared a dorm room and I'd seen them both naked more than a few times. I'd never seen them doing anything more than cuddling up in bed, but it wasn't much of a stretch to image the rest. I wriggled in my seat, suddenly restless.

Christie whispered, "You've got such a great tongue," and Kit laughed.

"Suck on it, then, baby."

More little *Mmm*s and the sound of lips pulling on something tasty. I flashed on Kit's smoky dark eyes and her fuck-the-world grin and her small, neat breasts and the trim dark triangle between her thighs. Out of nowhere, my belly twitched. Funny, the 4Runner felt warmer too. Of course, that could have been due to all the steam rising from the backseat. I folded my arms over my chest and willed myself to sleep.

"Ooh, honey," Christie hissed. "That makes me so horny."

"Yeah? Want more?"

"You know I do."

"What, baby," Kit teased. "What do you want?"

"Reach under my sweater and play with my tits."

Jesus. Christie was a talker. I knew that about her. It didn't matter what the occasion or who was listening (or trying *not* to)—the Super Bowl, a movie, a crowded elevator, or, apparently, in the middle of sex—she'd talk all the way through it. I should've told them right then that I could hear them. But just as I opened my mouth, Christie moaned. Now, I've spent a lot of time with Kit and Christie, and I've heard Christy laugh and curse and cry and tease. But I've never heard that little catch in her voice and the almost hurting moan that trembled in her throat. It was raw and beautiful and I strained with everything in me to hear it again. She was panting, hard and fast, and every few seconds she'd let out a tiny cry.

"You like that, don't ya, baby," Kit growled. "You like it when I squeeze your nipples like that, huh?"

"Oh yes," Christie whimpered. "Do it harder. Like that. It's so nice."

My head felt like an echo chamber, every word exploding like a rocket burst and careening around inside it. Every rustle of clothing and creak of the leather seats as they climbed all over each other was a knife slashing across the heated surface of my brain. My clit was a hot rock pulsing between my thighs and I spread my legs to get some relief. It might have worked, except...

"You're making me so wet," Christie gasped.

I didn't mean to, I swear I didn't, but I glanced up into the rearview mirror and saw them in the hazy moonlight that filtered through the snow. Christie's head was tossed back, her eyes nearly closed, and Kit's mouth was roaming over her throat. I felt the pressure of Kit's teeth skating along my skin, felt the hard points of pain and pleasure throbbing in my nipples, felt the come slick my clit. I tore my eyes away, but the image burned against my closed eyelids. I unzipped my pants.

"Give me your hand," Christie said breathlessly. "Oh God, feel what you did."

"Baby, baby... Jesus, you're so hot. You're dripping."

Kit sounded like she was going to cry. I wanted to too. I ruffled my fingers through the soft strands above my clit and imagined Kit stroking me and me stroking Christie and Kit's clit a smooth stone sliding over mine. The base of my clit was raised up and I was wicked hard. I bit my lip and tapped the hood. My legs jumped, and I hit it faster while easing closer to the edge of the seat so I could hear them better.

"See what you did to me," Christie sobbed softly. "You made me all wet. You made me so horny. Feel what you did to my clit. Feel...oh, yeah. Right there."

"You need me to take care of you, baby?" Kit crooned. "You need me to make this hurt all better?"

"Uh-huh. Uh-huh. Uh-huh."

The SUV started to shimmy again, but we weren't moving, and every few seconds Christie would whimper and say, "Squeeze me, honey. Oh, rub me harder. Oh, oh oh...so good."

I slid a finger on either side of my clit and followed her lead, squeezing and rubbing and sliding through the river of come.

"You gonna come for me, baby?" Kit whispered.

Yes! Soon, soon, soon! I pushed up my sweatshirt and slipped my hand under. My breasts were hot and swollen, my nipples as hard as my clit. I squeezed a nipple with one hand, my clit with the other, point-counterpoint…one-two, one-two, one-two, one…I was getting close to coming and breathing so loud I couldn't hear what was happening behind me. Christie was even louder, keening and gasping. I pushed both feet hard against the floor underneath the dashboard and fought back the pressure building inside my pelvis. My cunt was ready to spill over but I wasn't ready to let it go. I wanted to get off on Christie's come. Still, I needed to come so bad, I whined quietly. If she didn't come soon I was going to, no matter what.

"Honey, honey," Christie groaned in a tone I'd never heard—wild and half crazed, "fuck me fuck me I wanna come so bad."

That did it for me. My clit went ballistic, shooting daggers of pure pleasure into my cunt, and I started coming.

"Ooh, Go-dd," Christie wailed.

"Oh shit, oh shit," I whimpered, twisting in my seat while I grabbed my pussy and tried to squeeze every last drop of come out of it.

It felt like I came forever, curling up on myself and trying not to yell, and it was a lot quieter in the backseat when I finally got my hearing back. I stole a peek in the rearview mirror. Christie was cuddled up in Kit's arms, a dreamy little smile on her face. Kit had an arm around her shoulders and was slowly sifting strands of Christie's blond hair through her fingers.

Kit's eyes met mine in the mirror. "Warm enough up there?" she asked, her words slow and thick.

"I'm good," I answered, still watching Kit's face as I carefully circled the head of my supersensitive clit with one finger. Kit's eyelids slowly closed and then opened halfway a few seconds later. Her mouth went slack and she groaned softly and I knew Christie was doing her. I picked up the pace on my clit, which was all of a sudden pumped up again.

"Oh baby, yeah," Kit whispered over and over while she watched me watching her.

"Mmm, you're so hard," Christie cooed softly. "I love how hard you get right before you come."

My clit was dancing on the edge again and I could hardly keep my eyes open. The muscles in Kit's neck tightened and she bowed up off the seat, her face a mask of pleasure.

"You're making me come, baby," Kit groaned.

"Oh fuck, me too," I blurted.

Christie laughed and Kit and I both shouted while Christie brought us off together.

A minute later, I sagged into the seat, bathed in sweat and totally wasted. It took me a while to register that the ringing in my head was my cell phone. I fumbled around on the seat next to me and found it.

"Hello?" I croaked.

"Hello, dear, it's Irene from Emergency Services with an update. Are you still all right out there?"

I checked out Christie and Kit in the rearview mirror. They were kissing again.

"We're doing fine."

"That's wonderful. We'll have someone out to you in about two hours."

"Thanks." I disconnected and swiveled in the seat to give Kit and Christie the message.

Christie gave off sucking on Kit's lower lip and threw me a big smile. "So why don't you come back here and keep warm with us."

"Yeah," Kit said, grinning lazily. "We'll think of something to do until they get here."

What the hell, I thought as I climbed back between the seats, *what else is there to do on a road trip, anyhow, except play road games?*

MINE, HERS, AND OURS
KARIN KALLMAKER

I put my shoes back on and waited for my carry-on to reappear on the conveyer belt. When it didn't, I realized the object of attention at the scanner was something of mine.

Oh hell, like I didn't know what it probably was. Damn. I'd gotten the hand lotion and toothpaste into a Ziploc but had forgotten about that other little bottle because it was in a special velvet pouch.

My carry-on finally emerged and a screener picked it up, looking for the owner. I signaled it was mine, hoping I was reading her correctly. To me she looked friendly, professional, and a dyke. "I'm going to have to search the bag."

I nodded and watched her unzip it. "I can tell you what it is, probably."

She shook her head as I reached for the red velvet pouch. "I'm sorry, but you can't touch anything. Is it likely to be in there?"

I nodded. We exchanged glances.

"Perhaps we should go through it in the private screening area?"

I nodded and tried hard not to blush. I wasn't embarrassed, just highly amused. I swear her eyes twinkled for just a moment as well.

She turned to a supervisor and asked her to join us for a private screening. We proceeded to the little side room. The screener set my carry-on down with a thud in a small cubicle. The bag *was* heavy for its size. She got out the velvet pouch I'd indicated, but the supervisor said, pointing to the much larger, zippered leather black bag next to it, "Why not that one?"

The screener and I exchanged glances. Then I said, "It only contains recreational toys."

The supervisor bristled slightly. "We should still look—"

"In the interest of time, let's see if we can find the item the scanner revealed." The screener added, her face carefully neutral, "I'm looking for a small bottle, about three or four ounces."

"Yes, that's in the bag in your hand. I forgot to put it in the Ziploc with the other liquids is all."

She unknotted the smaller bag, showing no apparent response to the soft white rope and condoms that she moved aside. I was very glad she was wearing latex gloves—and I bet she was as well, though I knew everything was clean.

With a satisfied smile she held up the small black bottle of lube. "Do you want to put this in with the other liquids?"

"Sure. Thanks." I did just that as the supervisor hurried away.

We shared another I-know-you-know glance while I zipped my bag closed. When I finally picked up my carry-on, the screener said, "Have a really fun time."

I hoisted the little suitcase and couldn't help a crooked smile. "I intend to."

❖

Once I was out of sight of the security area, I put the lube back where it belonged. I didn't plan to waste a moment looking for supplies when I was finally alone with my girlfriend. Long-distance relationships can be stressful, and work demands had kept us apart for nearly three months, the longest gap since we'd started dating a year ago. A tech conference like the one where we'd first met was getting us together at last, and not a day too soon. The scent of her on the nightshirt tucked under my pillow had long since worn off.

The screener had been pretty hip, and no doubt if my slinky, sensual girlfriend had been with me in the security queue she might have even cracked a genuine smile. Yeah, I would have conveyed with a shrug, I'm carrying ten pounds' worth of sex toys for her. And then added, by way of a lopsided smirk, that she was worth it, which was an epic understatement.

I lined up for my boarding call and thought about the contents of my carry-on. I found myself wanting to explain to the screener, however, that I wasn't carrying the toys because I was butch and butches supposedly do the heavy lifting. It was more complicated than that—at least, it felt like it to me. There's that whole détente surrounding sex toys and who "owns" them given the who/what/when of their acquisition and the why/when/how of their use. I had once waxed lyrical on this theme with my girl; since at the time I had been in the middle of something she rather liked, her answer had been, "You think too much."

I had three more hours until I was with her, so what was I supposed to do but think? As I rolled my carry-on down the Jetway, I thought about the ten pounds of recreational sundries inside. One of the toys, the brown one, not so long but plenty thick, she'd bought "for me" last Christmas. It was never going to go inside me; I used it on her. From the start, though, we'd both always said it was "mine." She certainly called it mine when I was wearing it.

I made my way down the aisle in a daze, hearing the repeated purr of her sexy voice in my ear, telling me how much she loved my cock, how glad she was I was the kind of woman who liked to wear one. I wrestled my heavy case into the overhead compartment directly above my seat and settled down with relief. My knees were surprisingly weak.

I had also bought the purple one with the bumps to use on her, and we still called it mine, though lately…

I buckled my seat belt and tried not to visibly squirm as I recalled the little show she'd put on for me the last time we'd been together, using the toy herself and telling me just how much she liked it. So exposed and yet so confident, her bright blue eyes glowing with sensual pleasure, she had pushed it in slow at first, telling me how hungry it made her for me.

Arching into her thrusts, she'd said after that panting, sexy half moan of hers, "You like that sound, don't you? The sound of me all wet and juicy?"

When I could breathe I'd whispered, "You know I do." The closer she got to climaxing the sweatier her words were, carrying us both along the rising crest of her passion.

"Watch me, baby," she'd ordered. Plunging that toy in and out of her beautiful, red, slippery cunt, she'd said between groans, "You like watching me fuck myself? You know I'm going to need more when I'm done. You know I'm just getting ready for you."

I recognized the sharp gasp, then the even sharper cry as her hips lifted off the bed, and had knocked the toy out of her hand and given her what we were both crazy for by then, my cock in a long, single push, while she was still coming, and she started all over again. The vision of her pleasing herself so openly expressly to please me had made me want to take care of her every last itch. We'd been frantic into the night, fallen asleep, and reached for each other again in the morning.

The purple one with the bumps—that was her toy now, in my mind. Hers because she used it to please both of us. Yes, I was the one bringing it to our hotel room. I'd had such pleasure from it that I'd happily carry it anywhere she liked. No fools did my mama raise.

The man in the seat next to me fiddled with his tray table, jarring me out of my reverie. My pulse was racing and I felt feverish. I had entirely missed taxi and takeoff. The beverage service had started, and while I waited to ask for water I tried to get some control over my thoughts—no point in getting myself to a boil with two hours of flight as well as negotiation of a large airport ahead of me.

Right. Like I could stop thinking about what would happen when we were alone in the hotel room. I knew what I wanted to do to her: spread her out on the bed and taste her. She was sweet and copious at the start of an evening, and I enjoyed feasting on her. I closed my eyes and thought about the little gold flirt nestled in the leather pouch, every bit as effective in pleasing her as the larger toys alongside it. At first she'd been squeamish because it had been mine while I was still with my ex.

She'd said, during one of our three-nights-a-week phone calls that we'd started sharing after that first conference weekend, "You used it with someone else, and that seems a little…gamey to me."

"I understand, but you don't feel that way about my fingers, do you? Or my mouth?"

After a little pause, she'd said, "Well, no. I see where you're going with that idea."

"Sweetie, I don't consider the toys I kept after the breakup anymore sentimentally attached to my ex than parts of my body. I've boiled it several times. Believe me, I wanted all traces of her off *everything* of mine. Besides, the one I'm thinking about using always had a condom on it too."

"Oh? Will I like it?"

I'd made an impish noise into the phone. "I'll happily spend hours testing it out with you."

"I suppose," she'd finally said, after we'd discussed my intentions in minute detail, "that if everybody got rid of toys during a breakup it would be expensive and wasteful."

"That's right. We don't want to endanger the silicone supply."

"So you'll bring them with you next weekend?"

I had agreed that I would and felt I was quite the experienced lover. Then I'd realized that I had just talked a very good talk, and when we got together for our second weekend, with all my toys and hers, I would have to deliver on my bawdy, explicit promises.

When the stewardess gave me the water I wanted I drank thirstily, but I had no interest in the packet of peanuts. It was not at all the flavor I wanted in my mouth right now.

I don't know if it's part of the long-distance thing, but every time we were due to get together I had these same anxieties. We were sensuous and graphic on the phone—would all that magic happen again when we were most definitely in the flesh and expecting everything our bodies and ten pounds' worth of sex toys could deliver? The first weekend at the convention hadn't been planned, and we'd still done amazing things with some lube I'd found in my suitcase and the vibrator she always had with her. Amazing things. Epic things. Lost count of the times, shaky-legged, exhausted sleep, late to breakfast, lunch, and dinner kinds of things.

Now I was worried—like I always was—that I would look silly in harness and toy, or that I'd slip on lube or get the angle wrong, squish her hand with my knee, bump heads, or fall off the bed during some particularly energetic maneuver. I had ten pounds of sex toys with me— what if I couldn't please her with any of them this time? Silly, I scolded myself, because I knew my fingers, hand, and mouth could certainly do the job. Not that I was thinking of it as a *job*, goodness no.

Once I started worrying, I couldn't stop myself. What if this entire year had been a fluke? Just a flare of passion felt for a near stranger, and throwing all caution to the wind by going to bed? It had been wonderful and unexpected and naughty, as neither of us told anyone else at the time. What if the passion had run its course and now neither of us felt the same? Well, I knew I was still crazy about her. What if she didn't feel the same in spite of the repeated assurances on the phone?

Did she worry? Think about that toy of hers, the small pink one that had been bought in error, that we'd discovered really suited me? I'd never enjoyed that before, but with her and the things she whispered in my ear, I'd found a woman using a toy on me very pleasing. Size matters. In my case, smaller turned out to be much, much better. She was bringing that toy with her, she'd promised. It was very new to me to count on someone else that way.

I liked it. It scared me, but I liked it.

I stared at the compartment overhead, pictured the various items, and my memories again stopped at the one she called the brown bomber. Oh, that brown one, how we both enjoyed it. But my jaw had dropped when I'd opened it, and I hadn't been able to stop myself from saying, "Christ, honey, are you sure?"

For an answer she'd slipped a tape measure around the toy, then around my wrist. "I knew you'd worry about hurting me. So don't."

I'd blushed, sitting in my jammies under her Christmas tree, but not that night with that heavy cock strapped on. Sure, it felt a little silly fiddling with O-rings and buckles; if you think about it too long, sex *is* silly, except when you're doing it. It had felt really powerful to wear something she had specifically picked out for me to please her with. I did like that feeling of power, I liked that a lot. But when she wrapped her legs around my thighs and pulled me in, I found her power matched my own. I was only able to feel so powerful because she could take it. What good was that toy to me if there wasn't a woman I could drive to absolute abandon using it? It was now the biggest reason that bag weighed ten pounds. Yes, we called it mine, but without her, I mused, it was useless.

The feverish feeling was getting worse—I was definitely in a major lust for my girl. I could hear the sound of the brown one going inside her followed by the noise she made, a kind of oh-damn-yes-that's-exactly-it noise. Everything I did to her, especially when I told her in advance what I was going to do and then did it, made her happy. So why was I feeling so anxious?

Maybe it was the pink toy, the one I liked. I'd never been vulnerable like that before, and it was disconcerting to find I liked it. Maybe it was the conversation we'd had the last time we were together, those three long months ago, when she'd asked me, directly, what it was I really liked in bed.

"You," I'd said.

She'd snuggled close into my arms. "No, silly. I mean for yourself. I don't care what it is. I'm more than willing to explore it with you."

"I'm fine, baby, really. You are the best thing that's ever happened to me." It was the truth, and I didn't know what else to say. One of the things I loved about her was that she could ask for my touch, could put her desires into words and explain to me, show me, what it was she needed. I had never been capable of that kind of vulnerability. I just didn't have her courage. How could I tell someone my few kinky thoughts—what if they didn't want to share that with me? And it *was* so much fun taking care of her.

She'd propped herself up on one elbow to lock her gaze with mine. "Well, I'm a little self-conscious here."

"Why?" I was a goner. I knew that. Those blue eyes, that forthright gaze—how was I supposed to hide anything?

"I'm the one doing all the screaming. I mean, I know you come and it feels good." She kissed me softly. "I guess I'd like to make you crazy-wild-screaming too."

I shrugged. "I've never been that way."

To my surprise, she had smiled. "Good. Then we don't know for sure that you can't be that way, do we?"

With a start I realized my plane was touching down. My heart twisted against my breastbone and I grinned. Her flight landed twenty minutes ahead of mine and we'd arranged to meet at my baggage claim area if all went well. Otherwise, my cell phone would ring and we'd make new plans.

In just a few minutes I'd be holding her. Just a few minutes more until I smelled her and buried my face in her hair. I was foolish to be anxious. The fireworks would be there. Ten pounds' worth of sex toys, plus what she was bringing for me, would make for a wonderful time together. In addition, there would be the deeply satisfying falling asleep and waking up, the flush of laughing about nothing, the shared excitement over new tech that the conference promised, and the simple pleasure of holding her hand. Every day would have something new to enjoy together, and the more time we spent together, the more every day was filled with familiarity too.

The massive airport took time to navigate. I reached the baggage claim as quickly as I could and queued with my fellow passengers. Bags began chunking onto the carousel, and to my delight, mine was the second one down. I seized it, turned around, and there she was.

The wool coat was sleek and long, but I scarcely took note of it as I swooped her into my arms, spun her in a circle, and set her back down on what I immediately noticed were skimpy black stilettos—the kind of shoes that put the *fuck me* in footwear. My brain exploded with a hundred images of her in a hundred poses, all featuring her long, smooth legs and those shoes. I had her bent over my suitcase, on top of me on the baggage carousel, me grinding into her on the hood of the taxi.

"Shall we go?" That was all she said, in a very mild tone that was a flat-out lie compared to the way her eyes were gleaming with mirth and anticipation.

Laughing and chattering, we found a taxi and covered a million topics on the way to the hotel. All of her seemed alight with happiness, and it took my breath away to think that being with me might be the cause.

Fortunately, we ran into no one we knew at the hotel. By tomorrow we wouldn't be able to cross the lobby without a dozen hellos. But for the presence of the bellman, I'd have done naughty things in the elevator as a reward for that dancing look in her eyes.

After the obligatory tour of the small room and a parting tip for the bellman, we were finally alone. I put my carry-on up on the desk and unzipped it.

"I got searched at security," I said as I extracted the velvet bag.

"I didn't, and it's a good thing," she said from behind me.

Turning with the heavy leather pouch, all ten pounds of it, I started to say, "Why is that?" but the sight of her unbuttoning her long coat to reveal an exceedingly skimpy black negligee trapped the words in my throat.

The coat slid to the floor with a whoosh. She was smiling at my slack-jawed response. "Like what you see?"

"Hell yes." I swallowed hard as my gaze traveled from that sultry smile to the round invitation of her breasts, then past the tight black panties, all the way down her body to the stilettos. Thinking of the bumper sticker a friend had given her, I said, "Cute shoes. Wanna fuck?"

"Hell yes." She lifted one hand and I finally noticed that she was holding something.

At first I was puzzled. "I thought you were too sensitive to wear those."

"I am."

I studied the short length of chain dangling from her fingertips. At each end of the chain was a soft-tipped clamp. Then the significance of her answer sank in. My heart lunged up into my throat.

She moved in on me like a panther, backing me up against the desk. "Put the goodies down for now."

Not taking my gaze from hers, I set the leather pouch on the desk. I could not control a shudder as she pulled my shirt out of my pants and unbuttoned it.

The look in her eyes made my knees weak. It was the same proudly sensual woman who had used the purple toy with the bumps on herself to boil my blood.

She didn't break eye contact while she stripped off my shirt and sports bra. Still staring into my eyes she licked one of the open clamps, then took my nipple between her fingertips. Only then did she look down with a heated, sensual smile.

I felt faint when the clamp closed over my nipple—not too tight, not enough to get me to *ouch*, but tight enough that I could not forget it was there. As soon as she had both nipples in the clamps, she let the chain that joined them fall against my bare stomach. She looked up at me again. "Is that okay? Adjust them—fix it. It needs to be okay."

Trembling, I loosened one and tightened the other, then swallowed and found my voice. "It's okay. How did…I never said…"

"Baby, your body told me last time we were together. Thing is…" She leaned in to kiss me, and the silk of her negligee brushing against my taut nipples drew a moan from me. "The thing is, I like to toy with your nipples and it obviously feels really good to you, but when you're on top of me you do have a way of fucking me senseless and then I forget all about playing with you. This way…" She lifted one shoulder eloquently.

I was having trouble breathing.

She hooked one finger around the chain, gently moving it, and I couldn't believe the way it ignited all the nerves between my legs. "Now, what would you like to do?"

I exhaled explosively. "Fuck your brains out."

She grinned. "I was hoping you'd say that. For the record, these clamps are mine, because I think I'm going to love what they do to me."

Turning her attention to the leather pouch, she unzipped it and spread out the contents. She picked up the soft rope and brushed it lightly against my nipples.

"Fuck." The so-soft sensation was absolutely fantastic. My brain was narrowing in its focus and my vocabulary exited the room, because all I could find to say was, again, "Fuck."

"Oh, I knew you'd like wearing those."

I scrabbled on the desk for the harness and brown bomber. She was already undoing my trousers. Shoes and socks were flung into a corner. She fit the toy into the harness, then helped me step into it. I fumbled with the straps and told her, my voice raspy and low, "Get on the bed and spread your legs."

She ran one finger under the chain as an answer. "Feel good?"

I twined my hand into the hair at the back of her head and pulled her against me for a hard, deep kiss. Her warm body pressed against my nipples, sending pulses of fire down my stomach. Only when she gasped for air did I answer her. "It feels fantastic."

"Hot for me now?"

"I've been hot for you for weeks. I thought I'd burn up on the plane."

She brushed her lips against mine. "Poor baby. I think you'd better fuck me, then."

"Like I said"—I pushed her away from me—"get on the bed and spread your legs."

She did as I asked, finally, after pulling back the covers. She spilled over the sheets, abandoned and ready. I stripped the little negligee panties off her as I said, "I can't believe you wore this on the plane."

"Truthfully, it was under my clothes during the flight. All I had to do after I landed was take off—oh yeah. Please, baby."

I pushed her thighs apart until she bent her knees and those stilettos were resting on my shoulders. Every time I moved, the chain swayed and my nipples felt as if they were going to explode. My clit was so swollen it brushed against the leather of the harness. I looked down at her open cunt, one of the most beautiful things about her, about women, and it gleamed with wet and inviting red heat.

Usually I fell on top of her with possessive force and took her in a rush. She did like that, but the clamps made me move much more slowly this time. I stayed back on my knees as long as I could, watching the length of my cock ease inside her. I pulled back slightly, felt faint at the sight of how wet it was, and pushed in again. Her legs slipped from my shoulders and she wrapped them around my hips, reaching for me, her arms beckoning.

I lowered myself on top of her, and at the first twisting grind of my hard nipples against her soft breasts I felt a shudder run through me like I'd never felt before. The chain was caught between us, and every time I shoved all the way in it was like her fingers pulling at my nipples, except when she started to cry and toss under me, when she started to come and throw her arms over her head to brace herself for thrust after thrust, my nipples were still being pulled.

I lost control and fucked her, fucked her, my clit bumping against the leather of the harness in a tantalizing rhythm, making me desperate to come. She climaxed again and again under me, making those sounds of absolute abandon, little screams, her hands on my back, at her own nipples, clutching the sheets over her head. I couldn't stop fucking her and she didn't want me to stop. Every time I went all the way in I felt closer until finally my clit convulsed and I ground into her hard while she sobbed into my shoulder.

I felt unleashed, growling with pleasure and conquest, like something I'd always wanted was finally mine.

❖

Trembling in her arms after she helped ease the clamps off, she asked again if it was okay. Weakly, I mumbled, "What do you think?"

"I think it was more than okay."

I managed enough strength to take in her expression. "You're smirking."

"Who, me?"

I laughed, then said, seriously, "I've never done that before."

She grazed one of my still-hard nipples with a fingertip. I couldn't believe the powerful throb of response from my clit. "Come while fucking someone?"

"Yeah," I said, though it wasn't quite what I meant. I nearly let it go, then added, "I mean...gotten off by fucking someone. Fucking someone until I was done, not until she was." And I couldn't have had that if she hadn't been willing to explore it—to give that experience to me. No lover had ever thought so carefully about what might make me scream.

"It was the same thing right then, wasn't it? You did fuck me until I was done."

I thought about that while she kept lightly playing with my nipple. Though the clamps were off, the pressure and sensation was eased but still very present. Other parts of me were getting wet and swollen all over again. "That's never been true before."

She leaned into me until she could touch her own hard nipple to mine. I moaned. "For me neither. But I've always wanted to please my lover that way, to be what she needs, to take until she's done. It felt wonderful to me, it really did."

"There's no one else I would have let put those on me."

"No one's ever given me that kind of power before," she whispered. "Thank you. It felt amazing to me. To know you were letting me inside like that. To be as lost in sex with me as I am with you, every time I'm with you." She looked away.

"Is that what it's about?" I really hadn't considered it before, that she might be feeling like the one who was always more vulnerable because she got to a place where she *had* to come and couldn't stop. She'd gotten me to that place too and I wanted to be there again, in her arms. "Getting lost in it?"

"Getting lost together."

How did she manage to know so much, and how had I ever gotten so lucky as to be the one who held her? "What I just felt, is that what it's always like for you?"

"Since I met you, yes. Like that."

I had strutted over how good she felt. Smirked and skited, and yet I'd not understood, not really, that I wasn't taking from her, she was giving.

And I thought I knew all about sex.

I kissed her softly. "I guess I thought the point of really great sex was to be done. That it would be so good you'd be satisfied."

She snuggled against me. "And now? What's the point of really great sex?"

"Having more. What I just felt, coming like that, it makes me want more. It makes me never want to be done at all." I drew her hand between my legs. "Baby, please."

"After all that fucking," she whispered against my lips, "you want to fuck some more?"

"No, honey."

"Then what?" Her fingers found my clit and I twitched in response.

"I'm tired of living in two places."

She circled my clit with her fingers, then teased lower. "I want to talk about that too. Later. Are you sure you don't want to fuck some more?"

"No, honey."

She raised her head with an inquiring look, her lips parted as her breathing quickened, her hair a mess and a light in her eyes that warmed me in places I never wanted to be cold again. "If you don't want to fuck, then what do you want to do?"

I pulled her mouth to mine and arched into her touch. "I want to make love."

THE TWENTY-MINUTE RULE
ALISON TYLER

O f all the lies I heard when I moved to Los Angeles:
You're so pretty.
Of course you're a good actress!
Yes, I'll call you in the morning.
...none was quite so blatantly false as "the twenty-minute rule."
This insidious little lie claims that you can get anywhere you want in
Los Angeles—*anywhere* at all—in twenty minutes or less. Say you're
at UCLA, but you have tickets for the Hollywood Bowl. No need to cut
your last class short. You'll make it in twenty minutes, easy. Or maybe
you're working at the Westside Pavilion Mall, but you want to catch a
friend's new play in a warehouse downtown. Not to worry if your boss
keeps you late. You can get there in twenty minutes.

Who on earth came up with this insane concept? Some sadistic
demon with no geographical understanding of the sprawling region that
is LA? Or maybe the LAPD, hoping to generate more income from
speeding tickets. It's an evil little falsehood because you can't help but
think that the rule works for other people. Why else would you hear the
phrase so often?

I'll admit that I tried my best at first. For two years, I believed the
lies that Los Angeles tells on a daily basis.

I believed those women who promised they'd call after our
naughty nights between the sheets. I went on audition after miserable
audition. I gave myself twenty minutes to get to any appointment.

And then I got beaten down.

The one woman I truly wanted—a key grip in the movies—found
my roommate more interesting than me. The one coveted role I honestly
thought I'd landed went to someone else. Ultimately, the person I saw
in the mirror no longer reflected the compliments I received.

By the time I met Marlene, I'd stopped trying to find a steady girlfriend. I'd forgone any attempt at a serious acting career, studying to be a masseuse instead. Yet the twenty-minute rule was the most difficult to let go. I didn't want it to be just one more of Los Angeles's many broken promises, another glittery rhinestone-adorned carrot on the end of a fool's gold stick.

Marlene was a new client who lived out in Venice Beach. I made it to her house from my studio in Hollywood in a good fifty-five minutes flat. There was traffic, of course, and an injury accident, as reported over the radio. And the result was that I arrived half an hour late. The cottage sat on one of Venice's quaint canals, but I couldn't see the beauty of the location. Feeling sloppy and sweaty, I hefted my massage table through the tiny garden leading to the front door.

"Oh, good, you're pretty," she said when she opened the door. The lie just rolled off my back. *She* was the one who deserved the compliment, a green-eyed minx with hair the color of an Irish setter and a cinnamon-freckled complexion. She was built small and lean but looked plenty strong, proving her strength when she tried to wrest the massage table out of my hands.

"I can manage," I told her, feeling breathless from being late, as if I'd run to her place rather than fought my way through traffic.

"Are you sure?"

I nodded.

She led me through the house, which thankfully wasn't decorated as so many homes are in LA, in virginal all-white that makes me feel nervous to even breathe hard for fear of depositing a bit of the famous LA smog on the pristine interior. These anal clients who live in their all-white homes either insist I remove my shoes at the door or else hand over those little blue paper booties doctors wear during operations. But Marlene's place was wild, with splatters of paint on the walls, colorful metal license plates hammered directly into the giant wooden dining-room table, and clothes strewn everywhere. She had made no attempt to clean up, hadn't even seemed to consider where I'd put the massage table.

"How about here?" she asked, pointing to the wreck of her living room. The room contained two sliding glass doors, with a perfect view of the sun setting over the canal outside. Yet there was not even space for the two of us to stand side by side. "We'll just shove all this…" She started pushing the coffee table, made of some antique-looking chest, against the battered black leather sofa. Then she dragged several big canvases toward the kitchen, a tiny room I could see through an open hatch in the wall. It looked as if she'd never washed a coffee cup in her life.

"I have a show coming up," she explained, not bragging or sounding the slightest bit self-conscious, just matter-of-fact. "Things get out of hand before any one of my exhibits. The whole place becomes my studio."

I nodded and helped her shove, then set up the table and turned my back, giving her the chance to undress without me staring. But Marlene didn't seem to understand what I was doing. She moved around in front of me as if I'd been rude to turn my back on her, pulling off her white men's shirt—*once* white, I should say, now decorated with various interesting splotches of color—and kicking off her ripped jeans, more holes by now than denim. "It's next week," she continued, stripping off her candy-striped panties. She had no bra on. No real need. She possessed mere handfuls of flesh for breasts. "That's why I called you. Amanda Miller, the curator at the gallery, suggested I try to relax. And I'm lame at relaxing. I never got into that yoga craze, can't stand Pilates."

I was liking her more by the second, and when she hopped up on the table, I found myself hoping for the first time ever that she would be one of those clients who talked, rather than one who slept. The girl was interesting and she didn't seem phony in the slightest. Just the fact that she had proudly revealed her A-cup breasts in this world of silicone humps made me want to kiss her.

No, that's a lie.

I'd wanted to kiss her since I'd first stepped over her threshold. There was something about the look in her lake green eyes, the humor in her slightly wicked smile that made me want to press my mouth to hers, to lick in a line down the hollow of her throat. To devour her whole, so that I could own what she was.

To my great delight, she chattered throughout the entire massage. It was as if she'd never had a massage before, or as if she were simply getting a rubdown from a good friend. She didn't seem to want to relax in the slightest, more concerned with helping me to do my job well. When I lifted her hand in mine, she raised her whole arm for me, and

I had to tell her, "No, let me do the work. Let me position you," and gently shake the limb until she let loose. And when I rubbed the palm of her hand, caressing and soothing, she tried to return the favor, her thumb pressing back into my own palm, sending a wash of heat cresting over me.

Maybe she *was* stressed, but my fingers didn't feel it. There were no knots to discover in her back, no tight spots to slide away. Regardless, I gave her my best work, and she cooed and sighed between discussion of her art and her travels, but as far as I could tell, she was as easygoing as a house cat whose sole job is to find the best sunbeam to sleep in.

During the hour, she told me that she'd lived in the Real Venice—she said the words as if they were capped—and that she couldn't imagine ever living too far from water. She explained that she'd moved to LA because her work was marketable, and that she herself was marketable, admitting that her looks played an equal part in the value of her artwork. She was honest and open and I drank in every word, only responding when she asked me a direct question.

"How long have you been doing this?"

"Two years."

"You're good."

I thanked her and tried hard to believe she wasn't feeding me a lie.

Although I listened carefully, I also found myself fantasizing through the massage, imagining that this was my cottage, that I could sit on the tiny deck every morning and drink my coffee, watching the sunlight shiver on the little canal. Or that this was *our* cottage, where I would give Marlene massages every morning and she would paint me when she was in the mood.

"Your turn," Marlene said evenly when I was finished.

"My turn for what?" I'd been dreaming of what it would feel like to wake up at her side.

"A massage. Hop up on the table."

I looked at her, incredulous. "*I'm* the masseuse," I said, as if speaking to a child. Had she not understood what I was there for? She slipped off the table and pulled on her shirt and panties, leaving the jeans in their blue denim puddle on the floor. Then she scratched her chin and gazed at me with what I felt was an artist's eye, and suddenly I felt as naked as she'd been only moments before.

"But you look as if you could use a massage. In fact, you look as if you could use one even more than I did."

I hesitated. Nothing like this had ever happened to me before. Sure, I get those questions a lot from my friends, especially during a night out drinking: *Don't you ever fuck your clients? Haven't you ever been offered an extra twenty for a hand job?* The answers? No and yes. I've been offered but I haven't accepted. The twenty for an extra? Seems low for a fistful of pleasure.

"Come on," she said. "Do you have somewhere to be?"

"I've got another appointment at nine." It was my turn to lie.

"Give me twenty minutes." And when I looked at her, eyebrows raised at the statement, she whispered, "You know the rule of twenty, don't you? You can get anywhere you want to in twenty minutes."

"So I've heard."

"You don't believe it?"

I shrugged. "Never worked for me." That summed up LA in a heartbeat, didn't it? None of the lies worked for me. I'd tried to buy into them, I'd done my best, and I'd ended up in a dark studio apartment with a view of a wall, a one-time walk-on part on an infomercial, and a reputation for always being late.

"Try again," she urged. "Believe it one more time."

I looked at her. God, she was pretty. Not LA pretty, but *really* pretty. She wasn't like the ultra-young, ultra-chic, hipless starlets I saw every morning when I went down my street for coffee. She seemed—I fought for the word—real. And she seemed to really mean it about giving me a massage, straightening out the rumpled white sheets on my table, then crossing her arms over her chest and waiting for me to take off my clothes and hop on.

I hesitated another moment, and she shot me this wiseass smile and turned around as I had done at the start of the job, offering me a bit of faux privacy. I say *faux* because now that the sun had set, the whole room was reflected in the glass windows. She would be able to see me undress whether she faced me or not.

"What do you have to lose?" she asked, still keeping her back to me. I thought about that. Nothing, really. Or everything. If I let myself believe once more, put my heart out one more time, what would happen if this turned out to be just one more lie? That was easy to answer. I'd return to my depressing little hole in Hollywood and drink myself numb from my emergency bottle of JD.

"Twenty minutes," she cajoled, and I said to myself *fuck it*—and stripped. Off came my black drawstring pants, the tight black T-shirt. Down came my dark hair. I climbed onto the massage table and slipped under the sheet, reveling in the warmth left from her body moments before.

And as soon as her fingers touched me, I was gone.

I've never been a fan of receiving massages. I know that sounds strange coming from a professional masseuse, but I've always been the one to offer the back rubs, to stroke the sore muscles, to ease away the aches and pains. But Marlene was good. She knew instinctively how hard to press, not tickling, not messing around. Her fingers were warm and soft, and she slid them under my back and rotated in gentle circles, making the stress of not just my day, but my world fade away.

When she told me to roll over, I did so automatically, feeling intense pleasure as her hands smoothed over my back and down my legs. Feeling even more pleasure when she started to work her way back up from my feet, lingering at the insides of my thighs. Oh, so this was going to be one of *those* massages—at least, I hoped like hell it would be. When her fingertips ever so lightly brushed my pussy, I almost came. I trembled on the table, and she pulled back, but I rolled over and looked at her, the sheet falling away.

"Did I go too far?"

I shook my head. "Not far enough."

"We've still got five minutes," she said, glancing at the large round clock over the mantel.

I looked over as well. The clock had been in the same position since I'd arrived. Clearly, it was broken.

"Back down," she instructed, and I obeyed, feeling her climb onto the table with me, feeling her mouth against my pussy, her fingertips spreading apart my nether lips as her tongue sought out my clit.

I groaned and raised my hips as her tongue made circuitous routes around that pulsing source of pleasure. She was an ace driver. She knew just the road to take to get me off. I could feel her long, soft hair tickling my skin, could feel her smooth body against my legs, and I realized that she'd pulled her shirt back off and lost the panties, understood that we were both naked on my padded blue table, and even though I knew the thing could handle nearly four hundred pounds—I do occasionally massage the former football player—there suddenly wasn't enough room.

Hating to break the contact, I pushed her back and said, "Bed?"

She gave me an embarrassed look. "I sleep on the couch."

"Why?"

"I'll show you."

She slid off the table and I followed her naked down the hall to the bedroom, which had been transformed into a studio, covered with canvases and drop cloths and paint. So back we went, this time all the way through the house to the sliding glass doors. She opened them, and out we stood, neither of us caring what anyone else might think. She brought one of my sheets with us and spread it out on the wooden dock that led right to the canal. And then we were on it, and we were fucking. Fucking for real. Fingers and tongues and fists. I couldn't contain myself. The way I'd touched her before was as a professional. Now I touched her as a lover.

I didn't use the moves I'd learned in school. I used the moves I had wanted to use from the moment she'd opened the door. Making her stand up in front of me as I pressed my mouth to her cunt. Making her hold on to my shoulders for support as I nipped and bit my way to the center of her body. She drew her nails dangerously along my naked skin, then held on tight, coming like the relaxed cat I'd imagined during the massage, purring as I lapped at her clit, lapped and licked until the sweet cream spilled forth, until she could take no more, falling to her knees and curling into my arms to let me hold her.

And then it was my turn and she seemed to grow larger, to take up more space as she held me down on the tiny dock, wanting me on my stomach, one hand underneath my body, rhythmically pinching my clit, the other smacking my ass over and over, with just the force, just the heat, I craved. I don't know how she knew I'd like that, or that I needed that sort of touch. She just knew.

When I came, she moved her body so that she could press her mouth to mine, and it was as if she were drinking in my pleasure. Absorbing my moans and gasps into her own sultry body. Taking them for herself.

"Was that for being late?" I asked softly as I rubbed my sore ass. She wrapped us up in the sheet together and we stared out at the glittering water of the canal.

"No," she said, laughing. "That was for not believing."

"Not believing?"

"In anything. You let LA get under your skin. You can't do that. You have to hold tight to what you know. And you have to believe."

So I guess I was wrong.

I guess you *can* get anywhere you want in twenty minutes.

As long as you know where it is that you truly want to go.

OFF THE MENU
KIM BALDWIN

First off, let me say I didn't deliberately leave my umbrella behind. Honest. Amsterdam is just so damn capricious, rain one minute and sun the next, that it's easy to forget what the weather was like when you enter a place because it is almost always different by the time you leave. And I freely admit I'm sometimes forgetful, but it's one of my charms.

I go to Amsterdam a lot. It's one of my favorite cities, with its picturesque canals and refreshingly tolerant attitude about everything. And then there's the food. There are a thousand restaurants in and around the city, so there is always a new gem to discover whenever and wherever you get hungry. Indian, Greek, Spanish, Indonesian, Tibetan even—you name it, it's there.

On this particular night, my stomach began to growl as I biked past a little Thai place. It was Wednesday, always a slow night out anyway, and November, not the high season for tourism with its breezy cool temperatures and bone-chilling rains. So I wasn't too surprised to find only one couple occupying the ten or so booths, and they were on their coffee and dessert.

It had great ambience, the dark wood pub-style booths all plushly padded with leather the color of mahogany and subdued lighting provided by candles and tasteful wall sconces in an art deco style. Though the music had a definite Asian flavor, it was more new age symphonic than native folk tune—smooth and sensual. Oh, yes. For atmosphere, I gave it an A+.

One thing you risk in the tiny neighborhood eateries, though— once in a while, you run into the odd exception to the rule in Holland. No one speaks English. In cases like that, there are usually a lot of charades and pointing to other people's plates. And of course I hope

I can recognize a few words off the menu from previous forays into ethnic places. But yeah, I've made a few mistakes guessing and ended up with something that is disconcertingly unfamiliar. I still wonder what the meat was under that odd-tasting gravy I had in Nicosia.

I knew at once I was in for a challenge in this place. A frantically energetic young man of about twenty-two welcomed me in fractured Dutch and gestured for me to sit anywhere, then brought water and a menu. The latter was entirely in Thai characters and Dutch. By the time I had glanced through it thoroughly, seeking something vaguely familiar and finding nothing of the sort, the other diners had departed and only the waiter and I were left.

I pointed to an entree on the menu. He gestured indecipherably, muttered something in Thai, then Dutch. I pointed to another entree, with the same result. Smiling, he put up a hand to stop further questions and disappeared into the back. Soon after, *she* appeared.

She was of average height and rather slight of build, but her arms and shoulders said she worked for a living, really worked—physical labor, and lots of it. Or she had a passion for working out, or a hobby that demanded or developed impressive upper-body conditioning. Her long-sleeved navy T-shirt and blue jeans hugged her body like they were sculpted onto her.

She had skin the color of honey, short black hair, and warm, nut-brown eyes that shone with mischief no matter what else her expression revealed. At the moment, she looked…well, appreciative, as she crossed the room, her open appraisal of me from head to foot wonderfully disquieting.

She stopped beside my table and grinned down at me. "Welcome. I understand you have need of my services."

She spoke English with a British accent and her voice was honey-toned, too. Smooth, slow, and in a lower register than I would have imagined. I wanted it to be the flirtation it sounded like. Seemed so, from her very direct eye contact. Regardless of whether she was serious or playing, I wanted to play along. "I sure won't disagree with that."

"If you will put yourself in my hands, I promise you won't be disappointed." She laughed softly.

"You've certainly whetted my appetite," I replied, taking a long, appreciative look at her, just as she had with me. Up close her body was even more impressive. Martial arts, maybe, I thought. She also had a kind of graceful power in the way she moved and stood, and in the quiet, confident way she spoke.

"How hot can you take it?" Her smile crooked to one side as she tried not to laugh.

"Very." Oh, how I hoped I was reading that look in her eyes right. "Bring it on."

"My pleasure." She gave me a quick, flirty wink and a slight tip of her head, then pivoted and disappeared into the back.

A scant five minutes later, as I sipped my wine and relived the warm feeling of her eyes on my body, Frantic Waiterguy reappeared long enough to set a salad before me. Filled with colorful slivers of vegetables I couldn't recognize, it was heavenly and beautifully presented, although a rather petite portion, I thought.

The second plate arrived before I had even half finished the salad. The third and fourth were delivered shortly thereafter. By the time the little plates and saucers and bowls stopped coming, there had been more than twenty in all, and I was full to bursting.

Every single sampling had been a perfect gastronomic experience. And even more extraordinary, although I had been to Thai restaurants many times before, all over the world, I had not eaten even one of the twentysomething dishes ever before. And yes, many were decidedly hellfire spicy, so she took me at my word, and I ate every bit of *those*, you can be sure.

I wanted her to know that it wasn't all words. I can take the heat.

After forty-five minutes of eating, just as I decided *not one bite more or you will really regret it,* a half-drunken party of eight stumbled in, dashing my hopes that I would remain the restaurant's sole patron. I sipped coffee, willing her to reappear. Praying for her to, while wondering about her role in the place. Kitchen help? Chef? Owner?

Another couple came in and took a table near me. *Damn. What are you doing out in the middle of the week? Why don't you people go home?*

I lingered long after the waiter handed me my check. It read: *No charge. My pleasure.*

I lingered, hoping she would come out to ask what I had thought of the meal. And maybe more. But the restaurant only got busier and busier, and there wasn't even a glimpse of her. Finally, I took the hint and left.

I needed to bike away my disappointment, so I put on the headphones from my MP3 player and set off with no particular destination in mind, just hugging one canal for a while, then another, admiring the lights on the bridges and the security of people on the street wherever I turned. Ninety minutes passed in a heartbeat.

I don't know how I ended up back there, but just as I realized I'd wound my way full circle to the restaurant, the sky opened up and it began to pour. Of course it had been clear and full of stars a minute before. But that was Amsterdam, so that was nothing new.

And it was only then that I remembered that I'd left my umbrella there. Happy fate! But my heart sank quickly when I saw the restaurant was dark. I stopped anyway, because the place had a nice big awning and I just wanted a moment to think about her. Through the big picture window I saw a light on in the back and wondered if someone was still in there.

I didn't have to wonder long.

Her sleek and sexy silhouette appeared, unmistakable. Paused, froze when she realized I was watching, backlit by the street lamp outside. Then continued toward me. *Swept* toward me was more like it. Languid. Unhurried. I hopped off my bike and locked it to the nearest lamppost.

By the time I turned toward the ancient wooden door at the front entrance, it was open and she was there, leaning against the threshold watching me, arms folded across her chest.

"What a fabulous feast," I said. When I got close enough, I could make out her features. She was smiling broadly at me, eyes shining in the lamplight.

"Each and every dish. Exquisitely wonderful," I continued. "But it was just too generous of you to treat me."

"Not at all," she insisted. "A purely selfish gesture, I assure you. Part of my plan." She straightened and tilted her head toward the dark interior of the restaurant. "Come in?"

"Love to." I stepped inside and waited while she locked up again. "So you have a plan, do you?"

"Yes." She turned on her heel toward the back, knowing I would follow.

I did. "Going to tell me details?"

"All in good time," she said over her shoulder. She paused next to a long, deeply cushioned booth in the rear of the restaurant and lit the candle in the center of the table. "Cappuccino? Or perhaps some wine?"

"White wine would be lovely, thank you."

She was back with two glasses in the time it took me to remove my coat, scarf, and gloves. I slid in toward the back of the booth, inviting her to sit beside me, and she did.

"I'm very glad you enjoyed my efforts to please you." She gave me a long and deliberate once-over, lingering on my breasts before her eyes met mine with naughty promise in them.

"Oh, I more than enjoyed them," I said, relaxing against the plush seat back. "I savored every single bite. I am curious about something, though. I thought I was pretty well versed in Thai food, but I don't believe I've ever had any of those dishes before."

"No, doubtful you have. They were all my own recipes," she said, confirming what I had thought. No mere kitchen cook, but rare culinary artist.

"Magnificent creations," I gushed. "All such wonderfully complex blends of flavors."

"Well, perhaps it would be more accurate to call them potions, not recipes." She slid closer to me as she added this tidbit and rested her arm along the back of the booth so that her fingertips rested on my shoulder. Easy. Just barely touching, but I was hyperaware of that slight pressure. Of the musk of her perfume. And of those warm brown eyes boring holes into mine. She was gorgeous.

"Potions?" I repeated dumbly.

"Yes. And so far, every one is working perfectly, I might add." She licked her lips and leaned in closer. "The first dish was to keep you thinking of me until we could be alone together." Her hand began to gently caress my shoulder. "The second, to bring you back to the café if you left."

"Ah, I see," I played along. I shifted my body to reduce the distance between us, and put my hand on her thigh.

"That's the fourth one, there…" She glanced down to watch me slowly caress her from knee to hip. "The potion compelling you to put your hands on me."

"You skipped the third," I interrupted. She flexed the muscles of her thigh as I stroked her through her jeans and made me all too aware of how well conditioned her body was. I imagined her moving on top of me, and my heart began to beat a little faster.

"The third dish was to make you forget something you'd have to come back for."

I froze for a moment at this, surprised by the reminder. Busy in the kitchen all night, and she'd noticed I'd left my umbrella behind? "Well, I am kind of forgetful," I admitted.

She shook her head slowly back and forth. "It was the potion." She was staring at my lips, and I noticed she was breathing a little faster.

"Well, they all worked," I said. "I'm here."

"Not *all*, not yet. We're only just waiting for potion five to start working." She moved a couple of inches closer.

"And that one does what?" God, I loved the way she was looking at me. Like she was going to pounce any second.

"You will want me to kiss you. You will crave it. Need it. Be obsessed by the thought of it."

I nodded my head vigorously. "Oh, that one kicked in some time ago."

Her lips were on mine an instant later. She nipped at my lower lip and caressed me with the tip of her tongue before pushing hungrily into my mouth, wet and hot and insistent. I met her with equal enthusiasm.

"Six makes you want to take your clothes off." She was already reaching for the buttons on my shirt as she said this, and I was not about to fight the power of the potions. I smiled my agreement as she pulled my blouse out of my jeans and slipped it off my shoulders. I certainly hadn't gone out that day expecting to end up like this, but I had entertained the idea of enjoying myself in Amsterdam if the opportunity arose, so fortunately all the lingerie I had packed were things I was not ashamed to be seen in. Today it was a peach-colored satin and lace number that maximized my cleavage and left little to the imagination. From the look on her face, I'd say it was an excellent choice.

"Seven, you will crave my mouth on those beautiful breasts." Her voice had gone all husky.

"Oh yes. I ate every bit of that one." I straddled her, took her face in my hands, and kissed her.

As I teased her with a careful, controlled kiss, she deftly removed my bra. Then, as gently as I was kissing her, she tenderly cupped my breasts. She moaned, a low sound in the back of her throat, when her thumbs brushed over my nipples and found them rigid and erect. The sound and the sensations sent a warm twist of arousal through my lower belly and into my groin.

"Do it." I couldn't recognize my own voice.

She kissed my neck, sucking and licking and caressing with her tongue, down my chest to the right breast, cupped with her hands. She paused for a moment, looking, her pupils huge and black, before her mouth closed around my nipple and send a jolt through me.

I was instantly wet.

"God." I gasped. "That feels wonderful."

"Eight." She gave my left breast the same breathtaking attention, and I struggled in a haze to pay attention to the fact she was still reciting potions.

"Eight?" I repeated dutifully.

Her teeth briefly grazed my nipple before she replied. "The eighth ensures that you have fully complied with six."

"Six?" Okay, I admit by now I had lost count. All I could feel, all I knew…was her mouth.

"The you-want-to-take-your-clothes-off one," she reminded me as she gently nudged me to stand in front of her. Her mouth returned to my nipple as her hands dropped to my waist to undo the button on my jeans. She slowly lowered the zipper and I felt, more than heard, her moan against the sensitive skin of my breast.

She slipped her hands into my pants to cup my ass as she stood to kiss me again, her tongue invasive. Insistent. Intoxicating.

Her hands were cool, and I shivered a little as she caressed my thighs and calves while slipping my jeans and panties off. But mostly I trembled with the anticipation of what was to come.

"And nine has to be that I crave seeing *you* naked too," I said as she kissed her way up my body—across my thighs, breathily brushing over my sex to my stomach, a gentle nip at my breasts. Every nerve she passed came alive. She traveled up my neck to whisper in my ear.

"Undress me, then." She sucked hard on my earlobe, and I grasped her T-shirt and the tank top beneath it and lifted them up and off her. God, she had beautiful breasts. They were small, but perfect. Round and high, with the nipples dark and rigid. I wanted to put my mouth on them, but she kissed me again and guided my hands to the clasp of her jeans instead. I had her out of them in a flash, and then before I knew it, I was lying on the long, padded bench of the booth with her above me.

And damn, did she feel good up there. Our bodies found a rhythm, hard and driving and anxious, and she was kissing me again. I loved the way she used her tongue, and with the friction being generated between our naked flesh, I could easily imagine her using that tongue to get me off.

"Potion ten..." I hated giving up that kiss, but she was driving me crazy with her mouth and my heart was pounding like jackhammers were going at it in there. "All I can think of is you going down on me."

"Exactly right," she agreed and commenced to lick and suck her way down my body, pausing for a long moment at each breast. By the time she spread my legs with her hands and put her tongue lightly on my clit, I was so wound up and so damn wet I was ready to pop.

She was as talented with her tongue as she'd been with her cooking. I'd have bet money it wouldn't have taken any time at all, but she knew just how to prolong it to an exquisitely torturous level. Every time I felt the first stirrings of climax, she'd change her stroke just enough to keep me poised on the brink, screaming for it. Then back off enough for it to become a pleasant kind of pain. The kind that blurs all reason and caution and becomes blinding need.

"No more! Please make me come!" I panted, thrusting my hips forward to deepen the swipes of her tongue.

She was merciful. Her mouth closed on my clit and sucked, and I came hard and fast, an intense and driving climax that seemed to go on and on.

While I regained some semblance of strength and breath, she kissed her way up and down the length of my body. I watched her while she did, and she met my gaze. I love it when you can see in a woman's eyes how much you are turning her on. In no time I was ready and anxious to see her get off. "The next one...eleven, is it...involves you coming hard for me, in the way you like best."

I could feel her smile against my stomach.

"You're catching on nicely."

I raked my fingernails lightly over her back. Her body was so responsive when I touched her, it turned me on all over again. "Tell me what you want."

"I want to fuck you," she said, spreading my thighs as she moved up to kiss me again.

I tasted myself as her tongue gave me an idea of how much she wanted to be inside me. And I told her with my mouth what I thought of that idea. I sucked on her, played with her, worked her up until I could feel her heart thundering in her chest where it rested against mine. My clit twitched and I felt another rush of wetness at the thought of having her pump into me. We were in a city renowned for its sex shops. I suddenly wished there was one nearby that delivered. Fortunately we were on the same wavelength.

"I have a cock," she gasped when we broke apart, both struggling to breathe.

I wasn't about to question the how or the where or the why of it. I could only feel relief and a desperate anxious yearning. "Get it. Hurry."

She rose and disappeared in the direction of the kitchen. My clit was aching and my whole body was taut with expectation, but I lay back on the padded bench and resisted the urge to touch myself. I knew I'd blow at the first couple of strokes, and that was not what I wanted. Fortunately she was quick with her task, and the wait was most definitely worth it. She wore it proudly, turning to let me admire it on her.

The harness itself—a thong in the back—framed her tight ass in a way that made my clit throb faster. And the cock was a nice size for my body. Seeing it on her, I spread my legs without even realizing it. But it was the look in her eyes that made me desperate for her to fuck me.

"Get over here," I rasped and she was quickly on top of me, rubbing the cock over my swollen sex.

"How do you want it?" she asked as her hips rolled and bucked.

I wrapped my arms around her back and carved little crescents into her flesh with my fingernails while I tilted my hips to receive her.

"Just a little," I whispered, seeing in her eyes how desperately she wanted to impale me. She groaned when I took the cock in my hand and pushed it against her. "Watch," I urged, and saw her look down.

I gave the cock a couple of pulls and felt her body twitch with each one. When I put the head into me, she sighed approval.

She was fighting to go slow, I could tell; her thighs trembled from resisting the urge to drive into me. "So damn hot," she muttered as she watched me push the cock in only a few centimeters farther with each slow stroke.

We rocked together, both of us watching me take her in, determined to prolong it, but I was so wet and eager for her that my efforts at a slow build dissolved with three words.

"Please let me." The strain in her voice let me know how hard it was for her to maintain control.

"Yes. Now," I agreed, and she thrust hard into me, sinking the cock fully, so deep and quick and good that I gasped, and then we were into a driving rhythm that pushed me to the edge all too quickly.

"Touch me, and I'll come with you," she promised. I slipped my hand between her body and the harness to find her clit hard and swollen, and when I worked it in sync with the way she was fucking me it only took a few strokes for both of us to climax.

She stayed inside me as we lay panting, recovering, her body resting on mine.

"Damn nice," she groaned dreamily some moments later, and I hummed my agreement, too spent to move.

"Glad you had that handy." I moved my hips slightly to push the base of the cock against her clit.

She moaned and shifted and gave me back in kind, pushing the cock hard into me again, one quick thrust. "I live upstairs."

"Convenient."

"Very," she said. "You know, I hate to have you leave when there are still a few potions left to kick in. And besides, you haven't seen what I do with breakfast."

What can I say? Never argue with a woman who knows her way around the kitchen. You never know what she might cook up next.

HOT BLONDE ROAD TRIP
CRIN CLAXTON

I'd been watching her all night, propped up at the South London bar, pushing my back hard into the worn wood and fingered chrome of Tomi's counter. She was new and blond, not a natural blonde going by the depth of her long, dark lashes. I wanted her.

"There's a gorgeous pair of boots I just have to have."

"I know. Did you see the new pink Jimmy Choos?"

Fragments of conversation breezed over me from the table where she sat with her companion. I was seriously trying to work them out… femme friends?…femme girlfriends? There was a lot of touching, some stroking, an extraordinary amount of pouting. The hot blonde's eyes flickered to mine regularly enough for me to venture a smile. Hot Blonde smiled back. I took a breath, put a boot on the floor…and Femme Companion glared over at me, grabbed Hot Blonde's hand, and pulled her onto the dance floor. Disappointed, I rested back onto the tall leather bar stool.

"Hmm," Tomi said, clocking the femme-on-femme dance action, close enough to comfort any voyeur in the bar. "Wannanother beer?"

I nodded, and Tomi clipped the top off a Beck's.

"Blonde, huh? Having a change from the usual?" Tomi remarked, sliding the beer along the scuffed, dark counter.

"She comes in a hot package," I replied.

"Aha." We both took a moment to look Hot Blonde up and down, all the way up her shapely legs in stilettos and black stockings and all the way down her curving body, imprisoned in a tight, low-cut top that was crying out to be pulled off and tossed aside. I noticed Tomi was also checking out Femme Companion. She was sexy too, in that haughty, stern-faced way. Wasn't sure if I liked or didn't like Femme Companion's hands all over Hot Blonde's hips, back, and buttocks. I did like Hot Blonde blatantly staring at me while she did so. They were subtly grinding. Taking the fast track at half speed, Hot Blonde's leg between Femme Companion's, and pressing into her.

"So what happened to a quick beer after work, feet up in front of Jennifer Aniston?" Tomi mopped up a spilt rum and Coke.

"There's only so many reruns of *Friends* a guy can watch…" I told her.

"So this is you taking a risk, is it?"

"Huh?" I narrowed my eyes, hoping to hell Tomi hadn't discovered self-help books.

"Ain't that what Myra wants you to do?"

I continued to narrow my eyes.

"Your dating skills gotta be a bit rusty." Tomi buffed the counter, rubbing hard at a mark.

The song ended. Hot Blonde strutted back to her table, her short skirt flashing glimpses of her thighs. She stared straight at me so hard I swallowed, then she reached for her glass of champagne and necked it.

"Tomi, I think I'm gonna need champagne…" I murmured when Hot Blonde waved. Not waved me over. Waved good-bye. I frowned as Femme Companion drained her glass also, took Hot Blonde's hand, and pulled her toward the door. Even two fabulous booties strutting in high heels couldn't compensate for my letdown. I'd been enjoying the teasing, from the safe distance of my bar stool. At the door Hot Blonde turned and shot me a long come-hither. Not sure if I wanted to follow, I sat deliberating, watching Tomi dig around in the chiller. Hell, Myra was right. I needed to think outside the box.

"Gotta go," I muttered to Tomi's surprised face as she emerged with a dripping bottle of champagne.

The car park was quiet and deserted. It seemed I'd lost them. Maybe it was just as well…I wondered whether to return to the bar or get on my bike, gleaming quietly under the dull floodlight, and just take off somewhere. I headed for the bike…and a powerful saloon purred behind me. Hot Blonde was sitting in the passenger seat applying lipstick, silhouetted in the interior light. Okay, this was it: the second chance. I walked quickly over before I could talk myself out of it.

"Um…" I said.

Hot Blonde glanced at me, winked, and continued pressing

lipstick onto her pouting lips. The lips looked like they were enjoying the fondle.

"Yes?" Femme Companion said sharply.

"Um…hi," I managed.

"Hi." Hot Blonde said sweetly. Then she and Femme Companion stared at me. Not in a hot way. In a "what the hell do you want?" kind of way.

"Do-you-want-to-go-somewhere?" I said in a curious monotone forced by nerves.

"I'm in a bit of a rush, actually," Femme Companion said, leaning forward to reveal the tops of two very nice-looking breasts.

"I'm not." Hot Blonde was running a hairbrush lightly through her long blond locks. She swept a bunch off her gorgeous face and looked at me from under those long, dark eyelashes. I smiled.

"That's what I hoped." I boldly opened her car door.

"Well," Femme Companion pouted, "guess this means I'll see you later, darling." She smooched into Hot Blonde and snogged her with no regard to the recently applied lipstick. "Ta ta," she said to me like a sexy femme Mary Poppins, mouthed me a kiss, and gunned the engine.

Hot Blonde walked away from me, her buttocks swaying a sweet promise. She rested against my bike, putting one stiletto on the passenger footpeg. "I like motorbikes," she informed me, fingering my black pearl upholstery.

"What would you like to do?" I asked, stepping closer and trying to look moodily Brandoesque.

"Let's ride." She jumped astride the bike like a pro and patted the front seat, the tip of her tongue poking out between her teeth.

The Harley growled to life under my fingers, and I turned onto the busy main road, weaving gracefully through late-night club traffic. "Where d'you wanna go?" I shouted over the engine at lights.

"Surprise me," she mouthed, tucking strands of blond hair into her helmet.

I took off with the green light, musing how in a relationship, reading my girl's mind is the last thing I want to do. With a stranger, that's a lot of the fun.

I took the road out of town and onto the M25. The Night Train roared beneath us, responding eagerly to the throttle with a boom from the twin exhaust. A bit nervous, I relaxed as Hot Blonde nestled into me, her arms around my waist. I felt the hard plastic of her helmet where she rested her head against my shoulder blade.

On the M23, her fingers slipped inside my jacket. The hulking shadows of pine trees flanked the road, urging us southward. I opened the throttle so we could enjoy the awesome power between our legs, and the Harley swallowed the tarmac. Hot Blonde reached around me, her hand pushing my cock onto the bike seat so that the deep vibrations shot through to my clit. I smiled, imagining Hot Blonde behind me with her legs wide open to the same guttural force.

Brighton Pier was still lit up when I turned onto the lower seafront road. Clubbers were staggering out of rainbow-flagged bars. I cruised, as subtly as a Harley will allow, to a darker, quieter spot of beach. Hot Blonde stepped off the big bike smoothly, taking my hand. Free of the helmet, I faced the ocean and a salty breeze hit my nostrils and ruffled my hair. I stepped onto the pebble beach when I felt resistance from Hot Blonde.

"You don't expect me to walk on that in my Manolos, do you?"

I turned to see her frowning at the pebbles and then at her shoes.

I shrugged. "Should I carry you?"

With an easy sigh, Hot Blonde shook her head, kicked off her shoes, lifted up her skirt, and slowly unrolled her stockings from her dark legs till she was barefoot and my shorts were soaked.

We walked to a spot sheltered by a beach hut and a weathered, upturned rowboat. I laid my leather jacket on the pebbles.

"This is a nice spot you've brought me to," Hot Blonde said softly, looking out to the waves turning under a slowly brightening sky. "It's quite far to come with a stranger…"

"Do you go all the way with strangers?" I couldn't help asking. I dared to reach over and rest my fingers lightly on her bare leg, watching her face to see what she would do.

"Not every stranger. Why don't we make a start and see how far we get?" Hot Blonde pulled me into a kiss, tonguing my mouth while pushing her hands under my T-shirt, pulling it up to expose my back. I cupped her breasts out of her bra and popped them into my mouth, giving each of them a fair tonguing. The sea air licked my back and bare arms while I licked Hot Blonde's hard nipples. She moaned into the top of my head.

"What have you got for me in there, honey?" Her hands found my cock. She pressed it so the top of it pushed against my clit.

"That feels good." I sighed, unable to hold back. I slid up into her, pumping fast until she put her hands on my hips, pushed down, and breathed, "Take your time, baby. There's no place I have to be but here."

The easy rhythm of the beach washed over me. It was me and the hot blonde, and it was also the crash of waves, the salty breeze coming off the tide, the pulse of the sun-soaked shell and shingle, the sweet ancient rhythm of the earth beneath coursing through my body. She started to come, loudly. Staccato moans that spurred me on harder and deeper, and seemed to wake up sleeping gulls. The ocean itself crashed to the beat of her breath as her nails dug into my back and she cried out. Finally she lay back, dishevelled and panting.

"Wow!" I grinned. "You came so hard you knocked your wig off."

Laughing, she reached up to the gold silky hairpiece and stroked it tenderly. "It got you off." She smirked.

I allowed that. "It suits you…but then, I knew you weren't a natural blonde." I twined my fingers in her raven pubic hair.

"You know, in twenty years you've never fucked me on Brighton Beach," she said as I tucked myself in and she straightened her skirt.

"No, Myra. But we got quite far in the ghost train on the pier, a few years ago…"

"Sexy…but also a little creepy," Myra reminisced.

"How did I do?" I asked.

"God, you don't want marks out of ten now, do you?"

"No, I'm talking about my driving."

"Oh." Myra relaxed. "You drove my bike very well, darling. Might even lend it to you again." Her eyes misted slightly, staring out to a bank of gray cloud moving in fast.

"Do you think you could get passionate leave?" Myra asked wistfully, trying to smooth the wig back down on her gorgeous head.

"What kind of compassionate leave?"

"Not compassionate, passionate." Myra pouted. "Take me south, baby."

I thought about it, eyeing the Harley thoughtfully. Dover was only twenty miles away…

"Don't you need clothes and stuff?" I asked.

"Knickers…not even," Myra decided. "Anyway, the shopping's fantastic in St. Tropez."

"Okay. Let's go…hey, remember that peach orchard just outside Nice?" I said with a grin, getting to my feet. I remembered the sun on my back, the smell of the fragrant fruit.

"Peaches, hmm…sweet, plump, succulent flesh with juice that runs down your chin," Myra said, pulling me back, unzipping my flies. "Oh yes, I remember…"

ONE FOR THE ROAD
VK POWELL

No cop in her right mind would volunteer for night shift—especially not on a rainy Saturday night. And any lesbian with half a brain was at home making love to her girlfriend or, if like me she didn't have one, was out cruising for one in the bars or coffee shops. I closed my thighs around the sharp need that seemed to be a constant companion on long nights patrolling the mostly desolate tri-county area. As I maneuvered my police-package Impala along the rain-slick highway, the fire burned closer to the surface. Tonight the longing verged on being painful.

Why were cops so interminably horny, anyway? Maybe there was a cop gene. One had to be born with it to go into the profession and to chase sex so relentlessly. Some believe it's the uniform, like catnip to women of all persuasions and inclinations. My personal opinion, it's the power. Authority can be a heady aphrodisiac but a cold bedmate. Most of the time, I just wanted to let it all go.

I slid my right hand up the inside of my leg and into the heat between my thighs. The back of my thumb pressed against the hard prominence of my clit, sending a shiver into my gut. I rocked forward and the utility belt settled lower on my hips, increasing the pressure in my core. The air inside the car sweated moisture, adding to my discomfort. I surveyed the tools of my trade while rain peppered down on the roof like a calling.

My nightstick and flashlight were tucked into their usual spots between the passenger seat and back. It wouldn't be the first time I'd gotten off riding the ribbed handle of my baton or the dimpled shaft of my Maglite. Squeezing my swollen center, I felt the evidence of my arousal seep through the wool-cotton blend uniform pants. I reached for the nightstick and propped it in the seat between my legs, slumped in the driver's seat, and rubbed my crotch against the upright pole. A couple of long, easy strokes were all it would take to stop the jagged pain.

Scanning the road ahead, I looked for a safe place to pull over as my clit twitched with each agonizing touch. As I rounded the bend at Murphy's curve, the headlights of my cruiser illuminated a vehicle off the side of the road and a drenched figure with arms flailing. *Not now. Five minutes from now, but not now.* Returning the nightstick to its intended position, I cursed and pulled over, positioned the patrol car for protection, and activated my blue lights.

The bundled figure moved too quickly toward my vehicle, face obscured by a massive umbrella, right hand stuffed into a jacket pocket. Adrenaline that seconds before had pulsed between my legs shot like tiny pinpricks up my spine. Experience had taught me not to take chances out here, miles from the nearest backup. I stepped from the car, abandoning my raincoat, and ordered the person back between the two vehicles. My hand hovered above the Glock 40 on my hip.

"Stay where you are," I yelled over the deluge of rain. The figure continued to approach. Violation of safety rules one and two: *always* keep your hands visible and *never* move toward a police officer. The advance is always theirs. This one didn't get the memo.

"Driver, stop." Instinct took over. I surveyed the area around us and calculated my next move. The road was deserted as far as I could see in both directions. In one fluid motion, I unsnapped the holster, drew my weapon, and leveled it at the encroaching motorist. Preparing to duck behind the door of my patrol car, I gave another command. "Stop and show your hands."

Arms stretched skyward and the unseasonably heavy coat draped open. The umbrella fell to the ground and tumbled away in a brisk breeze. A figure that seconds before had seemed menacing and potentially dangerous was transformed into a half-dressed, very surprised woman.

Straight blond hair hung at shoulder length, plastered to her head. Her eyes were wide with confusion. Underneath the overcoat a lace thong teddy with a cutaway middle, made transparent by the rain, clung to the sculpted curves of her full breasts and hips. The light patch of hair at the juncture of her thighs changed from golden to silvery blue as the light bar flashed repeatedly. I was spellbound by a sight I'd never encountered in all my years of police work.

"Could you lower that thing, please?" The woman nodded toward the weapon in my hand, which was still fixed on her midsection. "As you can see, I'm not armed." She turned her body completely around to illustrate and ended with her hands perched defiantly on her hips.

When my alert status returned to quasi-normal, I holstered my weapon, closed the patrol car door, and stepped toward her. As I got closer, something about her seemed familiar, but I couldn't make a connection. It was just wishful thinking. What cop wouldn't want to drive up on something like this?

"What are you doing out here—like that?" I gestured at her skimpy outfit, an appreciative smile threatening to belie my professional tone.

She gathered the coat around her and gave me an up-and-down appraisal. "I was on my way home and this damn piece-of-junk car broke down. It's finally died, I'm afraid."

I gave her what must have been a skeptical look. "Guess I shouldn't ask where you've been in that outfit."

"It's a long story. Any chance you could give me a ride? It's just a couple of miles up the road."

"Sure. I'm about to go off duty anyway. If the car's locked, it should be okay here until someone comes out tomorrow." I motioned her toward the passenger side of my patrol car. "But I'll have to search you. It's policy."

"No problem, Officer." She slowly removed the weighty coat, held it at arm's length, and dropped it on the soaked ground. Placing her hands on the hood of the car, she stretched her legs out behind her and leaned forward, exposing bare cheeks separated by a single strand of lace. "Please be thorough. I wouldn't want you to miss anything."

I stepped behind her and positioned my right foot against the inside of hers. I reached toward my glove pouch, then decided against it. This was one search I wanted to conduct skin on skin. Our bodies were so close I could feel her heat through my rain-soaked uniform. Resisting the desire to merge her warmth with my own growing need, I leaned in and began the rote procedure.

I slid my hands up her firm arms, patted and squeezed the well-formed muscles, aware that the only thing concealed there was a sexual energy so strong it pulsed beneath my touch. When I reached her shoulders, I eased my fingers upward along her strong neck and into her long hair. I massaged her scalp and she gave a low moan. Or did I imagine it?

Returning to her back, I smoothed my hands along her shoulder blades, down and forward, lightly cupping the swell of her breasts. They fit so perfectly in my palms. I imagined their weight and texture sucked first delicately, then hungrily into my mouth.

"Umm," she groaned and eased slightly backward, bringing her butt into contact with my pelvis. I stifled an initial impulse to rock forward into her inviting ass.

I reached around her body and with the backs of my hands searched between her ample breasts. They were hot and supple against my skin, the nipples puckered and rigid.

"Oh," she breathed heavily. Her head slumped forward. "I'm sorry. Must be the rain. It always makes me horny, Officer."

The hint of irreverence and challenge in her voice excited me in a perverse sort of way. What kind of woman would travel half naked in this dreadful weather? Did she have a lover waiting at home as turned on by the thought of her as I was in her presence? I wanted such a woman, and my body emphasized how much.

I didn't trust myself to respond. The ache I'd felt earlier returned with a vengeance. I knew the slick wetness between my thighs had nothing to do with the rain. I'd never responded sexually to anyone while on the job, but she was different.

Resting my hands on her hips, I paused and drew a ragged breath. A wave of warmth sprang from my depths and burned the flesh where we connected. I kneaded the fullness of her thighs and headed toward her curvaceous ass. My clit pounded with an urgency that made me weak. Her hips ground back against my hands, humping the charged air between us.

As I smoothed my palms up the inside of her legs, she leaned farther forward on the car, splayed her hands across the hood, and hiked her ass toward me. "Oh, yes…higher, please."

Her words unleashed a primitive urge that warred with my experience and training. Blue lights flashed, reminding me of the potential exposure to passing eyes and professional censure, but my body was beyond reason. My hands quivered uncontrollably against the inside of her thighs. The back of my fingers brushed against the passion-drenched fabric covering her crotch, and this time, the moan was mine.

"Go ahead, Officer. Take what you want."

I knelt behind her and ripped away the thin string of cloth cutting through the center of her sex. She pushed down against my hand, swinging her hips from side to side.

"Fuck me, hard. I need it, now."

My dwindling control vanished. I reached around, grabbed an erect nipple, and tweaked it between my fingers until she moaned deep and throaty. I pressed my face against the exposed flesh of her hot ass and licked my way down.

"Fuck me!"

The words fanned my already out-of-control passion and I drove my fingers deep inside her slick, wet opening. She clawed the hood of the car and pistoned against my hand. It felt like something inside me ruptured as I clung to her and my own desire ran freely down my legs.

"I'm...gonna come...quick." She reached back, grabbed her ass, and pounded herself harder into my pumping hand.

"Oh, good God! I'm coming." She placed her outstretched hands on the fender of the car and braced herself. The cheeks of her butt slapped against my fingers with every upward thrust. Seizing muscles clamped around my fingers as her tremors began.

She suddenly pivoted on my hand, swung her leg over my head, leaned back against the car, and screamed, "Suck me!"

With my free hand, I pulled her to me and buried my face in the swollen folds at her core. I stroked the soft moisture of her insides with my fingers while I took her firm clit into my mouth and sucked. She exploded against my lips as her orgasm milked my thrusting digits.

"Oh, yes, that's it." Her legs trembled against the side of my face as she slumped forward. "Holy fucking shit." She reached down and cupped my face in her hands. "Take me home, Officer?"

I could barely breathe. The pain in my clit pulsed with unreleased pressure. I stared at her in disbelief. "Home?"

"You said you'd give me a lift." She retrieved her drenched coat from the ground, pulled it around her, and opened the passenger door of my patrol car.

I rose on desire-weakened legs and walked slowly toward the driver's side while my uniform pants chafed the raw flesh of my crotch. The short ride to her residence was a blur. When I pulled in front of her place, the rain had stopped. She directed me to follow the driveway to the back of the house. A U-shaped path led to the rear of the residence, a dense stand of cypress shielding the yard from view. I turned the car off and waited—for what, I wasn't sure.

She slid across the seat, ran her hand up the inside of my thigh, and grabbed my clit in her fist. "Aww…" My legs tensed as I pushed back to escape her grasp.

"I know you want this, Officer. The car reeks with the smell of your sex." She looked around the interior of the vehicle. "What's your weapon of choice…the nightstick, perhaps?" Retrieving my baton from the floorboard, she stroked its length and sniffed the handle. "Lucky guess, huh?"

"I…"

"Take this uniform off. I don't want to be charged with assault on an officer."

She tugged at the keepers on my utility belt. They unsnapped easily. I looked around the yard and tried to wriggle away from her.

"We're perfectly safe back here. The neighbors on both sides are gay boys, and I think they'd like what I'm getting ready to do to you."

Her lips covered mine. Her tongue plunged deeply and stroked the inside of my mouth, bringing chill bumps to the burning surfaces of my skin. Her fingers deftly unbuttoned my shirt, ripped the Velcro tabs of my vest loose, and shoved them both off my shoulders. She unbuckled the gear belt, drew it carefully from around my waist, and dropped it on the floorboard behind us. Unzipping the uniform pants, she slipped her hand into the wet curls at the base of my abdomen.

"Come on. Jerk me off." I tried to push her hand deeper but she resisted.

Muscles tightened throughout my body as I prayed for one swift, hard tug on my clit. That's all it would take. I leaned toward her, took a lace-covered breast in my mouth, and flicked the nipple with my tongue. The stroke resonated in my own breasts and pelvis. I pumped my hips toward her hand. She withdrew. "Oh, fuck!"

"I know you're hot, but it's not going to be that easy. Quid pro quo. Now lose these pants." She got out of the car and came around to the driver's side while I quickly shed my boots and the confining trousers. Opening the back passenger door, she motioned me inside. "Get in—on your knees."

I stood in her backyard naked and stared at her. Every rational thought in my head yelled "run" but my body craved whatever manner of pleasure or pain she intended to unleash on me. "I'm not sure I…"

"I'm sure, Officer." She reached down and ran a finger between my engorged lips. "Trust me." She licked the evidence of my arousal from her soaked digit and nudged me toward the backseat.

Desperate for release, the pulse in my temples pounding out the rhythm of desire between my legs, I stepped forward and pulled her leg between my thighs. Grabbing her ass with both hands, I stroked myself along the muscled length of her. My knees almost buckled. I knew I could come where I stood. I arched to ride her leg again but she backed away.

Blinded by the pain that soared through my pelvis, I bent over and pressed a hand against my distended clit. "Please…I can't stand it. I have to come."

"I know you're hurting, so just get your ass in the car so I can help you." Her hooded eyes flashed a combination of mischief and longing.

I climbed into the backseat on my hands and knees like the single-minded creature I'd become. Every movement chafed the flesh between my legs that hung hard as stone. I dropped my head, forehead against the cool vinyl seat, and waited.

After what seemed like an eternity, I felt the seat dip as she moved in behind me. I heard the distinctive rip of Velcro and the sharp snap of latex in the darkness. At the first sticky-cool touch of her gloved hands on the outside of my legs, I lurched forward, waves of need tightening in my groin. She caressed the length of my back and moved between my parted thighs.

"It's okay, Officer. I've got you." She pressed her hot center against my butt and leaned over, rubbing her lace-covered breasts against my back. She nibbled the side of my neck and slipped a finger into me. "Do you want me to fuck you now?"

I jerked so forcefully, I almost threw her off me. "Oh, God, yes. Please. If I don't come soon I'm going to explode." I rocked back into her hand. She simultaneously filled and stroked me toward orgasm, once, twice, almost there…

"I have a special treat for you," she whispered in my ear, withdrew her hand, and sat back on her heels. My disappointed groan brought a small chuckle. "Look at me." Her tone was more demanding.

Turning slightly, I rested my cheek on the seat and looked toward her. She was attaching a leather strap around the palm of her right hand. From the top of the miniature harness a small ribbed protrusion extended about four inches.

"What's that?" My expression must've relayed more than my casual tone.

"Don't worry, copper. It won't hurt—much. It's called a butt plug and…"

"I don't think I like…" I started to sit up. She pressed her hand against the small of my back and guided me down.

"I think you *do* and I'm going to prove it." She knelt behind me and lowered the plug toward my body, explaining as she went. "It needs lubrication." I felt slight pressure as the device slid easily into my vagina. My hips rocked to meet the welcoming penetration. "Back on all fours," she ordered before I could establish a rhythm. "You're gonna like this."

Any further objections vanished as her strong fingers kneaded the cheeks of my ass and teased them apart with her thumbs. When she rubbed my juices around the puckered rim of my anus, splinters of white heat torpedoed through me. "Oh God." I could barely breathe.

"Steady, girl." She massaged the slick heat around my tight opening with her finger first, pressing and loosening me for her entry. "That's it, baby. Just let me in."

She rimmed my anus with the rounded tip of the plug and began to slowly ease it inside me. Every nerve ending in my body coalesced at that point of contact. Ridge after ridge of the probe passed through my sensitive orifice and sparked straight to my clit.

"Fuck me, please. I'm dying here." I humped back toward her hand, desperate for more. She withdrew the plug, and with each retreating rib it felt like I was being jerked off from inside. My knees slipped in the juices that pooled on the seat beneath me. I reached down to stroke myself, needing the direct pressure on my swollen shaft.

"Don't." Her voice was raspy with desire.

I whimpered and started to tremble. I needed to get off so desperately. "It's so good. Faster." I dug my fingernails into the vinyl seat. Her hand quickened its pace, forcing the butt plug in and out of my anus with increased fury. "Can't take…anymore…"

Grabbing her left arm, I wrapped it around my thigh, closed her fingers around my throbbing clit, and squeezed. "Pull it. Hurry. I need to come."

She seized my painful flesh between her thumb and forefinger and stroked its turgid length. I rocked back and forth, unable to resist the sensation at either end. She drilled the probe into me harder. Her latex-covered fist slapped against my ass with each entry. The fingers of her left hand simultaneously milked my clit. I matched her motions stroke for stroke.

"Yes, that's it. I'm coming." The muscles in my body stiffened as every ounce of energy gathered between my legs. As the convulsions clawed their way through me, I struggled for breath, desperate to come but trying to make it last.

She buried the plug in my ass, draped herself over my back, and held on as I came in one hard burst after another in her exquisite hand. When the tremors finally ended, I collapsed onto the soaked seat with her still clinging to my back. I was vaguely aware of the probe being eased from between my butt cheeks.

"I knew you'd like it. You cops aren't as tight-assed as everybody thinks." She nuzzled the back of my neck and sat up. "Now, why don't you check off, D257, and come inside?"

Suddenly the vulnerability of my situation hit full force. "How do you know my call sign?"

"I thought you'd have figured it out by now—D257, go ahead for Comm Center."

The pieces fell into place. "You're the new dispatcher?" I breathed a heavy sigh of relief.

"And I've been trying to get your attention for the last three months. Guess this worked for you, huh?"

"But how did you know I'd—"

"You walk around like you've got a permanent stiffie. I just wanted to check out my theory." She leaned down, kissed me, and flicked a breast at the same time. "There's plenty more where that came from, Officer. You coming in?"

I smiled as she gathered the bits of my uniform scattered throughout the car and handed them to me. "Be right there." I reached across the seat, keyed the mike, and signed off duty.

DENVER, PART DEUX
THERESE SZYMANSKI

When I got into my car to drive to Denver, I couldn't help but think about my last road trip.

It'd been just a few years before, also when I was underemployed. Except that time it had been a fairly random, unplanned romp across the country and back again—this time it was to Denver and back with a very specific purpose in mind.

I thought about the hundreds of hours we'd spent on the phone together, and all we'd talked about during those long conversations. And all we'd done during those conversations.

"Take off your clothes," I'd said one night. Previously, when I'd asked her to take off her shirt, or maybe to think about touching herself, she'd turned me down cold, so it was anyone's guess why I'd become so bold and cocky. But finally, one night, when I'd carried through on a promise, when she started to realize she could trust me, she listened to what I said and took off all her clothes.

She'd never had phone sex before, so we were charting new territory right from the start. And I got more and more excited when she was really needy—like the hormonal night when we talked much earlier than usual and she came three times.

I could only imagine what I'd be able to do with her in person.

It made me wet just thinking about it.

When we first started with the phone sex, she was very quiet, even when she came, but still she moaned loudly when I told her I'd like to watch her masturbate—and when I asked her if she'd like to touch me back, she said, "Oh, God yes."

So I'd tell her to take off her clothes, *all* of them—to get naked for me—and she'd put down the phone for a moment while she did that, then she'd pick it back up. It was never the same twice, but usually

I'd coax her into fondling her breasts and teasing her nipples until she began whimpering.

"Can I go inside?" she'd ask a few moments later in a breathy, heated voice.

"Yes."

"How many fingers?"

"Two." And I'd tell her where to touch while I whispered what I'd be doing to her if I was actually with her—how I'd stroke her cunt, explore her inside and out…flick her clit back and forth with my tongue as I fucked her with my hand. How I'd run my fingers over her tummy and breasts and squeeze her nipples with my other hand. And all the while I spoke, and listened to her moans, my fingers would itch to touch her skin and I'd imagine how she'd taste and feel.

Thinking about touching her so intimately was not making my drive any easier. In fact, it was greatly inhibiting my lane-changing and fast-maneuvering abilities, so I determined to think about something else instead. Like how, during the few hours we'd spent together in real life, I'd neglected to do more than hug her or pick her up teasingly (of course, the last time I'd seen her, she had been wearing my shorts), or about how silky her hair might feel, how soft her skin would be, how good it would be to hold her in my arms and hear her moan into my ear. How nice it would be to finally be able to hold her tightly afterward, caressing her back and hair while whispering loving words into her ear.

Or that's what I couldn't help but *imagine*. We had yet to say certain words to each other, but I was pretty sure that's what we both were feeling. I knew I wanted to say them to her, and wanted the reassurance of her in my arms before I said them. But I also wanted to kiss her first, because…nothing was possible if you weren't kissing compatible.

But I was sure we were gonna be.

And I was sure I already was.

The last time I'd driven to Denver, it'd taken me thirty-one hours, but I stopped for two hours in Missouri to get my car serviced (which they hadn't been able to properly do), and an hour in Kansas to unsuccessfully attempt to take a nap. Also, I'd had to drive the Penn Turnpike in a storm, so it took *way* longer to make it than it should have.

I was leaving DC at 11 a.m., but it was a mighty long drive and a lot depended on whether or not I caught a break this time, so we really couldn't be sure when I'd get to hers, so she was leaving a key under her front mat, just in case I got there before our estimate of 6 p.m.

I was rather known for picking up women and having one-night stands. Alas, my last driveabout didn't include any one-nighters, just a beer run on a fire truck during a wedding (long story). And this time, I really didn't want a one-nighter. I hoped to have an every-nighter, plus some, in the future.

Aw, the hell with it. I wasn't looking for something temporary at all. And I was driving all this way because tickets for last-minute flights cost too much, and I had the time, and I couldn't wait to touch her, hold her, love her.

I drove, impelled by my need to be with this woman and Know For Sure. I drove on and on, hour after hour, occasionally wanting to undo my jeans and push them down so I could play with myself. But that was only because I was thinking about Her. Wanting Her. Needing Her. Getting really wicked turned on by Her.

The way she said, "Oh, God yes!" thrilled me all along my spine. Her asking, "Can I go inside?" made my clit twitch. Thinking about her in a certain dress (a little black one that she taunted me with), and thinking about me touching her in it, made me weak in the knees.

As the drive went on and day turned to night, and I found a semi to rabbit for me through two states, I couldn't help but remember all the times she'd told me what she was wearing. After the first time I asked, she volunteered. I loved how she'd also describe her underwear (although she wouldn't give me details if she didn't think they were particularly interesting, even though I always found it *all* fascinating and exciting because She was the one wearing them and She was inside them), and when she didn't, I knew she wasn't wearing any.

And that was hot as hell.

In fact, everything about her was hot as hell. Including her little Alabama accent.

Especially when she'd drop lines in e-mails like, "as long as I can be dressed at least some of the time you're here!" which made my knees disappear, just thinking about her planning on being naked so much of my visit.

And I drove on farther still.

And I thought, as night turned to day, about what it might be like when we saw each other again. Although I'd had sex with her over the phone, I hadn't really imagined exactly what it would be like to touch her, or what she'd look like naked. I didn't want to envision any of that too much, because I wanted to experience all the joy of our first time together—I wanted it to be our *real* first time together.

But I'd wondered what our first kiss would be like, how we'd touch each other—how I'd touch her face, caress her hair, bring her into my arms. I wondered if she'd wrap her legs around my waist. She'd already told me she wanted to straddle me, and that she liked to be carried. She was smaller than I, so we'd determined I could pick her up easily.

So I couldn't help but wonder if she'd wrap her legs around my waist.

That would be really hot.

I pressed down on the accelerator.

One day she'd agreed I was a perv and told me she'd thought about me that morning when she'd dressed without underwear. Even over thousands of miles, my guts turned to butter when she told me that.

I arrived in Denver at 11 a.m.

She wasn't home. I let myself in and brought my bag with. I was disappointed. (Well, actually, that didn't begin to cover it.) She wasn't there. My first-kiss scenarios were blown.

I couldn't walk through her condo, except to find the bathroom, which I simply used and then left. It felt too much like invading her space. So I drank a beer and went to sleep on her couch, falling into a realm where she *was* home, where she was there, or here, with me, and we were touching and kissing and…

She was running her hands lightly through my hair, saying, "Hey, baby."

I moaned, turning into her hand, kissing her palm. I opened my eyes, still unsure if this was yet another vivid dream starring her or if it was actually happening. The setting sun glowed through the blinds behind her, making her look like even more of an angel.

I ran one hand up her arm, thinking her skin was somehow softer than my imaginings, while I snaked the other around her waist, wanting to feel her near me, to know it was more than a dream.

My right hand found the back of her neck; I sat up and pulled her closer to me with my other hand.

First we hugged. She was warm and fit perfectly with me, her face burrowing into my neck.

Then I pulled back to look into her incredibly deep green eyes. I had to taste her. So I leaned forward to brush my lips against hers, fondling her lips with my own, until she deepened the kiss, entering my mouth with her tongue. I met her tongue with mine, brushing mine against hers.

The kiss test proved positive.

Then, as I realized I wouldn't be able to stand even if I wanted to (which I didn't), I nipped at her lower lip. She rewarded me with a full-throated moan that came from deep inside her.

I got still wetter.

She straddled me, a move guaranteed to drive me absolutely insane—I loved how she had to open up for me in this position and how her jeans wrapped oh-so tightly around her lithe body. She also had on a tank top, an *incredibly* soft cotton tank top with an unbuttoned men's work shirt over it.

I couldn't believe that I somehow got wetter from the fact that she didn't try to hide her bra straps.

She wrapped her legs around me and we continued kissing until I couldn't stand it anymore: I pushed her onto her back and stretched her out, lying on top of her, molding our bodies together.

I pressed my thigh into her pussy, tightening my muscles for maximum effect, to push against her as hard as I could.

She groaned in response. So I kissed her again, grabbing her by the hips and pulling her crotch harder against me as I pushed into her. She spread her thighs even more, opening herself up to me entirely. I let my hands travel over her curves, grasping her thighs, her hips, fondling her waist, going up her stomach to her breasts, which I held in my hands, outlining her nipples through her bra and tank.

"Yes, please," she whispered into my ear. I kissed and nibbled on her neck while I slid my hands down to the hem of her tank top, caressing her tummy before easing my hand under her back and quickly undoing her bra with a snap of my fingers.

"Sit up," I said, pushing up from her as I started to pull her top off.

She whimpered deep in her throat, then gasped and put her hands on mine. "Bedroom, please," she said, looking up into my eyes with her beautiful green ones. Her long black hair pooled around her shoulders and, yet again, I imagined her on top of me, with that incredible hair cascading down over my face.

I rose and, before she could follow, lifted her in my arms. She'd told me being carried made her feel safe and protected, so I carried her back to the bedroom, with her arms curled around my neck and her head tucked into my shoulder.

When I laid her on the bed, she released my neck and guided my hands to the hem of her tank. She kept her hands on mine as, together, we pulled off her top and bra. I knew she'd only been intimate with a few people in her life.

I leaned forward, kissing her, even as I held her. Going slow.

I wanted to make sure she knew I didn't just desire her…that I didn't want to just have sex with her…I wanted her to trust me and believe I didn't want to change her and didn't want her to change. I wanted her to know I loved her.

"You have no idea how truly beautiful you are, do you?" I pushed her onto the bed and let her continue covering herself. I let her be shy and humble and modest.

I caressed her arms and shoulders. I cradled her head in one arm and reached down to the fly of her jeans. She covered both breasts with one of her arms while covering my hand at her zipper with the other.

We looked into each other's eyes and I sat up to remove my own black T-shirt and black sports bra. I was modest myself, so she only got a vague eyeful before I bent to her again, kissing her, touching and caressing her…

I put my hand back on the zipper of her jeans.

She grasped my hand again. "No, you first."

I looked into her eyes, but she glanced down my body.

"I want you, but you need to…well…take off your clothes first."

"I have."

"I'll get naked only after you have."

My mind tingled briefly at the idea of being the first one naked. But then my butch persona stepped in and stopped that momentary thought of exhibitionism. "Don't you want to know me, personally, like you have over the phone?" I said. "Don't you want to come for me?"

She looked up at me, her left arm across her chest, her left hand cupping her right breast. Her right hand still covered my hand, my hand that was on the waist of her jeans, ready to open them.

"I'll let you get me naked once you're naked."

I already felt exposed, being topless in front of her, but she stayed my hand when I tried to undo her zipper.

"No. You naked first," she said.

So I stood, kicked off my boots, unzipped my Levi 550s, and pulled them, with my boxers, down and off my body. I was glad the room was dark, because I didn't like my body and couldn't believe I was standing naked in front of this beautiful woman.

I made to sit next to her on the bed, but she held up a hand. "No, wait, I want to see you. Turn on the light."

So I turned on one of the bedside lamps, then went to undo her jeans.

She reached up to cup my breasts and squeeze my nipples. She fondled me and then teased my nipples…hard. She squeezed them as hard as possible. She twisted them and yanked them and I was momentarily forgetting I was the butch and I was the naked one…

Finally I reached down, undid the zipper on her jeans, stripped her naked, and, before I could lie down upon her again, she slipped a finger up inside me.

My legs spread all by themselves. And I loved the light for letting me see her, in all her beautiful, naked glory. That same light made me feel self-conscious, made me want to cover myself, but I discovered I liked her looking at me, naked. And I liked that she could watch as that one—those *two*—fingers dipped inside me.

I liked being naked for her, and I liked the feeling of her inside me.

But I also loved touching her. I loved sliding my fingers into her, inside her. I sucked and kissed and bit and nibbled on her exposed nipples. I took one between my teeth and teased it, pulled it as hard and far as I could.

"Yes, please!" she cried.

I'd been dreaming—fantasizing—about us being flesh to flesh, bare skin to bare skin, since I first told her I'd liked her. And now she was naked, I was naked, and, as our bodies slid together, I pulled her hand from my body and held it over her head, against the bed, and fucked her cunt. And while I did, she held me to her with a hand around my neck.

As I kissed her, sliding my fingers in and out of her while flicking her clit with my thumb, I switched from holding her down to just holding her, and she moaned and writhed against me.

"You feel so good, honey," I whispered into her ear.

She wrapped a leg around me, pulling us unbelievably close together, and ran her fingernails playfully down my back. "Please, I've wanted…so long…"

I raised up so I could look into her eyes when I was inside her. She took a deep breath as she met my gaze. And then we kissed with our eyes open, looking into each other, seeing into one another's souls, entering each other's bodies with our tongues while I filled her with yet another finger…

She'd said that she wasn't sure how much she could take. She liked, when she was on the brink, hearing what I might like. Over the phone, with my voice guiding her actions and thoughts, when I told her something I might really like to do to her, that could be enough to send her over.

And now, I looked down at her—*"Soon you'll be looking up at me looking down at you,"* I'd said during our last phone call—and it was as if we were both thinking the same thing at the same time, because she spread her legs farther still.

"Yes," she said.

I slid yet another finger into her.

"Yes," she said.

She was naked for me. She was giving it up, for me. I was inside her, and she was enjoying it. "You have no idea how fucking hot you are, do you?" I said, taking in her full, lush breasts, the way she opened her thighs for me, the triangle of dark hair between her legs…

And I immediately realized I'd misstepped. I could almost feel her pulling away from me even as I looked down at her. *"I have a feeling you can get sex just by breathing,"* she'd said to me during one of our first phone calls, before she'd let me talk her out of her clothing.

I stilled my fingers inside her and pulled her tight to me with my other hand, holding her. "You know I want you and want to be yours, and yours alone, right?" I whispered into her ear.

I felt her relax under me again.

I lifted my head so she could see the truth in my eyes. "I love you."

She pulled me down, holding me tightly against her. "Please tell me you're not just saying that."

"I'm not just saying that. I wouldn't. I love you."

She put her hand over my hand, the hand between her legs, and slowly guided me in and out of her again. Slowly, cautiously, carefully.

"Will you be mine?" I asked. "Do you want me?"

"Yes. Yes, please. God, yes." She closed her eyes as her breathing grew harsher.

"No, look at me," I said. "Because I'm about to make you mine." I reached over to pump some lube into my hand.

She saw how deliberately I was coating my hand, and she knew what I meant to do. I felt her relax around and under me. "Yes."

And we both watched as I slid my fist into her. She began gyrating her hips harder and faster than before.

"Yes," was her mantra, urging me forth, making my fist go all the way inside her.

I lay down to explore her cunt with my tongue, with my mouth. I drove into her with my fist, licking her from top to bottom and back up again.

She yanked at my hair, drawing me closer to her, farther into her. Her legs tightened around my head, and I pushed them apart with my shoulders even as she arched to shove herself more completely into my mouth.

I moved my free hand all over her body, wanting her to feel every bit as naked and exposed as she actually was. I ran my hand up over her tummy, to caress one breast, then the other. To pull and tug at one nipple, then the other. I ran my tongue up and down her, sucking her clit into my mouth as I explored her insides with my hand.

"Yes, oh God, yes, please," she said, moving all over the bed, so I had to hold her down with my free hand. "Yes! Yesyesyes!"

❖

Well, maybe this is all in my imagination. Maybe just my hopes. 'Cause I didn't really drive to Denver. But I am flying there next week...

VARIATIONS ON A GAME
SAGGIO AMANTE

Marielle lifted the marble object from the blue velvet box, slowly separating it from the parchment paper in which it was wrapped. She unrolled the paper carefully and focused on words written in a familiar hand: *Those who have leisure for the diversions of this game cannot find one that is more advantageous or more satisfying—to the vanquished as well as to the victor. Which will you be?*

She lifted the paper to her nose and inhaled the sweet jasmine scent that lingered on its surface. A fleeting vision danced through her mind—a woman...tall, with eyes like coal...and golden skin... laughing...taunting...*Which will you be? Which will you be?*—before dissolving into nothingness.

She reached for the object that had been wrapped in the parchment, cradling it in her palm, caressing its smoothness. She rubbed it against her cheek and lips, savoring its coolness against her skin. The piece was black, elongated, and slightly curved. It matched precisely the seven other pieces of like shape that formed a row across the board, facing eight white clones that stood at attention on the other side of the checkered jade surface.

Flickering candles placed strategically throughout the room lent a dim light, and the figures arrayed on the inlaid board in front of her cast odd shadows against the tabletop. On opposite sides of the board, along the top and bottom edges, behind the tall sentinels, stood eight white and eight black figures, all in poses so erotic that the mere sight of them fueled her arousal.

She wore only a black silk robe, embroidered with gold dragons, which she had found lying on an enameled credenza against a red wall. The robe was tied at the waist with a single silk cord. Her long black hair was upswept and held in place by two red lacquered sticks. Her feet were bare.

She placed the final piece on the board and sat in the ornately carved dragon chair with her arms resting loosely on its arms. From across the room the soothing sound of water dripping from a bamboo fountain filled the air. The phone on a small side table to her left rang with the tone of a Zen gong, its vibrations caressing her skin. She lifted the receiver to her ear and waited, her breaths becoming more rapid with each passing second. She was wet with anticipation and ached to relieve the pressure that was steadily building between her legs. Yet she did nothing. Instead she sat, silent and unmoving, until she heard the voice she had been longing to hear.

"You look beautiful tonight," the voice purred. "I've been waiting for you."

Marielle's breath caught in her throat. "I want to see you this time," she said softly, "play you face-to-face."

A deep laugh echoed provocatively in Marielle's ear. "You'll see me soon enough, my darling. But I wonder—when you do, will you be the winner or the spoils?"

"I'll mate you in five moves," Marielle replied quickly.

Her opponent laughed again. "*Empecemos, entonces*. Let us begin, then. I'll even give you the advantage. Your play."

Marielle fingered the white pawn at rank 2, file f. "Pawn to f4."

"Ah, you are too easy," the voice teased warmly.

"I've only made one move. Don't you think you're being a bit arrogant?"

"Perhaps…or perhaps not," the voice taunted. "Confidence is not always arrogance. Pawn to e5. Your breasts are beautiful. Drop the robe off your shoulders."

"Where are you? Can you see me?" Marielle scanned the room. High in the far right corner a red light blinked at her. "You can, can't you?"

"Does that bother you?"

"You said I would have the advantage, but it appears the advantage is yours."

"Does it? Appearances can be deceiving, you know. Let me see your breasts."

The voice was gentle yet commanding, and Marielle complied without protest. With two fingers, she lightly scraped her nails across her left breast, sliding the robe off it carefully. She slipped her hand underneath her breast and pushed it up, twisting her nipple between her thumb and forefinger. "My pawn takes yours at e5. Are you trying to lose?"

"Ah…you tease me, but one breast will do for now. I'll fill my mouth with you soon enough. To lose a pawn is nothing. Sometimes it is the sacrifice that wins the game. Pawn to d6."

"Pawn takes d6. You *are* trying to lose." Marielle's voice cracked as the canvas of her mind filled with alternating visions of coal black eyes staring intently at her while a hungry mouth descended slowly toward her to suck first at her center and then at her breasts.

"Bishop takes pawn at d6. Am I trying to lose? Or am I coming after you?" The seductive inflection in her opponent's voice was unmistakable.

"And what will you do if you get me? Pawn to g3." Marielle reached between her legs and dipped one finger in the pearly dewdrops forming on her dark, silky hair.

"Queen to g5. You're wet, aren't you? Wet for me. And hot…so hot. I can feel your heat from here."

"The thought of *you* makes me hot. Queen's knight to f3. Are you touching yourself? Are you thinking about touching me?" Marielle stared directly at the blinking red light as she brought her finger to her lips and ran her tongue slowly along its length.

"Queen takes pawn at g3. Check." The voice laughed. "I'm thinking about winning this game, though I must admit you *are* an enticing distraction."

"Pawn takes queen at g3. You can't have been concentrating too hard on this game. You've given up your queen. Who has the power now?"

"I do, my love. I've always had the power," the voice replied as if the answer were never in dispute. "Bishop takes pawn at g3. Mate."

Marielle removed the white pawn from the board and held it tenderly, caressing its tip with her fingers. She ran her hand along its shaft slowly—up and down, up and down—enjoying the sensation of the cold marble against her palm and fantasizing its cool hardness slipping inside to fill her. She held the pawn toward the camera, then reverently placed it on the table. Finally, she turned her king on its side and conceded with a whisper, "Mate."

She stood and pulled the tie at her waist, letting the robe drape completely open and then slip off her shoulders to fall in a heap at her feet. She reached to remove the red lacquered sticks from her hair and shook the long blue-black tresses loose to tumble against her back and over her breasts. A sliver of light came from behind her and a large shadow moved across the floor. Her body shook involuntarily as she felt the feral heat of the body that had stopped just centimeters from her own.

"Which are you?" the woman whispered, reaching around Marielle to cup her breasts in the palms of her hands before bending her head to place small bites across Marielle's neck and shoulder.

Marielle pressed her breasts hard into the palms of the woman standing behind her and moaned softly at the sting of the teeth on her skin. She was in that place just between pleasure and pain, and every nerve in her body screamed for more. Marielle gasped as the woman removed her hands from her breasts, splaying one against her stomach to pull her closer still before sliding long fingers between her folds to circle with perfect pressure against her swollen clitoris. It was a familiar dance, one that they had played on other nights after other games, and Marielle's body tingled with anticipation.

With one long stroke through the thick wetness between Marielle's legs, the woman removed her fingers. She reached down to grasp the hard, curved object strapped between her legs, then moved it deliberately across the firm, round flesh of Marielle's buttocks before sliding it insistently between Marielle's labia.

"Which are you, the victor or the vanquished?" the sultry voice repeated with each stroke.

When Marielle didn't answer, her lover placed a hand on the small of Marielle's back, forcing her gently but firmly forward. "So this is how it will be," she rasped.

Marielle swept the marble forms from the table with one arm, barely noticing as they clattered loudly against the gleaming teak floor. Then she bent more fully, shivering with delight as her breasts replaced the scattered pieces against the cool jade mosaic. She spread her legs wider, groaning with pleasure as her lover thrust into her and began to stroke. Marielle lifted slightly, pressing the curve of her butt firmly against the woman's mound. She heard a muffled moan behind her and glanced at her lover from the corner of her eye. Her head was thrown back, her eyes closed, and Marielle was certain she had found just the right amount of pressure to please her.

They rotated their hips in mirrored rhythm, moving together in perfect unison as one pressed forward and the other back. Marielle felt the woman pushing harder into her and knew that her lover had arched her back to move even more deeply inside. One hand held Marielle firmly by the hip while the long, tapered fingers of the other reached around her once more to slide between her folds and thrum against her pulsating clitoris.

"Which are you, the victor or the vanquished?" the woman demanded.

"Both!" Marielle screamed as her body exploded in the liquid heat of an orgasm stronger than any she had ever known.

Nota Bene: The opening quote is a paraphrase of a statement by Benjamin Franklin in his essay *Morals of Chess* written in 1779.

Downside

NYRDGYRL

It's hot and I'm horny. Even in the twenty-third century, there are places where a woman shouldn't wander unaccompanied, and this street looks like one of those places. Safety isn't on my mind, though. Only sex, and I don't have a lot of time to get what I want. Technically I'm AWOL, having boarded a shuttlecraft disguised as the ambassador's staffer I've left dreaming in her quarters. Sometimes being a med tech is good for something other than saving lives. My rational side knows that I'm sunk if I get caught. A court-martial is definitely not part of my career plan, yet my desire is doing my thinking instead of my brain.

My ship, the *Tomasina*, has been orbiting the planet Jabib for weeks while the captain and the ambassador negotiate to bring their government into alignment with the rest of the sector. Until a successful conclusion of negotiations, no one goes downside except for the Marines and the negotiation team. Unfortunately for my libido, I'm just a spacer, two stripes out of boot camp.

The Marines are having a great time using the extended negotiations as R&R to alleviate their boredom with this assignment. The *Tomasina* is an embassy ship, strictly intended to transport the ambassador and her staff. The Marines on board provide security for our small contingent, and most of them yearn for more dangerous duty.

In contrast, I enjoy my work. It's safe and interesting and it got me off the hellhole mining colony I was born on. The only thing missing for me is regular company. Most of the women on board are either straight, coupled, or Marines. The Marines won't mingle, the couples are exclusive, and the straights just aren't curious. That's left me and my trusty right hand for far too long.

According to Sergeant Haran, the focus of most of my fantasies, the nightlife on Jabib is the best she's encountered in this sector. After combat, sex, alcohol, and gambling are her three favorite vices and she says they're available in abundance at El Kareen, a bar she frequents during her time off. After every trip downside, she comes back dreamy-eyed and sated, which makes my stomach twist with envy when she visits sickbay for a hangover hypospray. I want some of what she's found.

Desperation made me dose the staffer. Her name's Sarah and she's new and lonely and a little bit naïve. Her eyes lit up when I dropped by with a bottle of Montorian Port. We spent a pleasant half hour chatting before her voice slurred and her chin hit her chest. Seconds later she was out cold, so I tucked her in, borrowed some clothes and her ID, then boarded the next shuttle downside. It was a snap. She won't remember what happened and if I'm lucky, I'll remember tonight for a good long time.

El Kareen is just like Sergeant Haran described it: flickering strobes bounce off mirrored walls and ceilings, making the room look larger than it actually is. Sweet-smelling smoke hazes the air, and before long I'm light-headed from the combination of the smoke, women, and perfume that batters my senses. I stumble toward the bar and order a beer. It's stronger than what I'm used to but I swallow the first one in three large gulps. Wanting to stay sober, I sip the second while standing with my back to the bar and my head on a swivel so I can absorb as many sights and sounds as possible. A weight that's been crushing my chest eases; it's good to be back in the company of women.

Three meters away a woman sits alone, nursing a neon blue drink. She sips, then the tip of her tongue darts out to clean the edge of the glass she cradles in her left hand. How I wish I was that glass. Between sips, the woman watches the dancers while tapping the fingers of her free hand to the beat underlying high-pitched wavering pipes. I've never heard music like this before, yet my feet twitch and my breasts ache for the press of a warm, supple body. She's nodding in time with the music and her shoulder-length hair swings back and forth, back and forth, almost mesmerizing me when the strobes illuminate her face. Bolstered by beer, I approach.

"Want to dance?" I'm speaking Standard while pointing at the dance floor. Puzzled brown eyes stare at my extended hand until her face lights up with comprehension. Dancing is better than I remember, pressed breast to breast swaying in time with the music. Every cell in my body jangles and I know that even though we don't speak the same language, our bodies do. We dance, only stopping occasionally to refresh her drink, until my shirt's as damp as my underwear. I switch to water so that I don't miss a single moment. I want this woman and she wants me, if the way she's sucking on my pulse point is any indication of her intentions. My legs turn to jelly when she maneuvers me into a darkened corner. We kiss and I gasp when our lips brush together. Her breath smells like apples and her lips taste like wine, creating a heady mixture that settles in my belly. Our hands roam under our loosened clothing while our lips are locked in wet, open-mouthed kisses. I'm finally, finally going to have sex with something other than my own hand.

The room falls away and the only thing I'm aware of is the way this woman feels in my arms. She unhooks my belt and slides her palm down my belly while scraping her nails against my skin. I know as soon as she touches me I'm going to come explosively. My hips thrust forward and my head arches back as her fingers inch closer and closer to the sweet swollen spot nestled between my thighs. Almost, almost...

"What are you doing here?" My subconscious recognizes the voice and I snap to parade ground attention even though just a second ago I was on the verge of gushing on a stranger's hand.

"Jeeter, I asked you a question. What are you doing here?"

It's Sergeant Haran, and even though the light is dim, I can see her pulse throbbing at the edge of her collar. She's pissed, and the chill radiating from her pale blue eyes freezes the lust in my belly to a solid lump of dread. Starting at my feet, her eyes rake me from head to toe, taking in my rumpled clothing and flushed skin. I'm too scared to move, too scared to speak, and even though my body's locked at attention, my mind's scrambling for a way to escape. My dance partner's disappeared and Sergeant Haran's battle-hardened body towers over me.

"Are you going to answer me?"

"I...I..." Sergeant Haran grabs my collar and hustles me down a darkened hallway. I stumble after her but my lowered pants force me to take four or five mincing steps to each one of her long strides. At the end of the hallway she palms a portal open, then pushes me into a room furnished with a single sofa.

"Sit down." I'm shivering and half naked, and Sergeant Haran sneers at my fumbling attempts to cover myself. I can't think of a single thing to say that's going to explain how I got here. She folds her arms across her chest and leans back against the portal blocking the only exit. There's no way out of this mess. "Okay, Jeeter. I'm waiting. Tell me what you're doing here."

I'm crying, so my story pours out in fits and starts. The only thing that might save me is the truth. She's disgusted by my tears, amused by my lust, titillated by my interest in her as a sexual partner, and amazed at the devious way I got off the ship. When I've run out of words and stutter to a halt, the room is silent except for the sound of her pacing footsteps.

Eventually she speaks. "That's quite a story, Jeeter. Procuring ship medical stores for personal gain, assaulting and impersonating an embassy worker, abandoning your post, and who knows what else just because you were horny." She smiles and shakes her head, then says, "You're gutsy enough to be a Marine." The twisted admiration on her face makes me almost believe she's going to let me go until she says, "You realize I can't let you get away with this, don't you?" The small bubble of hope rising in my chest bursts and reforms that lump of dread.

Sergeant Haran's eyes are distant and she sucks her cheeks in silent contemplation. I can't stand waiting. If I'm going to be court-martialed, I'd rather get the ball rolling.

"What now, Sergeant?"

"Huh?" Her gaze focuses and once again rakes me from head to toe. Surprisingly enough, instead of freezing me in place, this time it warms my belly and melts my body.

"S-Sergeant? Wh-what are you thinking?" I'm shivering again but not from fear. My gaze is drawn to her broad shoulders and lean hips, and for the first time I notice the bulge tucked against her left thigh.

She speaks slowly. "I'm thinking you've gone to an awful lot of trouble to get laid and maybe I ought to accommodate you before I turn you in." I'm stunned when she bends down and cups my breasts in her palms, brushing her thumbs across my nipples. Warring impulses fire and I can't decide whether to pull away or press myself into her caress, so my body decides for me. I've wanted Sergeant Haran since the first time she sauntered into sickbay.

"Wait." She snatches her hands back and I lurch forward to grab her wrist. "If we're going to do this, at least let me get undressed." When she doesn't look like she's going to retreat, I stand up and do a slow striptease that raises her eyebrows and brings a flush of arousal to her cheeks.

"Nice. Very nice. Show me parade rest, Jeeter." Following her order, I brace my feet shoulder-width apart and clasp my hands behind my back, which lifts my breasts front and center. Sergeant Haran skims her hands across my bared skin, lingering in the areas that make me squirm and moan. Her touch is feather light and when she kneels to concentrate on my lower body, my knees quiver and I'm afraid I might fall. Instinctively I know better than to break position without asking.

"S-Sergeant, I-I don't know how much longer I can stand up." She purses her lips and blows a warm breath at the juncture of my thighs. The quiver that races up my spine makes her laugh and do it again and again. "Don't move until I say so, Jeeter."

"O-okay, Sergeant." The pleasure is almost painful, and goose bumps pepper my skin wherever she touches me. Lights flash behind my closed eyelids and I sway like a wind-tossed reed, desperately trying to stay on my feet. When my knees finally buckle, she catches me in strong arms, then lowers my body to the floor.

Her fingers torture my nipples, tweaking one and then the other until I'm panting and humping the air, desperately seeking contact with anything solid. "Had enough teasing, Jeeter?" When she lifts my legs to her shoulders I'm beyond speech, and the first hot swipe of her tongue against my clit freezes the breath in my lungs. She burrows in and I buck and scream until my throat is raw. I'm still throbbing when she lifts my limp body and bends me over the back of the sofa.

"It's my turn now, Jeeter." Somehow I've missed it but she's now naked from the waist down and her dildo brushes against my ass when she leans into me. I'm instantly wet again. One large hand holds me steady while the other guides her dildo against the length of my sex, gathering the moisture that's flowing down my thighs. I don't expect it but she's gentle, easing the head of the dildo past my greedy lips and setting a rhythm that electrifies my hips. Soon I'm groaning and thrusting back against her forward thrusts until she buries herself so deeply I can feel her in my throat. She's grunting and muttering, "Gonna come, gonna come, gonna come, baby," when my muscles clench and grab her tool. My body flushes hot then cold, and I'm coming and gushing. After a final thrust she comes too, falling against my back and pressing my belly hard against the sofa. Amazingly enough, I come again.

When my head clears, I'm stretched out on the sofa and she's across the room buttoning and straightening her clothes. I'm weak and my limbs are heavy when I try to sit up.

"Take your time, Jeeter. You can't be in a hurry to get thrown in the brig."

My lips twist in a wry grin and I agree, "No, Sergeant, I'm not." I'm still in trouble, but maybe my memories of the most incredible sex of my life will brighten my time under guard.

I need to be cuddled and it must show on my face, because she sits next to me and cradles me on her lap. Sighing, I relax against her chest and am lulled to sleep by the steady lub-dub of her heartbeat. After a while she jostles me. "Wake up and get dressed, Jeeter, we've got a shuttle to catch." I slide off her lap and fumble with my borrowed clothing, trying to press the wrinkles out with the width of my hand. When I'm dressed and standing before her for inspection, Sergeant Haran takes my elbow and leads me back to the bar.

Nodding at the barkeep, Sergeant Haran asks for a couple of screaming orgasms and a beer. She bends down and whispers in my ear, "Thought I'd commemorate our evening together."

I blush hotly and the barkeep takes in my glazed eyes and mussed clothing, then erupts in raucous laughter while she mixes our drinks. She slides them across the bar and tells Sergeant Haran they're on the house.

"Drink up." The sergeant pushes both mixed drinks toward me and keeps the beer for herself. When I hesitate, she quirks her cheek before saying, "I have to charge you with something. It might as well be drunk and disorderly."

I don't know how many screaming orgasms I had or how many I drank but when I woke up, I was dressed in my utilities and facedown on a bed in the brig. My head throbbed and I knew that when I moved, I was going to spew the acid that was eating my stomach lining all over my cell. My memory of the trip back to the ship was a drunken collage of images culminating with my cheek pressed against the cold deck floor and Sergeant Haran looming over me with a satisfied smirk on her face.

"You back with us, Jeeter?" I groan and swallow bile when I turn my head to see Sergeant Haran standing outside my cell with her hands braced against her hips and her smirk firmly in place.

I rasp, "Yes, Sergeant." My throat is sore and my stomach sour, but a delicious ache between my thighs and in my limbs makes my suffering bearable. Though the trip back was a blur, everything that happened before is imprinted on my cellular memory.

"Ready to get out? I've cleared everything with the captain." She lowers the security screen and joins me in my cell.

Moving slowly, I roll over until my feet find the floor and my head falls into the palms of my hands. Sergeant Haran's laughter reverberates off the plated walls, spiking my headache and making me clench my eyes against the pain.

Chuckling more quietly, Sergeant Haran dangles a hypospray off the tip of her finger. "Want some of this?" I peel my eyes open and extend my trembling hand—just one shot from the hypospray and my hangover will be all gone.

When I reach out, Sergeant Haran draws back and tucks the dose into her pocket. "Sorry, Jeeter. Can't have it. There's always a downside to rash action, and this is it for you." She stands up, then helps me to my feet, taking care to cradle me snugly against her side. If this is the downside, I guess I'll just have to live with it.

Two under Par
Erin Dutton

"I scouted out the perfect place during yesterday's round," I whispered to Grace.

"What hole are we up to?" Grace pulled her driver from her club bag and smiled.

"Eight," I answered, anticipation already pulsing through my veins.

"Show me when we get there."

We were about to start the fourth and final round of the tournament. Currently in first and second place, we were paired together and stood waiting at the first tee. While Grace was occupied readying her clubs, I studied her.

She was gorgeous. I had been hooked from the first time I saw her. Regular workouts combined with hours spent on the golf course kept her muscles lean and strong. My pulse quickened at the thought of those muscles rippling beneath my fingers. A natural redhead, Grace usually pulled a baseball cap bearing the logo of her sponsor low over her eyes to protect her fair skin. I knew without being able to see them that Grace's hazel eyes sparkled with pre-match anticipation. It was more than just a competitive gleam—she thoroughly enjoyed the game whether she won or lost. But I knew from experience that her post-win high jacked up her already healthy libido.

Still, it was more than just her great looks that attracted me to Grace. Ten weeks before, I had shown up for my first tournament, nervous and very much aware that I was now playing in the big time. I was paired with Grace Manning, a tour veteran. My anxiety increased exponentially—I'd be playing with one of my heroes of the game. It didn't take long for me to see firsthand why Grace was the top-rated player on the tour. She had a fluid, seemingly effortless swing and one of the longest drives in women's golf.

But as I soon found out, Grace was also very down-to-earth. Her easygoing attitude and natural sense of fun rapidly eased my jitters. We hit it off immediately. By the third hole we were exchanging teasing banter and laughing between shots. We played a round of golf reminiscent of a time when I played for my own enjoyment, before competition and ranking became so important.

"We're up," Grace reminded me only moments before she was announced as the next golfer.

She teed up a ball, settled into her stance, and paused for an instant with her club head resting behind the ball. Her long, lithe body created textbook lines from the beginning of her backswing through the top of her follow-through. I thought again, as I always did when I watched Grace play, I had rarely seen anything quite so perfect.

Grace kept her eyes on the ball until it rolled to a stop in the center of the fairway and then turned to me.

"Ryan, you're distracted," she accused.

"No, I'm not," I protested, wondering how Grace could read me so easily already. I grinned as I allowed my eyes to purposely drop down and trail lasciviously back up Grace's body. "I was simply admiring your—form."

"That might be the worst pick-up line I've ever heard," Grace shot back.

"Like I need a line to get what I want," I murmured, brushing my arm deliberately against her breast as I passed. I teed up my own ball.

Grace laughed, and my stomach tightened. I loved the sound of her laughter. She was so free with it. I envied Grace her lack of inhibitions.

I lined up with the ball off my left toe, shifted my stance, and placed the heel of my driver directly behind the ball. My swing was unique in that lining up slightly off center seemed to be the most effective method for curbing my natural draw. Giving in to various trainers and coaches over the years, I had allowed them to tinker with my swing. But this unorthodox approach had proven the most consistent.

I glanced over my left shoulder to find my target. Tucking my chin, I slowly drew the club back, slightly shifting my weight to my right leg. Years of practice had ingrained the feel of the swing in my body. At precisely the right moment, I instinctively began shifting back to the left and my downswing took shape. The club's impact with the ball was solid, as indicated by the indescribable but oh-so-recognizable sound made by good contact between ball and club. My ball came to rest a few feet from Grace's.

I turned in time to catch Grace jerking her eyes guiltily from the vicinity of my ass. She grinned as I narrowed my eyes suspiciously.

"You've got a rather interesting form yourself."

"You think so?"

"Sure. But it could be better."

I laughed. "Are you volunteering to help?"

"I could. But it will take a lot of personal attention and I have a very…hands-on…approach."

The image of Grace's hands on me nearly made me stumble as I handed the club to my caddy. Grace and I walked shoulder to shoulder down the fairway.

"So—eight, huh?" Grace whispered, letting me know that her thoughts weren't entirely on golf either.

"I'll show you when we get there." As we walked, I let my mind wander back to the events of the past two months.

The third week of the tour, late one night over drinks, we began flirting. The next night a walk on the beach ended in a kiss. Just a kiss. But there was a moment, when her lips opened and I slipped my tongue against hers—I knew from that moment I didn't want it to end there.

The walk back to my hotel room seemed endless. My blood ran hot, I was almost painfully aroused, and I could still feel the firm pressure of her hips against mine. *Just a kiss.* It was anything but *just* a kiss. She had moaned against my mouth and pressed closer. Just when I was thinking I could take her right there on the beach, she had pulled back, grasped my hand, and continued walking down the beach. It was more than a kiss. It was an amazing kiss with a gorgeous woman on a beach in Hawaii. Could there be a more perfect moment?

To top it off, I played the best round of my life the next day and took second in the tournament—second to that same woman. I could handle that. It was the wanting her that was going to kill me. Just the sight of her was enough to send my fantasies into overdrive, conjuring up all the things I wanted to do to her. Mercifully, it turned out I wouldn't have to wait too much longer for more than just a kiss.

"Keep it up and we won't make it until tonight," Grace hissed, interrupting my mental replay.

I fixed what I hoped was an innocent expression on my face.

"I'm not buying that look," she said. "I know what's going on in that precious head of yours."

"I don't know what you mean," I teased, but I was wet already and we hadn't even finished the first hole. "It's going to be a long eighteen," I muttered.

"Stop it right now." Grace was all business again. She moved away and conferred with her caddy.

Grace birdied the first hole, while I paid for my distraction with a par. But as we approached the second tee, I drifted back to thoughts of Hawaii. And Grace.

The night before we left Hawaii we had decided to take one last stroll under the palm trees behind the club. The courses always felt subtly different as night fell. I loved to explore them under the cover of darkness, and Grace seemed to share my feeling of enchantment.

It started innocently enough. We walked along the cart path, talking about the tour. Thanks to Grace, my transition had been smooth. I was having fun and playing better than ever. It was unheard of for a rookie to place in the top five in her first four tournaments. I was being touted as a rising star.

Grace dismissed all the press, telling me that she was responsible for my success. "Do you think you would be playing like this if I wasn't winding you up with all of this sexual tension?"

"What tension?" I arched an eyebrow. "I already know you're just a tease."

"Really?"

She stopped in the middle of the path. I took one more step and was jerked to a halt. She held my hand tightly and wasn't budging.

"A tease?" she asked, pulling me against her.

She cupped the back of my neck with one hand and cradled my jaw with the other. I leaned in, humming with pleasure and anticipating our kiss. I could get used to the buzz of excitement I felt just before Grace kissed me.

"I think you're getting a little full of yourself," Grace murmured as she drew back just inches short of the kiss. "I might have to put you in your place."

"I like the sound of that." I wondered how long it would take to get her back to my room and to get her clothes off.

She held her mouth away for a moment longer before she finally closed the distance and her lips caressed mine. But she still didn't give me exactly what I wanted. She was aggressive until I responded and then she pulled back, lightly stroking her tongue against my lips. Just as I was getting frustrated she gave me more, pressing into me until I could feel every curve of her body.

"Hmm...is this more of that tension you were talking about?" I drawled as she gazed at me. I tried to sound casual, but I was raging with anticipation. Every word was foreplay. Every touch made me wetter.

"Maybe." She skimmed her hands down my chest. Her fingers brushed my nipples and my breath hissed through my teeth. She returned, pinching them through the thin silk of my shirt.

She practically growled as her mouth claimed mine. When she spread her legs to straddle my thigh, I wondered if I would make it back to the room. All I could think about was being inside her. I didn't even care that anyone could happen upon us at any moment. I craved her in a way I never had anyone before.

"Ah, baby, there's no way I'll make it if we keep this up," I pled.

A spark of challenge set off the heat already smoldering in her eyes. Wordlessly she rolled her hips against mine. All thought of making it back to the room fled my mind as I felt the heat of her against my thigh right through my slacks.

When I palmed her breast she arched her back, pushing it more fully into my hand. *Jesus, she's not wearing a bra.* She opened several buttons on her shirt and shoved my hand inside. *Lord help me.* I stroked her soft skin, kneading and caressing.

"Touch me." She reached for the fly of her jeans.

"Oh God, I want to—just as soon as we get back to the hotel."

She sucked my earlobe into her mouth. She bit my neck just hard enough. I pressed my hips into her in an attempt to release some of the pressure pounding between my legs. Her hands found my ass and she pulled me even tighter to her, grinding against me. I fisted my hands in the back of her shirt and buried my face in her neck, inhaling the subtle woodsy scent of citrus and teakwood I'd come to associate with her. I had to taste her.

"Here." She spoke aloud the word that was screaming through my head.

"Yes." I was beyond hesitation.

I dragged her toward the green. My head swam with the feel of her beneath me as I laid her down on the neatly manicured grass. Moving over her, I reached between us and pressed my hand into her open fly, encountering warm, bare skin. *No panties either?*

I had to taste her.

Dipping my head, I nudged my face into the open vee of her shirt and pulled one of her nipples into my mouth. It grew impossibly hard against my tongue. *Oh yes, baby. Could you know how much I've wanted you all these weeks?*

"Ryan—please." She grasped my wrist and thrust my hand farther into her jeans. "Please don't make me wait any longer."

I groaned as wetness coated my fingers. Her hips jerked as I brushed over her clit and when I pushed inside, she squeezed around me.

I wanted her naked. Her jeans were still tight around her hips and constricted my movement. I wanted room to fuck her, in and out as hard and fast as she could take it. I wanted to drape her bare legs over my shoulders and push my mouth between her thighs. I wanted to feel her clit twitch against my tongue.

I had to taste her.

Instead, still conscious that we were in public, I contented myself with rocking my fingers into her, pressing the base of my hand against her clit. She met my thrusts, lifting her knee and pushing her thigh between my legs. My already aching clit throbbed in response.

"Grace." I was incapable of anything more than the strangled moan as she pressed her foot flat on the ground, her thigh driving against me. "Jesus, Grace."

I couldn't help myself, the pressure against the already sensitive flesh between my legs sent an almost painful streak of arousal through my cunt. I needed relief. She would own me until I got it. I needed it in order to once again form a coherent thought.

"Come on, baby. Let it go," she urged.

"Oh God, I-I—Grace." I've never been more inarticulate in my life. Her name spilled from my lips amidst reverent moans, and even that was nearly more than I could manage. The heady scent of her— the feel of her firmly against my center—her body pulsing around my fingers.

I lifted up, bracing myself on one arm, and rode her leg to orgasm. It was a tight flash of light behind my clenched eyelids—white-hot pleasure that lanced through me. My body tightened, my fingers hard inside of her as she came with me. I lost myself in her. In the way she cried out and shuddered against me. In the soft panting breath against my ear.

Her hands were in my hair and she tugged my head up to rest her forehead against mine. "I knew it would be like this," she whispered.

"I had no idea."

"Was it good for you?" Grace purred in my ear, dragging me back to the present.

I was still standing at the second tee. Shit, I'd just had an orgasm from the memory of our first time while standing amidst a crowd of spectators. My legs felt like rubber and my heart pounded. Grace gave me a self-satisfied look. She knew exactly what had just happened, because after that first time, it had become a game between us. Every tournament was a challenge to find a new place to play on the next hole. After the sand trap at the seventh in Orlando, we'd had to take an extra-long shower.

I glanced around, immensely relieved to find Grace was the only one who appeared to be aware of my mental lapse. Realizing it was my turn to tee off, I stumbled forward. My smile mirrored hers as I thought about my plans for her tonight at the edge of the water hazard on the eighth hole.

I finished that tournament at two under par. Grace shot three under, beating me by one stroke. First or second, I always won when I played with Grace.

A QUIET NIGHT IN
LESLEY DAVIS

The conference had gone on for what seemed like days before the guest speaker finally noticed he had most of us bored to tears and mercifully let us go. Shawn grabbed my arm, unceremoniously pulled me out of my seat, and led me out of the conference hall at a fast gait.

"If that pompous windbag had kept up any longer, I'd have decked him." Shawn hailed a taxi with one hand and kept me close with her other.

Once seated in the back of the taxi, I yawned so widely my jaw cracked. Shawn looked me over solicitously and ran her fingers along my face.

"You tired, babe?"

"A little, but I want a drink so bad I can taste it already. I'll have one beer with you, but then I think I want to go back to the hotel."

"You need to relax and work those kinks out of your spine from sitting all day listening to Motormouth." Shawn brushed my lips with hers and I felt my stomach alight with flames.

"I'll relax in our hotel room with you," I muttered, accepting her rough tongue between my lips and letting her take her time exploring me.

The taxi jerked to a halt and we were on the receiving end of a very censorious look by our driver. Shawn merely stared at him as she paid.

"He's just pissed because I'm more man than he could ever be." Laughing, she smoothed down her suit, unconsciously accentuating her androgynous look.

"Shawn, we *both* are." I indicated my own attire, a suit as dark as

Shawn's was light. I ran a tired hand through my short hair and squared my shoulders. "Ready to make the locals squirm in their seats?"

Shawn wrapped her arm about my shoulder. "They squirm because you make them hot."

"They squirm because they see us together and can't help but wonder how two handsome butches got to be lovers."

"Because I knew a good thing when I saw it, and you had the smarts to recognize my worth."

"God, you're arrogant." I laughed at her and received a swift kiss as my reward.

"And you love me for it."

"You know it."

Inside, I smiled at the bartender as she poured me my drink, and then sneaked a look at my lover, who was searching the bar with curious eyes.

"See something you like?" I asked. Shawn immediately turned her sights to me, ever attentive.

"Seeing someone I love," she replied smoothly and pulled me close to her at the bar so that her leg pressed between mine. I shivered at the pressure.

"I don't think I want to stay, Shawn," I admitted as I drained my drink.

Shawn cocked her head to the loud music coming from the dance area. "Madonna not doing it for you tonight?"

"You know Madonna never does it for me."

"Want me to come back with you?"

I shook my head. "No, stay. Unwind. Just get in before the sun comes up."

Shawn flashed the rakish pirate smile that always twisted my heart. "I'll bring you something back?"

I put my hand behind her neck and pulled her down for a lingering kiss. "You do that."

At the sound of the door opening a few hours later, I glanced away from the computer magazine I had been poring over to see Shawn saunter in with a woman in tow.

"Put your magazine down, Troy, we have a guest." Shawn grinned and gently pushed the woman toward me. My blond lover, tall and slim, was accompanied by a short, full-figured redhead I didn't know. I immediately got up off the bed to welcome our gorgeous visitor.

Shawn introduced us politely. "Troy, this is Cait. She was at the conference too today." Shawn grinned at me. "She works behind the scenes with Mr. Personality."

My face gave me away and Cait laughed.

"He's not so bad, really." Her voice lilted with a little bit of an accent. "But he does waffle on once he starts to get into his spiel."

"Would you like a drink?" Shawn asked, slowly undoing her tie. I had never seen anyone do such a normal task so sensually. Shawn laid a hand on Cait's shoulder, drawing her attention away from me. "Something to eat, maybe?"

I tried not to smile at her attempts to be a good hostess. We all knew exactly why Cait was here.

"No, I'm fine, thank you."

Shawn slipped Cait's coat from her shoulders while Cait kept her attention on me, her green eyes boring into mine.

"Had I known you were down at the Zenith, I might have made the effort to stay longer," I said. "Instead I had some quiet time here just reading."

Cait peered at the magazine I had placed on the table. "Computer programming? Shawn said you were an IT specialist."

I shrugged. "It's a cool job, but not as butch as Shawn's. I have to really make sure I don't get soft sitting at my desk while she's out installing the machines."

Shawn chuckled and wrapped her arm about my waist. "You won't get soft, sweetheart, I'll see to that." She ran her hand down my arm and flexed her fingers into the muscle. "See?" She reached over to take Cait's hand. "Tell her she's not soft."

Cait's hand felt slight on my arm as she squeezed the muscle I had meticulously built there. I couldn't help but marvel at how different the two women were, yet how both could make my heart race just that little bit faster.

Shawn draped her arms over my shoulders and hugged me from behind. I leaned back into her warmth, enjoying the feel of someone exactly the same height.

"I told Cait she could come and play with us if she wanted," Shawn said. "She yanked me from my stool so fast she nearly broke my neck getting out of the bar. Seems she noticed us today and liked what she saw."

Cait chuckled, tentatively exploring my chest and then Shawn's face, familiarizing herself with us, getting to know us. "I'd like to play with you two. I think we'd have fun. A woman would be a fool to resist such an offer from two handsome women."

I smiled at her. "We don't get to play too often now. It's not safe and not everyone understands the rules of our games." I cuddled farther into my lover's arms.

"I'll get both of you?" Cait qualified, her gaze still locked on me.

I was aware of her attraction to me and was highly flattered by it. A butch will always be drawn to a femme, but it was clear my heart belonged to Shawn alone.

"Oh, we'll both be participating," Shawn said, licking my neck and sending a shudder through my whole frame. "Neither of us is exactly the voyeur type."

"Think you can handle us both?" I asked, knowing too well the reply as her eyes sparked into flame.

She stepped closer and ran her palm up my body to finally rest it against Shawn's forearm. "I can handle all you two dish out and more besides."

"Confident. I like that trait in a woman, especially one as pretty as yourself." I leaned forward to nuzzle at her neck. Her head fell back to grant me easier access.

"I knew this conference would be a good one," Cait moaned softly. "I just didn't expect the fringe benefits when I slipped out for a swift drink."

I pulled her close and kissed her gently, learning her shape and taste. I felt her lips open to my questing tongue and then pressed harder once given entry. I felt Shawn's arms fall away and heard the rustle of clothing behind me. That's my girl, straight down to business. I pulled back slightly, enjoying the dazed look on Cait's face. Shawn stepped in and gave her a kiss of welcome all of her own. I watched as my lover kicked off her shoes and began tugging one-handed at her belt buckle to open it up. I helped her with the cumbersome thing and opened her top button so all she had to do was unzip. Cait tugged me close, alternating between kissing us both. Shawn waited her turn and then kissed me as only my lover could. I melted from the force of her lips on mine and sucked hard at her tongue, trying to devour her. She pushed me back a little.

"Get your glasses off before they get crushed," she teased while pulling Cait closer to the bed. There she gently began to strip her. She opened the silk blouse to reveal a very lacy bra that barely kept Cait's breasts covered. "Oh my," Shawn breathed, "I do like a big girl in lace."

I helped Cait out of her skirt and between us we had her nude in moments. She was as beautiful as I imagined, all soft curves and lush flesh. I felt my mouth water at the sight of her.

"Natural redheads, you can't beat them," Shawn teased and Cait laughed at her silliness.

"I'm all natural, baby, and you know it." She turned around to look at me. "Are you two keeping your clothes on or do I get to see a little muscle here?" She tugged at my shirt but it was Shawn who moved to divest me of my clothing, baring me to Cait's eyes. Cait immediately cupped my breasts and began chafing at my nipples. I choked down a groan as my most sensitive spots were expertly handled.

Shawn pulled her own shirt and bra off and pressed her body into mine. "She loves that," she whispered to Cait and undid my trousers to let them fall to the floor, leaving me naked between them.

Cait pressed closer, sandwiching me between the hard body of my lover and her soft, sweet curves. She kissed me, all the time pulling at my nipples and running her nails around the areolae. Shawn cupped my breasts from underneath, holding them still for Cait's pleasure. While she watched Cait suck at my breast, Shawn chewed on my neck, holding me tightly, marking her territory.

"Bed," I managed to say huskily and we all scrambled onto the large mattress. In the move, I got Cait beneath me and I paid her back in kind for her worship of my nipples. I noticed the sound of Shawn removing her trousers and with some pride heard Cait gasp as my lover removed her boxer shorts.

Shawn held her large dildo in a strong hand. "By the end of tonight, you will have had this in you so deep you'll wonder how you ever managed before you met us."

With Cait between us, Shawn and I sucked on her breasts until the tips were ruby red and so full they had doubled in size. Shawn tugged me over Cait and kissed me hard. I reached over and twisted her nipple until she grunted with the pleasure of it, then I caressed Cait, enjoying the softness and the roundness of her belly. I was sucking at her breast, Shawn was kissing her, and Cait had both our heads in her hands, urging us on.

I brushed at the patch of red at the top of her thighs, then slipped my fingers lower. Cait was wet, so wet my fingers slipped in amongst her folds and found her opening with ease. I entered her gently, just with one finger, and she bucked beneath us. I stroked inside her, enjoying the welcome of her tight muscles and the flow of juice as I journeyed deeper. The bed dipped as Shawn shifted between Cait's legs.

"Think she's ready for this?" she asked as she rubbed the head of the dildo above where my hand entered.

I glanced at Cait. Her mouth was open as she gasped for air. I then shared a special look with my lover and removed my hand from where Shawn intended to be. "Fuck her," I said.

Shawn pushed inside her with the thick toy. Cait's breathing hitched, caught, and then released on one long, protracted moan. Shawn lifted Cait's legs up to rest on her hips and Cait crossed her ankles behind Shawn's back. For a moment I sat back and watched my lover at work, watched her lithe hips pump to a rhythm that drove the woman underneath her wild. I looked on as Cait dug her nails into Shawn's back, trying to hold on as the steady slide in and out made her rock on the bed. I ran my own hand over the soft leather harness that secured the dildo to my lover's hips. My fingers brushed across her buttocks and then squeezed the hard flesh there. I moved to lie on my side beside Cait and tugged first at her nipples and then at the hard tips that hung from my own sweet lover's breasts. I inched up and kissed Cait's face, drawing her lips to mine while my lover pounded at her.

"God, you're tight," Shawn hissed as she thrust inside Cait's cunt.

"Fuck her good, baby," I said to Shawn, squeezing Cait's breasts while Shawn's strokes got shorter. Cait's breath all but stopped and then the most delicious wail was forced from her bright lips. Her body bucked as she came hard on Shawn's cock and her eyes rolled back before she finally collapsed to the bed.

I grinned at my lover and Shawn roughly kissed me before gently easing her dildo from Cait's body. She began to unbuckle it fast, haste making her fingers fumble, and I pushed her hands away to complete the task. She moaned as the dildo skidded off her clit, and she spread her swollen lips for me to see how hard she was. With all the strength I possessed I pushed her back on the bed next to Cait, who twitched and sighed. Shawn tried to push back but I boldly held her down, forcing her to stay put while I kissed her senseless. Her strong hands dug at my shoulders, then kneaded my back muscles, hard enough to leave small bruises in their wake. I kept her pinned, my kisses harsh and almost brutal, but Shawn matched me kiss for kiss. I rubbed her nipple, my thumb running round the hard tip and flicking it. Shawn bowed her back, still trying to knock me off, but I held firm. I worked my way lower, and Cait roused to take my place at Shawn's lips.

While Cait kept my lover distracted, I shouldered her legs apart and knelt on the floor between her spread thighs. She closed her legs forcefully, trying to crush me, but we'd played this game before. It's all a sport, this show of strength, two prizefighters showing off their best moves. I slowly spread her swollen lips and took a deep breath, loving her scent. Her clitoris was free from its hood, bright red and straining. I gently touched my tongue to it and Shawn jumped and groaned. She was already too worked up for me to go slow. I knew how my lover hated to be teased, so I swiftly flattened my tongue and licked the length of her slit, sliding my tongue inside her, then flicking over her stiffened clit. I chewed at her ruffled lips and darted my tongue into her wetness, lapping it all up.

I heard Shawn breathing hard but knew she wouldn't say a word, not while we had company. But alone, when it's just her and me, she'll whisper sweet words and beg me to fuck her raw. For now, I took her clit into my mouth and sucked. I held her lips open, forcing her clit deep into my mouth, and felt the shudders shake her body. I rested a hand on her stomach, kneading the tight muscles, held on tightly as she came with a forced growl of my name. For a long moment I just left my face buried in her cunt and savored the fragrance. Strong and addictive, just like Shawn herself.

The next thing I knew I was flung onto my back between Cait and a very wild Shawn. She kissed me hard and I felt the silent thank-you pass from her lips to mine.

Cait was already busy on my breasts. She had learned quickly that I loved having attention paid to them. I speared my fingers through her long hair, holding her to me as she sucked on me. I may be butch, but the minute someone wants me on my back to suck at my tits, I'm not going to argue. Shawn had one of my nipples between her teeth and was gently gnawing on it. She rubbed my belly, tugged on my pubic hair, and then pressed lower. The touch of her callused fingertips on my clit caused me to jerk and grab for someone, anyone. Cait instantly draped herself over my chest, and I watched through barely opened eyes as Shawn positioned me how she wanted me, spreading my legs wide. She licked me first, her tongue rough as she nipped at my flesh. All the time my arms were full with the femme who was lavishing kisses all over me while I fondled her buttocks. I felt Shawn's fingers enter me and I opened to her. She pushed in and twisted her fingers, stretching me, widening me. She pulled out a tube from the bedside table and I realized her intentions. I started to struggle.

"Hold her down, Cait," Shawn instructed as she swiftly lubed up her hand.

"Shawn…" I started, but Cait's mouth hushed me and then distracted me from what was happening. Her fingers brushed through my tight-cropped hair and tickled at my scalp. I felt strong fingers enter me, then leave only for more to return.

"Open for me, baby," Shawn crooned and pushed a little farther in, twisting her fingers, easing her thumb into her palm.

Cait straddled my chest, fondling my breasts and pulling on my nipples. The stimulation turned me on and I heard Shawn let out a grunt of satisfaction. With a push, she was inside me. I hissed aloud at the pain but it soon subsided as I got used to the feeling of fullness. Cait shifted and got off to watch.

"How deep can you go?" Cait asked, clearly fascinated by the sight of my lover's thick hand buried inside me.

"As deep as she'll let me."

Shawn started to pump gently and my chest constricted. We'd done this before but never with a playmate to view. But then, Cait was proving to be more than just any pick-up. She knew the rules of the game. She watched for a moment, then stretched out beside me and ran her hand over my lower belly as if trying to feel where Shawn's fist was.

"This is so damn sexy," she breathed in my ear and then licked my neck sensuously.

Shawn continued her slow push until I had to beg. "Harder, please, Shawn."

She speeded up and I was awash with the sensation of my heart thumping and my cunt pulsating to my lover's driving beat. While

Cait watched my lover fist me, she sucked my breast and shoved my hand into her crotch to rub her clit. Shawn worked her free hand firmly between her own legs, bringing herself off as she thrust inside me. The room was filled with the scent of raw sex and the sound of our moans as we all got closer to coming. I felt wide open, filled to the brim, loved beyond hope, and blessed beyond belief.

I came first with a hoarse shout that was echoed by a rough cry from my partner and a soft keening from our new lover as my climax ignited theirs. When the room finally stopped spinning, I found myself cuddled between Shawn and Cait. As I lay in the stupor only good sex can bring about, I smiled to myself in blissful satisfaction. There is really nothing more enjoyable after a hard day at work than a quiet night in, spent in the company of the woman you love and a new friend.

FREE FALL
JULIE CANNON

I've never wanted to jump out of a perfectly good airplane until I saw her standing under the sign that read *Skydiving*. It was our second stop on a ten-day cruise that the glossy brochure promised would offer adventure and excitement at every port of call. The dark-haired, full-figured lesbian behind the narrow counter was certainly a good start. I bravely stepped in line.

I was about to turn fifty and my friends had booked me on this cruise as a birthday present, telling me I really needed to let my hair down and have some fun. I always thought I was a fun girl—admittedly not an extremely adventurous one, but I rarely shied away from a challenge. Sometime during the last few days under the sun and the bright blue sky I had made the monumental decision that I was going to live my next fifty years much differently than I had my first. My friends would describe me as solid, dependable, and predictable. I would use a totally different adjective: dull. I hadn't been in a relationship in years, went to the same nine-to-five job every day for the past two decades, wore sensible yet stylish shoes, drove an eight-year-old sedan, and called my mother once a week. Eyeing the woman four feet in front of me made me realize that I couldn't remember the last time I got laid. Worse yet, I couldn't remember the last time I *wanted* to get laid. Until now.

The man in front of me completed his paperwork and stepped away. The darkest eyes I had ever seen nailed me with a look that said *I know you're a lesbian.* Her smile confirmed her gaydar sighting.

"Looking for adventure this afternoon?"

Holy shit, she didn't waste any time, and she certainly didn't say that to the man in front of me when it was his turn at the counter. I'm not used to women coming on to me, let alone a woman who was looking at me like I was the last lesbian on earth. Things were definitely looking up. "And how do you know that?" I replied, mimicking her husky tone.

She looked me over from head to toe, her eyes slowing at the all important places. I wasn't thin and had my share of excess body fat in the expected places—I was fifty years old, for Christ's sake—but her admiring, interested look clearly said she didn't mind.

"Besides the obvious fact that you're in this line?" She pointed to the sign and smiled mischievously.

I could have drowned in the dimples in her cheeks, and I'm sure my face turned as red as her shirt. *Duh.* She spoke again and saved me from complete humiliation.

"Actually, you're the most *interesting* customer I've had in quite some time. I hope you're here to enjoy the exhilaration of an experience you've never had before."

She winked when she said *interesting* and looked at me as if she had just decided to swap me for whatever she had packed for lunch.

"Are you interested in going solo or tandem?"

Her question was loaded with innuendo, and I knew she was not simply talking about skydiving. My mouth started to water and my fingers tingled with the desire to touch the skin that was peeking out of the neckline of her jumpsuit. I had been going solo far too long. "Tandem. Definitely tandem," I said with seductive confidence. She too read between the lines of my answer and smiled, knowing what was to come. The thought of her strapped tightly behind me as we fell ten thousand feet from the sky made my legs weak.

I have no idea what she said during the four hours of instruction. Every time she looked at me I felt devoured. Her body language spoke to me in a way that made my tongue move against my lips, imagining they were hers, and every nerve on my body started to come alive. She brushed against me as she said something about my parachute, and when she leaned over me to straighten the lines I felt her warm breath caress my ear just before she spoke.

"I can't wait to have you strapped against me touching your body, squeezing your tits, and sliding my hands into your pussy. I'm going to be in complete control of everything you do. It'll be an experience you'll never forget."

She stepped away and I had to lean forward on the table to regain my balance. I was surprised at the speed with which she operated, but quite frankly I was now so horny she couldn't move fast enough. Those few short words were enough to drench my Jockeys as all reason flew out the door. My hands were shaking in anticipation of the actions she'd so crudely described. Our eyes met and she knew the reaction she had caused in me. She smiled knowingly and winked before answering a question from the man to my right. My nipples had hardened the moment I saw her, and after her little teasing episode, they were screaming. I straightened and her eyes flew to my chest, which clearly displayed my arousal through my thin T-shirt. She licked her lips and my nipples ached to be sucked.

My hungry eyes followed her around the room as she provided tips and instructions to the others in the class as they adjusted their harnesses. My body tingled in anticipation as she slowly approached me and reached for the clasp between my legs. This time she leaned toward me and whispered, "Did I forget to mention that I'm going to fuck you senseless as we fall out of the sky?" Her tongue grazed my ear as she yanked the buckle against my already throbbing clit.

"Jesus." I grabbed the edge of the table to keep from falling. She definitely had me right where she wanted me and right where I wanted to be. One more comment or touch and I might come right where I stood.

She cast me a seductive smile. "No, you can call me Carmen."

❖

I was the only woman in the dressing room and was just stepping into my jumpsuit when I felt someone behind me. I didn't have to turn to know who it was, and I held my breath as she stepped closer. Warm breath tickled my neck as strong fingers moved through my hair. "Is there anything specific you want to experience?"

Her voice caressed my skin. It was soft and low and held just enough of a Jamaican accent to make it extraordinarily sexy. Of course, it could have been the fact that I was already so hot that her reading a nursery rhyme would make me come. "Besides your hands on my tits and your fingers in my pussy?" I leaned into her and rubbed my ass against her. "Oh yeah, don't forget you're going to fuck me senseless." Her sharp intake of breath and moan told me she was looking forward to it as much as I.

She started moving in rhythm with my ass and gathered me closer. Strong arms came around me and large hands wrapped around my breasts. "Oh yeah, I'm definitely going to fuck you. That's what you want, isn't it? That's why you stepped into my line. You took one look at me and knew I could make you come like you've never come before." One hand drifted down and circled in for a landing on my hard clit. "You want the thrill of a stranger's hands on you. Anonymous sex in a foreign country. No complications, no regrets, and no inhibitions because we will never see each other again."

My hips bucked in invitation, but she didn't move any closer. She laughed sensuously as she nibbled on my neck. "Oh yes, I know exactly what you want and I'm going to give it to you. You are going to scream with desire and come so hard your body will explode. And then you'll go home and tell all your friends what a wonderful time you had in my country. Am I right?"

I found my voice somewhere between my throbbing clit and the electric pulses shooting through my body from the fingers tugging on my nipple. One simple word was all I needed. "Yes."

She stepped away and I felt cool where her body had pressed against me but was on fire where her hands had been. I shuddered at the loss of contact, and her fingers teased my skin as she pulled the jumpsuit up my arms and over my shoulders. This time when she leaned toward me, she didn't allow our bodies to touch.

"Don't be late."

As she walked away I realized I was definitely going to enjoy being the teacher's pet.

❖

God only knows how I finished dressing and managed to find the plane that held the stranger who had me so tightly wound I could come at any moment. My clit throbbed with each step and my evident desire had seeped through my undies long ago. My nipples rubbed against the coarse fabric of the jumpsuit, my legs were shaking, and I couldn't get to the plane fast enough.

I joined my fellow enthusiasts and boarded the small plane. She was waiting for us, and when I stepped inside she licked her lips and drilled me with eyes filled with lust. "Ready?"

"Are you?" I countered with my best *come fuck me* look, surprising myself because I didn't know I even *had* a *come fuck me* look.

"Yes," she replied without hesitation. Like she would. Hesitate, that is. *I* was the one going on the ride of my life.

Her eyes raked my body. "You know we only have about seven minutes until we're on the ground?"

The phrase *seven minutes in heaven* jumped into my sex-starved brain. The effects of age had caught up with me; as best as I could remember, it usually took me much, much longer than that to come. I might not be the sharpest tack in the box, but today I knew that would definitely not be the case. Her eyes flew to my chest as I took a deep breath.

"Not a problem." I could feel her eyes on my ass as I moved on shaking legs toward an empty seat.

❖

The vibration of the plane only brought me closer to orgasm as we taxied down the runway. My unpolished fingernails dug into my palms and I tore my eyes away from simmering black ones. I knew I was dangerously close to coming, and since I hadn't been blessed with the multiorgasm gene, that would be a disaster. I forced myself to think about the items accumulating in my in-box and the mail piling up inside my front door while I was on my vacation. Thankfully my ascent to orgasm didn't match the climb to our jumping altitude.

She unbuckled her seat belt and stood, signaling to us to do the same. I bit my tongue as my hands reached for the buckle that was pressing against my pussy. One wrong move, one millimeter of increased pressure, and I was a goner.

Mission accomplished, I stepped behind the last man in line. My mouth started to water as I imagined the strong hands that were manipulating the controls on the door in control of my body. A deafening roar filled the plane when the door opened, and my libido plunged when I realized what I was about to do. The minutes ticked by like hours as I waited my turn to step onto the black rubber mat that was the last firm thing I would stand on before the seven minutes of free fall.

After the other students had all jumped, she turned to me. The wind whipping through the open door made conversation impossible and she signaled me to step closer. Being a compliant kind of girl, I obeyed. I noticed her hands shaking as she completed the pre-jump check of my harness. She stepped behind me, and I was so scared I was barely aware as she reached around, securing our bodies together. A thumbs-up appeared before my eyes and I mirrored her actions, noticing the complete contrast in not only the color of our hands, but the size. Before I could notice anything else, we were out the door.

The deafening noise in the plane followed us out the door. The force of the wind slapped me in the face like a bucket of cold water, jolting me out of my fright. I blinked a few times, grateful for the protective goggles I wore, and what I saw took my breath away. The ground below was a pattern of shades of green that were the most vivid colors I had ever seen. I didn't get much opportunity to savor the view before I became aware of my zipper inching open.

One of the things that I had noticed when I donned the jumpsuit was the two-way zipper that ran the entire length of my torso. It opened from both the top *and* the bottom, and right now the instructor's hands were moving the bottom zipper northward. I arched my back as she had instructed us to, providing her with another four inches to open. My clit came to life and began to beat in direct competition with my heart as we fell a hundred feet per second toward the hard earth below.

The cold air hitting my body was quickly replaced by her large, warm hand. Its sister was busy opening the top zipper, and before I knew it I had one hand on my pussy and one squeezing my breast. The sensation of free-falling both literally and figuratively was unlike anything I had ever experienced, and I moaned. She responded by tweaking my hard nipple, and her fingers dipped into my pussy.

She expertly used her fingers to explore, unconcerned that we were quickly approaching the point where the FAA recommended we slow our ascent. My eyes rolled back in my head at the first touch on my clit. She obviously felt my reaction, because her fingers quickly moved away to less sensitive areas. I felt her fingers approaching the opening that few had ventured into in the past few years, and as she paused at the port of entry, she screamed, "Pull the cord!"

That scared the crap out of me, jolting me back to reality, and I grasped blindly for the bright red handle that would save my life. It slid easily out of the enclosure at the same instant her fingers entered me. The jolt of the chute opening slammed her palm against my clit, and I unexpectedly came hard in her hand.

Suddenly there was nothing but silence—and the aftereffect of my orgasm ringing in my ears. I blinked several times as I became aware of my surroundings. I took stock of my body and determined that everything was present and accounted for, and much to my delight two additional hands had obviously found a home inside my jumpsuit.

"That was the first one."

Warm breath tickled my ear an instant before her tongue entered. The way she said it and the resulting chill that ran down my spine left little doubt that I wasn't finished. The only response I was capable of came from between my legs, and her hand was filled with the juices of my expectation.

"That's right. I'm not finished with you yet," she murmured into my ear as her fingers started moving again. Her tongue quickly mimicked their cadence, darting in and out of my ear in slow rhythmic pulses. I clenched my legs to savor the feeling, and her chuckle joined the wet sounds of her tongue.

"You are so wet," she purred like a satisfied lion. "Your pussy is warm and soft in all the right places." Her fingers continued their exploration, coming closer and closer to where I needed them to be. My hips arched in anticipation.

Somehow I was able to enjoy the view as I kept falling, in more ways than one. However, it did nothing to match the view that formed behind my eyelids as her hands continued to move against me.

"Do you like the feel of my fingers on your pussy? Do you like it when I stroke you like this? Do you like it when I make little circles like this? How about when I rub you long and hard, touching you from the back all the way to the front? Or do you prefer light little flicks?" Her voice was husky and clear and her questions rhetorical as she described what her magic fingers were doing to me.

She had explored almost every millimeter of my pussy, and my clit was crying out to not be left out of the attention. I timed her teasing strokes, and at just the right instant my hand closed over hers and two sets of fingers pressed my throbbing clit. Like a dancer, she followed my practiced motions, and only a few seconds later the world exploded behind my eyes once again.

"That's it, baby. Show me what you need. Show me with my fingers on your pussy what you like. There is nothing more hot than a woman who knows what she wants and isn't afraid to get it." Her words surprised me. Not that she said them, but that they were true. I was touching myself in ways I only did in the privacy of my bedroom. My inhibitions fell out of the sky with us, and I was overcome with a feeling of freedom I had never experienced before.

My hand continued to guide hers, and the more she talked the bolder I got. "Oh, man, that feels good. That's it. Show me. Show me how you like it." I did as I was told—she was the instructor, after all. "Your clit is getting hard again. I feel your pulse beating on my fingertip. God, that feels good."

Even though *her* fingers were on *my* pussy, I instinctively knew that she was getting as hot as I was. I felt pressure against my ass and quickly realized that her other hand had left my breast and moved to her crotch. The thought of her mimicking my motions was all I needed for number three.

Explosions rocketed through my body as each second passed. I recovered quickly, wanting to have a little piece of the sky myself. My hand still clenched the rip cord and I let go, my fingers tingling to touch something more enjoyable. I reached behind me with both hands and quickly found a zipper. I slid it up, and in an instant my hand was inside. She wore men's boxers and my fingers slid easily inside and met hot, smooth flesh. Her body jerked at the contact, and I knew I had found my mark.

She changed the stroking on my pussy in such a way that I knew what she was doing was what she wanted done to her. Ever the astute student, I did exactly as my teacher showed me and was rewarded with a gush of warm Jamaican juice. My hand was at an awkward angle, but I was not going to let a little pain stop me from having what I wanted. Her hips ground against me as the pressure of our fingers increased. She slid one finger into me, and I quickly followed with two of my own. In and out we went, slowly at first, teasing each other as if to say *I can last longer than you.* We both lied.

Unintelligible words filled my ear as hot wetness overflowed into my hand. Amazingly, the pulses of our orgasms matched beat for beat as we floated back and forth across the sky. I wasn't sure if I had numbers four, five, and six or the biggest single orgasm of my life. It started in my toes and didn't stop until it blew out my mouth in a scream. I was still convulsing when insistent words pierced my muddled brain.

"We're getting close," she said as she pointed to the rapidly approaching landing zone. "As much as I'd like to do that again, we need to pull it together before everybody on the ground knows *exactly* what we've been doing."

I had certainly lost all sense of propriety in the last seven minutes but was still enough of a prude not to want my fellow students to see my current state of disarray. It was bad enough that anyone with any sense would be able to see that I had that *just fucked* look all over my face. I laughed. There was something different yet closely related that I wanted all over my face, and I shuddered when I thought about it. The wetness on my fingers reminded me that I was in possession of a substitute, albeit a poor one.

My hand cramped as I slowly withdrew it from the warm place I knew I'd never visit again. It was almost a sad parting, and I quickly brought my fingers up to my nose and inhaled the deep musky fragrance of the woman still firmly secured to my back. As I was memorizing her scent, she removed her hand and reluctantly moved our zippers back to their pre-fuck locations.

This time when she spoke, it was quick and all business as she gave me instructions on our landing.

Forty-five seconds later I was back on the ground, struggling to remain upright as the wind pulled our downed chute in the opposite direction. She released our tether and I was once again alone. With a parting glance filled with passion, lust, and just a little bit of cocky accomplishment, she gathered up our chute. The group that had previously exhibited sheer terror was now abuzz with excitement. As I watched from a few feet away I saw that she had everyone's attention, but none had hers like I had for ten thousand feet.

With one last knowing smile I turned and walked toward the hangar, knowing that I would never again be the woman I was before I jumped out of a perfectly good airplane.

TRUCKING
CHERI CRYSTAL

Rule number one: Keep the femme happy and life is good.

No way. You just got home. Let someone else go."
Gwen was taking my news a lot worse than I expected.
Lately she seemed edgy, going off at the slightest provocation. But
even when she was angry, I couldn't resist Gwen in her skimpy black
waitress uniform pulled tight across her well-formed breasts. The little
white apron hugged her narrow waist and the short skirt showed off her
impossibly long legs. It took all my strength not to take her right then
and there, but I knew from experience when to back off.

"It's good money, babe. Just a week more and I promise I'll be
home longer."

I was working like a dog and I was hardly ever home, but I was a
woman on a mission. I had to get through the means to make it to the
end.

"Tomorrow's our anniversary." Gwen's pout had the power to
bring me to my knees even though I'd known her for most of my life.

I pulled her full hips close and licked the cherry gloss right off
her sensuous lips. "Hmm. You taste so good." Her body relaxed in my
arms.

"Stay, then. Please, baby."

I loved when she begged, but I had almost enough money saved
for a surprise trip to Australia and New Zealand. We were in dire need
of a second honeymoon and I was going all out, taking a month off and
sparing no expense. I hoped it'd put the light back in Gwen's eyes.

"I'd love to, but you know I gotta work." I deepened my kiss and
started unbuttoning the top of her uniform. I sighed at the first glimpse

of sheer black lace barely covering her porcelain skin. Her nipples hardened as I brushed her bra with the backs of my fingers.

"I can't now. I have to leave for my shift." Gwen took a step back.

"A few minutes," I moaned and eased her bra up over her breasts. She held me off with her hands, then pushed me away. It was my turn to pout.

"Can't. You're not the only one with a job, you know." Gwen straightened her uniform and smoothed out the imaginary wrinkles. "The diner's a zoo now that Sylvia's gone, and Mary's out on sick leave."

"Aw shit. I'll be gone a week." I didn't start out as a trucker but the pay and benefits were better than my last job as an auto mechanic. Trucking did have its perks, though. I enjoyed the scenery, the freedom, and, at times, the solitude, but the traveling wreaked havoc on my marriage.

I fetched my jacket from the closet, pulled the printout of my route from a pocket, and handed it to her. "Here's where I'll be, give or take, depending on traffic and the size of the cargo we have to load."

"Be careful."

"I love you. Miss you, mucho."

"I know. Me too." Gwen kissed my cheek and called out, "Happy anniversary," as she turned to leave.

I watched her pull the Jeep out of the driveway, shook off the ache in my heart, and headed to the dock. Once there, I rigged my truck, helped load her up, and in less than fifteen minutes I completed the pre-trip inspection. As soon as I was on my way with nearly forty thousand pounds in my sixty-foot rig, the adrenaline rush kicked in. Religiously, I kissed my fingers and placed them on the picture of Gwen that I had plastered on the dash.

I listened to the weather report and then turned up the volume on the local station to tune out the other truckers on the CB—obviously they were just as horny as I was, and I really didn't need the reminders. It had been a while since Gwen and I did the nasty, and I was about to die from sexual frustration.

Not fifteen minutes into the trip the heavens opened up on the desolate highway. My windshield wipers were flapping, Shania Twain sang "Forever and for Always" in the background, and I thought of

Gwen because Gwen had a thing for her. Shit, I wanted Gwen in my arms. We used to go at it like rabbits most every night and even in the morning, but now I was hardly ever home. Her love was like medicine and I hated to keep skipping doses. I felt sick when I left. Every nerve in my body felt like it would shrivel up and die from lack of use. My clit ached from neglect. How could I concentrate on driving when my thoughts were on my crotch?

I thought about going down on her. The cab got very hot even with the air on. I opened the window and felt my face sizzle when raindrops blew in. It felt good, but I still wanted my girl. I'd rub my hands lightly over her breasts, tweak her nipples, and tease my way down her slightly rounded abdomen to her belly tattoo of the phoenix rising from the ashes. From there it was a quick trip down to the familiar folds that parted for my tongue as I lapped at her creamy center. A shot of electricity went straight through my pelvis at the thought of her screaming my name as she came.

I slammed my hands on the steering wheel. What would be the big deal if I bought the plane tickets and the other surprises next year? It was too late to turn around, so I tried to grin and bear it.

Twenty more miles to my first stop and it couldn't come a moment too soon. I pulled off the highway, weighed in, and took care of business at the rest stop. I reached for my cell phone to ring Gwen at the diner but then figured she might be busy with the after-movie midnight rush. It was time I took a break, so I plopped down on the bed in the back, not even bothering to get under the blanket Gwen had neatly tucked into the corners. Still horny and thinking of Gwen, I unzipped my jeans, jerked off hard, and exploded within seconds. Instead of feeling satisfied, though, I was more strung out.

I must have had a perpetual hard-on, because I found my hands in my pants when another come woke me up in a sweat. Too restless to sleep, I figured I might as well drive. I popped a piece of spearmint gum into my mouth, hopped out of the cab, and headed into my favorite roadside diner.

"Sam, what the hell you doin' back here so soon, honey?" Sylvia, my favorite waitress besides Gwen, asked. She acted surprised, but she righted the cup and saucer on the counter.

"Hi, Syl. Doing another run." She poured my coffee before I sat down. "What've you got that's good?"

"Something special—go on back and shower first. Use the one in the employee washroom. It's cleaner than the public one."

"Yeah?"

"Why not? You're a regular. The boss won't mind, and besides, he ain't here." Syl winked. She'd known me for years from when she'd worked at the diner with Gwen.

"Okay then. Wouldn't mind a private shower."

It felt great to get out of my boots and jeans and under the hot spray. I don't think I was in the shower five minutes when I heard the door open.

"Syl? Is that you?"

The next thing I knew, I wasn't alone, and some naked redhead slicked her hands all over the front of my body.

"Who are you?"

"Ginger Snap." She flicked her wet fingers and a droplet flew in my eye. I blinked and almost expected her to be gone when I opened my eyes. But she was still there.

"You can call me Gwen, though."

"No, I'm...I can't." I pushed her away and accidentally brushed her large nipples. Ginger's sizable breasts made her waist look even tinier. A thin strip of red hair peeked out from between her thighs.

"Why don't I help you wash so we can go have breakfast in your truck?" she purred while teasing me with her trimmed, brightly painted fingernails. She was doing her best, but I had to be good for my girl.

"No thanks. I already ate," I lied.

Ginger Snap went for my tits and I pushed her away harder than I intended.

"You like it rough?" She licked her lips and threw her head back, exposing her neck. "Gwen told me you were an animal."

"What?"

"Gwen sent me to surprise you."

Shock and arousal threatened to land me on the floor. "How do I know you're telling the truth?"

"She said that I should call you Beaufort and tell you that your Lucretia Belle loves you mucho. Now, do you want your anniversary present or what?"

I was so confused that this time when Ginger pulled me closer, I was too slow to fight her off. She went to work soaping me up between my legs, and Jesus, I was so horny and Gwen—*Ginger* separated my folds with her fingers and rinsed off the soap with the handheld nozzle.

I couldn't help myself, my clit was thumping. "Don't stop…"

She bit my nipple and I sucked in my breath. Her fingers were soon swallowed up deep inside, with only her thumb left to fondle my clit. Ginger's fingers fucked me, but I imagined it was Gwen taking me all the way. Goose bumps traveled the length of my body, starting with my puckered nipples, and I came like a bandit.

"Oh, God. What did I just do?" The guilt hit me and I leapt out of the shower.

"You came."

"Yeah, and now I have to go. See ya." I grabbed a towel that barely covered my body.

"Let me help you get dressed."

"No! I got it."

I don't remember the last time I dressed that quickly, but I was out of there and running past Sylvia without so much as a good-bye. I felt cold, lonely, and miserable.

"My keys? Where the fuck are my keys?" I dumped the contents of my backpack onto the pavement. Grabbing the keys, I shoved my stuff back into my bag and hopped into the cab. I rested my head on the steering wheel, not ready to start the truck and certainly not thinking about my delivery schedule.

"What's the matter, Beaufort?"

I turned toward the voice and Gwen's lovely head poked through the partition.

"Happy anniversary, sweetie."

"Oh, Gwen, babe, I…"

"Didn't you like Ginger?"

"Yes. No. What are you doing here?"

"I'm here to give you the second part of your surprise. Ginger was just to get you warmed up. Was she as good as the fantasy you told me about? I wanted her to be."

"I felt like I cheated on you."

"Shh, your fantasy is about to get better." Gwen pulled me closer and bit my lower lip, drawing me to her for a mind-blowing kiss.

I couldn't imagine anything better than having her there in my cab until she revealed the rest of her body, clad in a leather bra minus the cups and a thong minus the panty. I had no idea what they called these things, but I grinned from ear to ear like a damn fool. I pulled her to me by her beautiful bare behind and ravished every bit of her skin with my lips, teeth, and tongue.

"Oh, God, you shaped your pubes in a heart for me. You're full of surprises today, aren't you?" I buried my nose in her crotch and laughed.

"There's more."

Just then, Ginger poked her head out from the back, sporting a matching leather outfit and a big thick dick. Ginger snapped her fingers and I did a double take when a third girl, a Shania Twain clone, appeared in a sheer teddy and high heels.

"You always said you wanted a blonde, a redhead, and a brunette all at the same time," Gwen said. "I was going to dye my hair all three shades, but thought you'd get more of a kick out of this."

I had three incredibly sexy femmes with nothing else to do but please me. Was this for real?

I had a second's worry about messing up the sleeper when Ginger poured caramel syrup onto Gwen's breasts, butt, and inner thighs while the brunette lathered me up in dark chocolate—Gwen's favorite—but this was too appetizing to pass up. I loved caramel and went right for my favorite breasts. After all, I'd make sure nothing dripped anywhere except my mouth.

"Ooh, yeah," Gwen moaned as I licked the syrup right off her breasts. She took a taste of my chocolate and lost herself licking me clean. I loved it.

Ginger spooned me and nibbled on the back of my neck. I dipped my fingers into Gwen's pussy, mixed her juices with some caramel, and tasted it before sharing some with her. While she licked my fingers, Ginger and the brunette untangled themselves from us and started making out like they had done that dance before. Gwen nestled her naked ass neatly in my lap as we watched Ginger fuck her friend. Each time the dildo pounded the brunette's pussy, it may as well have been mine. I played with Gwen's clit and she pulled at my hair and dragged my mouth to the space between her neck and shoulder. I gave her a hickey for old times' sake, as if we were teenagers back in school behind the bleachers at the homecoming game, the very first time we kissed. Thirty blissful years went before my eyes in a flash.

"I love you," I whispered, teasing her opening.

"Me too. Oh, in, go in, Sam."

I slid my fingers in and she squeezed around my hand. I shifted Gwen onto her back so I could fuck her properly while next to her, the brunette's breasts bounced wildly and her tight stomach muscles rippled every time Ginger drove in the dick. I dove between Gwen's thighs and found the spot I longed to eat. When I sucked on Gwen's clit, she screamed. I bit gently and she scratched my back. Then I licked all around it, and she nearly punched me. The brunette carried on like she was about to come and Ginger panted and fucked her harder.

"Ohgodohgod, stop teasing, ooh." Gwen screamed some more and the brunette joined in. I tongued Gwen's clit the way I knew would make her come—long, hard, and fierce. I wanted it to be as perfect as her present was for me.

"Oh, Sam, baby, oooh, yeah." Gwen shuddered and bucked under my face, but I didn't quit until I was sure I got every last drop.

Looking bleary-eyed like she'd just got off too, Ginger pulled out of the brunette, who was sprawled out totally wasted. I motioned for Ginger to take Gwen while I watched, but to my surprise, she put the harness on me. Then she quickly slapped on a fresh condom and slicked it with lube. I wasted no time thrusting into my very best girl in the whole wide world.

I fucked Gwen for everything she was to me and then fucked her some more. The base of the cock dug into my clit and took me for a ride too. With my baby beneath me, I claimed what was mine and forgot we had an audience, my ultimate fantasy, or so I once thought. Finally, I exploded all over Gwen and collapsed on top of her, every muscle in my body exhausted. We never even noticed how or when Ginger and her friend let themselves out. Turned out Gwen was the only fantasy I ever needed, and I knew that it was the same for her.

"Do you really have to be away so much? I want us to be like this for always," Gwen said, nuzzling my neck with her teeth.

"I was trying to save enough to get us that trip to Australia you always talk about."

"Oh, Sam, I don't need a trip. All I need is you for another twenty-five years or more."

"You got me. Always and forever." I sealed the deal with a kiss. It was the happiest anniversary ever, and lucky me, there were a lot more to come.

PENDULUM
GABRIELLE GOLDSBY

The pendulum is bound to swing in my direction at some point, right? I mean, how many times can a person get screwed over in one year?"

"I think your record is three, but it's only September. You still have time to break it."

"Thanks for keeping count, Ciara."

"Welcome," she said as she tossed the last of four suitcases into her trunk and slammed it closed.

"You enjoyed that, didn't you?"

"Yup, I did. See, that's your problem."

"I have a problem?"

"Yeah, you make it fun for people to be mean to you, Leigh."

"Well, why do I have to be the brunt of every joke?"

Instead of answering, Ciara unlocked the passenger door of her car and left it open.

"Seriously, if you know I wish you'd tell me." I relinquished my perch on the fire hydrant and looked back at the house that, until forty minutes earlier, I had shared with my girlfriend. *My now ex-girlfriend.*

"Hey, don't look," I whispered. "I think she's peeking through the curtain. Act like we're having fun."

In typical Ciara fashion, she ignored my instruction not to look and squinted at the darkened house. "Nope," she said as she walked around the car, "that's just the heater kicking on and making the curtains billow."

"Oh." I slid into the car and slammed the door shut. "You think she'll give Yoshi back when I get a place?" I asked once Ciara was sitting next to me.

Ciara snickered, shut her door, and fastened her seat belt. "I think you just lost your cat."

"But he's mine. She didn't even like cats until she met Yoshi."

Ciara shook her head. "Then why didn't you bring him with you? Buckle your seat belt."

I found it tucked into a crevice of the seat and fastened it with a flourish. Ciara wouldn't start the car until she'd heard my seat belt click into place. She was kind of quirky that way. "It's cold out there, I didn't want him…"

"You didn't want your cat to be cold, but you let her put you out on the corner at ten o'clock at night?"

"She didn't put me out. I left."

"Why didn't you wait inside?"

Ciara pulled away from the house and the only regret I felt was the fact that I was leaving Yoshi behind. "She made it clear she didn't want me there."

"Did she at least tell you why?"

I shrugged. "I didn't ask her because I don't care." Her silence prompted me to tell the truth. "She said I was boring."

"She told you that? To your face?"

"No, she sent an e-mail to my mother and asked her to tell me. Of course she told me to my face."

"Let's take stock, shall we? Your girlfriend just dumped you because she said you weren't exciting enough."

"Boring. She used the word *boring*."

"Did you at least deny it?"

I wanted to deny it, but how could I? The truth is I *am* pretty boring. My idea of fun is the day Ciara and I ditched work and drove to the beach. We ended up huddled together on an isolated sand dune, miles from our car. We talked for hours about everything and nothing. Fun was the time she caught chicken pox at the ripe old age of eighteen and I climbed into bed with her and read *Little Women* out loud until my voice gave out on me. And then there were the Sundays Ciara and I wasted sitting in a mom-and-pop coffee shop, arguing politics and current events. *Boring* was the wrong word. I was pathetic. What else would you call being in love with your best friend?

"When are you going to start standing up for yourself, Leigh? You can't keep letting women walk all over you."

"I don't think she's walking all over me. We aren't compatible—"

"So that's it? You just move out? Leave most of your stuff, your cat—you loved that cat."

"He liked her better anyway." My shoulder bumped into the passenger side window when Ciara jerked the steering wheel and pulled the car over to the side of the road. "What's wrong? Why are we stopping?"

Ciara hadn't looked this grave since the day I told her that I was moving in with the eventual cat stealer.

"We're stopping because you're starting to get on my nerves."

"I'm sorry." I unbuckled my seat belt and reached for the door handle. I'd spent the first few years of our friendship fearing that she would say those exact words. Even with all that pre-worry, the pain still took me by surprise.

"Damn it, Leigh, stop being such a wuss and grow some tits, for God's sake." She grabbed the back of my hood and wrenched me back into the car so forcefully that the door slammed shut.

"What?" I froze as she kissed me hard, pushing my lips back against my teeth. I started to relax moments before she broke the kiss. When I realized that she was unzipping my jacket, I grabbed her hand to stop her. "Ciara, wait. I don't think we should."

"Why not?" Her question came out in a rush of warm, sweet-smelling breath against my cheek.

"I think you're doing this out of pity."

She released me and sucked air between her teeth. "Jesus...no wonder she put you out."

Ciara pulled the car back onto the road. And an odd heat settled in my chest. After all these years, what would posses her to kiss me like that? I was minding my own business, sitting on my fire hydrant. I had called her to tell her I was going to a hotel. Who asked her to come pick me up? It wasn't like I didn't have a good job and plenty of money and...

"Who the hell needs you anyway?" I hadn't intended on yelling, but I was close to tears. I wasn't just boring. I was frustrated, scared, and stupid too.

The car veered toward the curb and I fumbled with my seat belt and the door handle. She snagged the back of my hood again and when I turned around to tell her to quit, she grabbed my jacket and jerked me into another long, hard kiss.

If I wasn't so fucking boring, I wouldn't have just allowed myself to be kissed. I would have stuck my tongue into her mouth, grabbed her breast or something sexy like that; but instead, a sob threatened. When she released me, I tugged and pulled my jacket until it was in some semblance of order. I was both confused and aroused and I was still too fucking boring to do anything about any of it. I put my fingers to my sensitive lips and asked, "Why do you keep doing that?"

"Because I think something's wrong with you."

"Oh that's just great; something's wrong with me, so you—"

"Because I want you to stop…when are you going to get it?"

"Get what?"

"Oh my G—you need to stop dating these women that treat you wrong. There are people out there who…like you for you."

I don't ever remember having a hard time meeting her eyes. Even after I realized that my crush was turning into something more painful, I could still meet her gaze. Tonight was different. Tonight I couldn't look at her without feeling as if my chest was going to explode. The grinding of gears warned me to refasten my seat belt seconds before we gunned away from the curb.

"You are the most interesting person I know. You're also smart and warm and too sweet for your own good. You don't deserve to be treated like crap." She spoke with such vehemence that I blushed.

"Darn right I don't. Just once I'd like to be the one to dish it out. I'm tired of people fucking me over. I'd like to be the one to do the fucking for once."

"No, you wouldn't."

I stole a quick glance at her profile to see if her face looked as tense as her laugh. "Yeah, I would."

"You wouldn't know what to do with it if you could."

"Yes, I would." I didn't say it with any real conviction, because I was still trying to get a handle on the fact that Ciara had just kissed me. Twice.

"All right, fine."

"Fine what?"

"I'm going to give you that opportunity. The pendulum just swung in your favor, my friend. Let's see what you do with it." The last time Ciara had this look on her face we had been caught dumping soap suds and food coloring in the water fountain at school.

"Where are we going?"

"My place."

"Good, I'm tired." I leaned back against the headrest and closed my eyes.

"No sleep for you tonight," she said.

I opened my eyes wide. I wanted to ask what that was supposed to mean, but I didn't. I never did. I had known her since high school, but we were so different, I still didn't understand how we became so close. Remember that boring thing?

You probably already guessed this, but she was the popular one. You've heard the stories about the girl who screwed around with the captain of the football team's girlfriend and even got her to dump him a few days later? Well, Ciara was that girl.

I was the one with the glasses, the cheap haircut, and the pass to skip English Lit because I had already read the books over the summer. I didn't mind being unnoticed, but I had expected things to change when I left high school. And they did, to a certain degree. I got to go to all the good parties because I was Ciara's roommate. I got to walk around campus with the hottest lesbians because I was Ciara's best friend. I even got to see most of them naked because, well, Ciara was not shy. Why she continued to let me, the boring one, hang around was beyond me. I'm sure her girlfriends wondered the same thing.

She pulled the car into her driveway and got out. "Leave the bags, we'll get them tomorrow." She was already at the front door inserting her key in the lock when I stepped out of her car.

"Maybe you should take me to a hotel." I was trembling, and it had nothing to do with the cold.

"Don't be silly." She disappeared into her house and I was forced to make a decision. I could call a cab to take me to a hotel, where I would spend the rest of the night wondering what might have been, or I could follow her and hope for a repeat of the kisses we had shared in the car.

I closed and locked her front door and stood shivering with my arms crossed in front of my chest. I had been here at least thirty other times. I'd had my own key since the day Ciara moved in, but tonight was different. The off-center feeling that began when she kissed me hadn't left. It didn't help that the house was dark save for a small hint of light coming from the direction of her bedroom.

"Why would you want to go to a hotel when you could stay here with me?" she called from her bedroom. If the kisses hadn't happened, I would have followed the sound of her voice, plopped down on her bed, maybe snooped through a drawer or two in her nightstand to keep myself entertained until she finished whatever it was she was doing.

"Because you're scaring me." I raised my voice so that she could hear me.

"Come in here so we don't have to keep yelling to each other."

Before I realized it, my feet were responding to her request. She hadn't turned on the bedroom light, but a soft triangle of yellow spilled from her closet; her shadow flitted across the carpet like an apparition. "You need to stop being so scared of everything. Would I ever do anything to hurt you?"

"No, of course not," I said.

"Do you trust me?"

"Implicitly."

"Good, I trust you too. Here."

Something dark came flying from the closet. Instinctively, I put my hands out to protect myself; my fingers closed around a thin strap of leather just before something firm smacked me across the face. At first I thought she was tossing me a belt, but the weight of it told me I was holding more than a strip of leather. The light from the closet struck the tip of a six-inch black dildo hanging from a leather strap.

"Have you ever worn one of those, Leigh?"

"You know I haven't." I swallowed hard.

"I didn't know. You never talk about your sex life," she said as she walked out of the closet.

"One of us has to have secrets. You took your clothes off."

"You should do the same."

Her laugh was unconvincing. *She's nervous.* I shook my head and dropped my eyes to the floor. The dildo still dangling from my hand cast a shadow across the floor that advanced on, and then retreated from, her bare feet.

"Why are you doing this?" My question was directed to the shadow because I was afraid that if I looked at her, I would find her fully clothed and dialing the number to the nearest mental health facility.

"Because you said you wanted to know what it felt like to fuck someone."

"That's not what I meant."

"You mean you don't want to fuck me?" The sound of her voice sent a shiver down my spine so violent that the dildo began to sway again.

"No, that's not what I mean either. Are you doing this to teach me a lesson?"

"Come here." I obeyed because I wanted it too much not to.

Instead of yanking me toward her and kissing me hard as she had in the car, her lips were gentle. I didn't protest when she pushed my jacket off. I jumped, but nodded to her quiet "okay?" after her fingers grazed my ribs as she pushed my shirt over my head. I kicked off my shoes and socks and she helped me out of my pants. I had been nude in front of her before, hadn't I? We lived together as roommates for four years, surely we—

"Leigh?" She expected me to look at her now. *Don't fuck it up, Leigh. You've been waiting too long. If you wake up tomorrow and it's just a dream, you'll have a wonderful dream to remember. Look at her.* I started at her feet and worked my way up long legs, hips, and flat stomach. Her smile was tremulous. "Not boring. Beautiful."

She took the strap-on from my hand and held it for me. I didn't hesitate this time. She tightened it at my sides. "How do you feel?"

"Scared. Sorry."

"What are you afraid of?"

"That we'll do something to mess up our friendship."

"Even with this thing on and me standing here naked, you're worried about damaging our friendship?"

"Yes." I hated myself; I really did. But I'd hate myself even more if I lost her just so I could have sex with her for one night.

She nodded. "Now you know why I'm doing this." Her lips met mine again—soft, sweet. Several minutes passed before she pulled away. She sounded as out of breath as I felt when she spoke. "I promise nothing we do tonight will affect our friendship. Tomorrow we can act like it never happened, but tonight I need something from you. Will you do it?"

"I'll try," I said, my stomach turning into a warm, churning mash of nerves.

"I want you to fuck me like I'm a complete stranger."

"I can't." I was trying hard to keep a whine out of my voice. I mistook the warmth of her hand on my chest for excitement.

"Are you sure?" she asked as she pressed me back onto the bed and straddled my hips. She hesitated briefly, as if waiting for an answer, and then she lowered herself onto the shaft. My hands went to her hips to steady both of us. I was too afraid to move, too afraid to hurt her, but I wanted to push inside her with it. I lay still and she rocked her hips forward. She arched her back and leaned back, her hard nipples calling to me, and I released her hips and covered both of them with my hands. Pinching them between my fingers, I swallowed as I imagined taking them in my mouth. She lost her rhythm and I urged her on. Each time she lifted I caught a quick glimpse of glistening silicone before it disappeared inside her; I imagined it stretching her, filling her just the right amount before leaving her. Her clitoris was swollen and proud, pushing its way from between her lips. I latched on to some courage and ran my thumb along it, lifting it and gathering her moisture until my thumb glistened more than the toy disappearing into her body.

"Oh," she whispered, and if the sound of her voice didn't inflame me, the sound of her wet pussy stroking the dildo did.

I guided her movements with one hand on her hip. All of my fear had long since gone. Her hair was draped forward and—almost as if she sensed what I wanted her to do—she leaned back so that I could see the passion on her face. I felt another sharp pang of arousal followed by the irrational fear that she would realize that she didn't want me like I wanted her. With all the strength I could muster, I pushed her over onto her back.

She moaned a protest when the dildo slipped from her body. I shushed her, even though I reveled in the pure sexuality of the sound. She writhed beneath me for that instant it took me to poise myself at her entrance, just for the moment it took me to make sure I was still wet enough, to make sure she was still wide. I plunged into her. She yelled my name. A shot of adrenaline exploded through my body.

"Oh God, Leigh, please." Her legs encircled my waist and her hands clutched and kneaded my ass cheeks. I gritted my teeth to sustain control. I felt powerful, aroused, desired—and not the least bit boring.

"Harder, baby," she moaned and I gave her what she wanted. I was holding on to her hips, pounding into her so hard that the entire bed was slamming into the wall, and still she begged for more.

The sounds of us coming together caused heat to travel over my face and down my neck.

"I've been waiting so long," she moaned, and a hot flood of pleasure centered my soul and focused my hips. I felt it when my thrusts found the right spot and I almost screamed with triumph and wept because her legs went limp even though I knew she hadn't come yet. She called my name and I lifted my head to see the look of shocked surprise. I forced myself to slow my movements. She inhaled as I eased all but the tip out of her. I was supporting her legs now, and her eyes were fluttering shut. "Open them," I demanded, and she did. I felt powerful, complete, as I thrust into her again. She was trembling and I knew I had one, maybe two more thrusts before I lost her. "Every time"—I faltered when she bit her bottom lip —"every time I had to listen to them not giving you what you needed. I knew I could do better." I thrust until I could get no deeper and I saw her eyes glaze over. "Look at me."

She did, by God she did. "Every time I heard you telling them not to stop, I wished that it was me...do you know how hard that was?" Another deep thrust. She was still hanging on. *One, maybe two more.* "In my mind I've made love to you so many times, in so many ways, I knew what you needed. I've always known."

A new sound came from the back of her throat, a sound so low and feral that the one other time I had overheard it, my dreams had been haunted for weeks. I gave up my last tether on control and pounded into her. Her moan turned into a long, keening sob of pleasure. Her toes pinched the tender skin on the backs of my knees and her fingernails bit into the sensitive flesh of my ass.

I was on my knees lifting her with each thrust, and still she pulled me closer.

"I can't," she murmured and I stopped. Despite not having any breath left, I covered her lips with mine to stop them from telling me to get off. I wasn't ready for it to end. Who was I kidding? I'd never be ready. She was still holding me close, so I lifted my head and looked at her. Her eyes were shining with tears.

"Oh, Ciara, I'm so sorry." I kissed her twice, desperate to stop the tears before they fell.

She slapped me on the ass and glared at me. "Don't you apologize! You just fucked the hell out of me...never apologize for that."

"Sorry—I mean," I reached back and rubbed my ass, frowning at her, "so it was all right?"

She shrugged, a light sheen of sweat glistening on her upper lip. "It was better than all right," she said and I flushed with pride.

"So, what now? We act like this never happened?"

She stiffened. "If that's what you want."

"You know it isn't."

"Well, what do you want?"

"I want to do that again, and this time I want you to last a lot longer. I want you to make love to me real sweet until I come myself into exhaustion, and then I want you to wake up and make me breakfast like you did for those sluts you used to have in our apartment all the time."

"And then what?" she asked as she laced her fingers with mine. Our eyes locked. She was scared too; I could see it.

"And then I want to tell you how I've been in love with you since high school."

"You want a lot," she said, but she was smiling and her voice had a delicate tremor to it that I had never heard before.

"Yes, I do," I said with a cocky smile. "Let's start with the first want. We can work our way through the rest."

A Tangoed Web
MJ Williamz

The morning sun shone brightly through the worn curtains of the dingy motel room. Not quite awake, I squinted against the painful rays and tried to remember where I was. My head was lying on a fishnet-clad thigh, the scent of sex heavy in the air. The source of that scent wasn't much of a mystery, as there was a glistening wet pussy mere inches from my face. Whose pussy? Oh, yeah. Rizata's.

The previous night came back to me as I ran my hand over the crisscross pattern of the stocking. It had been my first night as a chaperone for a troupe of traveling tango dancers. The troupe had just lost a dancer who'd gotten pregnant by her dance partner, and we were on the road holding tryouts for a replacement for her. My main objective was to be sure there was no further hanky-panky between the male and female dancers.

No need to worry about that, I thought as I rolled off Rizata's thigh, spread her legs wider, and licked deep inside her. I felt her stir when my tongue stroked the length of her, teasing her, coaxing her clit out of hiding. She pressed her hand to the back of my head, urging me on.

I sucked on her, feeling her grow between my lips while I filled her pussy with three fingers, sliding them easily into her. The thick sound of her moving on my fingers fed my desire. I wanted to take her back over the edge. She was so very wet; her come flowed down my wrist.

Her movement stopped abruptly. Rizata tensed, hips arched and hands holding my face hard against her clit, before she let out a long, guttural moan and relaxed into her orgasm. I licked her spilled juices while my fingers continued to move in and out of her.

"Ladies! Ladies! Are you up?" I recognized Paolo's voice over the pounding on our door. "Come on. We're moving out in half an hour. Let's go!"

"*Cállate!*" Rizata yelled, bringing a smile to my face. I wouldn't have minded continuing what we were doing, but I knew we had to hit the road. There were more *estancias* to visit, more dancers who wanted to show us that they could dance the tango well enough to join our troupe.

I sat up. "Okay, Riza. You heard him. Let's go. You get the shower first."

"You could join me," she purred, running her fingers through my short, dark hair.

"I could," I told her. "But we'd never be out of here on time. Now go."

I spanked her high, firm ass and she disappeared into the bathroom. I lay there on the bed, listening to the shower running, fantasizing that I was a drop of water covering every one of her sixty-seven inches, from the top of her cinnamon-colored head to the tips of her perfectly pedicured toes. I imagined that drop of water flowing down her high cheekbones, her neck, traveling over one naturally large breast, teetering briefly on a tawny nipple before continuing down her taut stomach. Oh, to be the water slithering past her shaved mons and trickling through her lips, down her thigh and calf and finally to her foot.

What a lucky drop of water, I thought as I slid my hand between my legs. Fuck, I was wet. Not surprising after eating Riza for breakfast. I slipped my fingers inside, moving them in and out while I imagined it was Rizata fucking me. When I had myself teetering on the edge, I traced my shaft with my slick fingers before pressing them hard into my clit, gasping as the familiar bright light exploded behind my eyes and heat radiated over my entire body.

❖

I worked with the rest of the road crew setting up our equipment on the makeshift stage in the barn on an *estancia* in the Andes foothills. In the pampas, there were miles between the *estancias*, but word traveled fast that a tango troupe from Buenos Aires was looking for a new dancer.

The previous day's auditions had been hideous. The girls were either too short, too out of shape, or simply couldn't dance. None of us had much hope for that day being any better. Hope or not, the speakers had to be set just right, the cords all out of the way. The last thing we wanted was a heel catching, sending its owner sprawling.

By midmorning the orchestra was set up and the six musicians were warmed up and ready to torture some poor country girl. The director, Miguel Jovenes, took his seat in front, with artistic advisers and choreographers on either side of him. I settled into a chair and waited.

"Madeira?" Miguel called. "Is Madeira here? She's next." He looked around, then at his choreographers, who shrugged. "*Dios mío.* A no show. *Mierda,*" he spat as he sat down.

The silence was broken by the telltale click of stilettos on the plywood stage. Sure and unhurried, the most stunning woman I'd ever seen made her way front and center.

"You're looking for me." It was more a statement than a question.

Leaning forward, I rested my elbows on my knees. Damn, she was fine. She wore six-inch stilettos—bright red—a perfect complement to her black dress with its red piping. Her full lips, slightly parted, were painted blood red. I felt my own blood start to boil.

"Nice of you to show," Miguel attempted to insult her.

"I know," she replied, arching one perfectly plucked eyebrow.

The smile spread across my face before I could stop it. Her gaze landed on me. I swallowed hard, barely able to breathe. What were her eyes saying? That she wanted me? Maybe. To go to hell? Possibly. I couldn't read them at that distance.

Leaning back in my seat, I rubbed my palms on my jeans before folding my arms. I hoped I looked cool. She finally broke the spell and looked at Miguel.

"You want to see me dance." Again with the statement. She was hot and she knew it.

"Yeah." Miguel nodded. "Yeah, we wanna see you dance."

The music began and Madeira stomped her foot and raised her hand above her head, snapping her fingers, commanding the attention of an imaginary partner. She turned away from her audience, holding our gazes until the last possible minute.

Madeira's dance was the epitome of sensuous. Her feet moved quickly, kicking dramatically at all the right times. She grabbed her skirt and swished it this way and that, flashing stocking-clad thighs with each turn, each movement leaving me hoping she'd lift it higher—just a little higher. She was the mistress of the tease. When the song ended, she gracefully walked back to the front of the stage. My clit was bulging, pressing against my wet jeans. I felt like I'd just fucked this woman. That was the intent, I knew. She was that good.

I was about to take off to find Rizata to ease the ache when Miguel called to me.

"Aleja! Come here. Dance with Madeira."

"*Perdóneme?*"

"Dance. You be the man. I want to see how she does with someone leading."

My legs were shaky as I climbed the steps to the stage. Her gaze followed me the whole way. Trying to assume a cocky swagger, I crossed the stage and held out my arms. She stepped into them, standing a good inch taller than my five feet ten inches. My work boots didn't have six-inch heels.

Our eyes met and I refused to look away. Nothing was said. Nothing needed to be. The music started and I dipped her. Big mistake. The urge to bend over and suck on her exposed neck was hard to fight. Her mahogany breasts pressed against her bodice, begging to be freed. I roughly pulled her up and held her close. Then we danced, her movements fluid; she turned and dipped on cue, responding to the lightest of touches. The tango we performed was one of love lost, and every time she danced away from me, I felt a void, a chill where the warmth of her body had been.

As the song neared the finale, our eyes met and held until the very end. Both of us daring, challenging the other. Was it really just a dance? The music ended and I held her to me, her arms around my neck, her leg wrapped around mine.

"Bravo! Bravo!" Miguel and the others were standing. I had forgotten we had an audience. I stepped away, immediately missing her closeness.

Forcing myself not to look back, I walked off the stage and returned to my chair while Miguel approached the stage to hire her. I looked up only when I heard the clicking of her stilettos walking back the way she'd come. Again our eyes met, and she fixed me with a smoldering glare. She had to feel the heat. Or had I just been burned?

"Why are you looking at that *puta*?"

Where had Rizata come from?

"I saw you dance with her. You want to fuck her, don't you?"

"Easy, Riza, you got no claim on me."

"What?" She sounded indignant. I sensed a diva-sized tantrum building.

"I'm sorry," I cooed. The last thing I needed was her making a scene. If Miguel found out about us, my job would be over in a heartbeat. I tried to lay it on thick. "I just meant we hadn't talked about *us* yet. You know—what you want out of this and all."

She was still pouting but seemed placated until she whispered in my ear, "Just be sure you're in *my* bed tonight."

Miguel was looking over his shoulder at me. I was fairly certain he hadn't heard our exchange, but I didn't see any reason to stick around. I left the barn and stepped out into the blazing beacon that was the Argentine afternoon sun.

"So you enjoyed the dance?" A resonant voice flowed from behind me.

Turning, I stood face-to-face with Madeira.

"You liked what you saw." Again, statement or question?

Glancing around to make sure Rizata couldn't see us, I focused my attention on the enticing woman in front of me. My appreciative gaze started at her sexy shoes, moving leisurely up her shapely legs. I licked my lips as I took in her firm thighs, brazenly lingering where they disappeared under her dress. I longed to run my tongue up to where they met.

During the dance, I got up close and personal with her ample breasts, so I didn't give her the satisfaction of drooling over them again. Instead I looked at her face—her lips full and inviting. Her black eyes weren't. She cocked an eyebrow, and I realized she was waiting for a response.

"Yeah. I like what I see."

She looked bored. "Your boss just hired me. Told me to find you. Something about a chaperone?" She smiled wickedly at that. I didn't know if it was the idea of a chaperone or the idea of me as her chaperone that amused her.

"Yeah. It's my job to keep an eye on you ladies. Gotta make sure you're in your rooms without male companionship come bedtime."

"What? You're gonna stand guard outside our doors or something?"

It was my turn to grin wickedly. "No. I sleep in the room with you. Believe me, I'll know who's in your bed."

Her tongue slid out and caressed her upper lip provocatively. She looked like she was about to say something, but remained silent as she turned and walked away.

Holy fuck. I wanted that woman and I wasn't doing much to hide it from her. I wanted my tongue to caress her blood red lips. Whether she wanted to take me to bed or just tease the hell out of me was unclear. I watched her hips sway as she strutted away from me, imagining grabbing them and pressing her into me.

"Yo, Leja!" Paolo interrupted my fantasy. "Get over here. We need to get things loaded. Miguel says he's ready to hit the road."

One last glance at Madeira and I was happy to move equipment or do anything else to alleviate the tension that had mounted in the hour since that woman had first stepped onstage.

"Where we headin' now?"

Before Paolo could answer, Miguel's right-hand man walked up.

"Change of plans. Seems the hot new dancer is the daughter of the owners of this *estancia* in Rosario. To show their gratitude, they've invited us to stay for a fiesta. Miguel wants everyone to head around to the courtyard there."

The courtyard had been arranged with several long tables at one end, which I knew would soon be filled with enough food to feed a poor family for months. Small round tables were interspersed, and Miguel and his *compadres* sat at one with a man I assumed was Madeira's father. Rizata and Madeira occupied another with their male counterparts. Lust oozed from the very pores of every man there. The women just appeared bored with them, but the animosity was palpable.

"Come on." Paolo motioned to three empty tables where we could hang together.

"You go on. I'm gonna look around," I said before leaving the courtyard and turning left to explore behind the house. A copse of *ombús*, large evergreen trees, barely concealed an intimate circular swimming pool. I slid between the trees and stood gazing into the clear water, the lights on under the surface now that night was falling. The pool looked inviting, the coolness beckoning to me after an afternoon of laboring in the heat.

"It's tempting, isn't it?" Madeira's voice interrupted my musings.

"I assume you mean the pool?" I cocked an eyebrow.

"Where did you learn to dance like that?"

"I grew up in La Boca, the barrio where the tango got its start."

"But you danced so well—like a man."

I didn't feel that warranted a response.

"Something tells me you do other things well, like a man."

I grinned. "Most things I do better."

"Why do I get the feeling that you don't often bypass temptation?" she taunted, offering me the back of her dress. My hands itched to comply.

I looked around, fearing that someone might walk up.

"What are you doing?"

She pulled her hair to the side. "I'm going swimming. Now unzip me."

She stepped out of her dress and stockings in one movement before adeptly removing her bra. I was pleasantly surprised to note that her tan did not vary from head to toe. With the grace she'd demonstrated onstage, Madeira sauntered to the steps and, staring into my eyes, slowly descended into the pool. I didn't know if it was the water or excitement, but her dusky nipples peaked temptingly toward me.

"Are you really going to let me swim alone?"

"I don't know that me getting in there with you is such a good idea."

"I think it's a wonderful idea." She swam to my side of the pool, resting her arms on the edge, her long legs gracefully treading underwater, her rounded ass just breaking through the surface.

"You're scared of me."

"I'm not scared of anything," I lied, still concerned that one of her brothers, her father, or even Miguel might walk in on something they shouldn't.

She pushed off the side and swam away from me on her back, her breasts floating in plain view but her legs never separating enough to show me what she knew I wanted to see. My desire overrode my concern and I quickly stripped out of my jeans and black T-shirt. I stood naked before her and admired her eyes admiring my tight body. My breasts were small, but she seemed to like them.

"Are you coming in?"

"I hope to," I cracked. "Are you through staring?"

"What if I say no?"

"Then I stand here and let you stare."

"I'm more into touching than looking."

I sat on the edge, dangling my feet in the water. "So touch."

Madeira glided over to me and slid her wet arms over my thighs.

"I thought you were gonna touch."

She didn't say a word. There was no need. I lowered my mouth to hers. Her lips parted, and my tongue greedily claimed hers. I felt her hands on my hips and shivered as she pulled me closer. We groaned into each other's mouths as I slid down her, my wet cunt gliding easily over her firm breasts. I gasped when my hard clit moved over a rigid nipple.

The pool was shallow, so it was easy for us to stand pressed together as one, hands exploring, mouths open, tongues teasing each other. I finally pushed her away and walked back to the wall, where I spread my arms out and lazily kicked my legs.

"What?" she asked.

Grinning, I replied, "I like to make it last. I'd be lying if I said I didn't just about fuck you right then."

"I wouldn't have complained."

She swam easily to me and placed her feet on my shoulders, keeping her upper body afloat with a graceful motion of her arms through the water.

My gaze didn't remain on her eyes but dropped to her shaved pussy. My mouth watered as I longed to bury my tongue inside her. My hands propped up her legs as I slid her swollen lips closer to my mouth.

"What's going on here?"

Turning, I saw Rizata standing, hands on her hips, fire in her eyes.

I slid Madeira's legs off my shoulders.

Madeira looked from Rizata to me and back again. She sidled up to me, running her fingers over my hair. "She's too much for you, Rizata."

I pushed her away. "We're just messin' around, Riza. Why don't you come on in?"

Rizata continued to glare at Madeira.

"I'm serious, baby. Come on in. The water's fine."

"She wouldn't know what to do with you anyway, Leja," Madeira said. "Let her go back to the fiesta. She can find a nice man to please."

Her glare never lessening, Rizata unzipped and stepped out of her skimpy denim shorts. Her thin cotton T-shirt was next and there she stood—tanned, toned, and tempting.

Without saying a word, she walked toward us and sat, legs spread, her pussy inches from my face. Her scent beckoned to me, daring me *not* to feast. I slid her closer to me and ran my tongue the length of her, aching, needing more. My hand cupped her ass, pressing her harder into me.

"Hey!" Madeira pulled me away. "Anyone can spread her legs and let you eat her cunt." Her hand slid between my legs, spreading my lips and exploring inside me. "But not everyone knows how to please another woman."

Madeira's mouth closed over mine, her tongue immediately pressing into my mouth. I welcomed her eagerly, happy to share Rizata's flavor. I felt her fingers slide out and circle my clit, which swelled at her touch. I tried to tell myself to make her stop, to remember that Rizata was there, but the thought of her watching Madeira please me was only arousing me further.

"You think you know so much." Rizata slid in the pool and pushed Madeira's face away from mine. "You don't know what she likes." She lowered her mouth and took a rock-hard nipple between her teeth.

"Oh, shit," I groaned, relishing the feel of her light bite. The shock waves shot down and met with the ones Madeira was creating between my legs. My knees were growing weak.

"Easy, you two, there's plenty of me to go around," I managed to say, though I wasn't sure I wanted either to stop.

"I can make you come so hard, *mi* Leja," Madeira whispered.

"But you two need to enjoy this too," I said. "I don't want it to be all about me."

"After last night, I'm ready to please you again and again and again," Rizata whispered against my neck, her fingers taking over for her mouth on my nipple.

"You've had *her*," Madeira countered, pinching my clit. "You know you're ready for some new blood."

"I'm ready for anything." I tried hard to stay focused. "But I can't enjoy myself with you two fighting like this," I lied. "Tell me, Riza, are you turned on?"

"Of course, Aleja," she whispered, nibbling my earlobe.

Dios mío. I'm not going to last.

"Madeira, touch Riza. Tell me if she's wet."

"What?" they cried in unison.

"Riza, you do the same. I need to know you're both dripping with desire."

It took them a minute, but they seemed to come to a silent agreement and somewhat begrudgingly moved away from me, reaching between each other's legs. The moans that escaped them were obviously involuntary.

I backed away and watched, as aroused at the sight of the two beauties fingering each other as I'd been when they touched me.

"Tell me," I said. But it seemed I was forgotten as they pressed against each other, their full breasts flattened together as they tried to get even closer. The water churned around them as their fingers worked more quickly. Finally, their open mouths met and they kissed with a hunger I definitely shared.

Madeira pulled away first and looked at me with eyes that didn't quite focus.

"But it's you we want," she breathed.

I took them both by the hand and walked them to the steps. When we got there, I put their hands together.

"Ladies first." I sounded like a gentlebutch, but I really just wanted to enjoy the vision of those two sexy asses climbing out together. I wasn't disappointed. When they reached the top, they turned and faced me.

"Please kiss again," I said as I followed.

When they eagerly complied, my temperature shot up. I took their hands and pulled them down onto a large mat where they lay together, mouths still locked, legs wrapped around each other.

Disentangling their legs, I slid between them. I licked up one of Madeira's thighs while my fingers grazed the inside of Rizata's. Both sets of legs parted. The women groaned, hands moving over each other. I glanced up and saw Madeira's hands cupping Rizata's breasts as Rizata pinched Madeira's stiff nipples. The only neglected body parts were the nerve centers between their legs, which were swollen and wet, begging for attention. I was happy to oblige.

My tongue slid inside Madeira while my fingers spread Rizata's lips. Madeira's musky flavor and the feel of two wet pussies at once made mine nearly burst. I slid three fingers inside Rizata and fucked her while I sucked on Madeira's engorged clit. Both women writhed, their moans growing louder. Madeira pressed my head harder into her, riding my tongue as I licked the underside of her clitoris.

Rizata grabbed my hand and pushed it into her open cunt. Madeira ground into me as Rizata took my hand and pressed it against her hardness.

Their heady scents alone were enough to drive me crazy, but combined with the sounds—my sucking on Madeira, my slick fingers sliding over her, the suction of my fingers moving in and out of Rizata—I was amazed I could function.

They panted, grinding into me. I sucked harder on Madeira and pinched Riza's clit while I pressed into her and was rewarded with both of them screaming at once. Loud, piercing screams that came from deep inside as they gave themselves over to the orgasms we all had a hand in.

I hadn't planned to stop until I was sure they were finished, but the sound of footsteps approaching and voices calling out in concern forced me to change my mind. I was on my knees, Madeira and Rizata sprawled contentedly on the mats, when Miguel arrived at the pool.

Expecting the worst, I was surprised to see him smiling.

"Aleja! You dog! You keep these ladies happy and you'll be with the troupe for a very long time."

He was laughing as he disappeared through the trees.

Relieved at his response and horny after theirs, I lowered my cunt to Madeira's mouth, all in the name of job security.

TAPPED OUT
RADCLYFFE

No matter how many times I experience it, an airport crammed with lesbians always makes me high. Today was no different as I watched dozens of jostling, laughing dykes of all ages, sizes, and descriptions converge on the baggage carousels in the Albany airport. Waving to familiar faces and calling out greetings, I squeezed my way through the ocean of women lugging bulging equipment bags and six-foot-long sheaths crammed with bo sticks and jos and Kung Fu swords. The Third Annual Women's Martial Arts Tournament was underway, and my favorite weekend of the entire year was about to begin.

"Sorry," I murmured automatically as I jumped out of the way of yet another woman pushing a baggage cart piled so high it should carry a hazard sign and veered into someone next to me.

"That's quite all right, darlin'," a woman drawled in a voice sweet and thick as molasses.

I stiffened because I'd heard that voice before, only then I'd been flat on my back with her hard thigh jammed between my legs, her small, firm breasts crushed to mine, and her hot mouth skimming my ear.

I'll never forget what she whispered to me then, flouting every rule of fair play I'd ever heard of and some I probably hadn't.

"You'd better tap out, darlin', before I break your wrist."

She was right and I knew it, but I'd hesitated for just a second because I was stubborn and because a small part of me liked being pinned by the weight of her hot, hard body. She sensed my conflict and shifted her thigh, rolling it over my crotch so imperceptibly no one but I could have known. I moaned softly and she laughed against my neck. When I felt my clit swell, I was furious at her for making me feel something I wasn't supposed to want and at myself for not being able to stop. With the arm that wasn't vised between hers, I rapidly slapped the mat as hard as I could, tapping out and thereby signaling that she had bested me in the finals of the senior black belt jujitsu division.

We hadn't said a word after the finals last year, not even at the closing ceremonies when we'd stood together to receive our trophies. I'd avoided her at the party later that night, even though I'd caught her watching me more than once. She didn't look any different now than I remembered, still lean and taut, her skin the color of honey and her blond hair bleached to spun gold by the Georgia sun. Small crinkles radiated from the corners of her summer blue eyes as she smiled at me.

"Good to see you back, Cassidy," she said as we both reached for our bags.

"Hi, Robideaux," I managed, though my jaws were clenched so tightly my teeth felt cemented together. Lee Robideaux was a legend in martial arts circles, the highest ranking woman judoka in the United States. She'd earned her rank, no one questioned that, but she was flashy and arrogant and God damn it, sexy as hell.

It had taken me months to forget the rush I'd gotten from being helpless underneath her, and it didn't help that almost every time I'd masturbated, no matter who or what I started out thinking about, I always ended up coming with her hot breath in my ear and my clit exploding against her slick, tight thigh. Just thinking about it now sent a ripple through my cunt, and that pissed me off so much that I jerked my equipment bag off the conveyor belt with a snarl.

"Need a hand with that?" Robideaux whispered in the proximity of my ear.

Yes! my clit screamed. *No!* my brain shouted.

"I'm fine." And I was, other than the fact that the muscles along the length of my jaw had gone into spasm and I had an ache between my legs so huge that I was going to need a private moment very soon or suffer for the rest of the day with terminal priapism. I hated that just looking at her could make me wet and, worse, that closing my eyes and imagining her grinding her hips between my legs could make me come. I swear she was laughing as I heaved my bag onto my shoulder and stomped away.

Luck was not with me. The rooms we'd been assigned at SUNY where the tournament was being held weren't ready yet, so I couldn't even soothe my agitated body with a brisk round of solitaire.

Unfortunately, I'd never developed a knack for making myself come in a public bathroom, which was my only alternative. Besides the fact that it was frustrating to try and fail, it was embarrassing that just seeing Robideaux could get me so horny that I was almost willing to give it a shot.

Fortunately, I spied one of the tournament directors who I'd trained with years ago, before she'd moved to another state, and I flagged her down.

"Hey, Mel, are the practice rooms ready yet? I'm competing in the first round tomorrow morning, and I wanted to work out a little bit. I'm really stiff from the plane ride."

Melissa took a quick look around, then pulled a key off a ring that she wore on her belt. "We're not supposed to let anyone in down there until after registration is finished, so lock up when you're done and bring the key back to me."

"Absolutely. Can I stow my suitcase somewhere?"

"Behind the desk with the security guard," Melissa called over her shoulder as she hurried off to intercept a group of newcomers.

I remembered the layout from the last two years, so I skirted around the swarm of athletes waiting for the elevators and took the stairs down a level to the hallway that connected the dorms to the adjoining building where the practice rooms were located. The locker room was empty, and I quickly removed my sneakers and socks and stripped. I stowed my T-shirt, jeans, and underwear in a locker and pulled out an old pair of white cotton gi pants that I kept in my equipment bag to practice in. I didn't want to wrinkle my tournament gi before I competed. The pants were practically threadbare at the knees and the seams were spreading in the crotch, but they were comfortable. The white T-shirt that went with them was just as worn and practically see-through. Once dressed, I padded in rubber flip-flops toward the practice room.

As I inserted the key in the lock I heard footsteps behind me and looked over my shoulder. Robideaux approached wearing a pristine white gi, her black belt frayed on the edges from years of use.

"I thought I'd get in a little workout," Robideaux said.

"The practice rooms aren't open yet," I said.

Robideaux looked pointedly at the key in my hand. "Seems you've solved that problem."

"You're not supposed to be down here," I said inanely.

Robideaux leaned one arm against the door frame and bent close so that her eyes were inches from mine. "Are you going to report me, darlin'?"

Her breath slid along my throat, sweet and warm, just like her voice.

"I don't kiss and tell," I muttered.

She grinned. "I'll remember that."

I unlocked the door and held it wide. Robideaux edged past me, managing to brush her crotch against my thigh, and stopped at the edge of the tatami mats that took up most of the twenty by thirty foot space. We both kicked off our shoes, bowed, and stepped onto the mat. I walked away from Robideaux to the far side, knelt in *seiza*—legs folded beneath me, hands palm down on my thighs—and closed my eyes to center myself. After a few minutes of deep breathing, I stood and started my stretching exercises. Out of the corner of my eye, I saw Robideaux sitting with her legs spread almost a hundred and eighty degrees and her torso bent forward to rest on the mat, her arms extended straight out in front of her. She was flexible as well as strong, but I knew that from having grappled with her. A disturbing image of her legs scissored around my waist flashed through my mind, and a warning tingle stirred in my crotch. Abruptly, I turned my back to do a series of standing shoulder rolls from one side of the mat to the other. I lost count of how many I had done, until I came up out of a roll to a standing position and found Robideaux an inch from my face.

"Warm enough yet?" Robideaux asked.

"For what?" I asked, just a tiny bit breathless.

"To practice with me."

I shook my head and indicated my attire. I wasn't wearing my gi jacket or my black belt, and many of the holds and throws required using the uniform material for leverage. "I wouldn't want to take advantage of you."

"Not even if I wanted you to?"

I felt my face go hot and I searched hers, but saw nothing except cocky assurance in her eyes. Annoyed at my reaction, I said more sharply than I would have if she didn't always manage to get me off balance, "That's not my game."

"Then what is, darlin'," Robideaux said softly, settling her hand lightly on my hip.

"Nothing you'll ever fi—"

She slid her arm around my waist, bent her knees to lower her center of gravity at the same time as she drove her hipbone into my crotch, and launched me onto my back with an effortless hip throw. I'd been thrown thousands of times, and she knew it. I merely relaxed into the fall, tucked my chin, and slapped the mat with my arms extended to absorb the force of the impact. There was no chance that I would be hurt, but I was surprised and irritated. Fortunately, I glimpsed a blur of white coming at me and rapidly rolled to one side just as Robideaux dropped on her stomach onto the spot where I had been lying, clearly intending to pin me. She hadn't even fully landed before I catapulted onto her back, clamped my knees on her waist and dug my heels inside the curve of her hips in front, and wrapped one arm around her neck from behind. Then I let the momentum carry me onto my back so that she was stretched out on top of me, her back to my front, her butt nestled in my crotch. All I had to do then was arch my back with my legs folded around her waist and tighten my arm around her neck, gripping my own wrist with my other arm behind her head, and choke her. Which I did.

After a second, she tapped out on my arm, two quick slaps of her palm against my skin, and I let her go instantly. She rolled off and lay on her side facing me, breathing fast and grinning that infuriatingly sexy grin.

"Nice move," she said.

"What did you expect?" I shifted onto my side too, and I couldn't help but stare into her eyes. They were bluer than I remembered, the pupils wide and dark. "That I was just going to lie there and wait for you to pin me?"

She eased close, so close I could feel her lips move against mine as she whispered, "That's exactly what I was hoping."

"Well, think again." I intended to get up, I really did, but she slid her hips a little closer until our thighs touched and I was suddenly frozen to the spot. I felt her fumble between us and I looked down to see her untie her belt and pull it off. Her gi top fell open and I groaned. She wore nothing beneath it, not even a sports bra. Her breasts were as golden as the rest of her, the nipples small and tight in the centers of two perfect, tawny circles.

"How about if I even the field?" Robideaux shrugged out of her top. "Better?"

"What are you doing?" I whispered.

"I propose a rematch," Robideaux said, pushing me onto my back and straddling my waist. She knelt above me, her hands braced on my shoulders. "No holds barred. Whoever taps out first loses."

"What makes you think I want a rematch?" I said, trying to sound tough, but I couldn't take my eyes off her breasts. They swayed ever so slightly with each breath, tantalizingly close. I wanted my mouth on them. I wanted to tighten my teeth around her nipple until she moaned. Her crotch was hot against my stomach and I twisted my hips, trying to dislodge her before I lost my mind and clamped my mouth to her flesh.

"Your cunt felt so good against my leg when I beat you last year," Robideaux said softly, rocking on my belly. "I made you wet that day, didn't I?"

"Fuck you."

"Maybe." She lowered herself, still pinning my shoulders, and kissed me, her tongue teasing my lips before dancing inside my mouth. I gripped her forearms and jerked my pelvis into empty air, aching for contact. I moaned into her mouth and sucked on her tongue. She pulled back, laughing.

"I bet you still think about it, don't you? Do you come, thinking—"

"Get the fuck off me."

"Make me."

I planted my feet flat on the floor, thrust my hips, and torqued my shoulders, throwing her to the side. I was on her in a second, my legs scissoring her thighs, but she was naked from the waist up and I didn't have anything to hold on to. I tried for a front chokehold, but Robideaux twisted the back of my T-shirt in her fist, jerked it tight around my neck, and almost executed a reverse choke. I managed to twist away just in time but lost my grip on her legs. She pumped her hips and flipped me, and the next thing I knew I was on my back with her forearm across my neck and her body pinning my chest. She licked my lips, then nipped at my chin.

"Are you going to tap out?" she murmured.

I turned my head away as much as I could so she wouldn't see what the weight of her body was doing to me. I couldn't move, and if she leaned a little harder with her arm on my neck, I wouldn't be able to breathe, but my cunt was swelling and my clit was hard and all I wanted her to do was press harder, everywhere. She inched up until her breasts met mine and I groaned.

"All you have to do is tap, darlin', and I'll let you up," Robideaux whispered, one hand dropping to my waist. She pulled the ties on my pants and I felt cool air against my belly.

"No," I moaned, turning my head back and searching for her face. Her eyes were hazy and her lips parted in a half-smile far sexier even than her cocky grin.

"You make me so hot," Robideaux murmured, shifting ever so slightly until her crotch rode my thigh. She slid her hand down my pants and cupped my cunt while pressing a tiny bit harder against my neck. "Ready to give up?"

"No." I jammed my leg into her crotch and she groaned, her eyes closing and her grip on my neck relaxing. I thrust my hips to throw her off, but she stayed with me, squeezing her hand between my legs and catching my clit in her fingers. I yelled, "Oh, fuck!" and went completely still.

Robideaux trembled and jerked her crotch against my leg. "Nice...try." She shuddered and shifted her arm from my neck to cup my cheek in her palm. She was shaking so hard I knew she'd come soon.

"Tapping out?" I gasped, my clit twitching between her fingers. I could have bucked her off then, except her grip on my clit felt too good. I wanted to beg her to make me come, but it was so much better than I'd imagined all those times I'd teased myself to orgasm while thinking about her that I never wanted the reality to end.

"I can last as long as you can," Robideaux said, but she sounded about to lose it.

I shoved my shoulders up while I still had enough strength in my stomach to do it and caught her nipple in my teeth. She moaned as I sucked her, but I couldn't hold it long. I fell back and she almost followed.

"Concede?" I asked weakly. I couldn't breathe. God, I was close now.

"You wish," Robideaux grunted, milking my clit with long, firm strokes.

"Robideaux," I groaned. She was making me come and I couldn't stop her. Didn't want to stop her, didn't want the terrible wonderful pressure building in my cunt to stop, ever. I gripped her hips to keep her centered on my thigh and pushed and pulled her along my leg. The muscles in her stomach went board hard, and she threw her head back and came with a loud cry, soaking her pants and mine. She didn't let up on me but just kept pulling my clit while she writhed on top of me, still coming, and I exploded seconds after her.

I lay there panting, spent and weak, Robideaux's body pinning me to the mat, her hand still between my legs. She shivered and I felt around on the mat for her jacket and dragged it over her. Robideaux bit my neck, then nuzzled my ear. I kissed her. When she rubbed my clit in slow, firm circles, I moaned.

"You might want to tap out before you get hurt, darlin'," she murmured.

"Are you crazy?" I laughed and bumped my clit against her palm, already hard enough to come again. "Feel that?"

"Mmm, yeah."

"Does it feel like I'm ready to tap out?"

Robideaux heaved herself up on an elbow and grinned at me, her eyes soft and satisfied. "Up for another match?"

"I'm here, aren't I?"

She leaned down and kissed me. "Same rules—you tap out, you lose."

I just nodded and kissed her back, thinking that win or lose, it was going to be one hell of a tournament.

HEARTS ON WHEELS
LC JORDAN

"Come on, baby. Open up for me. I know you want to."
The words, barely a whisper, were swallowed by the darkness that pressed in close all around me. Sight was useless to me now, so I closed my eyes and concentrated as my hands moved unerringly over the smooth curves in front of me.

I felt a slight resistance and rotated my wrist, ready to use more pressure. My heart was pounding so hard I felt the pulse all through my body. It was the same rush I got every time I was so close to claiming another beauty.

Just as I was about to rock forward and put my weight into my movements, the unmistakable jingle of keys next to my ear shattered the moment. Startled, I lost my balance and dropped the slim jim. The thin metal tool sounded like a cymbal crash as it clattered against the car door, then the pavement.

Quickly reaching into my hip pocket, I pulled out a penlight and flashed it behind me. A woman shaded her eyes from the white halo. I lowered my aim a few inches, only to spotlight a pale triangle of skin and subtle swell of breasts framed by the dark vee of a pullover. Unreasonably embarrassed, I flicked the light to the side.

"What the hell are you doing?"

The words came out in a loud whisper because I hoped the owner of the car I was trying to repossess was still asleep. The woman in question obviously saw no need for stealth and replied in a soft but normal voice.

"I could ask you the same thing, but I think I already know the answer. That's your tow truck parked just down the street, isn't it?"

Before I could deny or confirm anything, she tilted her head slightly and shook the keys again. "Wouldn't it be easier with these?"

It clicked then that she must be the car's owner, or rather former owner, since the dealership was repossessing it. I'd been doing repos for a couple of years and was usually in and out before the owner knew what happened. After the first few times of getting cussed, kicked, and chased, I learned to be quick, quiet, and keep a close eye on the house. Nobody had opened that front door while I was watching.

"Where did you…" My question was cut off by her short laugh, though it sounded more derisive than amused.

"I wasn't hiding in the bushes, if that's what you mean."

She stepped forward and unlocked the car door. The dome light was just bright enough to let me see her fairly well, so I clicked off the penlight and picked up the slim jim.

"That's not what I thought," I told her, although I was beginning to wonder. "So you must be Anne Shaffer."

"I must. Couldn't sleep, so I decided to take a walk," she said simply as she held the keys out to me.

Checking my watch before opening my hand, I couldn't help voicing a question. "Do you really think that's wise at two in the morning?"

Something short of a smile but not quite a smirk lifted the corners of her mouth. I made the mistake of noticing her lips. They were full, but naturally so, and came together in a perfectly shaped bow. The color was a darker shade of pink, perhaps made more so by her light complexion. The dim glow of the car interior reflected tired but not defeated eyes. I nearly forgot why I was there in the first place.

If Anne realized I'd been staring, she made no comment. Instead, she dropped the keys into my hand. They were warm, and the tips of her fingers grazed the skin of my palm. It felt electric and I closed my fist tightly around the keys, whether to prolong the sensation or dispel it, I wasn't sure. I swallowed and spoke again, more harshly than I intended.

"You really shouldn't be out walking by yourself at this hour. It isn't safe. That's just asking for trouble."

Anne folded her arms across her chest and leaned back against the car. "Not safe, you say? Meaning I might run into all kinds of unsavory people like muggers, car thieves, that sort of thing?"

The car-thief comment stung a little. "Look, I'm sorry," I told her and immediately knew I had a problem. I never said I was sorry; you couldn't let yourself get emotionally involved in any way and do this sort of job.

"No, I apologize. That wasn't fair of me to say that. I'm just angry." Anne pushed off the car and turned away from me.

"You have a right to be angry," I told her. "I'm jackin' your car." It was a lame attempt at humor, but I was rewarded with a brief laugh from Anne. Turning around, she swiped a thumb beneath one eye and looked somewhere past my shoulder.

"You know, you live with somebody, you plan a life together, you buy a house and two cars. You pick out furniture and dishes. Then one day she tells you she loves somebody else and you're left with extra sheets and more bills than you can pay." Anne looked at me then with a mixture of defiance and a need for acceptance. "I decided the house payment was more important than the cars."

I didn't know what to say so I broke my cardinal rule again. "I'm sorry. I wish there was another—"

"Don't." Anne stopped me in mid-sentence. "You have nothing to be sorry for. Besides," she flashed a genuine smile, "I defaulted on her car too because they were financed together. So if you're coming after mine, that means someone will be repossessing hers."

I held my breath, hoping my face didn't give me away or that Anne didn't connect the dots. Just like with poker, I had no such luck.

"Wait, are you also picking up a car registered to Kim Powell?" Anne took a step toward me as she asked the question.

Shaking my head, I pocketed the nearly forgotten keys and started walking down the street to get my truck and finish the job. "I can't give out that kind of information," I called back over my shoulder.

The sound of a car door slamming was followed by rapid footsteps on the pavement. It didn't take Anne long to catch up with me.

"Look, I know this may seem crazy, but if you are towing Kim's car I want to be there."

We were almost to my truck, but that brought me up short. "Absolutely not."

Anne wrapped slender fingers around my wrist, causing me to feel that strange electric current again. "Please, I need to do this. I'm just asking that you take hers first and let me watch. Childish, I know."

I didn't immediately answer and Anne interpreted my silence as a final refusal. Her hand slipped from my arm, but I could feel her eyes on me as I crossed to the passenger side of the truck.

"Get in."

I faced Anne as I opened the door and waited. She approached slowly, as if she expected me to change my mind any second, jump in, and drive away.

"Thank you."

The words brushed against my cheek as quickly and softly as her lips did. Before that I had been wondering how I lost control of the situation. After that fleeting kiss, I decided I didn't care.

The trip across town was made with little passing traffic and even less conversation. About a block from my second repo address I cut the engine and coasted within site of the target house. The windows were all dark, just like at Anne's, but I wasn't taking any more chances. I was about to explain the rules to Anne when she turned mischievous eyes toward me.

"So what do we do first?"

"We," I stressed the word, "don't do anything. I unlock it, roll it into the street, hook it up, and drive away fast."

"But surely there's something I can do to help." Anne sounded both frustrated and excited. In turn, I didn't know if I should laugh or be worried.

"No. You do nothing but sit right here, understand?" I tried to make myself perfectly clear.

"What if I have the keys to this car too?" she baited.

"Do you?" I doubted it but couldn't resist playing along.

Anne blew out an exasperated breath. "No," she admitted. I grinned at her painfully honest answer.

"I don't need them anyway." I held up two bright new keys. "Masters from the dealership. I'll be right back."

As a repo artist, legally I couldn't open a closed gate or garage or move another vehicle to get to a target. This particular job was classically simple, though. I had the door unlocked, the car in gear, and was rolling it backward into the street in well under a minute.

Turning the steering wheel with one hand, I noticed that the car had become easier to push. When I glanced back toward the hood, my suspicion was confirmed. Anne was there shoving with both hands.

"That's enough," I whispered loudly as I eased down on the brake, stopping the car. "Wait right here," I tapped on the hood. "You are in so much trouble."

Anne grinned, not looking the least bit contrite. "I think I like it," she confessed, making me smile in return and blow my authority act.

I quickly started the truck and backed up to the car. Jumping out to set the winch, I didn't see Anne anywhere. The hydraulics lifted the front end of the car as I scanned the street, then the yard for Anne.

"Holy shit." I froze for a moment when I spotted her standing on the front steps of the house, ringing the doorbell.

A light flicked on in an upstairs window. I watched in disbelief as Anne pushed the button one more time, then sprinted down the sidewalk toward me. Another light came on downstairs, jarring me out of my stupor. I threw on the tow straps and boots, securing the car as fast as possible.

"We need to go now," Anne needlessly informed me as the front door opened, revealing a very irate woman even from a distance.

"There you go with the *we* again." I gave Anne a push into the cab and made a not-so-graceful slide into the driver's seat. Chancing a look back at the house calmed me a little when I saw the woman still on the steps and not in hot pursuit. She must have been too stunned to give chase.

Pulling away from the curb, I glanced right just in time to see Anne roll down the window and lean half her body out, waving. Reaching over the seat, I grabbed the waistband of her jeans and tugged her back inside. She landed halfway over the console and partly in my lap.

Her face was flushed, her hair windblown, and she was smiling and trying hard not to laugh or maybe cry. Something that sounded like a combination of both escaped her. Without thinking, I loosened my hold on her jeans and slid my arm around her waist, lifting her up a little.

"You okay there, trouble?" I asked as she sat perfectly still for a moment, then gave me a repentant look before dissolving into a fit of laughter. I could tell it was probably fifty percent induced by nerves and the rest a kind of catharsis. In any case, it was infectious and I joined in. It lasted exactly one block and then Anne moved back into the passenger seat and angled toward me.

"That was the most fun I've had in a long time. I can't remember when I've laughed like that," she confessed. Some of the humor left her voice as she continued, "So how angry with me are you?"

"I didn't leave you back there, did I?" Her expression was beyond priceless when the implications of that possible scenario sank in.

"It never even occurred to me…"

"Well, for the record it didn't to me either, until just now," I teased. "I'm not mad. You are definitely a hazard to my insurance policy, though."

"I may be bad for your business but I'll bet I'm good for your heart rate." As soon as the words were out, Anne looked mortified. I tried not to laugh, especially since I realized there was a fair amount of truth to that statement. We were at her house by now, so I pulled over and turned the engine off. Adopting an innocent expression, I made no comment.

"That didn't come out right," she tried to explain.

"It's all right; I know what you meant." My tone was faintly disappointed and Anne didn't miss it. She just gave me a curious stare and started to speak twice before finally getting anything out. Even then, she sounded as unsure as I felt.

"Do you want a Coke or some coffee…water…" Her voice trailed off, leaving me to imagine other options on the menu. Shaking my head, I declined.

"I really should go." It was as much a statement to myself as Anne. It just didn't sound very convincing to either of us.

Anne wouldn't face me, but her words were clear. "I really wish you wouldn't."

"Coffee," I blurted out.

I made the choice without thinking. Normally I didn't even drink coffee, but nothing about the night had been normal so far.

"Coffee it is," Anne said as she got out of the truck and headed for her house, not waiting to see if I'd follow but simply trusting that I would.

My eyes had to adjust to the lights in the living room as I entered the open door, closing it behind me. Anne was standing near a hallway, one hand on the wall and the other combing through amber hair. She started to enter what I assumed was the kitchen, then paused.

"Do you really want coffee?"

"Not really." I had to give her credit for cutting to the chase.

Anne crossed the room and stood a few feet from me. "I've already asked a lot of you tonight. I don't know why I think I have a right to ask for more. But it's been a long time since I felt like anyone wanted to be here, with me. I just…just lie to me if you have to."

She met my eyes, and there was no apology there, nothing but want and need and honesty. That took a hell of a lot of courage.

Slowly I closed the distance between us, stopping close enough that our thighs touched. Cupping her face with both hands, I feathered my thumbs over the delicate skin before I lowered my mouth to Anne's. Neither one of us moved or breathed, just concentrated on the sensation of that connection.

Pulling back, I waited until Anne opened her eyes. "No lie," I whispered, making sure she understood. "No lie," I repeated before I kissed her again, rubbing my lips against that incredible softness before giving in to the need to taste the warmth beyond. Anne curled her arms around my neck, matching every stroke of my tongue.

My fingers trailed down her neck, brushing past the outside of each breast, and settled on her ass, nearly lifting her off the floor. Every squeeze brought an answering tug from fingers wound in my hair. Sometimes it was almost to the point of pain, but it only fueled my desire. I needed more.

A hurried inventory of the room convinced me the couch was a fine idea and much closer than a bedroom. I slowly backed with Anne in tow until I felt the cushions against my legs. As I lowered my body, I raised her sweater until her bare stomach was even with my mouth as I sat.

The small dimple of her navel was too inviting, tempting me to taste it before covering it with my lips. Anne's stomach muscles fluttered away from the touch while her hips rocked forward. Small goose bumps appeared on her skin as warm breath traveled upward. Without my urging, she lifted the sweater over her head and tossed it on the floor. I held her hands when she would have unclasped her bra, preferring to do it myself. The satiny material slid down, revealing small, perfectly round breasts and deep pink nipples.

Sliding all the way against the back of the couch, I coaxed Anne to follow. Placing a knee on either side of my thighs, she braced her arms on the cushions behind me and leaned in. Both breasts were within easy reach of my tongue, teeth, and lips, and I took the invitation seriously. Whichever nipple wasn't in my mouth was between the fingers of one hand while the other had wandered down to the bare skin above her waistband. Anne was too preoccupied to notice until I dipped lower, barely touching soft curls and then pulling out.

"Oh."

It was one word, and I wasn't sure what it meant so I repeated the motion and got the same response. Using both hands now, I opened the buttons of her jeans and touched damp silk before pushing past it to wet heat. Anne's arms trembled and we both groaned as I used two fingers to trace along slick folds before pressing deeper. I closed my eyes and clenched my own legs together as I felt Anne contract tightly around my fingers.

Holding perfectly still, I waited until the warning spasms stopped, then eased slowly out and back in again. Anne's back arched in time with my movements, so I let her set the pace. Hips rolling forward, breasts swaying, and the stroking of my hand reminded me of rhythmic waves on the ocean. It was at once hypnotic and beautiful to watch.

Anne's rocking increased in speed as a thin sheen of perspiration painted the skin of her torso. I stretched my thumb out, touching her clit for the first time. Throwing her head back, Anne came down hard on my hand, forcing my fingers deeper still and grinding her center against my lap. My hand was trapped between us, but I didn't care. The combination of Anne riding out her orgasm and the resulting friction was enough to throw my own painfully neglected clit into overdrive. Surging up to increase the pressure, I hit just the right spot and came as Anne's arms finally gave way and she collapsed against me.

Several minutes passed before Anne's breathing slowed and she raised her body enough to look at me. My arms were loosely wrapped around her back, stroking the now cool skin there.

"You're awfully quiet."

"I was just thinking," I answered, but didn't give any more detail.

"About?" Anne prompted when it was obvious I wasn't going to say more.

"About taking Kim's car for a ride and hoping I get lucky."

Anne narrowed her eyes, trying to decide if I was serious or not. Without warning she jumped off my lap and grabbed her sweater. Not bothering to find her bra, she yanked the shirt on and inched toward the door. "First one there gets to drive." She already had her hand on the knob.

I didn't rush to beat her, only reached in my jeans pocket and produced the keys. "First one there with the keys gets to drive," I corrected her.

"Works for me." Anne jingled her own set of keys and raced out the door.

Jumping off the couch, I ran after her. "You are in so much trouble," I said out loud. The thing was, I meant myself, not Anne. But I kind of liked it.

GIGOLA
CLAIRE MARTIN

Jen closed the door to the stateroom suite after hanging the privacy sign on the handle. She rested her forehead against the door for a moment and took a deep breath. She didn't dread the next item on the evening's agenda, but it had already been a long day and her work was not done. Such was her life as a gigola, currently on duty as the companion to Rosalind Humphries on board a lesbian cruise of the Greek Isles.

Roz was in her fifties, the owner of a successful advertising agency, a powerful woman with a full life. Her partner of thirty years had died two years earlier and Roz had no interest in trying to replace her. She simply craved a little uncomplicated companionship and a lot of sex. They'd met in person the previous month in Roz's vintage row house in the Gold Coast neighborhood of Chicago. Roz had explained over the phone that she wanted to review with Jen exactly what she was looking for in a companion and fill her in on the details of the proposed trip. Then they would both decide whether the arrangement suited them.

Jen arrived exactly on time, dressed in a black turtleneck, black jeans, and black cowboy boots. She carried the keys to her motorcycle, a slender wallet tucked into her back pocket, and a small satchel. She was just running her hands through her windblown hair when Roz opened the door and surveyed her with a look of surprise.

"I know it's bad manners to stare, but I'm finding it hard to believe my luck. Please tell me you are Jen."

"I am. Is it rude of me to stare back?"

Roz pulled Jen through the door. "Come on in and let's be rude in private." She led the way down a short hall toward the back of the house, coming into an area where several walls had been knocked down to form a large comfortable space with the kitchen as its focal point.

Roz went straight to a bottle of wine to finish uncorking it and poured a glass of the cold white for Jen. Roz led Jen to an overstuffed couch on the other side of the room that looked out over the small backyard with a flagstone patio and flower beds.

"Jen, our mutual friend has told me a little about you and I'm sure she's told you a little about me. But I want to be very up front with you about what I'm proposing."

"Absolutely."

"The impetus for this trip is that I've been wanting to go on this lesbian cruise to the Greek Isles for a very long time. In fact, it was all booked for Dorothy and me the year she fell ill, so the trip never happened. Frankly, I don't want to go alone. I also don't want to go through the bother of trying to find a new girlfriend. I don't have an interest in a new relationship. Dorothy was it for me and we had thirty great years together. But there are times like a trip when it just feels better to me to have a companion."

"I'm sure we'd have a great time together."

"Specifically *how* great is the other part of the arrangement I want to discuss with you. Obviously you are known to provide certain... services to the women you spend time with."

Jen smiled and took a drink of wine. She always enjoyed seeing how the women handled themselves when it came time to talk about sex. Roz did not seem in the least bit embarrassed. "You're talking about a sexual arrangement," Jen said.

Roz was small but quite powerful looking, her body in great shape and her demeanor relaxed but in command. She looked at Jen for a few moments before slowly holding a hand out to touch her on the cheek. "Yes, I think quite a lot of sex is going to be an important part of our arrangement."

Jen listened to Roz's proposal, including the financial arrangements, and then put her wineglass down on the nearby table. "Let me propose something before we shake on this deal."

Roz raised an eyebrow. "And what would that be?"

Jen scooted closer to Roz, taking her wineglass and putting it down as well. "I propose that I audition for you. After all, you are hiring me to play a part in your life, aren't you? Don't you want to be sure you're hiring the right woman?" Jen leaned in and touched her lips to Roz's, hearing the slightest sound as Roz gasped.

"I'm listening," Roz said, holding herself motionless.

"So, I propose that I make love to you right now. Then you tell me whether you want to take me on this trip at the terms you've outlined."

"What a wonderful idea." Roz moved her hands up Jen's arms and across her shoulders. "Since you're auditioning for this role, let me very temporarily play director. Here's your motivation. You're about to make love with a woman who spends all her waking hours in charge, making decisions and issuing orders. What she wants is to have someone take her to bed, make the decisions, and issue the orders."

Jen smiled as she stood up, taking Roz by the hand. "I appreciate clear direction," she said, grabbing her bag with her other hand and leading Roz to the stairway. "But starting right now I don't want to hear another sound from you. Is that clear?"

❖

"What are you doing?" Roz asked. She watched as Jen attached a restraint around her wrist and then to the bedpost.

"Don't talk," Jen said. "I don't want to hear a word from you, except for the word *stop* if that's what you mean for me to do."

"But…"

"Not a word, Roz. No noise whatsoever." Jen attached the other wrist and then moved the sheets and blankets to the bottom of the bed so that Roz lay exposed, her body naked. She knelt between Roz's legs, pulling them up by the knees and spreading them wide. Roz watched her carefully, her breath coming a little quicker now. As she saw Jen's hand approach her cunt, a moan escaped her lips and Jen's hand immediately retreated.

"Now, we're going to have a problem here, Roz, if you don't do as I say. No noise. None. The second I hear a noise from you, I'll stop. Is that what you want me to do?"

Roz shook her head, her eyes a little wider. Jen's hand approached again and she began to caress the soft skin at the top of her thighs, moving in closer and circling around her opening, dipping her finger in slightly. Roz was very wet and the moisture spread easily as Jen continued to move her fingers slowly around Roz's cunt, skirting around her clit. Roz twisted her head back and forth, biting her lips, but when Jen's finger found her clit and rubbed just to the side of it, back and forth, she was helpless to stop the moan from escaping. Jen's hand immediately pulled away and she leaned over to hover over Roz.

"I guess you want me to stop."

"No! Don't stop."

"Oh, I will stop. I told you what would happen. And if you make any noise as I leave you, I'll untie you and we'll be done for the night. Now, lie still. I'll be back. Eventually."

Jen chuckled at the look on Roz's face, a combination of arousal, frustration, and fury. She checked to make sure Roz was comfortable and then walked out of the room, closing the door behind her. She went downstairs and took her time having a drink and a snack. Then she geared up and headed back into the bedroom. The fury was gone from Roz's face in favor of heightened arousal and her eyes seemed to glaze over as she watched Jen approach her, the long dildo bobbing in front of her. Jen resumed her place between Roz's legs, lubing herself up as she did so.

"Are you ready now for me to fuck you?"

Roz nodded.

"Are you going to be able to be quiet while I fuck you?" She spread Roz's legs wider, moving them so they were aiming toward her head. "Because I'm going to fuck you until I come. I won't know if you come or not, because you're not going to make any noise. And actually, I don't care if you come or not."

Roz's mouth dropped open as Jen pushed her cock in, its length gliding smoothly into her. Her expression was almost wild as she fought to be silent, moving her hips in sync with Jen's as Jen found a powerful, steady rhythm. Soon Jen was grunting, crying out, talking into Roz's ear as she held herself above her with her muscular arms. "God, it feels so good fucking you. All the way in you, can you feel? Yes, yes, God, it's pounding on my clit. So fucking good." Jen shifted slightly and really started to stroke, her head down to watch the cock slam into Roz, hearing the slight noises erupting from Roz but too far gone to pretend to want to do anything about it. In a moment Jen threw her head back and roared out, coming with a fury, narrowly avoiding collapsing her entire body weight onto Roz as she fell to her side. As soon as she could move she reached over to remove the cuffs, gently bringing Roz's arms down by her sides and then pulling her close to snuggle against her shoulder.

"You can talk now, you know," Jen said, kissing Roz on the top of the head.

"That was one humongous orgasm. You should have heard the screaming inside my head."

"Oh, good, I'm glad you came."

"I thought you didn't care." Roz looked up at Jen with a wry smile. "That's what you said, anyway."

"That was Fantasy Jen, as I like to call her. And she didn't give a shit. But that's not really me."

"Well, you nailed the audition, as it were. You're hired. That is, if you agree to take the job."

Jen squeezed Roz closer to her. "I look forward to it."

❖

"Darling, I'm drawing my bath now. Give me time for a good soak." Roz's head peeked out of the bathroom door and she looked at Jen, who was now standing in the bedroom. "Christ, you look done in. Feel free to call it a day if you want, sweetheart. I'm perfectly fine."

Jen returned her look with a smile. "Is that what you really want?"

"No. What I really want is for you to fuck me blind. But I'm not an unreasonable woman, you know. I don't want to wear you out."

Jen approached the bathroom and opened the door wider, taking the naked Rosalind into her arms. She lowered her head to kiss her neck. "Don't worry about me," Jen murmured. "There hasn't been a time yet that I haven't had plenty of energy for you."

Roz laughed and pushed Jen away. "You're sweet. Now, go rest and I'll be out soon."

Jen got out of the dinner clothes Roz had delighted in buying for her and carefully hung them in the closet. Naked, she moved to the chest of drawers and pulled out her leather harness and the two dildos that lay next to it. One was a standard-size silicone model while the other was smaller, sized more for the activity Jen suspected Roz was in the mood for.

Jen strapped herself in, fitting the smaller dildo snugly against her, turned down the lights, and lay on the bed, her cock erect, its companion and various accoutrement tucked under the pillow beneath her head. Roz did not say a word when she walked to the side of the bed, removed her robe, and climbed on top of Jen. Her petite form felt as if it weighed nothing. Jen pulled Roz down to her, kissing her slowly and deeply, feeling Roz's body begin to respond as she caressed her. She clasped her hands firmly on Roz's hips and urged her forward, stopping her when her breasts were overhead. She pulled Roz down so that the nipple of one breast dropped into her mouth. Jen licked and sucked it, closing her teeth together and holding it as her tongue flicked back and forth. She pressed her teeth more firmly together and bit, feeling Roz begin to writhe above her. She bit harder and Roz gasped.

"Jesus, I could come just from this." Roz squirmed as Jen held her firmly by the hips and by the lock of her teeth on her nipple. Just as the pressure became nearly too intense, Jen opened her mouth and soothed the nipple with the flat of her tongue. Then she moved to the other breast and started all over. Roz began to pant as the medley of sensations overtook her.

Jen pulled her forward again until Roz's cunt was over her face, but when Roz immediately lowered herself in search of Jen's mouth, Jen held her up and away.

"My tongue is going to touch you now," Jen breathed, the air hitting Roz's clitoris an inch or two away. "But it will only touch you twice."

"God, you're a sadist," Roz said.

"You wish," replied Jen, placing the tip of her tongue at the base of Roz's opening and moving slowly north until it shuddered to a stop at her clitoris.

Roz tried to grind herself on the tongue but it slipped away as Jen raised her up and repositioned her for another run. Roz swayed on her knees, keeping herself upright by grasping the headboard in front of her. She hung her head down and watched as Jen slowly made her way from cunt to clit with her talented tongue.

"I can't stand much more. Can't I order you to fuck me now?"

Jen slid out from under Roz and came up on her knees behind her in one smooth motion. She quickly lubed up her cock and grasped Roz again by the hips. "You can't order me to do anything, remember? But you can beg me to fuck you in the ass. And that's what you want. Isn't it?"

"Please," Roz said, "just do it." Roz gripped the headboard tighter and spread her knees wider. Jen lifted the cock and placed the tip right up at the opening of Roz's ass, poking ever so slightly at the entry.

"If you want this to go in, you'll beg me to do it." Jen reached a hand around and placed the flat of her middle finger on Roz's clit and pressed. Roz's hips rocked back and the cock was right there, pressing at the opening. Jen spread more lube around the head of the cock and pushed it in a little bit. Roz threw her head back and made a growling noise.

"Fuck me, please."

Jen pushed a little farther, then started slowly pulling back. "I'm sorry. I didn't hear any begging." Jen's hand returned clitside and Roz's writhing ass started to work its way onto the cock.

"Please push it in. Please fuck me. Please make my ass hurt. Please, God, just do something."

Jen grabbed Roz's cheeks and spread them wide, advancing the cock slowly, past the resistance, past the point of no return as Roz started making ferocious noises, groans, and moans and screams as Jen pushed all the way in. Just as she began to pull back to complete the stroke, Jen picked up a bullet vibe and twisted it on, placing it up against Roz's clit, eliciting more screams. She held the vibe tight against Roz as she started to stroke in and out, the pressure from the base of the cock noticeable against her own clit. But long before Jen could get close to coming, Roz cried out a final time and stopped rocking, pulling her ass away from the cock, leaving it behind to bounce on its own.

"Holy Christ," Roz murmured as she collapsed. "I'm done. Done in." She mumbled a few other unintelligible words before falling asleep, still face down on the bed.

Jen got off the bed and slipped off her harness before pulling the covers over Roz. She looked utterly content and deeply asleep, apparently able to make the transition unfettered by any of the doubts and uncertainties that plagued Jen when the night went dark and quiet. She picked up Roz's robe and wrapped it around herself, moving into the sitting room to make herself a drink, then on to the verandah to gaze out at the Mediterranean. Somewhere out there was the island of Lesbos, a stop strangely omitted from the itinerary. Jen thought about the irony of that. She also thought about the 1,200 lesbians on board the ship and wondered how many of them had just finished making love. She hoped it was most of them.

LAP TOP
RENÉE STRIDER

I stepped out of the air-conditioned yellow cab into the heat and
noise of an early afternoon in June in the middle of Chicago.
After hauling my bags and my jacket out with me from the backseat, I
paid the driver and walked up the steps into the hotel, barely noticing
my surroundings or acknowledging the doorman's greeting. I was
distracted, eager to register and get to my room as soon as possible. I
had stayed here before and already knew that I liked the place. It was
an old hotel, beautifully renovated and smaller and more intimate than
the monster hotel and convention center a couple of blocks away where
most of the actual conference was being held.

A small crowd was waiting at the elevators, some people already
wearing name tags: American Library Association Annual Conference.
I recognized one of them from a previous conference, a cute young
woman with a sprinkle of freckles on her nose and fiery red hair pulled
back into a loose chignon. I peered at her tag. Marion somebody. The
woman noticed me looking and blushed as our eyes met.

Now I remembered. Marion had made very clear her interest in
me before, but my attention had been elsewhere then. It still was. We
smiled at each other.

"Hi, Alaine."

"Hey, nice to see you again, Marion."

"Are you presenting again?"

"Tomorrow morning. At the session on integrated library systems.
We've been beta testing a new one at UW, in Seattle, so I'll report on
that. How about you?"

"Not this time. I'm just here to attend some of the sessions—like
yours."

One of the elevators pinged and, as we got on, I admired her from behind. Short skirt, round ass, long legs. But I always checked out pretty women, and my attention to Marion's attributes was mostly from habit.

"See you later, Marion." I had reached my floor first. Wrestling with my belongings, I pushed awkwardly through the other passengers.

"I hope so, Alaine. I'm two floors up." That made me look up from my bags. Marion winked at me just as the elevator doors closed. I grinned, then promptly forgot about her. I just wanted to find my room quickly. My breathing was slightly erratic, and it had nothing to do with this Marion somebody.

The room was too cold. I don't like air-conditioning unless it's absolutely necessary. I dropped my brown leather bomber and the larger of two bags on a luggage bench. The other one with my laptop I placed on the queen-size bed, then found the switch and turned the cooling unit off. Fortunately, a couple of the windows could be opened enough to let in a breeze. The air was warm and no doubt polluted, but it made me feel less claustrophobic. I could hear the dull roar of traffic; this high up it was almost soothing, just background noise. I pulled the drapes aside farther and for a moment stood looking out at downtown Chicago, at high-rises blocking out all but a bit of hazy blue sky.

The room itself was quiet, no hotel sounds or voices in the corridor. I stripped down to briefs and tank top, pulled my bra out from under the tank, and dropped it over the T-shirt and black trousers I'd draped on the back of the chair. Then I washed my hands and face in the bathroom and splashed cool water on my cropped hair. After toweling off, I combed the damp hair back with my fingers and examined myself in the mirror. I liked the way the white tank accentuated my shoulders. I rolled them to loosen up from the stiffness of travel. My face was slightly flushed—from anticipation and low-level arousal. I took a deep breath.

I retrieved my laptop from its case, pulled back the duvet, and got comfortable on the crisp white sheet, sprawling against the pillows I had plumped up against the headboard. With legs bent and bare feet flat on the bed, I placed the laptop on my abdomen and opened it, raising my knees till the monitor was at the perfect angle. It was a slim new Sony SZ, so the keyboard wasn't heavy as it rested on me. I switched it on. From the brilliant blue screen, I opened the browser, which immediately brought up the hotel site and connected wirelessly. Then I signed into my instant messaging account.

Chandra's icon wasn't highlighted but that didn't mean she wasn't online. She had probably signed in as invisible to other IM lists.

A: r u there

Waiting for Chandra to answer, I held my breath.

C: Al, finally! About time! God!
A: sorry my plane was late and then traffic

I paused, conscious of the beating of my heart.

A: are you on a chair, bed?

I like to picture the scene exactly.

C: Chair at desk. You? Are you still dressed?
A: lying on the bed in underpants and tank
C: Ooo. Just how I like you.
A: but this is about you, what are you wearing
C: Linen slacks, navy. White cotton blouse.
A: under the shirt
C: Just a bra, white.
A: fastened in front?
C: Yes.
A: unbutton the shirt and undo the bra

My breathing picked up as I waited. I could feel the quickening of the beat in my throat and chest. That's where it always began, slowly spreading through my body to my stomach, the arousal heavy there, then settling down between my legs.

C: Done.
A: pinch your nipples, are they hard

I brought a hand up from the keyboard to touch my own nipples through the thin cloth of the tank top. They were stiff and pointed, as Chandra's must be. I groaned when a current of sensation arced to my clitoris as I tugged on them with thumb and forefinger.

C: Yes! I'm so turned on. Tell me what else to do.

My fingers quickly returned to the keys.

A: hold your breasts in your hands and stroke your nipples with your thumbs

I waited. I knew exactly the sound Chandra was probably making—that sharp intake of breath. I imagined the fullness of those tan breasts in my own hands, their dark peaks. The throbbing between my legs increased.

A: are you doing it
C: Oh god

I bit my lip; Chandra wouldn't last long. I would, though. I got as much pleasure from leading Chandra to orgasm, from controlling when and how, as from my own—more—so I always staved it off. And Chandra was well aware of it, I knew. That, and letting me take charge and deciding when she could come, always excited her immensely.

A: move your hand slowly down your belly, tell me what you feel
C: mys kin, so hot and damp. from persrpr pir sweat.

My skin was, too. I smiled at the typos. And no more upper case; she had to type with one hand now.

A: undo the zipper
C: yes
A: leave your fingers outside your panties. describe them
C: white slik, below my belly button. hurry, want to come

I pictured white silk against the smooth olive skin of her abdomen, now rising and falling from her ragged breathing. My fingers stumbled over the keys. I deleted some nonsense, trying to keep my breathing under control.

*A: i can feel you through the silk, soft warm, put your fingers
just inside your panties, no further
C: god. m dying, i'll come without touching
A: no you won't, only when I say! slide your fingers down
slowly through your hair and stop, don't touch your clit, just
the hood*

I knew she would be whimpering by now. I moved the laptop
aside a bit and slid my own hand under the white elastic band of my
black Jockey briefs and down, following my own instructions. It was
as if I were caressing her.

*C: hurry al please
A: slide one finger slowly through your cunt past your clit
then inside, tell me how it feels
C: oh god slippery hot tight feels so good*

Heart hammering in my chest, I pushed a finger down on either side
of my clit, then pulled back, careful not to touch the tip. Imagining her
scent, I brought my fingers up to my nose; imagining her taste, I licked
them. I wiped them on my Jockeys and returned to the keyboard.

A: touch yourself, you can come now.

In my mind, I could see her fingers stroking herself, probably
just one fast, hard pass over the swollen clit, her head thrown back, a
cry ripping from her throat. I thought I could hear her and moaned in
sympathy.

Putting the laptop aside, I sat up and swung my feet over the side
of the bed and waited, aroused still, the pulse in my throat echoed by
my throbbing clit.

The door to the adjoining room opened and Chandra stood
there, leaning against the doorway, just as gorgeous as she had been
four months ago with that shimmering black hair and those dark eyes
smiling at me dreamily. She looked like she'd just been fucked. By me.
Her clothes were still in disarray, undone, waiting for me to remove
them. I stared at her bare breasts, the nipples just hidden by the edges
of the open shirt.

"That was amazing. I came so hard," she said with that throaty laugh.

"I heard you," I said.

"I wanted you to, so I was extra loud. I know it turns you on.'"

"Yeah, it does. Come here so I can finish taking your clothes off."

She stood in front of me, between my knees, and started to reach for my breasts through the tank top. I pushed her hands away and she grinned knowingly, continuing the caress over my bare shoulders, up my neck to my hair. I let her.

"I thought you'd never get here," she murmured. "It took much less time to drive here than I expected. I waited two hours. I tried to work on my presentation but couldn't. Way too horny."

Chandra was coordinator of the digital art collection at a university library not so far from Chicago, in Michigan. Our common interest in library automation was what first brought us together at a conference three years ago. The fucking had been frenzied, especially after Chandra, normally not even remotely the submissive sort, had discovered to her surprise that letting me top her and giving me control of the scene gave her the best sex she'd ever had. So we'd repeated our games at subsequent conferences and sometimes via laptop when traveling.

She ran her hands over my mostly dark brown hair.

"This is new. The bleached tips—and it's so short. I like it," she said approvingly.

"It gets too curly and uncontrollable." I closed my eyes, enjoying the sensation of her strong, slim fingers caressing my head.

"And we both know how important control is to you," she murmured, an almost imperceptible catch in her voice that I knew signaled arousal.

"And we both know you want me that way," I replied.

Chandra arched against my hands as I rubbed the palms gently against puckered nipples under thin cloth. I pulled the shirt and loose bra down from her shoulders, letting them fall to the floor. Cupping her still-covered ass, I pulled her toward me and licked a brown nipple. She lifted the full breast with both hands to give me better access.

"Suck it!" By now she was panting softly.

"Nuh-uh, I'm in charge, remember," I admonished and pulled her hands away, holding them tightly against the small of her back. She knew she wasn't allowed to help. But I drew her nipple into my mouth and she moaned.

Still gripping her hands behind her with one of mine, I used the other one to push her trousers down over her hips to the floor, then brushed the backs of my fingers lightly to and fro along the crotch of her silk panties. It was more than damp. She writhed and moaned again. I tugged them down, too. Her feet were already bare and I let her step out of her clothing. Shoving one of my knees between her legs so that she'd spread them, I pulled her hips toward me and sank to my knees by the bed. She tilted her cunt toward my face. This was what I'd been waiting for—her scent, her taste. I groaned loudly. Holding on to her so she wouldn't fall, I licked her and rubbed her till my face was wet. She was gasping, and just before she went rigid, I stopped and pulled my mouth away.

"What are you doing! Jesus, don't stop!" she pleaded, trying to pull my head back to her, but I grabbed her hands again.

I stood up then and kissed her, my tongue driving into her mouth. She sucked on it frantically, in a rhythm like fucking. I knew she could taste herself on my tongue.

"I'm going to fuck you first. Then I'll let you come." My throat was tight, my voice hoarse.

I nudged her down to sit on the foot of the bed. She had calmed down a little and smiled provocatively, raising her eyebrows in that way she had. Deliberately, she leaned back on her elbows, thighs splayed wide, exposing her cunt to me. The light from the windows was bright enough to see everything: the soft, wet triangle of dark hair, the glistening dark red of the labia and swollen clit, the darker center.

I couldn't look away. Standing in front of her, I pushed my Jockeys down slowly till they fell to the floor, and stepped out of them. I left my tank top on. She stopped smiling as her eyes locked on my groin. I slipped two fingers into my own cunt, then held them up so she could see how wet they were. Her eyes widened. There wasn't a sound in the room except for our labored breathing and the low snarl of traffic coming through the open windows.

"Move up on the bed and lie flat. Keep your legs spread. Clasp your hands above your head."

She did. I got up on the bed too and kneeled over a firm, muscled leg. She reached for my swaying breasts under the tank top, teasing me.

Not allowed. I seized her hands and placed them back up above her head. This time they stayed there.

Leaning on one elbow, I lowered myself until my swollen and aching crotch rested briefly on her thigh. I needed to feel her naked skin against my clit just for a moment. It was almost as hot as my cunt. I had to lift off again or I'd come instantly.

Chandra was shivering slightly, clutching one of the pillows still leaning against the headboard.

"Please fuck me, Al, let me come," she begged, raising her hips.

"Wait. When I say."

I stroked between her moist lips, my fingers entering her, in and out, palm sliding against her clit. I could feel the tension in her whole body as she hovered on the brink, waiting for permission. I gave it once more.

"You can come now."

Immediately her whole body stiffened as she arched off the bed with a strangled cry, at the same time shoving her thigh against my clit. I grunted and almost came too. She fell back down, moaning and shuddering. I held her till she was still, burying my hot face in the silky waves of her hair, all the while conscious of my sex against her skin.

Chandra's thigh was still between my legs. I moved my cunt against her in a slow rhythm. I wanted the pleasure of the slippery friction to go on and on, but I couldn't last much longer. I felt myself begin to come and moved up fast for a final hard thrust of my distended clit against her hipbone, barely aware of her hand moving down to my ass. Just as the orgasm tore through me, she drove a finger into that orifice. I exploded, crying out with each spasm. Then I collapsed half on top of her.

She eased her finger from inside me and got up off the bed as I rolled over on my back. "I'm going to wash my hands. Be right back," she said, a satisfied smile on her face.

By now I'd recovered somewhat physically if not mentally. This was my first experience with anal penetration. I was in shock.

"You fucked my ass! Why did you do that! I should have tied your hands like before. I'm supposed to be the top! I've always been a top. I'm supposed to control the scene. You've just ruined it!" And so on. I was deeply offended.

"I wanted to give you the most mind-blowing orgasm ever," she said matter-of-factly. "Tell me if I didn't."

During the bathroom sounds, I lay there looking up at the ceiling and reflecting. I had a feeling that this was about more than wanting to give me the ultimate orgasm.

When she came back, she stood by the window and looked out for a bit before turning back to look at me. She was still naked but the light was behind her so the details of her body were indistinct, as was her face. I sat up on the side of the bed, facing her, still wearing my white tank top. It was late afternoon now and hot in the room. I wanted to go out and come back in to see how strongly it smelled of sex. I could hear the faint wail of a siren in the distance and from below in the street, surreally, the barking of a dog.

"I'm driving back tomorrow afternoon," she said. "After my presentation."

"Oh. Okay." I was surprised and waited for more.

"I won't be going to any more conferences, Alaine. At least not this kind. I won't be seeing you anymore."

"Ah, so that was symbolic. But what do you mean?" I was stunned. It's not as if there was ever a question of anything more between us. We weren't interested in joining our lives, just our bodies. I didn't want commitment, just hot casual sex.

"I've been thinking for a while that it's time for me to go home— I mean really home. I've been offered a position at the provincial museum in Toronto, digitizing its art collection."

I felt a pang of regret. But that ass fuck—which was also a mind fuck—changed everything, and it wouldn't be the same anymore. That had been her intention, of course. The sex had always been so good, though; what we both wanted. How do you find that again with someone else?

She sat down beside me and kissed my cheek.

"I'm sorry, Al. It's been fun, though, hasn't it?" She smiled but her voice quavered slightly.

"The best," I sighed, my eyes blurring.

She put an arm around my shoulders. "Want to go and hear the keynote speaker tonight? We should clean up and get something to eat first."

Tonight would be our last night together. I'd make sure she didn't pull anything like that again. Maybe she'd let me tie her up. Still, that was some orgasm…

And about tomorrow, I decided I'd better skip Chandra's presentation. Watching her in her element—cool, authoritative—always made me wet because I'd be sitting there visualizing her as just the opposite during sex, whimpering and begging me for release. Better to avoid that. It might kill me.

I sighed again, then remembered the attractive woman at the elevators. Marion somebody, two floors up, had said she'd be at my session in the morning. The thought of that cheered me up considerably. Maybe she'd even be there tonight. I'd make sure to speak with her again, get to know her a little better. I wondered where she lived. Not too close to me, I hoped. I wondered if she had a laptop.

MERMAID
FIONA COOPER

I loved this Harley before I loved you. Loved the ultra-classic louche chrome curves, the studded panniers, the glossy lung of the gas tank with the mermaid I had airbrushed there. When I rode the switchback coast highway, a rainbow pennant whipping and cracking over my head, the mermaid's breasts nudged against my black leather thighs, the gleaming scales of her tail curved right into me, and the fiery 1450 engine pulsed through my bones. I was flying like an elemental dragon. I liked to ride alone, Nina Simone filling every cell of my head with her blues spell of love and longing.

I'd stop at a roadside bar when I felt my fingers welding into my gauntlets, let the engine drag my toes through the dust, peel my gold-flake helmet from my soaking hair and swagger round the cooling beast, sunlight blazing rainbows against my shades. Old boys would gather like flies round shit, reminiscing about the bikes their wives had made them trade for family-size four-wheel stability. Truckers talked too, hypnotized by the white line and the endless freeway.

Sometimes a waitress would come on to me for a ride, and we'd take off up the road, I'd drive into the hills and stop for the view, and more often than not, the heat and the power of the bike had them wet and horny and I'd fuck them under the pastel overall—of course they were *never* like this as a rule, they said, thrusting against my fingers. They didn't usually fuck back. And that suited me.

Then there was Ruby, she had her own café, and when she rode back of me, her hands pushed inside my jacket and burned my breasts while her teeth teased my neck and she told me go left, go right.

I stopped when she told me, and she slid one thigh over the pillion and stood there laughing. Ruby had magenta lips, bronze eye shadow, and dark eyelashes heavy with mascara. She unbuttoned her overall like a stripper, she had a bra that unclipped at the front and a purple slash of silk around her ass. She pushed my hand between her thighs and unzipped my leathers, stripped me bare, and pulled me down beside her on the grass. Her strong thighs clamped my hand and she pushed herself upright to look down at me. Ruby kissed like she wanted to swallow my face, her hand stroked my nipples very softly and ran over my belly and hair like a butterfly.

"You want me?" she asked, laughing. One of her fingers ran between my thighs so strong I gushed against her palm.

"You want me," she said, one arm round my shoulders holding me so her eyes and lips locked with mine.

When her finger slid just inside me, she kept it there, moving round and round, stretching me so I could feel oceans erupting from deep inside me.

"Let's dive," she said, and her tongue filled my mouth as her fingers surged right inside me.

"Let's dive together," I said, fighting to touch her too, but she said *no!* and kept right on inside me, her eyes hypnotic.

"Come on, baby," she said, "Come on, baby, give it up, give me it, come on…"

I welded to her in the heat and shuddered over and over, and Ruby slowed a little, then fucked me like lightning until my head exploded. She rocked me against her breasts and laughed again.

"I need a cigarette," she said.

I watched the blue smoke rise from her lips and nostrils as I came back to earth. She reached for her overall as I reached for her, and one powerful hand held my wrist.

"I don't want that," she said, smiling, "that's the way I am—do you have a problem with it, bike dyke? It's nothing personal."

"I got no problem," I said.

"Good," she said, and we sat there for a while before she kissed me on the cheek and dressed.

"Business as usual," she said. "Café won't run itself."

I dropped her by the dusty gas pumps and she said, *Anytime you're passing, drag your black leather ass my way.*

I loved black leather before I loved you, got fucked by Ruby a few times before I loved you. The afternoon I found you I had ridden hard past Ruby's place, teeth clenched, determined not to stop. The thrill had gone. I always rode any distance along the highway alone—until there was you.

You were sitting looking at the wide Pacific when I first saw you. *God damn it,* I thought, *this is my place.* It was miles between towns or even motels or roadside stops high above the beach. You looked like a surfer hippy, white vest, white shorts, sun-white hair. I'd passed a bright orange beach buggy a mile down the road and guessed—rightly—that it was yours. You have baby blue eyes and a goofy smile and you never stop talking, so I knew a lot of your life within a half hour. Divorced, semi-broke, children you never saw, artist, drifter, clapped-out car, rented apartment with the rent overdue, wondering if your luck had run out totally or had it even ever begun?—and I could see your blah blah blah was a shield for tears, your laugh was a brake on screaming—I knew that you were probably nuts and maybe a whole lot of trouble and definitely the most beautiful creature I had ever seen.

I think I was supposed to tell you about me, but I don't do that.

I just said to your questing eyes: "I follow the sun."

"Sounds romantic," you said and I felt my throat closing so I had to swallow deep.

"It can be," I said, acting cool.

You pushed your hair away from your face and took your eyes from mine.

"If you want it to be," I said, wondering what fool had come out with those words.

I don't say those words, I don't feel these things, I don't do falling in love with a total stranger. But you seemed eager to ride with me, hell, you even left your shoes behind.

So you rode barefoot pillion and we picked up your bag from the dead orange buggy and you just moved in like you were meant to, like you belong. I said I'd sleep on the couch and you looked hurt and shrugged, your eyes searching mine. You kissed me very lightly on the lips. I tried not to grin like a crazed fool. It was no good.

"Whatever you want," you said.

"I want to sleep with you," I said.

You shuddered in my arms, kissed my shoulder, held on to me like I was trying to escape, which I wasn't. It was weird and wonderful to be in bed with you, first time anyone had been in this bed with me. Amazing to be naked between sheets with your lovely body twined round me. I held you as close as my own skin. And we did it too, we slept together.

Morning I woke first and we were in the same position. Your upper lip sucked your lower lip and you looked about three years old. When I eased out of your arms, you wrapped them round the pillow and kicked the duvet off your beautiful curves. Your ass was like two peaches. I did coffee and stretched beside you.

I thought you were still asleep when your hand flopped on my thigh. Then, your eyes still closed, you climbed over me and pushed your head between my thighs. Your fingers unfolded me, and your tongue ran against me.

"Mmm," you said, "You taste amazing. Put your coffee down, you're in for a bumpy ride. Okay?"

"Be my guest," I said, speechless with desire, loving the strength of you.

You giggled as you ate me, then swam up on top of me after I came, licking your fingers and kissing me open-mouthed and salty with me. The sun through the blinds made rainbow scales over your back all the way down to your toes. Your shoulders were the color of pale wild honey, your hair a tangle of sugar spin. A gust of laughter seized me and you looked concerned.

"I'm just really happy," I told you, "really happy."

"Good," you said, "I just want to make you happy. I don't seem to have done much of that so far in my life."

We finished our coffee, then I kissed you, and your tongue played with mine, you teased my lips with your teeth, you let your mouth fill with the juice from mine and our tongues swam round each other like twin dolphins in the waves. My feet flippered down the bed and pulled me to hover over you. I nuzzled your hair and let my nose rub against the steaming smooth skin taut and trembling as you jackknifed your thighs apart for me. And what did you taste like, my darling, you were a rock pool at sunrise, fresh and salty, and your hair was feathery fronds of seaweed dancing in the tide. You were soft as an oyster, the pearl of your passion rising to my lips on the undulating crest of wave after wave.

"Does this mean we're going steady?" you said to my neck as we held each other, beached on the pillows.

"Uh-huh," I said.

I wanted to marry you right that moment and the thought made my heart thunder like it would burst out of my chest. But I remembered you didn't seem to like marriage too much, remembered that falling in love had always been a deep whirlpool for me, knowing I was already helplessly spinning into you. Thought that not using the words might just be a good idea.

So we went on for the next couple of months, me dispatch riding, you waitressing, us making love more and more, my bare apartment filling with rainbow junk, music, and the sparkle of you. Never mentioned love, either of us, like you don't walk on the cracks in the sidewalk, or under ladders. For all you had told me your life story I never told you mine, and I knew there was a lot more to you than that hurried bio on the cliff top by the coast road. I just thought some day you'd up and leave, and though you were closer than my skin my heart prefers nonverbal. That way you can be in the moment, not fretting over a future that no one can tell.

Then there was the Tuesday when everything changed.

We had a day off together and you turned to me in bed and said, *I want to take you somewhere. It's really important.*

I got that kicked-in-the-gut feeling as we dressed—hell, it was just too perfect with you and already my head was hurling smart one-liners for when you dumped me, each word sharp and accurate as a dart dipped in curare. You just hummed some shoo-doo-be-wop song, kissed my cheek, stroked my face, looked into my eyes—just the way you usually did, only I was reading good-bye in every gesture. But just like *love*, the word *good-bye* is one I didn't want to use. Not with you.

So then we were driving along the highway, as we'd done a hundred times before, only this time you said you'd tell me the way. We took the inland fork, and after a while, everything was greener, avocado orchards lining the road. We stopped at a taco stand and the sun dazzled off your hair and I was the fool wanting to say, *Don't do this, I'm in love with you.*

"Good coffee," I said.

"Not far now," you said and my heart stabbed as you put one golden thigh over the Harley. Well, I'd have the Harley once you'd gone, and the engine roared right through my body—only the feel of your arms round my waist roared even more powerful through my heart.

You tugged me right, then left, and we were virtually dirt-biking for the last few miles before you said *stop.*

This was the end of the road anyway. I had never seen a place

so green—a grassy dip fringed by trees. I peeled off my helmet and
stood there while you walked a little way like you were looking for
something.

"This way," you said, taking my hand, your eyes shining as if
we'd been making love.

Through the trees and over a low rise, and we were on the shore
of a lake, silver and hazy right into the distance. Turquoise dragonflies
skimmed the surface and a heron stood some twenty feet from us and
never moved. You were still like I'd never seen you before—poised
like a wild creature scenting the wind, your muscles quivered in the
sunshine and your eyes were huge and radiant.

"Sit with me," you said and you slid your arm round my shoulders
as we sat on a curved rock.

"Something I have to tell you," you said.

I braced myself. Hell, I'm a big girl now. All my wisecracking
would have to get me out of the hurt I knew was coming.

"Look," you said, "I have to tell you about when we met."

So now you were going to say it was a habit of yours to hang
around the highway and pick people up. Like I did with waitresses.
Something to do. And it would be something to do again, even if I was
a walking riding dead person doing it.

"I don't know what you're thinking," you said, "but you've been
strange all morning. Don't be a stranger to me—please."

"Okay," I said, letting our eyes meet, struggling to keep all my
armor shiny and well buckled.

"When you saw me I was working up the guts to just jump over the
edge. I could picture myself flying out and down and hitting the waves,
and going deep like a mermaid, bubbles streaming in my hair, the salty
water filling my lungs and the riptide tossing me about, carrying me
deep beyond it all. I had just prayed for a reason not to end it all.
Prayed for an angel. Then you came roaring up, you and your bike, and
there was the mermaid—and I don't believe in coincidence."

You looked at me and my armor was rust blowing in the wind.

"I've never brought anyone here before," you said. "I found this
place once and used it to cry in. Then to connect. The ripples on this
lake gave me the strength to leave that marriage, the sparkle of these
dragonflies kept me moving and sparkling. You might think I'm crazy,
well, you won't be the first."

I kissed you, just a gentle lip-to-lip kiss, and held your hand. Jesus! You were almost not here and my heart thundered till my head was pounding—I had almost stopped at Ruby's that afternoon as well, then simply did not wish to, never wished to do that again.

"I know you're crazy," I said, "I'm crazy too. And I want to tell you I'm crazy about you, even if you don't want it, well, it's a good feeling to have. It's good to feel. Don't worry about it."

Your eyes widened for a second.

"You too?" you said. "I thought you just tooled along Pacific picking people up. Wondered when you'd change the locks, tell me it was fun while it lasted."

I groaned from deep inside.

"Do you think talking is a good idea?" I said, "Like me talking—you've just said what I've been thinking all morning."

"I am shit at mind reading," you said. "And so are you and so is everybody. Talk to me, no matter what, or I'll just go ahead and fill the silences. As you know."

Our embrace filled the silence. I breathed in your hair, your skin, my body breathed you.

"So are we going steady?" you said.

"I want to marry you," I wanted to say, the throbbing heat in my head unbearable. Instead I said, "Oh yeah!"

We were naked in seconds. You pulled me to my feet and we ran into the lake, water like silk rising along our legs, clusters of bubbles caught in your hair. Maybe I should have said marry, what the hell, you hadn't dumped me, you drew me into your arms, your legs curving and strong as a mermaid's tail. I dived to catch your beautiful breast, floating in the clear water, you gasped a deep breath and undulated down to suck my toes, nibble my knees like a grazing fish, the feel of your hair sweeping over my skin was electric.

"Float for me, darling," you said.

I floated like a starfish and you were my fifth arm, darting into me, spouting clear water over my belly as you rose to gasp for air and dive again. Your toes wriggled a frill of bubbles on the surface, your widespread hands splashed me and the sun dazzled me even through closed eyelids. *If I drown now,* I thought, *I die happy.* My nipples stung as they clenched erect, I was so hot suddenly the water was icy cold and every nerve in my body plugged into the main grid as your lips gripped me and your tongue was hot as a geyser. You slid along my shuddering body as I came over and over, convulsing from deeper inside me than anyone else has ever been.

Our wet faces kissed and you lay on my arm, and I trod water as my hand spread between your thighs, fingers finding your wonderful hot wetness, my thumb coaxing the fabulous fins of your sex stiff and trembling.

"Live with me forever," I said to your sky blue eyes and your mouth whispered

Yes

And then you gasped and screamed *yes* to the wide blue haze spinning high above our heads.

"Let's ride round the lake naked," you said. "No one ever comes here."

"Just you and me, huh?" I said, and our laughter was echoed as a skein of waterbirds clattered up from the reeds.

"And," I said, "going steady? I want to marry you."

"I was going to say that," you said. "You really mean it?"

"I do," I said.

"Okay then," you said, drawing a silver ripple round us for a ring.

We staggered to the shore along a path of sparkling sunlight like we'd rescued each other from drowning.

OPEN VIEW
GUN BROOKE

The glass elevator slowly ascended the amazing height of the
hotel. Through the window, Deborah saw the lights of San
Antonio glimmering like precious jewels against the velvet night sky.
Behind her, she felt the heat emanating from her lover's body. When a
soft kiss landed at the back of her neck, she gasped in surprise.

"Hi, beautiful," Haylee whispered, raising her hands to Deborah's
waist. "I trust you remember what you promised me?"

"What?" Deborah managed.

"You know what I mean, love."

"Ah. That." Deborah felt her cheeks warm. She had tried to keep
from thinking about her promise. "Do it for me, as a present, and I will
return your kindness...in full," Haylee had said before they left for the
formal function that had brought them to San Antonio.

Being without panties was one thing, but an entire evening of
"going commando" among the top brass of her agency had made her
feel entirely vulnerable, and every time Haylee caught her glance across
the room, Deborah had blushed profusely. She had also feared that her
increasing arousal would give her away. Fortunately, scents of ladies'
perfume and men's aftershave, together with the drinks and finger food,
drowned out any of her pheromones.

"Yes, *that*." Haylee spoke with a low purr, and there was something
indefinably dangerous in her tone. She stepped closer; Deborah felt the
fabric of her black pantsuit against her back.

"You like my dress, though?" Deborah tried to change the subject
as Haylee pressed close against her back. At the outer perimeter of her
mind, she thought she noticed the glass elevator moving slower.

"I like your dress very much. I think you look amazing in that
blue color, and the sequins over your breasts have lured me all evening.
There's only one other thing you look even better in."

"And what would that be?"

"Nothing. You look best wearing absolutely nothing." Haylee didn't move, trapping Deborah at the window. Haylee slowly caressed Deborah's shoulders and played with the spaghetti straps holding the dress up. "You smell divine," she murmured.

"So do you," Deborah said, swallowing against the dryness of her throat. It was true. Haylee's signature scent of citrus and musk was making Deborah lick her lips. Her knees threatened to give out when Haylee pressed her lips to the base of her neck and kissed her way along her shoulder.

"Mmm," Haylee purred. "So soft. So tasty." She nibbled the skin and let her tongue caress the little bites.

Deborah tipped her head back.

"Oh, Haylee," she sighed. "Let me turn around. Let me hold you."

"No, sweet thing. You're fine just where you are. I can see your reflection in the glass while I'm touching you. Stay as you are."

"If I can," Deborah murmured. "My legs seem awfully weak."

"Don't worry. I've got you."

Haylee slid her hands down Deborah's arms, causing goose bumps to appear and her lover to gasp out loud. Not missing a beat, Haylee gently raised Deborah's wrists and guided them to the window frame.

"There, hold on," she said huskily.

Deborah nodded and gripped the frame on both sides of the large window. She saw herself reflected in the glass. Her eyes were wide and her ragged breath produced a steamy little circle, distorting the image of her flustered face.

"Now, where was I?" she heard Haylee say quietly behind her. Determined hands pulled at the dress and began to slide the soft fabric up her legs.

"Oh yes, you know how I like you," Haylee said. "Naked. Especially this part of you."

Deborah could only nod. It excited her that Haylee liked to watch her, observe her in the most intimate of ways. Haylee bunched the silky garment up over Deborah's hips and held it there with one hand, resting the other one on her hip.

"Mmm, you feel so soft. I have wanted to do this all evening, you know. I've been such a model of restraint." Haylee caressed Deborah's hips and left no crevice or curve untouched.

"Yes...you have," Deborah had to agree. "But please let me turn around. I'm half naked in front of a window on an elevator, for heaven's sake. What if someone's out there?"

"We're high up. Unless they have binoculars. Then they'll get a bonus show they didn't count on, trust me." Haylee kissed her way down Deborah's neck. "Besides, doesn't the thought of some stranger standing in a dark room, watching us—maybe jerking off at the sight of my fingers in your wet pussy—make you hot? I think so. Just hold on like that." She put her arm around Deborah's waist and held her up. Sliding her hand beneath her raised dress, she caressed Deborah's hot center. Deborah shivered, unable to take her eyes off the alluring image reflected in the window. "That's it. Spread your legs, sweet thing." Haylee ruffled the soft strands of hair between Deborah's legs.

Deborah inhaled sharply at the no-nonsense tone of voice and complied. When Haylee commanded her like this, she knew she had no choice but to surrender. It was as if Haylee had a sixth sense about when to take control. It had scared her the first time and she felt a little apprehensive even now, her breath coming in excited gushes. Slowly she spread her legs, giving Haylee access to the swollen heat between her legs.

"Good girl," Haylee cooed. "You know just what I want, what to give me, right?" She trailed her fingertips through the wetness and spread the moisture over Deborah's sex.

"Oh, Haylee," Deborah moaned. This immediate assault on the sensitive area made her cling harder to the window frame. Watching their reflection in the glass added to the fire at her core. "What are you doing to me?"

"Taking you," Haylee said breathlessly. "Making you mine. Making you never doubt that you belong with me."

Haylee's fingers performed a tantalizing drum roll on the ridge of nerves between Deborah's legs. Shivers coursed through Deborah, making her gasp out loud and throw her head back. Wetter than she'd ever been, she envisioned their nameless onlooker, a women their age, standing with her binoculars, or perhaps even a telescope. Would she push her hands into her panties and fondle herself as she watched the two strangers in the glass elevator?

"You *are* mine, aren't you?" Haylee asked with a growl. "You're all mine."

"Yes, yes," Deborah sobbed quietly, nearly there, feeling pleasure bordering on pain. It was as if tiny scorching flames licked her from inside. "All yours."

"You see all of this in the glass, don't you?" Haylee urged her on. "You see my hand and what it does to you?"

"Yes. I see everything…oh, God, I do—"

"It's driving you crazy but you can't stop looking, can you, darling?"

"No, no…"

The probing fingers found her entrance and pushed inside.

Suddenly dizzy, Deborah couldn't hold herself upright any longer and bent forward to brace her elbows against the window ledge. Haylee shifted her grip and slid into her.

"Ah!" Deborah groaned.

"So this is what you want?" Haylee kissed Deborah's neck. "You want me to ravish you from behind like this, hmm?"

"I…yes!" Deborah hadn't known she'd wanted it, but the thought of Haylee fucking her like this made her sex tingle madly.

Haylee plunged two fingers into Deborah, setting up a slow but forceful rhythm, pressing her fingers down against a spot that drove Deborah crazy. "Mine!" Haylee murmured as she pressed her body against Deborah's, forcing Deborah's sex to slide along the window ledge.

"Yes!" Deborah replied with a sob. She shivered as a shattering feeling built inside. Just when she thought she couldn't take any more, Haylee added another finger, filling her, stretching her beyond what she thought possible. The relentless hand driving into her and the husky, whispering voice in her ear finally became too much. Deborah's heart thundered as the elevator slowed. With a whimper, Deborah gripped the window ledge and began to convulse. Light-headed and trembling, she let Haylee hold her up as she came. *Are you watching, out there?*

"Ah!" The orgasm swept through her, flooded her, and she slumped against Haylee with a moan. Haylee slowly slid from her and cradled her in a soft embrace.

"Hi, you," she murmured. "Are you okay, sweet thing?"

"Mmm," Deborah managed. "Very okay."

"I think we're here."

As if on cue, the elevator stopped at their floor. Haylee quickly smoothed the dress down Deborah's hips and swept her up in her arms. Deborah clung to Haylee's neck, hiding her face as her lover murmured "'scuse me" to the people waiting for the elevator. Haylee strode down the corridor with Deborah in a firm grip. "If you only knew how much I want you, love," she whispered throatily. "I want your mouth on me. Now. I can't wait."

"I want to taste you," Deborah murmured. "I want to make you come, Haylee. My love."

Haylee put Deborah down, produced the card key, and opened the door. Once inside, Haylee eagerly tugged off her suit, stretched out on the bed, and spread her legs wide. She rasped, "Now, sweet thing. Now."

Her voice was even darker with desire, and ripples of renewed lust made Deborah groan. She crawled between Haylee's long legs, feeling more aroused than she'd ever been. It was time for her to take over this adventure. Time to teach Haylee she wasn't the only one who could reduce a lover to a whimpering, pleasure-ridden mess. Deborah licked her lips. "Mmm," she purred and took one lick along Haylee's drenched, slightly parted folds. "You like this, hmm?"

"Deborah…" Haylee said, her voice suddenly just as weak and as submissive as Deborah's had been earlier.

"You like this too?" Deborah asked casually as she licked along her lover's labia, one languid lap after another. Haylee's taste was familiar but always addictive, and Deborah pushed her mouth harder against the fragile tissues.

Haylee's husky murmur increased in volume as Deborah danced her tongue over her most sensitive spot. Hungrily, Deborah caressed the delicate inner lips and the distended clit without mercy until Haylee's legs began to tremble.

Deborah took the quivering, hard clit between her lips and fluttered her tongue over it, feeling wetness soak her chin. She greedily tasted it and reveled in the effect she had on the woman she loved.

Determined to not let go, to see Haylee through, Deborah hooked both arms around Haylee's legs. When she felt Haylee's orgasm against her lips, her own clit began to burn again.

"Deborah!" Haylee arched fiercely beneath her. Her orgasm hit hard, almost throwing Deborah off.

Not wanting to leave her lover, Deborah ground her hips against the mattress. She desperately needed to come again, and the lingering spasms of Haylee's orgasm only fueled her desire. She moaned.

"Oh, Debbie, come here." Haylee pulled Deborah up her sweat-soaked body and pushed a leg between her thighs. "I know where it hurts. I know." She grabbed Deborah's hips and pushed her up and down her slick thigh. "That help, sweet thing?"

"Yes," Deborah sobbed. "Yes. Oh, like that. Yes!"

Haylee held her tightly, and Deborah knew she wouldn't last long. She pulled one of Haylee's dark, puckered nipples into her mouth and sucked as her hips undulated feverishly against Haylee's thigh. Her clit was painfully hard, and every stroke against Haylee's slick leg sent prickles of pleasure bordering on pain up Deborah's groin.

When the second orgasm hit, tearing through already inflamed tissues, she let go of the now deep red nipple and cried out. Deborah tossed her head back, pressing her pussy against Haylee, drenching her even more. Eventually her muscles gave out and she slumped onto Haylee's body.

"Deborah."

Deborah found it amazing that a voice, speaking a single name, could say so much. The pillow was cool against her hot cheek as she gently stroked Haylee's breasts. "I love you."

"God, I love you right back." Haylee's voice was husky in the aftermath of their lovemaking. "I love you so much."

Tipping her head back, Deborah sought Haylee's eyes in the dusky room. "Thank you."

Haylee smiled. "You're welcome."

"Happy anniversary."

"Happy anniversary, sweet thing. Five years."

"Can I have, like, fifty more or so?" Deborah slid her hand around Haylee's back and hugged her tight.

"Fifty sounds good to me. A nice round number."

Deborah grinned. "I like nice round things too." She cupped one of Haylee's butt cheeks. "Like this one, for instance."

"You're insatiable!"

"Yes."

"Greedy, even."

"Yes."

Deborah rolled Haylee onto her back. "And I'm also fair. Just so you know."

"Okay. And by that you mean?"

Deborah nipped at Haylee's still swollen nipple. "I got two. I owe you one, babe."

"Owe me...? Oh!" Haylee arched into Deborah's mouth. "Yes, you're very fair."

Deborah gazed lovingly up at Haylee, a slow fire igniting in her eyes. "Then, my love, let me settle the score."

'57 BUICK
KI THOMPSON

I love my car. It's not just your average automobile tooling down the road. It's a '57 Buick, dark blue, with blue fabric interior. The backseat is bigger than my couch at home and has been used the same way, if you know what I mean. The car once belonged to my dad and then he gave it to me when he bought his newer, more reliable car. He buys Japanese models, which I suppose are very reliable when you compare them to the Buick. But my car has personality. She's an individual that stands out in a crowd of sameness. She has her moods and can be downright ornery at times, but she loves me too, and I know it.

What I love most about my car is the way it turns women's heads as I pull into the parking lot of the local hangout. I tend bar there, Geraldine's it's called, and you can find me most nights pouring shots and drafts. I'm the one in leather with tattoos from the neck down. Oh yeah, and I'm always packing. Say what you will about it, I like the way a rubber cock feels in my pants, especially when the pants are tight and press into me whenever I move. It keeps me turned on all night long so that I'm always ready. And the ladies that come to Geraldine's, well, they like that.

The owner of the bar, her name is Maude. Geraldine's has been around for a long time and had several owners, but they always kept the name. I guess they didn't want to confuse people. Anyway, Maude has been getting on in years and has always treated me like the kid she never had. She says that one day the bar will be mine, so I've been saving up for the day when I can take it over and make it my own. My name's Kevin, but my friends call me Kev. I know it's a guy's name, but that's what my parents called me. And truth be told, I kind of like it.

It was closing time on a Saturday night and I was finishing up behind the bar, washing glasses and balancing the cash register. Maude had gone home hours ago, as usual, so it was just me, the waitress Connie, who was cleaning tables, and a lone woman who was leaning against the jukebox. She was swaying slightly to the plaintive cry of Annie Lennox and appeared to be a bit tipsy but still in control. Her cream-colored silk blouse was partially open and her tight black miniskirt revealed long, shapely legs. Connie kept giving her the evil eye, annoyed that there was still a customer in the place when she wanted to get home to her girlfriend.

"It's okay, Connie," I said, "you go on home, I'll lock up."

"What about her?" Connie tossed her head in the woman's direction.

"I'll take care of *that* too."

"She looks a little out of it. You want me to call her a cab?"

"At this hour? It's raining. I'd be lucky if it got here by noon. Nah, I'll just drop her wherever she needs to go. No need for you to hang around, though."

Connie gave me that grateful look that says, "I owe you one," tossed her bar towel into the cleaning bag, and headed out the back door. I put the cash drawer in the vault, spun the dial, and turned off the lights in the back room. After grabbing an umbrella and my keys, I sauntered out from behind the bar.

"Lady, it's time to go. I gotta lock up."

The brunette glanced up and seemed to focus in on me from some faraway place. She wasn't drunk, I realized, just lost in a world of her own, and I was surprised to discover what a knockout she was. I usually notice that kind of thing even when the place gets really busy. I gave her the once-over and she did the same to me, and more. If it was possible for a woman to fuck you with her eyes, then she was doing a pretty good job of it. She left fingerprints all over without even touching me.

"Time to go?" she asked, as though it wasn't obvious from the empty room.

"Yeah, do you have a way home, or can I give you a lift?" I crossed my fingers, hoping I'd get lucky.

"Oh, yes, thanks, I would really appreciate a ride. My friend left hours ago."

I frowned, wondering what she meant by *friend*, and why anyone would leave such a beautiful woman alone, especially on a night like this. Locking up the bar behind me, I led her to the passenger side of my car, holding the umbrella over our heads.

"Is this your car?" She stood back admiringly.

"Yeah," I said casually, trying to be cool about the best car ever.

I opened the door for her and she crawled in, her eyes scoping out the roomy interior. I slammed the door shut and ran to the driver's side, tossing the umbrella in the back. I turned the key in the ignition and the old bomb roared to life.

"Nice." She took in the big backseat. "You could have a really good time back there, couldn't you?"

A smile was my only answer. I reached up to the steering column and shifted the car into drive, and the big Buick lumbered out onto the street.

"Where to?" I asked. It felt like she was a mile away on the other side of the big front seat, and I grinned as I noticed her scooting my way.

"Anywhere you like," she said throatily, her hand pressing against my leather-clad thigh.

"Now that's what I like to hear." I pushed down on the accelerator and the car labored to increase speed.

I drove up into the wooded hills outside the city and found my favorite parking spot overlooking the town. The rain had all but stopped and the skies were clearing. A few brave stars managed to make themselves visible through the clouds, and as the air heated up, so did the interior of the car. Her blood red fingernails traced the lump in my pants and I felt myself grow hard in anticipation. Of their own accord, my hands reached out and fondled her taut nipples through the silk fabric of her blouse. She moaned and pressed them into my palms.

"Pinch them," she whispered in my ear.

I was more than happy to oblige, feeling the stiff points harden between my fingers. She climbed onto my lap, sitting with her back against my chest, and I reached down to the handle and pushed the bench seat all the way back. Her miniskirt slid up her thighs and I ran my hands down the outside of her legs, reaching her knees and then returning up the inside. Reaching her triangle, I cupped her already damp panties and quickly found her swollen clit with my thumb. I teased it in slow semicircles, feeling it rise in response.

"Oh, that feels *so* nice." Her ass writhed against my cock.

With one hand still at her center, I slid my other hand inside her blouse, pushing the lacy bra aside and finding a hard, hot nipple. While I pinched the tip, I tickled up and down her swollen mound. I let one finger slip inside her panties, finding a deep pool of wetness, and she nearly jerked off my lap.

"Hold still, baby," I cooed. "I want to tease your pussy some more. It's so hot and wet. I want to feel inside, see how hot you really are."

She spread her legs wider, inviting me in, and I slid one finger in effortlessly. She was creamy and soft and I pressed my cock upward, straining to get at her. Knowing what I was about, she reached down and slipped her panties down around her ankles and onto the floor. She then reached behind herself, rising up slightly to get at my zipper. Quickly she grabbed hold of the cock, yanking it out of my pants. Free of its constraints, it soared upward, ready for action.

"Oh, you're so hard," she murmured. "I love a hard cock. Does it want me?"

"You know it," I panted. I love a good tease, it makes me so horny.

She lowered herself slowly but purposefully onto the shaft and I thrust my hips to meet her.

"Oh yes!" she shouted.

She rose up a few inches and then dropped down as I slammed into her. All the while I worked her breasts, smashing them hard into my palms, twisting and turning her nipples. She was screaming now, one hand clutching the door, the other the steering wheel in front of her. She rode me hard and fast, and I felt the sweat trickle down my chest from the exertion of keeping pace with her. She clearly knew what she wanted, and while I was more than willing to give it to her, I could tell that we were in for a long night. It was as though she craved the fuck, wanting it to never end. Each time I slowed to catch my breath, she moaned impatiently, speeding up her rhythm to keep her excitement peaked. I used to pride myself on my stamina, but it was going to take everything I had to keep up with her.

Several minutes into it I could tell something was wrong. She couldn't seem to get off and I could sense her frustration mounting.

"Let's get in back," she growled.

She let the cock pop out of her as she climbed off me and over the front seat into the back. I sat in the front for a moment, trying to unscramble my brains, stunned at her ability to stop in mid-thrust without a *fuck you very much*, and then jumped in after her. She was already flat on her back, knees bent, hot and waiting. Damn, she wanted it badly.

"Take your clothes off," she commanded. "I want to feel all of you, all over me."

I've never stripped faster in my life. I was so aroused I could feel it on my thigh as it trickled down to rest behind my knee. But if you wear leather pants you know how hard they are to take off, and in the Buick, half crouched and horny, it was no easy feat. Added to that, the rubber cock kept getting in the way, and my companion was no help either. She kept grabbing my ass and pulling me into her, pressing the cock into my swollen clit until I thought I would explode.

"Jesus, let me get out of these pants so I can fuck you," I complained.

I finally managed to get them around my ankles and I fell on top of her. As I guided the cock back into her with my hand, she took both of my breasts in her own hands and began to suck each taut nipple, tugging gently on the nipple ring in my left breast.

"Oh, yeah, yeah, do it like that," I moaned.

I was on the edge and I slammed into her hard until she cried out. Each slight withdrawal nearly took my breath away as my clit ached to feel the press of the rubber toy once again.

"Yes, harder, faster, just do it! Make me come!" She clawed my back, urging me on.

I thought I was going to pound right through her, like a jackhammer on hard pavement, and I wasn't going to stop until I hit bottom. She rose up off the seat, meeting me with each thrust, bucking and rocking over and over again. The sweat poured down my back and between my breasts, as if every pore in my body had released its pent-up juices just for this one earth-shattering climax. I felt like an animal in heat, blind with lust and the call of the wild, with no awareness or control over myself. My entire being was wrapped up in this one great fuck.

"Oh, oh, oh, yes!"

She hissed one last syllable and then I felt it—like an underwater explosion that first draws in and then gushes out. Her insides clamped down on the cock and nearly lifted me off the backseat, and I had to grab hold of its edges to keep myself grounded. She screamed, she cried, she laughed hysterically, all the while drawing me deeper and deeper inside. With one last thrust I felt myself coming. I came and came and it just felt so damn good that I began to cry at the sheer need of it. When it finally stopped, I knew she had wrecked me for anyone else.

We lay there for I don't know how long. I'm not even sure I was fully conscious and I think I must have slept. But after what felt like a few seconds, she was up and on me, wanting more. I laughed—surely she was joking. But when she reached for the limp dick, slippery with her come, my eyes went wide with shock.

"No way!" I protested. "Baby, I can't. I gave it all I had."

"Come on," she pouted, tracing the outline of my tiger tattoo.

I could barely lift my arms, let alone lift anything else, and despite her protests, I managed to get dressed. She asked me to drop her at an all-night club where I later found out she went home with two other women. One of them, Carrie, was a regular at Geraldine's, and she told me the blow by blow. Turns out, the brunette was insatiable and needed sex like I need to breathe. Carrie said she couldn't walk for a week. I knew the feeling.

The backseat of my car was never the same either. Three different springs in that old couch in the back had unfurled and strained to poke through the fabric. No one could sit back there without getting hurt, and it cost me big bucks to get it fixed. But you know, it was okay. I didn't mind, really. I figured I got away easy.

DRIVEN TO DISTRACTION
EVA VANDETUIN

It's past midnight when my flight comes in, and I stumble off the plane exhausted, but with nerves buzzing excitedly. It's been months since I've seen her. Being that we live on opposite sides of the country, our hands are often tied by busy work schedules, or, more often, doomed short-term relationships that lack the spark we have when we're together.

I admit it. I am here to fuck. I am here for the bed frame–breaking, nail-gouging, screaming, sweating, thrashing, all-out debauchery that I never get at home. This would be uncomplicated if we didn't love each other too, and if we weren't so devoted to our separate careers that neither of us is yet willing to move. And so I am here again, smelling like airplane under my perfume, dragging my roller bag behind me through the mostly deserted airport.

She's standing by the baggage carousel, turned away from me but instantly recognizable from her broad shoulders and the explosion of dark, wild curls barely contained in her ponytail. My stomach tingles in anticipation, not unpleasantly. Walking toward her, I wonder if I'll be able to sneak up on her. Her smell is already in my nostrils, earthy and oddly intoxicating.

One of the ironies of our highly physical relationship is that she's such a perfect gentleman. We met while I was in town for a conference and made a date for a local pub, where I, as the poster child for lightweights, managed to get staggeringly drunk on two beers. She walked me back to my hotel and I invited her up, not prepared to get naked but not wanting the evening to end. Maybe I was tipsy, and maybe I just had her read right: we talked, she gave me a foot rub, kissed me on the cheek, and went home.

After that I could hardly wait to fuck her. And after I had, I just wanted to do it again.

Is it still an addiction if it's good for you?

A year later we're still on opposite coasts, working jobs we love, trying and discarding girlfriends that leave us both dissatisfied. And so here I am, my eyes fixed intently on the back of her head, my lower lip between my teeth, coming closer, closer to coming.

I'm still a few yards away when, as if she felt my eyes boring into her, she spins around and returns my look. As I close the distance between us, she opens the laptop she's holding. A cheerful graphic of fireworks and brightly colored text lights the screen. "Marianne"— she taps a key—"you were missed."

She looks at me, half smiling, her eyes intense, but almost shy. "Geek," I mutter inappropriately, and my voice comes out breathy with lust. Her smile broadens as I slide my fingers into her hair and lean in to kiss her.

She keeps her lips closed and chuckles when I squawk with frustration. "All in good time, my dear," she says, taking my bag and offering her arm. Her half-rimmed glasses have slipped down to the end of her blunt nose, and she shoots me a look full of wry and mildly wicked humor. I know that look. She intends to tease me mercilessly. I want to kill her. No, I want to throw her onto the cheap airport carpet and tear off her clothes. Then she'll regret this "all in good time" nonsense.

Instead, I allow her to lead me to the parking garage, docilely enough, I suppose. She asks after my cat and my mother and my best friend who just got married, and I answer, my eyes still drilling into her head as she loads my bag into the trunk and opens the passenger door of her car. I get in and tuck my skirt in behind me, and a moment later she swings into the driver's seat. She adjusts the rearview mirror and I lean closer to her. Our eyes meet in the reflection. Putting my hand on her thigh, I caress her through the fabric. "Come on, Robbie, baby," I purr, and turn to look at her directly. The scent of her body mixes with the hint of jasmine perfume I splashed on in the airplane bathroom; out of the corner of my eye I can see her smooth hand resting on the wheel, and the memory of what those fingers have done to me makes me long to rock back and forth in my seat. My cunt swells comfortably against the cushion. I reach for her and maneuver her hand under my skirt. "It's a long drive home, honey. C'mon. No one will see."

She's absolutely getting wet, I know it, but she's restraining herself. Robyn takes her hand away from me and caresses one of my small breasts, squeezing the nipple. I moan, and she chuckles, maddeningly. I give her an accusatory look. "Robyyyyn—" I start, and she puts her fingers to my mouth.

"Shh. It'll be more comfortable at home. You can wait." The corners of her eyes crinkle when she smiles. I vow silently that she'll be walking funny tomorrow. She's older than me and I can outlast her. No mercy. None.

We pull out of the parking garage and get on the road, heading away from the city. The roads are almost deserted at this time of night, and through the car's sunroof I can see the faint twinkling of the stars, muted by the bright face of the waxing moon. Robyn flips on the radio and turns it down low, and the faint sound of jazz saxophone floats from the speakers as she coaxes small talk from me. I can't help it; she makes me laugh.

After about fifteen minutes there's a lull in the conversation and I sit back silently, watching her drive. Outside, the dim outlines of trees whip by; a car passes us on the opposite side of the road, and the thick silver rings on Robyn's fingers glimmer suddenly in the momentary flash of headlights. She takes a sip of coffee from a travel mug, and I watch the movement of her mouth, the swell of her throat as she swallows.

I hate waiting. And suddenly I have a lovely, terrible, wicked idea.

I settle myself back in my seat and slide down, letting my legs fall open as I gaze casually out the window. Moving slowly so as not to attract her attention, I work my hand under my skirt and into my panties. The hard nub of my clit is pushed out to meet my fingertips. I dip a finger into myself and spread the moisture over my clit as I begin to rub in slow, rhythmic circles. My head falls sideways, my temple resting against the coolness of the car window. One, two, three, four. Little currents of pleasure shudder down my thighs, up the small of my back, and I suppress a moan, breathing more quickly, waiting for her to notice.

"Annie, you asleep, honey?" she asks after a minute. I don't answer but watch her from under lowered lids. The smell of my cunt is noticeable now, and I see her nostrils flare. I hold back a giggle. She's glancing over at me but still trying to keep her eyes on the road. I thrust into my cunt, letting out a telltale squelch and a choked sound of pleasure. Oh yes. Now I can see the whites of her eyes. "Baby, I'm *driving* here."

"Yes, I can see that." Smirking, I flick my clit faster and writhe a little in the seat, sighing and then catching my breath with a gasp. Her hands tighten on the wheel. "Don't worry, we'll be there soon. You can wait." Robyn groans and chews her lower lip in frustration. "Oooh, I'm *so* wet tonight. My cunt's been aching and aching, I had to give it a little attention. And it's so lovely and warm." Smiling at Robyn, who is still watching me out of the corner of her eye, I put a finger in my mouth and deliberately suck off my juices with a satisfied slurp. Then I brace a knee against the dashboard and start to fuck myself methodically, fingers plunging in and out of my cunt with a sucking sound. The radio has changed over to some kind of electronic dance music, and I moan softly to the beat, arching my back against the seat as my pleasure builds.

Robyn is sweating. I can see beads of moisture forming at her hairline, though the air in the car is cool. Her fingers flex on the wheel as she accelerates, five miles per hour over the speed limit, then ten. I laugh in my throat, pulling my shirt up over my breast to fondle one nipple as the car hugs a tight curve. Robyn mumbles what sounds like imprecations under her breath. Fifteen miles per hour. "Don't you dare come," she says, pinning me with her eyes for a split second before looking back at the road. This time I laugh outright, delighted with my own naughtiness, as we speed down the final stretch of road toward Robyn's house.

She reaches for the garage door opener before the house is even in sight. The car slides into the garage as the door is still going up, and she brakes neatly, just at the edge of safety. The headlights flick off before the car has even rocked to a complete stop. In the darkness, she says, "Oh...you...little..."

And then she's on me, ignoring the cramped space of the car, the parking brake digging into her thigh as she pins me to the seat with my still-buckled seat belt and knocks my hands away from my body.

Robyn's mouth is hard and demanding on mine; her tongue thrusts into my mouth as she inhales, taking my breath, then filling my lungs with hers.

No longer laughing now, I shut my eyes and let her take over, giving myself to the darkness and to Robyn and the jumble of sensations contained by the awkward space. The seat belt releases with a click and then her hands are rough on my thighs, pulling me toward her across the middle of the car. Fingers pinch my nipples hard, and I feel her hand on my shoulder, pressing me back against the car door, my head propped against the window. Under my skirt, she finds my cotton panties pushed halfway down and rips them away. A groan of pleasure escapes me as I reach over my head to grip the discarded seat belt. I know I'll need to hold on when she—

—pushes her hand into me suddenly and hard, and there's a bit of pain to it but I'm so wet and ready that pain is just a welcome spice. Is that two fingers, three? She tosses my skirt back and kisses my exposed belly, and I feel a finger plunge into my anus. Shuddering with the abrupt sensation of fullness, I cry out and buck against her hand. Her thumb claims my clit and I thrash helplessly in the uncomfortable car, in an impossible position, with my neck shoved miserably against the car door as her hand penetrates me expertly and her low voice rasps as she tells me, "Marianne, come!" A roaring starts in my belly and rushes out through my limbs, exploding out my feet and hands and the top of my head, and from far away I hear myself scream, the sound weirdly muffled by the upholstered interior. I come, and I come, and I come.

I feel Robyn caress me, and as her hand withdraws I notice my cramped neck and reach up to find the door handle. The car door clicks open. I slide the rest of the way down in the seat, my head hanging over the edge and out the door. Out of my line of sight, Robyn opens the inner door of the garage and flicks on the kitchen light. Water runs in the sink. I breathe.

A few minutes later, she returns and helps me from the car, her arm resting warmly around my waist as I make my trembling way to the living room. She guides me to the couch, then turns and gives me such a serious look that I'm afraid for a moment that I've actually upset her, but she pulls me against her and I can feel that she's packing. I tilt my pelvis and rub against her cock gently, pressing it into her clit, and she moans.

"Am I wicked?" I ask her in my sweetest voice as I unzip her fly.

"Oh, God, yes," she says, and takes me by the shoulders, forcing me face down over the arm of the sofa. I rest my cheek against the smooth leather of the cushions and smile as she yanks my skirt from my body and pushes the thick head of her cock against the lips of my cunt.

"Good," I tell the cushions smugly. "Because I won't ever change."

Night Train
Stacia Seaman

"leeping car, berths seventeen and eighteen. Have a pleasant
"journey," the conductor said in her earthy Polish accent. She
smiled and tipped her hat and the door clicked shut. Sarah and I turned
to each other, grinning like idiots as the train pulled out of Prague's
Hlavní Station. We were on our way to Warsaw.

We'd eaten at the little Indonesian place on the way to the train
station, and now we split a beer and sat on the low seat, looking out the
window at the fading lights of the city.

Our sleeping compartment was designed for three people: three
bunks along one wall, a small bathroom opposite, and a tiny sofa
beneath the window. So far we'd been lucky that we had the room
to ourselves, as we didn't particularly want to share. Of course, we
could have avoided the whole issue by paying another five bucks each
for a first-class double, but we were both money-conscious students
and, as Sarah pointed out, who the hell went to Poland in late October
anyway?

"Those bunks look pretty solid," I said, looking around the small
compartment.

"Yeah, they do," Sarah replied, handing back the bottle and
snuggling close.

An hour later, the second beer was half gone. We turned off the
compartment light; we were well north of the city and even through
the clouds the moon and stars shone bright. Snow was beginning to
accumulate on the fields and on the barn roofs.

"I never thought I'd be happy to see snow in October," I said,
Sarah's arm warm on my shoulder.

"But you're right, it's so," her voice trailed off for a moment,
"rural. Pastoral."

"It still throws me when I see a horse pulling a plow," I said. "I'm used to big old green John Deeres."

We both laughed for a moment, then finished our drinks and got ready for bed.

"It's nice to have our own bathroom," Sarah said, rubbing a white towel over the damp skin of her face and neck. "And not have to worry about bringing our own sheets," she added, slipping into the already turned-down lower bunk. "Unheard-of luxury."

I got into the bunk with her, pulling her tight against my body. "I think this might be a bit wider than the dorm beds." My lips traced a path on her neck.

"You think so?" Her hand wandered down the curve of my hip.

"Definitely."

"Did you lock the door?"

I slid a hand into her flannel pajama bottoms and teased the skin at her waist. "Can't."

"What?" She pulled back from me. "Why not?"

"No locks," I said.

"But what if—"

"Stop worrying." I kissed her softly. "Nobody's going to come in, and if they do, it's too dark to see us anyway."

"I don't know," she said.

"Think of it as an adventure."

Sarah rolled her eyes. I had always been the more impetuous one, though I appreciated her pragmatism, which had kept me out of trouble more than once. In fact, it was why we were on our way to Warsaw instead of Transylvania for Halloween weekend—she'd convinced me that no, two years after the fall of Ceausescu's communist regime, the wilderness of western Romania was not yet a tourist mecca.

I kissed her again, knowing she'd probably turn me down because of the unlocked door but wanting to see how far she was willing to go. I traced her lower lip with my tongue and when she opened her mouth, I slipped my tongue in, then pulled it back, making her come after me.

She whimpered, putting her arms around my neck. "If you're sure..."

"I'm sure," I said, trying not to sound surprised. "Now come here and kiss me."

She obliged, tentatively at first, then with more enthusiasm. Our mouths moved against each other, sometimes gentle, sometimes hungry, our tongues teasing and retreating, then teasing again.

Sarah rolled onto her back, pulling me on top of her.

Thump!

"Ow."

"You okay?"

"Yeah. Thought that bunk was a little higher, is all."

"Mmm." Sarah rubbed the back of my head. "Poor baby."

"I'm not sure this is going to work here," I said, disappointed, as I rolled over onto my side with my back pressed against the wall. I hadn't assumed that anything would happen between us tonight, but something had—it wasn't much, I know, but now I wanted more.

Sarah moved into my arms. "Maybe we should just try to get some sleep."

"Don't feel like sleeping." I meant it. I'd never be able to sleep, not with Sarah so near and so warm, her body pressed against mine in this tiny space, not after those kisses. I traced a finger lightly along her upper arm before moving under her shirt and caressing her stomach. "Do you?" I dipped a finger into the waistband of her pajama bottoms.

"No, I don't," she said, and I pushed her onto her back intending to kiss her, and this time slammed one foot into the wall at the foot of the bed.

"Okay, this isn't going to work," I said, lying on top of her, stroking her long, silky hair with my right hand. "Why don't we just move onto the sofa instead?"

"That sofa?" Sarah asked doubtfully. "It's, like, four feet long."

"We can work around that." I pushed her hair away and kissed her neck, inhaling her bedtime scent—the soap and the Nivea cream she used every night.

"And if anyone opens the door?"

"Nobody's going to open the door." The faintest remnant of her perfume lingered at her pulse point. Sarah had the sexiest clavicles I'd ever seen, just barely visible under her skin. "Stop worrying."

I moved up again, into a soft, gentle play of lips—the kind of kiss that makes me melt—enjoying the feeling of her hands in my hair, on my shoulders, on my back. I could feel the pressure build between my legs, and suddenly kissing wasn't enough anymore. Mindful of the small space, I maneuvered my way to the bottom of the bunk and curled up by Sarah's feet.

"Take off your top," I said.

She did, revealing small, perfect breasts. My mouth was suddenly dry.

"Touch them," I said. "Play with them for me."

She hesitated at first, but whether she was being coy or shy—the door was unlocked, after all—I couldn't tell.

"Please," I said, hoping she wasn't going to think better of this, and ran one hand up her left calf.

She cupped her breasts in both hands and squeezed them. My breathing grew ragged as she rolled her nipples between her fingers, then tugged at them. Her eyes fluttered shut; her hips began to rise and fall in rhythm with the movement of her hands.

I moved forward and kissed the skin of Sarah's stomach, then gently peeled the flannel pajamas from her body. The bunk was warm—very warm—and the scent of Sarah's arousal lingered in the air.

"God, baby," I said. "You smell so good."

I rested my cheek on her thigh, enjoying her scent, and slipped one finger into her silky heat.

"Am I wet?"

"God, yes." I stroked her again before dipping inside her. "So wet." I pressed one finger, then two, into the slick heat. "So good."

I turned my head so that I could taste her. Almost immediately her clit pulsed and she tightened around my fingers. "So close already?" I murmured.

"Please," she said, draping her legs around my shoulders and squeezing them. "Don't stop."

My fingers moved in and out of her pussy as I flicked my tongue back and forth against her clit. She was unbelievably hot and wet, and she came all too quickly, her muscles pulsing around my fingers and her legs tight around my shoulders. I stayed where I was, enjoying the aftershocks as her body calmed.

"Kiss me," Sarah said, and I moved up beside her. Her kisses were long and slow, and the arousal that had simmered in me all evening flared anew. Together we pulled off my sweats, and at the first touch of her fingers, my hips jerked forward.

Sarah moaned and pushed me down onto my back, and I closed my eyes as her mouth burned a trail down my neck and along my collarbone. I whimpered when she pulled away.

"Did you hear that?"

"I didn't hear anything," I said, but I tugged on my sweats anyway.

Sarah pulled up the bed sheet. "I thought I heard—"

There was a tap on the door, then the conductor poked her head into our compartment, backlit by the dim illumination in the corridor.

For a moment I froze. Had she heard us? Not that it mattered; all she had to do was look at us to know what was going on. Sarah's mouth was kiss-bruised, and I was certain my frustrated arousal was obvious. Oh God, what if she threw us off the train?

I moved closer to the door, blocking the shaft of light that fell directly onto the bunk—and Sarah.

"Tickets, please," the conductor said, a hint of amusement in her voice and in her eyes.

"Oh. Right." I rummaged around in Sarah's backpack, then produced the tickets. "Here you go."

The conductor punched the tickets, then handed them back to me. "Sorry to have...disturbed you," she said. "*Dobranoc*. Enjoy the rest of your evening."

My legs almost buckled when the door closed, and I couldn't help laughing.

"It's not funny," Sarah said. "If I hadn't heard something—"

"But you did," I said. "And it's fine. She didn't see anything."

"Easy for you to say," she groused. "You're dressed."

"So I am." I quickly undressed and slipped back into the bunk. "Now, where were we?"

"Oh no," she said. "There's no way."

"Come on. She's already taken the tickets, she's not going to come in again. And nobody's going to get on a train this late. We've got the compartment to ourselves."

I pressed up against her, her breasts just below mine, barely able to resist the urge to grind myself to orgasm against her thigh.

"Really, baby, I can't," she said with a sigh. "Let's just try to get some sleep." She turned on her side and I curled up behind her.

I tried to go to sleep, but it just wasn't possible. The memory of Sarah's scent, of her taste, was too fresh. Not wanting to keep her awake, I slid out from under her warm body, pulled her pajama top on, and sat down on the seat, looking out the window. The countryside was absolutely still. I half expected the moonlight to reflect off the snowy fields, but they were eerily dark.

Unfortunately, my attempt at distracting myself failed. The rhythmic sound of the train, combined with the swaying motion as we glided along the tracks, was a counterpoint to my arousal. My clit was so hard it almost hurt. I had to do something to relieve the tension. I shifted slightly and pressed my thighs together.

"What you looking at?"

I jumped and turned around. Sarah stood in front of me, wearing my sweatshirt, her hair tumbled across her face.

"Just outside." I patted the seat next to me. "The contrast."

She sat, curling against my side. "In what way?"

"The cities are so urban, you know? The huge apartment blocks and factories right in the middle of town."

She nodded.

"And then you get out here, and it's like it's not even been touched."

"Come back to bed."

I leaned forward, tracing her cheekbones with my thumbs as I kissed her. "I don't think so," I said. "We have some unfinished business."

"But the conductor—"

I grabbed her hand and put it between my legs. "I don't care."

"Oh," she breathed. "Oh God."

I pulled off the pajama top, and immediately Sarah dropped to her knees in front of the sofa. Her mouth closed hot and wet on one nipple, and her fingers rolled the other one, tugging it until I felt the fire shooting straight to my clit.

"Please," I said. "Please." I was swollen with need, and it was all I could do not to press her hand against me until I came.

"Mmm." She stroked me once, then lifted her finger to her mouth and sucked it. "God, you taste good."

I grew still wetter as I watched her, and my clit throbbed. I wanted her inside me; I wanted—I needed—her mouth on me.

My head dropped back against the cushions when she opened me, and the first swirl of her tongue almost pushed me over the edge.

"Easy," she murmured. "I'm not going to let you come just yet."

She slid two fingers inside me, then pulled them out, slowly repeating the motion. My hips rose to meet each thrust, and my legs were spread impossibly wide.

"I love how open you are for me," Sarah said. "I love watching the way you move."

"Feels so good," I said. "I love when you fuck me."

I heard her sharp intake of breath, then felt her mouth on my thigh. She was taking her time, kissing my inner thighs, keeping up the gentle thrust of her hand.

"Wait," she said. "I think I hear—"

"It's nothing." Which was true, but even if there was someone in the corridor, I didn't care. There was no way I was letting her stop now. "I don't hear anything."

"But—"

"Please, baby, I need you."

I pushed my hips up against her, and her mouth closed on me again. I reached down for her free hand. My eyes closed as our fingers entwined. Her tongue was just where I liked it—above my clit, moving back and forth, hard and fast. I was so close—I opened my eyes and looked directly into the eyes of the conductor. She glanced down at Sarah, then back up at me—and I came, loud and hard, a series of waves that went on and on. When I opened my eyes again, the door was closed and Sarah was curled up on the sofa beside me.

"That was incredible," she said. "You were amazing."

Dumbly, I nodded, still a bit hazy and completely unsure of what had just happened. "Sleep," was all I managed to say.

The compartment had cooled down considerably and I pulled on my sweats before lying down on the bunk. Sarah had just snuggled up against me when there was a knock at the door.

"Passport control." The conductor, brisk and efficient, gave no sign that she'd opened the door minutes before. She stamped our passports and handed them back, then closed the door.

Now hopelessly confused—had I really just imagined it?—I drifted off to sleep.

We woke up late, then hurried to get ready, knowing we'd reach Warsaw in about half an hour. It was a crisp, cold day, the sunlight bright against a crystal blue sky. We stared out the window, silent, then closed the curtain and finished packing up our things. The train's whistle gave a shrill cry when we pulled into the station.

Sarah hadn't said anything about the conductor's presence in our room last night, and I certainly wasn't going to bring it up. I picked up my backpack and followed her out into the corridor.

As soon as the door opened, Sarah jumped down onto the platform. The conductor winked at me as she helped me step down. "Have a wonderful time in our lovely city," she said.

Box and One
Nell Stark

At the shrill of the whistle, I pulled up from my practice drive to the basket and popped a quick jump shot. *Swish*—a good omen. Heather snagged the ball with one hand and gave me a thumbs-up with another.

"Go time," I said. And then I took a deep breath, because I knew that when I turned around, I'd see Jordan Cassidy waiting for me at center court.

I had resisted the urge to look at her during our warm-up. Would her hair still be as long as it had been last semester? Would I spot a new tattoo peeking tantalizingly out from beneath her jersey? Would she still look at me the way she had four months ago?

I turned around. She stood next to the ref, palming the game ball and surveying the court as though she were its queen. Which made me the general of an invading force, sworn to defeat her even as I couldn't help but admire her greatness. And her beauty.

I jogged to the parley. My hands were clammy.

"Casey," she said. "Good to see you again." The grin that curved her lips told me that what she really meant was that it would be good to fuck me again, once all of this was over. I found myself wishing, as I had every time we'd played State since my freshman fall, that the ref and our teammates would just disappear.

"Likewise." I tried to outwardly keep my cool. Her sweat-slicked skin glimmered beneath the harsh neon lights. When I licked my lips, she laughed softly.

The ref was oblivious. "You ladies know the drill by now, yes?"

"Yes," I said, holding out my hand. Her palm was calloused and hot as it slid against mine.

She used her grip on my hand to pull me a little closer. "Same rules as always, I presume."

My fingers trembled against hers. I cleared my throat. "Works for me."

"Glad to hear it," she said, her teeth flashing. "Good luck."

"And you."

As I jogged back to the sidelines, I thought back to my first game against State freshman year. Jordan Cassidy had wreaked havoc on our defense during the first quarter of that game, until our captain had us switch to a box and one. She chose me as the one, telling me in no uncertain terms to stick to Jordan like glue and shut her down.

So I did. And by the end of the game, I was utterly, hopelessly in lust. I can still remember how the butterflies churned in my gut when she winked at me after the final whistle. I didn't care that despite my valiant efforts, we'd lost—I just wanted to feel her body pressing me into...anything. A bed, a wall, the backseat of a car—nothing mattered but *her*.

I must have been about as transparent as glass, because I got my wish later that night in her dorm room. And that was the beginning. Every semester since then, we've played a box and one against State. If we win, Jordan's in charge for the night...and if they win, I am.

It's a beautiful, beautiful system.

At our bench, Heather handed me a water bottle. I took a long swig, then adjusted my headband. "Same old, same old," I said. "I've got Jordan."

A few people snickered. Our center, Val, wolf-whistled. I rolled my eyes at them and stuck my tongue out at her. "Let's kick some ass, okay?"

"You sure it's kicking you want to do with her ass?" Val persisted.

I refused to rise to the bait. "For now," I said.

That earned me a laugh, and I bounced on my toes as that pre-game rush of adrenaline kicked in. It was finally time for the showdown—the last time I'd ever play State. The last time I'd ever face off on a court against Jordan Cassidy. I tried not to think about how it was also probably the last time I'd ever be in her bed. *Not now. Focus.*

I squared my shoulders. "All right, girls. Let's get out there."

❖

"One minute!" someone shouted from the sidelines. I resisted the urge to wipe my stinging eyes and focused warily on Jordan, who had just received the ball at the three-point line. This was the kind of moment every player lived for—a tied ball game with less than a minute to go.

Shut her down. The mantra beat inside my head in time with my racing pulse. *Shut her down.*

I watched her eyes. Dark blue, almost black—they were mesmerizing. But I resisted their hypnotic pull, drawing strength from the solid box of my teammates' zone behind me. *Shut her down.*

And then the air around me changed as someone rushed up to set a pick. I spun aside just as Jordan began her drive. Her perfect eyebrows arched in surprise when she found me still with her, and she pulled up sharply. A head fake. A pump fake. But I was still watching her eyes, and I could tell when she finally settled her attention on the basket.

The world slowed down as I jumped. Somehow, my fingertips grazed the ball just enough to interrupt its perfect arc—just enough to let Val step in and fiercely grab the rebound.

I sprinted across the court, ignoring the burn of the lactic acid in my quads. Jordan stuck with me, of course, so close to me that it was impossible to tell her ragged breathing from mine. I went down deep as Heather brought the ball across center court, then I darted back toward the top of the key.

Her pass was immaculate. I caught the ball in front of my body, then brought it down to shield it from Jordan's wily hands. My fingertips slid over the bumps of its surface, gently caressing its grooves. Taming it—lovingly bending it to my will. Making it one with me, an extension of my palm.

Left. I had to pivot left. She wouldn't expect that.

I faked right. I spun. Caught off guard, she jumped immediately— and I waited for her to fall. As I cradled the ball and bent my knees, I remembered what I was fighting for: the right to be beneath her, tonight. The right to surrender.

I jumped as her shoes hit the floor. The ball rolled off my fingertips, spinning unimpeded toward the hoop. Crescendo, decrescendo.

Swish.

A second later, the buzzer drowned out the cheers from our bench. Heather and Val sandwiched me, hugging me tightly and shouting in my ear. When I could get my arms free, I high-fived them triumphantly before making the hand-shaking rounds with our opposition.

Jordan and I saved each other for last, of course.

"Nice shot, Case," she said, pulling me into a hug. She caressed the taut muscles of my back, and I tightened inside at the sensuous promise of what was to come.

"It was a sweet game," I murmured against her shoulder. God, her body felt so good pressed up against mine—lean and soft and slick.

As we pulled apart, I watched a smug grin curve her lips. I shivered. She noticed, and the grin grew wider.

"Better put a sweatshirt on, champ. And once you've showered, meet me outside the gym."

"Okay," I said, loving to obey her. "See you soon."

She looked me up and down and I watched those dark eyes go hazy. She hummed deep in the back of her throat. "Yes. Hurry."

❖

I showered in record time, then dressed in khakis, a white oxford shirt, and loafers. I left two buttons of the shirt undone to show a little cleavage—and to make it easier for Jordan to take off. When I stepped into the cool, early spring air, I saw her slouching against the wall, both hands jammed in the pockets of her well-worn leather jacket. Her dark hair curled around the collar in damp waves.

"Hi," I said.

"Hey. You look nice."

I was about to echo her when I realized that *nice* was a completely inappropriate adjective. "And you look dangerous."

She laughed and sauntered toward me. "Just the way you like me?"

It was my turn to hum. Unfortunately, before I could elaborate, several of her teammates exited the gym.

"Yo, Jordan, you guys coming to Ronnie's?"

Jordan looked me over again. She didn't turn back to face her girls. "Don't think we'll make it this time," she said. "Have fun, though."

I was mildly surprised. Ronnie's was the local pizza place and a favorite post-game hangout. Usually, we made a token appearance there before retreating to Jordan's apartment...but tonight, apparently, she had other ideas.

Once the others had moved away, she stepped closer to me. "If you're starving, we can stop by," she murmured. "But to be honest, I don't want to share you with anybody tonight."

My throat went dry at her possessive words. "You're in charge," I said hoarsely.

"Damn right I am." She took my hand and tugged. "Let's get out of here."

We didn't speak as we walked. Jordan drew circles with her thumb on the back of my hand, and with every stroke, I felt myself become wetter, more swollen. She was previewing how she'd touch me, and I knew it.

When we finally reached her apartment, she led me straight to the bedroom—then shut the door and pressed me up against it. I groaned softly and rested my head against the wood as her hands found my breasts. She kneaded them firmly through my shirt.

"I love how you dress," she said. Her voice was harsh and ragged as she unveiled the force of her desire. "So proper and preppy—you fool everyone. But I know what you're like when you're naked with me...wild, so fucking responsive...I know."

And then she slid one thigh between my legs and kissed me, hard. Her tongue slid past my teeth, thrusting in time with each squeeze of her hands. She pinched my nipples through the fabric and I cried out against her mouth.

My knees buckled when she brought her lips to my ear and sucked my sensitive lobe. "I'm going to fuck you," she whispered, her breath hot and moist. "Gonna fuck you as hard as you played today."

"Please—" I gasped, then moaned as she sucked briefly at the skin just below my jawline.

She unfastened my buttons, then roughly pulled the shirt over my shoulders. While she undid my belt buckle and pushed my pants down my hips, I struggled with my bra. Somehow, I managed to kick off my shoes and keep my balance as she pulled my slacks over each foot.

Now on one knee before me, Jordan traced the swollen ridge of my clitoris through my underwear with one fingertip. I wavered on my feet.

"Mmm," she said, pressing a little lower. "Wet already—I can feel it."

"For you," I managed to gasp.

Breathing heavily, she got to her feet and fumbled with her own belt. Her fingers were trembling, and I felt my body grow even heavier with desire. God, I loved that I could affect her so strongly.

"Take those off," she told me as she began to unbutton her jeans. "Take them off and get on the bed on your hands and knees."

I swallowed audibly as I pushed the thin cotton down my legs. Unsteadily, I walked toward her bed and climbed on top of it. I hesitated. Her demand was so...wanton, somehow...and for a moment, I wasn't sure I could do what she'd asked. But this was Jordan—Jordan, who saw me for who I really was. Jordan, who had been the first woman to show me what my body could do. I trusted her, and I wanted her so damn badly.

I got on my hands and knees, facing the headboard, and then I spread my legs as wide as I could, presenting myself to her. *See me. Take me. I'm yours tonight.*

"Fuck, Casey...you are so fucking gorgeous, you know that?"

I concentrated on breathing deeply as I listened to her rummage around in a drawer. And then the bed dipped with her weight, and I trembled in anticipation of her touch.

She knelt beside me and put one hand on the back of my neck, massaging lightly. She reached under me to tease my breasts with her other hand. I groaned as she slowly tugged and twisted my nipples.

"I'm gonna bring you up so high," she murmured. "Bring you up so high and keep you there so long before I let you go..."

I groaned, my hips thrusting helplessly against the empty air. She traced a path down my back as she continued her teasing strokes, then finally slid her hand beneath me. My hips jolted when I felt her playing with the fine hairs at the apex of my thighs.

"Please," I whispered harshly. "T-touch me, please."

But she held off for several more minutes, tickling and stroking my belly, touching me everywhere except where I needed her most. And then, when I was almost sobbing in frustration, she slid her thumb into me and lightly circled my clit with one finger.

"Fuck," I groaned, already so very, very close. She stilled her hand, then moved away from my clit and slowly worked two fingers into me, inch by inch. I shivered and clenched hard around her knuckles.

"Relax," she said softly. "Just relax. I'm not going to let you come yet—no tightening up. Be open for me. God, Case, I'm going to make you feel so good—I promise. You're exquisite."

I wanted to laugh hysterically at the idea that I could relax while she was buried inside me, but I did my best to do as she asked. My head hung down between my braced hands and my arms shivered even as I focused on breathing deeply.

"Yeah, baby, that's it," she crooned. "Good, very good." She thrust into me gently, curling her fingers up on every stroke, moving her other hand to the small of my back to steady me.

And then she pulled out of me—slowly—but even so, I cried out at the loss.

"Shh, Casey. It's okay—I got you." She moved an object into my field of vision and I struggled to focus on it. Silvery, long, textured. A dildo. "I'm going to fuck you with this now. Gonna get it all lubed up and then slide it into you and make you come."

I felt myself get wetter at her words and tossed my head, suddenly frantic to feel her guide the toy inside of me. "P-please," I groaned. "Oh God, please..."

A moment later, she touched the cool, slippery head to my clit, rubbing it against me in firm circles. My hips jerked and I gasped low in my throat—just a few more seconds like that and I would come, so hard...but she could tell, and so she moved it away.

"No, please!"

"Am I keeping my promise?" she said, just before teasing at my opening. I shifted my hips, aching inside, wanting nothing more than to take what she was offering.

"Fuck, yes....do it—"

I pressed my forehead into the blanket as she slowly and deliberately pushed the dildo into me, as the gentle pressure of her thrust gradually opened my body. When the toy was all the way inside me, she rocked it in and out just a little. I groaned.

"This is so sexy," she whispered. "I love taking you this way." And then she twisted it inside me—first back and forth, then spinning it in a gradual circle. The sensation of the ridges brushing against my inner walls felt incredible, but I couldn't come without her fingers on my clit, and I needed to, so badly.

"Fuck oh fuck gotta come please touch me *please*—"

She held off for a few more seconds before finally taking pity on me and reaching around my body. She leaned against my back as her fingertips worked their magic, massaging my clitoris insistently even as she spun and thrust the dildo inside me.

"Coming—" I managed to choke out before the white-hot waves

of ecstasy engulfed me, before my arms gave out and I slumped forward onto the bed, bucking and shivering, dying and being reborn.

A long time later, she rubbed my back as she slowly worked the toy out of me. And then she lay down and pulled me into her embrace, and I snuggled up against her until my strength returned.

"Amazing," I said, shifting in her embrace to meet her gaze. "You're...you're incredible, and you know it."

She flashed me a smile that was half smug and half wondering. *Adorable.* I moved again until I was lying on top of her, my stomach and breasts pressed to hers. And then I kissed her chin, just because I could.

"So," she said, smoothing my hair with one hand and tracing the length of my spine with the other. "Senior spring, huh? What are you doing next year?"

I didn't answer right away, because I was too busy kissing her neck. Besides, I didn't want to think about the fact that next fall, there wouldn't be a game against State to look forward to. That next fall, she'd be out of my life. But finally, I lifted my head long enough to say, "Grad school. Boston. You?"

She laughed softly. "Art school. Also Boston."

I raised my head to look at her, unable to suppress what I knew had to be a goofy smile. "Really? That is very, very cool."

"Really. And, um, I agree." She looked away and cleared her throat. "So...uh...d'you have a roommate yet?" The question came out in a rush. "Because I'm still looking and I was thinking all of a sudden that maybe—"

I cut off her babble by lunging forward to kiss her. And once I was sure she wouldn't be able to form words for the next several minutes, I kissed my way down her body until my shoulders were pressing her thighs apart.

"This means yes," I whispered, just before leaning in to taste her.

DAISY'S CHAIN
JD GLASS

Act I

D ammit, Annie! You're so...so..."

"What?" she asked, hands on her hips as she stood by the door of the hotel room. "So damned what?"

I stared at eyes that glared glacially back at me, a snap of crystal flame that made me wonder, and not for the first time, if she knew how soul-appropriate the sword charm she wore around her neck was. "*American*," I said finally. "So fucking stubborn!"

"Well, I don't care—I'm not going," she said. "I absolutely refuse. I've got a sound check—I'll see you at the club." She whirled and slammed out of our room. The rattling door echoed in the sudden silence.

Shit. That was *not* how I'd intended to spend the little time we had before tonight's gig at La Rocca Ballroom. I knew how nervous Ann was, making her debut singing lead on more than a few songs on the new Loose Dogs album. It was rough luck that the debut performance was Belgium instead of London, where she would have been much more comfortable. And worse, the club the label had selected was known for playing recorded music, not live bands, which meant double the pressure to win over the crowd. But the rottenest cut of all was that Ann, with that quick and clever mind of hers that I found so sexy, knew, without anyone saying a word, why the tour was starting in Belgium instead of London or Berlin where the band had tremendous followings: it wouldn't damage their reputation if the album bombed. Not that it would, or should—the music was good, and Ann was phenomenal— but still, the undeniable pressure was there.

"The only good things in Belgium besides the people are the

chocolate and the beer—and I don't even *like* beer," she'd said during a fit of nerves on the flight over.

But fuck all and fuck it twice, she should have been here with me for the next hour or so, balanced on the tip of my tongue, buried inside my cunt, letting me ease the tension I hadn't had the opportunity to soothe over the last week during the prep for the tour, a tour that would last three months. There were other pressures, too, but we didn't need to discuss those.

But we really had to discuss the trip I was set to take after—Rude Records wanted firsthand information on what was happening Stateside, wanted to bring bands there, wanted to scoop and sign new talent. I wasn't just tour manager, I was also A&R—artists and repertoire—and part of my job was doing exactly that: discovering and signing new blood.

It would have been perfectly fine for Ann to travel with me and she knew it too. The band would have time off, it was no secret that we'd lived together for the last few years, and as far as cost, well, the label had offered to pay her if she'd provide technical specs of the sound systems at the venues we'd investigate, but no, not Ann: she simply refused to return to the land that had birthed her. And…I knew quite well why, even if I suspected she might be wrong.

I ran the water for my shower as I mused. I should have dropped the topic when it came up, saved it for another day. Foolish on my part, because right now, all Ann should be focused on, *could* be focused on, was the show, this first show. She was an amazing performer, charismatically edgy, with razor-sharp sensuality, but if she came before a show, or even if she didn't…if she hit the stage that stimulated, she was positively deadly; she made the audience want to come with her. It was no small secret at the label as to why she was being not-so-subtly nudged to lead singer.

I was five years older, it was three years after "discovering" Loose Dogs in a pub in London and a bit more than two and a half since we'd started going together, living together, and I still wasn't immune to her, not since I'd caught that flash of her eye the first time I'd seen her onstage, then found her after to offer the band a contract, only to find myself a few hours later back in my flat and on the hot end of one of the most exquisitely wanton fucks I'd ever had. She might have been young, but she'd made up for what she didn't know with a libidinous creativity that left me amazed and breathless, and a complete mastery of the techniques she had in hand, so to speak.

She'd learned quite a bit more since then and we'd grown quite fond of each other in the interim, but we had only one real rule between us: share the girl or the story. Frankly, it didn't matter which end you were on with my Annie, it was always hot.

Poor Ann, I thought, stressed about the tour, stressed about my trip, and almost a week since either one of us could relieve that tension in the way that suited us best, which meant, of course, that neither one of us could be anything other than off-tempered.

I'd just have to make it up to her, I decided as I went through the luggage and selected my clothes for the evening, something in a shade of blue that would match Ann's electric eyes.

The local radio station had made a prize out of having listeners attend the sound check. There were bound to be a few girls there that would catch her eye, and most of them would be more than happy to… meet…their favorite female rock musician before she went onstage for the actual performance.

Maybe…we'd share her, maybe not. It would be nothing new or unusual since it was something we both enjoyed, but tonight? I'd leave it up to Ann. It made no difference to me how it went, because she'd be brilliant onstage, and after?

I stepped into the shower and shivered involuntarily, unable to discern whether it was the anticipation of what I knew to expect later or just the shock of the water as it hit my skin.

Either way, I knew it didn't matter—in the end, Ann would pour what she had into me.

When I hit the club less than an hour later, after the requisite small talk with the owner, a small-detail review with the promoter, and a checklist of personal requirements with the manager and technical ones with the sound and lighting techs to make sure everything was dead-on right, I looked up from my clipboard and found what I was looking for: stage left, a nice body decked out in typical underground style—tight, short, silver skirt and combat boots with a face that stared with rapt fascination at my Ann as she worked out the kinks in the sound. In less than thirty seconds I knew who she was: part of the tour, lead singer for the opening act, and a bass player as well, as opposed to the typical fan. The fact that she was out there, so clearly focused on Ann instead of backstage with her band… This would be extremely easy.

Add to it that she was a musician, and not a typical groupie? So much the better.

"Are you Marguerite?" I asked over her shoulder as she leaned against the column.

I couldn't help but smile as she whirled to answer.

"Yes, yes I am," she answered, and I was pleased to see the appreciation in her eyes as she took me in. Well, this *was* going to be fun.

"I'm Candace, Candace Neils, the tour manager for Rude Records, specifically for Loose Dogs," I informed her as I held out my hand. "Your band got added to the tour so quickly—have you met Ann yet?"

Act II

You know, it's the reason I got into rock and roll in the first place. Loose Dogs played my little suck-water town, and the next thing you know, every girl who liked girls and all the boys who liked them were forming up into bands, learning to fake it through the songs, that sort of thing. It was Ann, the bass player Ann R. Key, who fired my imagination: tough, cool, and she played a fuckin' low end that could get the crowd moving from one end of the hall to the other end of the country, and everybody knew it. There was no one, no one at all, who could touch her in terms of pure creativity and technique, though she inspired many to try.

I watched her run through the sound check, playing with the pre-show crowd that was there, courtesy of a local radio station promotion.

Tough and tight, that was how she looked and how she played too, a low-slung pair of laced-up leather pants and a sheer blouse that hung open almost to her navel, the only part of her skin that showed except for the occasional flash above her hip when she turned. Those flashes shone edibly.

I couldn't help but lick my lips every time I saw that; she was fucking hot—and this was just a rehearsal, a sound check, a "just getting those last touches right" thing.

But I had to get my head out of my crotch because I had my own stuff to take care of before the show, and I decided I needed two things: a bottle of water and a cold shower.

"Are you Marguerite?" a low and beautifully modulated voice asked right over my shoulder.

"Yes, yes I am," I answered, as I turned to face an incredible pair of tits. I raised my eyes to find a sexily curved smile, sharp cheekbones, and drop-dead-gorgeous green eyes.

"I'm Candace, Candace Neils, the tour manager," she informed me as we shook hands. Whatever else she said faded to hearing as well as memory when she asked, "Have you met Ann yet?"

I shook my head numbly as I tried not to stare quite so avidly at the woman before me. I recognized her from photos I'd seen in several articles about the band. General rumor said she was Ann's lover, though Ann refused to discuss her private life in interviews, while inside buzz said she was quite—well, it said enough. Just thinking about it made my mouth go dry.

Candace's eyes seemed to sparkle even brighter and she gave me what could only have been an amused smile. "She'll be done soon. Let's take you round to the dressing room to meet her then, shall we?"

I nodded as dumbly as I'd answered before when she gave me the barest hint of a wink and took my arm. From the tone of her voice and the lift to her lips to the way her fingers closed over mine, I knew this wouldn't be a simple hello: I'd just been chosen.

I don't know what kind of questions Candace asked as we walked to the dressing room—surely they were about my band and the tour, and I'm sure that I must have tried to thank her for this opportunity— but before I knew it, we were through the corridor and at the door. Candace let me in, told me Ann would be there shortly, to make myself comfortable, she'd personally come back and in plenty of time to get ready for curtain.

I barely had a moment to look around and to register that this dressing room was a fair bit bigger than the one I shared with my band before Ann stepped in, holding her bass in her left hand.

"Hi. Who are you?" she asked, her manner very direct as she carefully set her instrument down in a nearby stand.

"Marguerite. Candace said—"

"Candace, huh?" she interrupted and faced me, her expression shifting, flowing, from guarded friendliness to a sultry contemplation.

"You were standing stage left, by that pillar, yes?"

My mouth went dry as she closed in on me and I realized she'd seen me, seen me practically drooling over her.

"Did you enjoy the sound check?" she asked, her voice low, unmistakably sensual, her softened American accent making even the most meaningless of her words both strong and sensual.

I forgot why I was there, forgot I was in a band, forgot even my name as baby-soft lips kissed me and my heartbeat tripped over itself when her tongue skated over mine.

She was a phenomenal musician; she kissed even better.

When her hands reached for me I moved my own automatically and opened the laces to the pants that covered those amazing hips.

My nipples were aching hard under her palm, between her fingertips, and I slipped my hand into her pants. She wore nothing beneath them and that jumped my blood, made me go from hard to ready, ready for whatever would happen next.

"You kiss so beautifully," she murmured into my throat, leaving one of those hard points lonely cold as she caught my hand in hers and gently stopped me before I could really do anything but feel the heat of her cunt. "I'd love to feel your mouth on me," she added, then sucked gently on my fingertips.

Ann R. Key, bassist for Loose Dogs, and my own real live hero, had just asked me to go down on her. I shifted the light leather of her pants when I knelt to discover that Ann kept that pussy tightly trimmed, and as she leaned against the wall, I got my first real taste of rock stardom: sweet.

She was hard, just fucking rock hard, and she was hot, and wet, and I couldn't resist flicking the tip of my tongue into that tasty tight opening that yielded to me, then licking from that spot to her fat clit, only to start the delicious trip all over again.

The feel of that smooth cunt on my face, sliding against my mouth…it was getting me so hot, so fucking wet, I could *feel* it, and I shifted to relieve the ache in my throbbing clit, ready to take matters into my own hands.

Either she watched, or she guessed. "Don't touch it, baby," she groaned as I applied the flat of my tongue to the underside of her hard-on. "I promise I'll take care of you—God…" The word scraped from her throat as her head snapped back against the wall.

I gave her slit one last long taste and glanced up at her. Those beautiful blue eyes had closed and when my lips pushed back the hood that hid her hard-on, I sucked it in.

"Just…like…that…"

Act III

I thought of a girl, *the* girl, three thousand miles and six feet away. I closed my eyes as the girl with me—the one between my legs—mouthed me, intermittently flicking her tongue into my hungry cunt. "Yeah…that's nice." I drifted three thousand miles away, to a shore that looked on this one.

I needed relief, quick, fucking relief, while my head rested against the wall of the dressing room and my mind drifted across an ocean. Just as her kiss had promised, she did nice work with her tongue.

"Just suck me, baby," I told her.

She might have nodded before she did, it didn't matter because she closed her lips tightly around my swollen clit; she sucked me nice and hard, she licked me good and slow.

"Yeah…" I groaned, fucking her face, "that's it, now."

I threaded my fingertips through hair the same color as *hers*, close enough to remember texture, close enough to bring me back to the beach and an almost-kiss I should have never missed.

It might have been too long ago, too far away, and way too damn late, but I remembered it vividly, the one that happened months later, and for a moment, it was my mouth on *her*, the wished-for feel of her riding me, sweet and wet, beautiful and *mine*, on my lips, that most intimate kiss, a kiss I wanted desperately to return.

"You got me, shit…that…ah shit yeah…" I choked out as she found the right rhythm, the sweet spot on my clit that brought me out of my head.

My fingers convulsed in her hair as my clit throbbed like it would explode and I could feel her jaw, her chin, pressed tight against my cunt, working me beautifully, bringing me off.

"Oh yeah, that's good, really good," I encouraged, as her tongue played a slick and steady beat against the hard-on I'd been carrying for what had been too long, and I was dying to come while wishing I wouldn't before the dream ended, three thousand miles of long ago and far away, where it was me and *her* like I knew it would be, like it should have been, soft skin and warm sighs, a melt into the warmth of her depths, into mine, her light and my dark, and her cunt clasped around me…

"Fuck!" I spat between clenched teeth, the final surge of blood fattening my clit when she sucked harder, and for a moment, *she* filled my cunt, was a scream through my blood, in my heart, a heart that didn't understand the realness of dirt the way my head did and then I was coming, coming sudden and hard on her face as her lower lip dragged against my dripping cunt.

I opened my eyes to the room and leaned my spinning head back hard against the wall as I gently stroked the temples of the head between my thighs and caught my breath. I was in a backstage dressing room in Belgium, with a girl who needed to come kneeling with her face against my cunt right before I had to get onstage.

Finally, I looked down at her, only to see her staring up at me, an uncertainty in her eyes as she chewed her lips, lips that had just done such very good work.

I was going to have to remember to thank Candace for sending this girl to my dressing room when we saw each other later; we'd quarreled earlier because she told me she had to go to the States, do some research for the label we worked for, and I had flatly refused to go with her. I wouldn't go back, I had no reason to, and she knew damn well why. But there was no need to think about that now, I thought as I smiled at what was very obviously Candace's apology with my come on her chin.

"That was really fucking nice," I said softly. I cupped her chin in my hand, slick under my fingertips from my cunt, slick from my come. "C'mere. Marguerite, right?"

I gently pulled her up to me until she stood between my legs, the laces of my pants still loose and wide and hanging as I kissed her, kissed my come off her chin, licked the taste of my cunt on her tongue. I reached around her, a firm grasp on her hips, before I let my hands wander, up silky-smooth muscles, under Lycra and rayon and shiny, shiny silver.

The tiny bit of whatever she wore under that short little skirt might as well have not existed as my fingers eased unimpeded past it and along her creamy slick folds to squeeze her clit between them. I gripped her ass and pulled her closer to me with my other hand.

"Ooh…yeah," she said, a warm rush of air against my throat before she licked it. "But…oh…everyone calls me Daisy."

"You're with the opening band?" I asked, the name kicking something off in the back of my head as I played my fingers in the rich heat of her cunt. She was so slick and swollen; those pretty pussy lips had parted and her hips lightly pumped her clit between my fingers.

"Uh-huh," she sighed in agreement to the question, to my hands about to fuck her, my thumb on her hard little clit, fingers coaxing, teasing, a little dip into her hot hole, not so tight now, and definitely ready. She leaned heavily against me and widened her stance between my thighs. "I sing," she breathed out against my throat.

Huh. I laughed to myself. I'd thought she was another groupie or a fan, let in during sound check by the radio promoters as a prize or something. Instead, she was the lead singer for our opening band. Very, very, nice prize; it was rare for bands to intermingle on this level—it was all partners or groupies, true love or true lust. I'd really have to thank Candace for stroking my ego so nicely.

"Fucking gorgeous," I growled, then nipped lightly at her ear as I thrust my fingers into her waiting cunt—it had waited long enough and eagerly drew me in.

She gasped softly and pushed her face into my neck. I thumbed her clit and reached with my other hand farther around her ass to spread her hungry pussy a little more. Marguerite was so fucking wet, and as I spread her hole just a bit more, I knew what I wanted to do.

"You're gonna like this," I promised, and she shuddered against me as I filled her cunt from both sides, alternating my rhythm.

"That's…that's so…fuck!" she groaned into my ear.

"It is," I agreed. Her back arched slightly as she took me in deeper and in reflex surged forward, not knowing which way to move as I bounced her cunt across my fingers. "Knew you'd like that," I murmured.

"Fucking good," she agreed, rubbing her cheek against my neck.

"Lean into me." I could feel the tension in her body as she rested her weight against my chest. I was *so* fucking hard again, but it was good, I was back in the here and now, deep inside Marguerite's cunt and loving it, the heat, the soft, slipping grip on my hands as her fingertips dug into my biceps. I rested my face against her hair.

"Thirty minutes to curtain."

I glanced up to see glittering green eyes.

"Plenty of time," I smirked at her as she approached. There was no way I was going to stop what I was doing—Marguerite's pussy felt too good in my hands, the low sounds she made, the breath against my neck that fanned down my chest, across my breasts, tightening my nipples, bringing my blood where I wanted it to go.

My smirk widened. I could tell from the appreciative expression on her face that Candace knew exactly...

Marguerite stirred in my arms and I pulled her closer. "Shh...stay, baby, you're fine..." I assured her, and I worked her cunt harder to prove it. She gave a short, sharp, little cry as her cunt opened beautifully, and I was that much deeper inside her.

Candace came closer, then kissed me over Marguerite's shoulder, fucking my mouth with hers when she recognized the taste on my tongue. Her hands had traveled along my forearms, until they came to rest, one over my knuckles where they disappeared into Marguerite's steaming cunt from behind, the other holding me firmly inside her.

"You remember Candace, don't you?"

Marguerite lifted fuck-heavy eyes to mine and nodded. What pretty eyes she had, blue and gold, I noted briefly.

"Hey, love," Candace whispered behind her. She grinned at me and I knew what she was going to do even before she bit down, then trailed her lips along Marguerite's neck: we'd done this before, and we drove her crazy, a pattern of touches and teases meant to torment, distract, take her to the very fucking edge and over it, cunt squeezing and screaming.

Marguerite's body trembled between us, the anticipation sending a fresh flood of hot silk down my hand. "You can take it, baby," I murmured, then kissed her neck.

Candace's fingers slowly inched over mine as I gently withdrew from behind Marguerite, slid them from that hot little space, slid the others just enough to have those new fingers meet and twine with mine, pad to pad.

I brought my free hand to Candace's cheek and she caught my fingers in her mouth, sucking on them delicately, flicking each of the tips as if it was my clit.

"Oh guy—Christ!" Marguerite groaned as our joined fingers filled her cunt.

Her pussy tightened as we worked it, a stepped and paced rhythm as Marguerite's fingers clasped even harder around my biceps, and I increased the pressure on her clit, which jumped under my thumb. Candace pushed her harder onto me and licked long strokes along her neck. I joined her from the other side until our tongues tangled again and I knew she'd be *very* ready for me to fuck her after the show—and so would I.

"Sorry," I mouthed to her, an apology for my fit of pique, when we broke for air.

"Forgiven?" Candace mouthed back.

I grinned at her in answer, because I knew what that slick tightening around our fingers meant—our guest was going to come.

I carefully shifted my fingers around Candace's in that slick space that hugged me so tightly. Marguerite stiffened.

"Oh fuck," she groaned, "holy fuck." Her fingers now dug into my arms and her hips trembled between my thighs.

She had nowhere to go, nowhere to move, trapped between me and Candace as we fucked her, a good, hard, and steady drive into her cunt, while her clit pulsed under my thumb. A small, high-pitched noise came from her throat.

"Welcome to rock 'n' roll, love," Candace murmured into her ear before scraping it with her teeth, "the pre-show's a blast."

Marguerite gulped, then nodded, tossing her head back to rest against Candace's shoulder.

"I'm gonna…I'm gonna—ohgod…"

"Oh that's nice, yeah," I encouraged, because this was getting me so fucking hot. "You're so fuckin' nice and tight…you're gonna come just like this. C'mon baby…."

"Uh-huh," she squeaked out as she pushed off my arms and bore down on the twin pressures invading her cunt as it spasmed, then spasmed again and again, a lovely wet kiss on our fingers as we held her between us.

"Too…much…" Marguerite finally managed to weakly say.

I kissed her forehead and Candace nuzzled her neck as first I eased my thumb and then my fingers off and out of her pussy.

"Time, Ann: you're cutting it close," Candace reminded me after I sucked on her tongue while Marguerite breathed along my collarbone.

"I've got to get ready, and so do you," I murmured into Marguerite's ear. "I'll bet you knock 'em dead." I kissed her softly again; she'd been a good sport, and she had a job to do.

Marguerite held Candace's hand as they walked toward the door, but shocked me when she turned around and threw her arms around my neck, then kissed me soundly.

"Going to the after-party?" she asked after she let me go.

I quickly glanced over at Candace, who grinned at me before I smiled down at the young woman who pressed herself against me. "No, there's a show tomorrow," I told her. "But…I will be early for the sound check."

Another night in Belgium, I thought as she released me and opened the door. Candace waved to me before shutting it behind them. Another gig. Considering the plans I'd just made, maybe it wouldn't be so bad after all. This was gonna be a great show.

TEST DRIVE
RADCLYFFE

The minute I walked into the luxury showroom, three guys converged on me like I was live bait tossed into the shark tank. Maybe it was the short red skirt that clung smoothly to the curves of my ass (I knew that because I'd checked it out before I left the house). I guess it might have been the tiny wisps of white lace and silk that peeked out through the opening in my almost-see-through blouse. I'd left the top three buttons undone so when I leaned forward a little bit, the inner curves of my breasts would show. The thin cups of my bra and the black silk blouse didn't hide the round, firm prominences of my nipples, either.

Looking for a little action?...How about something special?...You came to the right place.

Even if I hadn't been able to read it in their body language, I could hear the word *baby* at the end of every sentence. I smiled sweetly (the mirror again) and kept walking, adding just a little bit more sway to my hips than my heels actually called for. All three of them followed until I was in the center of the showroom.

"Maybe you can help me. I'm looking for…" I waited until they leaned forward just a little, moving in unison as if pulled by an invisible magnet centered directly between my tits. "Blaze Vernon."

I might have imagined it, but it seemed as if they deflated just a little, like someone had let the air out of a tire. One, with curly dark hair and a five o'clock shadow, said gruffly, "You sure? Because I think I might have just what you're looking for."

"I don't think so," I said lightly, stepping slightly to one side so I could see the rest of the room. Another dark-haired, curly-headed sales rep came forward, but this one was a head shorter and a hundred pounds lighter than the three in front of me. She held out her hand, her dark eyes wary but interested.

"I'm Blaze."

While I clasped her fingers and smiled into her eyes, the other three melted away. "You don't remember me. I'm—"

"Miranda Sullivan," she finished for me.

Surprised, I nodded and reluctantly let go of her hand. We had only been introduced once, at a party the month before, and I was certain she hadn't taken notice of me. But *I* had noticed *her*, and I'd checked around later to ascertain her vital statistics. The most important one checked out just fine—single. The others weren't as important, but put together, they made a very nice package. Thirty years old, new in town, ex-jock of some kind—no one was really sure exactly what sport. From her rangy build I would have guessed basketball or golf or lacrosse. She seemed like speed came easily to her. Unfortunately, she had also disappeared from the scene as quickly as she'd appeared. It took some not-so-subtle probing, but I finally tracked down where she worked and, well, sometimes you just have to take the wheel.

"Mira," I said. "Call me Mira."

"What can I do for you, Mira?"

I pointed toward a sleek two-seater. "I'd like to take that out for a test drive."

Blaze nodded seriously, and maybe she really even believed me. "I need to make a copy of your license."

She was only gone for a few minutes, and then she courteously held open the passenger side door for me. "I'll drive it out of the showroom," she said, "and then you can take her for a spin."

"I'm happy for you to drive," I said as I slid onto the low, body-hugging seat, my skirt riding high on my thighs. "I'm not all that used to handling a stick."

"That's fine." Blaze hurried around the front and settled into the driver's seat. "You just let me know when you're ready."

Once she exited the parking lot and headed toward the expressway, I leaned across the narrow center console, feigning interest in the gauges and dials on the dash. The outside of my left breast rubbed against her arm.

"This model features the standard front-engine, rear-wheel drivetrain common to most high-performance sports cars," Blaze said, staring straight ahead.

"Nice and smooth," I commented, my nipple tightening as Blaze brushed against it while reaching for the stick shift.

"Sixteen-valve, six-speed transmission." Her voice was just a little strained.

"I imagine it handles well." I pressed a little harder against her, my nipple resting on her arm just beneath the edge of her short-sleeved shirt. Her tanned skin was hot and my breast tingled. "If you're not afraid to let all that power out."

"Front wishbone/rear multilink suspension." Blaze wrapped her fingers, which were long and tapered with short, smooth nails, around the head of the gear stick and pushed it into fifth gear. Her knuckles slid along the bare skin of my thigh with the forward motion. As she pulled her hand back, her fingertips followed the path her knuckles had just forged, and I shivered at the unexpected surge of heat.

"That must make for quite a ride." I let my hand fall casually onto her thigh. The muscles underneath my fingers were as hard as stone.

"Zero to sixty in 7.9 seconds," Blaze murmured.

"It feels even faster than that," I breathed.

Blaze signaled with a tap of her fingers over the blinker and cut across traffic into the fast lane. We were still under the speed limit, but just barely.

"Does the speed bother you?" Blaze asked, glancing down quickly at my hand on her leg, then back up at the road. She shifted into sixth. My clit buzzed at the sound of the engine's roar.

"No." I eased my fingers higher until they were an inch from the vee between her legs. "I like a little bit of danger with my pleasure."

"Do you want to drive?" She covered my hand with hers and squeezed it so fleetingly over her crotch that I might have imagined it. But when she gently deposited my hand back in my own lap, she was breathing hard and a muscle rippled along the edge of her jaw. My palm burned from the waves of heat pouring through her pants. I hadn't imagined it. It took me a few seconds to catch my breath.

"Not yet," I said shakily.

We finished the test drive and returned to the showroom and I told her I'd think about it. She gave me her card, asked for my number in return, and told me to call if I had any questions. I said I would and left without looking at the three men whose eyes followed me out of the room. Then I climbed into my car, which I'd left parked at the far side of the lot, eased my seat back, and slipped my hand under my skirt.

I was wet and it only took me a few seconds to come, Blaze's card still between my fingers. When I opened my eyes and glanced across the parking lot toward the building, I saw Blaze framed in the open doorway. I smiled and drove away.

Two days later she called and left a message, asking if I'd made any decisions about the car. The day after that I went back, and this time when I walked in she was the first one to reach me.

"Still thinking about that car?" Blaze asked, her gaze slowly traveling from my eyes to my mouth and back up again.

"Just about nonstop." I turned a little, pretending to look at the car, and brushed my hip against her crotch. "I can't get any work done, thinking about it."

"I've been a little distracted myself," Blaze said. "We could take it out again, if you're not sure."

"I think I'd like to see how it does on the open road."

Blaze smiled. "You're going to love the way she maneuvers."

"That's what I'm hoping."

She took us out of town onto the tight, narrow, twisting back roads, pushing us through hairpin turns, accelerating up hills and blasting down the other side. I turned in the seat and watched her handle the stick, her long fingers caressing the leather-covered head with obvious pleasure. The powerful engine hummed, and the vibrations tingled in my clit. I'd worn a skirt again with nothing underneath but bikinis and I was already wet.

"I saw you in your car the other day," Blaze said, her eyes on the road.

"I can't resist hard, fast driving."

"Then you must be enjoying yourself today." Blaze smiled softly and flicked a glance at me, her eyes dropping to my lap.

I trailed my fingers up the inside of my thigh, pushing my skirt high enough to expose the pale silk covering my pussy. "I am. Even more than the first time."

"You don't have to wait," Blaze said hoarsely.

"I don't want to distract you," I murmured, but I couldn't resist pressing my fingertips to my hard clit. I moaned softly.

"Do it," she whispered, and pressed down on the gas pedal.

The force of the engine accelerating surged through me, and I drew the slip of silk aside with one hand and stroked my swollen slit with the other.

"Zero to sixty," I gasped, letting my head fall back against the window as I started to come. "In...oh, God...right now."

Blaze laughed and reached across the space between us to caress my cheek softly. "That's what I call high-performance."

"It's not the engine," I murmured drowsily. "It's the driver."

She took us back to the showroom while I dozed. When she pulled into the parking lot, I straightened my clothes and stroked her arm. "That was one ride I won't forget."

"Any time."

I didn't call, but I came every night thinking about her. Two days later she left another message, but I still waited. That night, my doorbell rang just after eight. Blaze stood on my porch. A bright new shiny sports car stood at the curb.

"I think you'll like the feel of this one," she said.

I grabbed the waistband of her pants and pulled her inside. "I told you, most of the time I like to sit back and enjoy the ride."

"Most of the time?" Blaze raised an inquiring eyebrow.

"Mmm."

I led her to the sofa and curled up next to her. She put her arm around me and kissed me. Her lips were soft, her tongue was firm. Her mouth was hot. After a few minutes, she pulled back and whispered, "My engine is about to red-zone."

Laughing, I popped open the button on her fly and unzipped her pants. "You mean it's not just *my* idle that's running high?"

"Definitely not." Blaze nibbled on my lower lip. "I couldn't even make it through the whole day after that first test drive. I've been spending a lot of time in the bathroom at work."

"Well, we can't have you blowing a piston, now can we?" I pushed my hand down between her legs and slid her clit between my fingers. It swelled as I stroked it. "Nice. Responsive."

"You like the feel of that?" Blaze asked, her voice tight.

"It's got more flex than I anticipated," I teased, flicking the tip with my finger.

"Keep it up," Blaze laughed quietly, "and it won't do that for long."

"What do you—oh, I see. It's getting quite a bit stiffer now." I jiggled it around a little and she jerked as if someone had hit her. "Does that feel good?"

"Oh yeah," she groaned. "It feels great."

"What else do you like?"

"Why don't you…run the gears. Push it back and forth and…yeah, like that. Side to side…" Her legs tensed and I saw her grip the edge of the sofa, hard. She was breathing fast and when I skimmed her ear with my lips, she moaned.

"Is that right? Is that good?"

"So good," she whispered, but she sounded like she wanted to cry.

"Are you sure? Because I can stop if it's not…"

"Faster," she groaned. "Oh fuck, my clit is so hard."

"How's that? You like it there?"

Blaze cupped her hand in her crotch on the outside of her pants, over mine, and moved my fingers just a little lower. "That's it. You're there. Right there."

"Will this make you come?"

"Like you wouldn't believe."

"You want to?" She gushed over my fingers. "Is that… are you…" I tried to tell if it was what she needed, but her eyes were cloudy and unfocused and I didn't think she was listening.

"I'm starting to come," she whispered, but I think she was talking to herself. She stared down at our hands, mine inside her pants, fingers circling between her legs. "It's good. Really good…oh baby, you're making me come."

Everything was hot and wet and hard and when I found just the spot that made her cry out, I rubbed it harder until her hips came off the couch and her head jerked back and she twisted and pumped under my fingers.

"Christ," she groaned a minute later, looking sheepish. "Sorry. I didn't mean to do that so fast."

"It's okay," I murmured while I kissed her neck. "Just don't fall asleep, because I'll overheat and explode."

She laughed a little shakily. "Are you kidding?" She skimmed her fingers under the edge of my skirt. "Take this off."

I rolled away and opened the drawer in the table beside the couch. I pulled out a harness with my favorite dildo attached and dropped it in her lap. "Put this on."

I held my breath while she stared at it for a second, then sighed in sweet anticipation as she grinned.

"Looking to go for another test drive?" She stood and pushed down her pants, then strapped on.

"I've been waiting all week to try out this model," I said, sliding out of my skirt. I grasped her shoulders and pushed her back down on the couch, then straddled her hips. "Hold it for me."

When she reached between my legs to grasp the cock standing up from her crotch, her knuckles brushed my clit and I whimpered. Then she glided the head back and forth along my slit and I couldn't breathe. Every time she rolled the cock over my clit it felt like she was turning her fist deep inside me.

"Don't do that," I moaned. "You're going to make me come. I'm not ready yet."

"What about lube?" she whispered.

"Touch me. What do you think?"

She groaned this time as she cupped my pussy and I filled her hand with juice. She eased a finger inside me and I tightened around it. Her palm grazed my clit, on purpose now, and I wanted to come.

"Please stop," I whimpered. "Please don't make me come."

"Isn't that what you want," she demanded, pushing more fingers inside me. "Because that's what I want. I've watched you come twice. Now I want to feel it."

She pumped me harder and my stomach convulsed. I needed to come but I fought not to let go. "I want your cock in me. I want to come on your cock while you're fucking me."

She pulled her fingers out and grabbed my hips, centering me over the head of the dildo. "Put both hands around it," she ordered, staring down the length of her body to the shaft that bobbed between my legs. When I did, her hips twitched. "Now jerk it off a little bit until you get my clit nice and hard again."

She lowered me enough so that every time I manipulated the shaft over her clit, the head bumped mine. Pretty soon my hand was a blur and we were both whining. I was ready to come and from the desperate sounds she was making, so was she. Just before my pussy let loose, she pushed my hands away with one of hers and steadied the cock against my opening.

"Now fuck it," she groaned. "Slide down that hot stick and fuck it until you come."

I dug my fingers into her shoulders and took her in deep in one long, fast plunge. Her cock was fat and filled me up, stretching me, making me ache inside. The muscles in my thighs had gone soft but I managed to push almost all the way off, until the head rubbed against that one spot inside me that always makes me want to come. Then I dropped down hard again, impaling myself on her.

"God," I said through gritted teeth, "I'm going to come so hard on you."

"Open it up, baby," Blaze urged, her hands guiding my hips. "Let's hear that engine purr."

I pumped my hips, working my pussy up and down her thickness. I was boiling over, creaming on her like mad, and I couldn't hold my head up any longer. Leaning my forehead on hers, I moaned, "Ten seconds."

She wasn't content to let me drive to the finish alone, though, and thrust her hips every time I slid down, jamming the slick leather around the base of her cock into my clit. I wanted to ride her forever, but I couldn't stop what was happening inside me. The muscles of my cunt clamped around her cock and my clit swelled against the shaft.

"I'm coming," I whispered and she kissed me.

I came on her, her mouth swallowing my cries as I went rigid and my cunt shuddered. When I thought I was done, she stroked her thumb over my clit and set me off again. She kept revving me up until I slapped her hands away and dragged myself off her relentless cock.

"I'm out of gas," I groaned, collapsing next to her.

She pulled me close and nuzzled my neck. "I've got a great car parked right outside," she whispered. "Full tank."

"Give me a minute, and we'll take it for a test run." I pulled lazily on her cock and teased her mouth with my tongue. "Except this time, I think I'll drive."

CONTRIBUTORS

SAGGIO AMANTE was born in the North, grew up in the South, and lives in her head, where fun-filled fantasies occasionally make it from her imagination to the printed page. A recovering Catholic, she once thought she wanted to be a nun but, like Mabel Maney, "then (she) realized that what (she) really wanted was to be a lesbian." One of her favorite quotes is a Kate Clinton classic: "Some women can't say the word *lesbian* even when their mouth is full of one." To which Sage replies: "Bon appétit!"

KIM BALDWIN has published four books with Bold Strokes Books: the intrigue/romances *Flight Risk* and *Hunter's Pursuit* and the romances *Whitewater Rendezvous* and *Force of Nature*. She is currently at work on her fifth, the romance *Focus of Desire*. She has also contributed stories to three previous books in the BSB Erotic Interludes series. A former journalist, Kim lives in Michigan. For more info visit www.kimbaldwin.com.

GEORGIA BEERS was born and raised in Rochester, New York, and still lives there with Bonnie, her partner of thirteen years, and their two dogs. She's hard at work on her fifth novel, *Mine,* as well as a script for a short film and several short stories. When not writing, Georgia enjoys reading, movies, hiking, and watching too much television.

Born in North Carolina, RONICA BLACK now lives in the desert Southwest, where she spends her time creating the images in her mind. Ronica is the author of *In Too Deep*, a Lambda Literary Award finalist and Golden Crown Literary Society Award winner, and *Wild Abandon*. Her latest romance, *Hearts Aflame,* is coming from Bold Strokes Books in July 2007. Ronica has also contributed short stories to *Best Lesbian Erotica 2005* and *Erotic Interludes 2* and *3*. Visit Ronica's Web site at www.ronicablack.com.

Award-winning author GUN BROOKE, residing in Sweden, loves to write romance and science fiction. She has published *Course of Action, Protector of the Realm, Coffee Sonata,* and *Rebel's Quest* with Bold Strokes Books and she is currently writing her fifth novel, *Sheridan's Fate*, due in October 2007. Gun also has several short stories published in different anthologies. If you are curious about this writer, she welcomes you to her Web site, www.gbrooke-fiction.com.

JULIE CANNON is a native sun goddess born and raised in Phoenix, Arizona. Her first novel, *Come and Get Me*, was released in April 2007 and *Heart 2 Heart* will follow in December 2007. Julie's day job is in Corporate America, and she and her partner Laura live in Phoenix with their seven-year-old son, six-year-old daughter, two dogs, and Spencer the cat.

CRIN CLAXTON writes novels, short stories, and the occasional poem. Her queer vampire novel *Scarlet Thirst* is available from Red Hot Diva Books. Excerpts from her second vampire novel have been published by Suspect Thoughts 'zine. Her short stories have been published in anthologies by the Women's Press, Diva Books, Bold Strokes Books (*Erotic Interludes 3* and *4*), Carve online 'zine, and *Diva* magazine. More info at www.crinclaxton.com.

FIONA COOPER has published a short story collection, *I Believe in Angels*, and nine novels including *Rotary Spokes*, *Jay Loves Lucy*, *Serpents Tail*, *The Empress of the Seven Oceans*, and most recently *As You Desire Me*. She has contributed to many short story collections as well as zillions of gay magazines. She works as a medium, soul regression therapist, and psychic artist, and recently gave a one-woman show, *Dinosaurs and Dykes,* at the York Lesbian Arts Festival to rapturous acclaim. She is never happier than when she is under a rainbow by the sea with an icy glass or three of New Zealand fizz by her side.

CHERI CRYSTAL enjoys reading, writing, exercising, eating, having sex, and multitasking. With five published erotic short stories, including "Debut" in *Erotic Interludes 3: Lessons in Love* and "Escort" in *Erotic Interludes 4: Extreme Passions,* Cheri strives to write the great American lesbian novel. She considers herself fortunate to have the best role models to emulate and look to for guidance. She thanks her friends and family for their love and support.

LESLEY DAVIS lives in the West Midlands of England with her American partner Cindy Pfannenstiel. She has five published works available, *Keeper of the Piece* and its two Adepts of Calluna sequels, and *Cast A Wide Circle* and its follow-on that tell tales of magic. She also is proud to have had a piece in *Erotic Interludes 2: Stolen Moments*, published by Bold Strokes Books.

Born and raised in upstate New York, ERIN DUTTON moved to Nashville, Tennessee, eight years ago. No longer a Yankee, and yet not a true Southerner, she remains somewhere between the two and is happy to claim both places as home. She is the author of *Sequestered Hearts*, May 2007, and *Fully Involved*, December 2007, from Bold Strokes Books.

EVECHO loves writing lesbian sex stories. Her simmering ambition (other than eating her way around the world) is to retire from the legal grind and open a bed & breakfast—where service comes from a personal touch. She is grateful to Radclyffe for including her in the fantastic Erotic Interludes series from Bold Strokes Books. Evecho may be contacted at everwrite@gmail.com or via www.thesandbox101.com.

JD GLASS lives in the city of her choice and birth, New York, with her beloved partner. When she's not writing, she's the lead singer (as well as alternately guitarist and bassist) in Life Underwater, which also keeps her pretty busy. Her novels include *Punk Like Me, Punk and Zen*, and *Red Light* from Bold Strokes Books.

GABRIELLE GOLDSBY (gabriellegoldsby.com) is the author of four novels, the newest of which, *Such a Pretty Face*, will be published by Bold Strokes Books in 2007. When not writing, Gabrielle spends her free time reading, lifting weights, and backcountry hiking. She resides in Portland, Oregon, with her partner of eight years.

LC JORDAN is a thirty-nine-year-old Midwestern woman with a lifelong passion for reading and writing. She has been fortunate enough to have some of her stories published in print anthologies. LC's search for the perfect alchemy of words is a never-ending process.

KARIN KALLMAKER is best known for more than twenty lesbian romance novels, from *In Every Port* to *Finders Keepers*. She has also earned a naughty reputation with novellas, novels, and erotic short stories, including *18th & Castro*. In addition, she has a half dozen science fiction, fantasy, and supernatural lesbian novels (e.g. *Seeds of Fire, Christabel*) under the pen name Laura Adams. She likes her chocolate real, her Internet fast, and her iPod very loud. You can find out more about her work at kallmaker.com.

CLAIRE MARTIN lives in Chicago, where she sells real estate. When she's not driving around from property to property, she is busy writing and reading, reading, reading. She has been previously published by Bold Strokes Books in *Erotic Interludes 4: Extreme Passions* and also has a story in the Cleis Press anthology *Best Lesbian Romance*. She is currently finishing up her first novel. Claire lives with her partner of ten years and their 2.2 spoiled cats.

NYRDGYRL lives with her lovely in the Rockies and works in emergency services as a firefighter. She has a story in *Erotic Interludes 3: Lessons in Love* titled "The Decision Coin."

MEGHAN O'BRIEN lives in Northern California with her girlfriend, their son, and evenly matched teams of cats and dogs. She is the author of *Infinite Loop* and *The Three*, both from Regal Crest Enterprises, and has contributed short erotica to three other Erotic Interludes anthologies. You can find her online at www.meghanobrien.com.

A retired assistant chief of police, VK POWELL lives in North Carolina and is a member of the Golden Crown Literary Society and Romance Writers of America. She is the author of two erotic short stories: "Toy with Me," which appears in *Erotic Interludes 3: Lessons in Love*, and "Dessert, Anyone?" in *Erotic Interludes 4: Extreme Passions*. Her novel, *To Protect and Serve*, is slated for release in 2008 from Bold Strokes Books.

RADCLYFFE is the author of over twenty-five lesbian novels and anthologies including the 2005 Lambda Literary Award winners *Erotic Interludes 2: Stolen Moments*, edited with Stacia Seaman, and *Distant Shores, Silent Thunder*. She is the recipient of the 2003 and 2004 Alice B. Readers' award, a 2005 Golden Crown Literary Society Award winner in both the romance category (*Fated Love*) and the mystery/intrigue/action category (*Justice in the Shadows*), and a 2006 GCLS winner for mystery (*Justice Served*). She has selections in multiple anthologies including *Call of the Dark*, *The Perfect Valentine*, and *Wild Nights* (Bella Books), *Best Lesbian Erotica* 2006 and 2007 (Cleis), *First-Timers* and *Ultimate Undies: Erotic Stories About Lingerie and Underwear* (Alyson), *Naughty Spanking Stories 2* and the upcoming *A is for Amour* (Cleis), and *Sex and Candy* (Pretty Things Press). She is also the president of Bold Strokes Books, a lesbian publishing company.

STACIA SEAMAN has edited *New York Times* and *USA Today* best-sellers and numerous award-winning books, and has herself won a Lammy with coeditor Radclyffe for *Erotic Interludes 2: Stolen Moments*. She edits everything from textbooks to popular nonfiction to mysteries and romance novels. She lives with her cat, Frieda, and enjoys being silly.

NELL STARK is a graduate student of medieval English literature in Madison, Wisconsin, where she lives with her partner and their two cats. Her first novel, *Running with the Wind*, was published by Bold Strokes Books in March 2007 with her second, an urban fantasy titled *Free to Fall*, coming in 2008. She thanks her beta reader, Ruta, and her partner, Lisa, for their helpful and encouraging feedback. Visit her at www.nellstark.com.

RENÉE STRIDER settled down in her favorite Canadian city after bouncing from place to place in Europe, Canada, and the U.S. for most of her life. Besides getting a great deal of pleasure from writing lesbian stories, she occasionally writes about art and translates poems and fiction into English from an endangered minority language. Speaking of games, she shuns snow and ice sports as they only encourage winter, but she likes summer games like sailing. Contact her at reneelf@cogeco.ca.

THERESE SZYMANSKI has been shortlisted for a Spectrum and a few Lammies and Goldies, and made the Publishing Triangle's list of notable lesbian books in 2004. She's written seven Brett Higgins Motor City Thrillers; edited *Back to Basics, Call of the Dark, Wild Nights,* and *A Perfect Valentine;* has novellas in *Once Upon a Dyke, Stake through the Heart*, and *Bell, Book and Dyke*; and has a few dozen published short stories.

KI THOMPSON began her writing career when her first short story, "The Blue Line," was included in the Lambda Literary Award–winning anthology *Erotic Interludes 2: Stolen Moments* from Bold Strokes Books. She also has selections in *Erotic Interludes 3: Lessons in Love* and *Erotic Interludes 4: Extreme Passions* and *Best Lesbian Romance 2007* (Cleis Press). Her historical romance novel, *House of Clouds*, is forthcoming from Bold Strokes Books (Oct 2007). Contact her at www.kithompson.com or www.boldstrokesbooks.com.

Called a "trollop with a laptop" by the *East Bay Express*, ALISON TYLER is naughty and she knows it. Her short stories have appeared in more than seventy anthologies including *Sweet Life, Sex at the Office,* and *Glamour Girls*. She is the author of more than twenty erotic novels (including *Tiffany Twisted* and *With or Without You*) and the editor of more than twenty-five anthologies, including the brand-new *A is for Amour*, *B is for Bondage*, *C is for Co-Eds*, and *D is for Dress-Up*. Catch up with her at www.alisontyler.blogspot.com.

EVA VANDETUIN is a religious studies graduate student. She sees sex and spirituality as being closely intertwined, and the relationship between the two inspires much of her fiction. You can find more of her work in the web archives of *Clean Sheets,* as well as in the anthologies *Erotic Interludes 3: Lessons in Love, Erotic Interludes 4: Extreme Passions,* and *Ultimate Lesbian Erotica 2007*.

MJ WILLIAMZ lives in Portland, Oregon, where she crunches numbers by day and indulges her true passion of writing lesbian fiction by night. Her erotic short stories have appeared in *The Good Parts*, *Back to Basics*, *The Perfect Valentine*, *Blood Sisters*, and most recently her story "The Presentation" appears in *Ultimate Lesbian Erotica 2007*.

Books Available From Bold Strokes Books

Sequestered Hearts by Erin Dutton. A popular artist suddenly goes into seclusion, a reluctant reporter wants to know why, and a heart locked away yearns to be set free. (978-1-933110-78-3)

Erotic Interludes 5: Road Games ed by. Radclyffe and Stacia Seaman. Adventure, "sport," and sex on the road—hot stories of travel adventures and games of seduction. (978-1-933110-77-6)

The Spanish Pearl by Catherine Friend. On a trip to Spain, Kate Vincent is accidentally transported back in time—an epic saga spiced with humor, lust, and danger. (978-1-933110-76-9)

Lady Knight by L-J Baker. Loyalty and honor clash with love and ambition in a medieval world of magic when female knight Riannon meets Lady Eleanor. (978-1-933110-75-2)

Dark Dreamer by Jennifer Fulton. Best-selling horror author Rowe Devlin falls under the spell of psychic Phoebe Temple. A Dark Vista romance. (978-1-933110-74-5)

Come and Get Me by Julie Cannon. Elliott Foster isn't used to pursuing women, but alluring attorney Lauren Collier makes her change her mind. (978-1-933110-73-8)

Blind Curves by Diane and Jacob Anderson-Minshall. Private eye Yoshi Yakamota comes to the aid of her ex-lover Velvet Erickson in the first Blind Eye mystery. (978-1-933110-72-1)

Dynasty of Rogues by Jane Fletcher. It's hate at first sight for Ranger Riki Sadiq and her new patrol corporal, Tanya Coppelli—except for their undeniable attraction. (978-1-933110-71-4)

Running With the Wind by Nell Stark. Sailing instructor Corrie Marsten has signed off on love until she meets Quinn Davies—one woman she can't ignore. (978-1-933110-70-7)

More Than Paradise by Jennifer Fulton. Two women battle danger, risk all, and find in each other an unexpected ally and an unforgettable love. (978-1-933110-69-1)

Flight Risk by Kim Baldwin. For Blayne Keller, being in the wrong place at the wrong time just might turn out to be the best thing that ever happened to her. (978-1-933110-68-4)

Rebel's Quest: Supreme Constellations Book Two by Gun Brooke. On a world torn by war, two women discover a love that defies all boundaries. (978-1-933110-67-7)

Punk and Zen by JD Glass. Angst, sex, love, rock. Trace, Candace, Francesca...Samantha. Losing control—and finding the truth within. BSB Victory Editions. (1-933110-66-X)

When Dreams Tremble by Radclyffe. Two women whose lives turned out far differently than they'd once imagined discover that sometimes the shape of the future can only be found in the past. (1-933110-64-3)

Stellium in Scorpio by Andrews & Austin. The passionate reuniting of two powerful women on the glitzy Las Vegas Strip, where everything is an illusion and love is a gamble. (1-933110-65-1)

The Devil Unleashed by Ali Vali. As the heat of violence rises, so does the passion. A Casey Clan crime saga. (1-933110-61-9)

Burning Dreams by Susan Smith. The chronicle of the challenges faced by a young drag king and an older woman who share a love "outside the bounds." (1-933110-62-7)

Fresh Tracks by Georgia Beers. Seven women, seven days. A lot can happen when old friends, lovers, and a new girl in town get together in the mountains. (1-933110-63-5)

The Empress and the Acolyte by Jane Fletcher. Jemeryl and Tevi fight to protect the very fabric of their world...time. Lyremouth Chronicles Book Three. (1-933110-60-0)

First Instinct by JLee Meyer. When high-stakes security fraud leads to murder, one woman flees for her life while another risks her heart to protect her. (1-933110-59-7)

Erotic Interludes 4: Extreme Passions, ed. by Radclyffe and Stacia Seaman. Thirty of today's hottest erotica writers set the pages aflame with love, lust, and steamy liaisons. (1-933110-58-9)

Sleep of Reason by Rose Beecham. Nothing is as it seems when Detective Jude Devine finds herself caught up in a small-town soap opera. And her rocky relationship with forensic pathologist Dr. Mercy Westmoreland just got a lot harder. (1-933110-53-8)

Punk Like Me by JD Glass. Twenty-one-year-old Nina writes lyrics and plays guitar in the rock band Adam's Rib, and she doesn't always play by the rules. And oh yeah—she has a way with the girls. (1-933110-40-6)

Wild Abandon by Ronica Black. From their first tumultuous meeting, Dr. Chandler Brogan and Officer Sarah Monroe are drawn together by their common obsessions—sex, speed, and danger. (1-933110-35-X)

Chance by Grace Lennox. At twenty-six, Chance Delaney decides her life isn't working so she swaps it for a different one. What follows is the sexy, funny, touching story of two women who, in finding themselves, also find one another. (1-933110-31-7)

Turn Back Time by Radclyffe. Pearce Rifkin and Wynter Thompson have nothing in common but a shared passion for surgery. They clash at every opportunity, especially when matters of the heart are suddenly at stake. (1-933110-34-1)

Justice Served by Radclyffe. Lieutenant Rebecca Frye and her lover, Dr. Catherine Rawlings, embark on a deadly game of hide-and-seek with an underworld kingpin who traffics in human souls. (1-933110-15-5)

Justice in the Shadows by Radclyffe. In a shadow world of secrets and lies, Detective Sergeant Rebecca Frye and her lover, Dr. Catherine Rawlings, join forces in the elusive search for justice. (1-933110-03-1)

A Matter of Trust by Radclyffe. JT Sloan is a cybersleuth who doesn't like attachments. Michael Lassiter is leaving her husband, and she needs Sloan's expertise to safeguard her company. It should just be business—but it turns into much more. (1-933110-33-3)

Storms of Change by Radclyffe. In the continuing saga of the Provincetown Tales, duty and love are at odds as Reese and Tory face their greatest challenge. (1-933110-57-0)

Distant Shores, Silent Thunder by Radclyffe. Dr. Tory King—along with the women who love her—is forced to examine the boundaries of love, friendship, and the ties that transcend time. (1-933110-08-2)

Beyond the Breakwater by Radclyffe. One Provincetown summer, three women learn the true meaning of love, friendship, and family. (1-933110-06-6)

Safe Harbor by Radclyffe. A mysterious newcomer, a reclusive doctor, and a troubled gay teenager learn about love, friendship, and trust during one tumultuous summer in Provincetown. (1-933110-13-9)

Honor Reclaimed by Radclyffe. In the aftermath of 9/11, Secret Service Agent Cameron Roberts and Blair Powell close ranks with a trusted few to find the would-be assassins who nearly claimed Blair's life. (1-933110-18-X)

Honor Guards by Radclyffe. In a wild flight for their lives, the president's daughter and those who are sworn to protect her wage a desperate struggle for survival. (1-933110-01-5)

Love & Honor by Radclyffe. The president's daughter and her lover are faced with difficult choices as they battle a tangled web of Washington intrigue for...love and honor. (1-933110-10-4)

Honor Bound by Radclyffe. Secret Service Agent Cameron Roberts and Blair Powell face political intrigue, a clandestine threat to Blair's safety, and the seemingly irreconcilable personal differences that force them ever farther apart. (1-933110-20-1)

Above All, Honor by Radclyffe. Secret Service Agent Cameron Roberts fights her desire for the one woman she can't have—Blair Powell, the daughter of the president of the United States. (1-933110-04-X)